"A stick and book, grey street sign and a purple door… they all fit but how?" I murmured to myself.

I nodded and threw the ball some more. "A staff like a cane with runes carved in it… a spell of some sort I'm sure." I bounced through twice more while sorting and then stopped and looked at the ball.

Bouncing it again. "The book isn't a book, but a journal that's very old… not printed but written because it was seen." I reversed the direction of the throws. "Written like a prophecy in a leather-bound journal. Need to find out what prophecy he's trying to break."

More bouncing, a little faster. "Grey street signs, but the street signs aren't grey." Bounced slower again, too chaotic with the fast rhythm. "A sign that isn't grey, but white only seems grey under a street light." I rocked my head to the motion of the ball. "A sign that isn't grey but a sign is something used for directions, so you find your street. Grey street. That was so obvious I didn't see it."

I caught the ball and nodded once, then threw it again. "Okay." Wall to floor to wall again. "Purple door. Purple is no longer my favorite color for reasons that are carved into my back. Purple, mage… a magical place? A door to go through?" I reversed the rhythm of throwing. "Or is it as simple as a purple door on grey street at night?" I bounced it harder, trying to see. "Underneath the door doesn't make sense… unless it's a tunnel and the door is above."

I caught the ball and held it in my hand. "Oh, I *know* where Marcus will be, and what he's doing. I have to go tell them."

I spun around and then jumped and screeched when I saw all of them standing there, silently watching me. "I…"

Also by J. Risk

The Alterealm Series
The Huntress
The Seer
The Empath
The Witch

Writing As: Jacqueline Paige

Dreams

After the Silence
Volume 1 Bree

Animal Senses
Heart
Scent
Passion

Magic Seasons Romance
Beltane Magic
Solstice Heat
Harvest Dreams
Autumn Dance
Winter Mist

Single titles
Solitary Witchling
Cafe Serenity
Salvation

The Seer

Alterealm Series

Book 2

By J. Risk

Family tree at the end of *The Huntress*

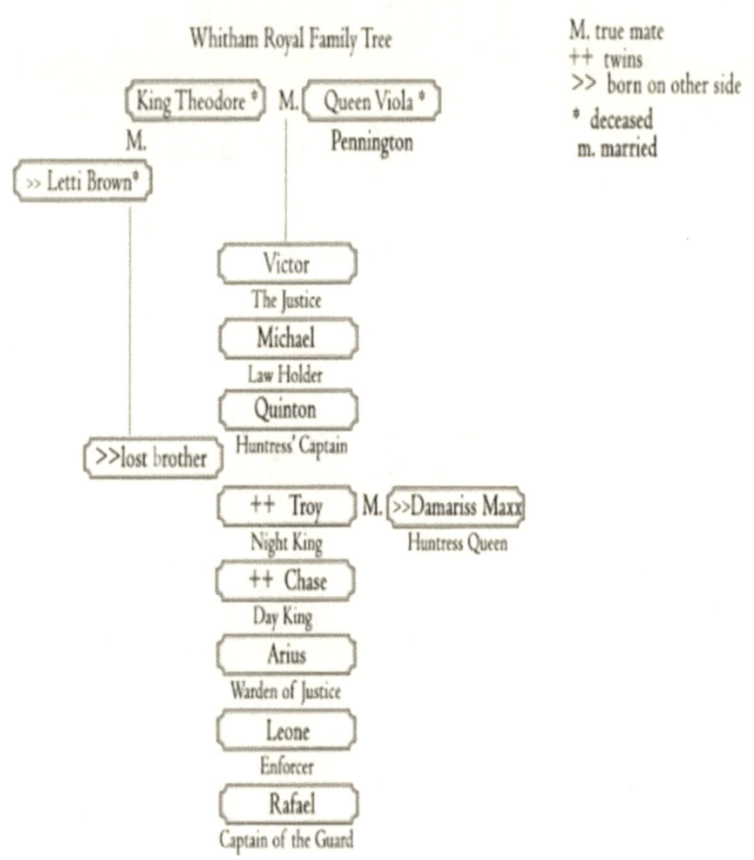

Published by FRP
Copyright © 2018 Roxane Kerr
Edited by Gaele L. Hince
Cover art by: Off the Wall Creations

Updated 2020

ISBN (paperback): 978-1-7773723-5-4
ISBN (digital): 978-1-7773723-4-7

Prologue

I patted her cheek again. No reaction. She didn't even stir. Looking around to make sure we were hidden in the shadows, I sat down beside the crazy woman with the fantastically bright red hair, trying to figure out what I should do.

This was a complication. I didn't do complications. In fact, I did everything possible to avoid them. Go out each night, do what was inevitably necessary. Go home. A perfect complication free routine.

I looked back down at her. I'd seen her around a few times, sure, but that didn't make us friends. I didn't even know her name. Then again, I tried not to get close enough to know them. It never ended well. That was one thing I learned many years ago. While friendships and love may relieve the endless loneliness, it wasn't worth the heartbreak. Watching friends die was something you could never get used to, and they always did.

Do I sit here until she comes to? I didn't even know why she sat down and then fell over. I reached over to check her pulse, it seemed strong enough, not that I would know, but I did know alive and she was that. Her skin wasn't clammy in the way the drug users got when they overdosed. So, what was wrong with her? Did I call for help? Then what? Calling for help lead to questions—that I'd most likely prefer not to answer.

Shit. I couldn't just leave her lying in an alley. There were too many creeps and sickos in the neighborhood to do that. As a woman, I knew what could happen in the wrong places, never mind when unconscious. I looked around, checking we were in the shadows and no one was lurking close by.

She needed to wake up and explain how she knew I was freaked out by the weirdo in the yellow contact lenses. My skin had been crawling when I'd been near him, then she breezes by and grabs me to rush me out of there. Why had she said I was being followed, and we had to hurry? Hurry to where? Followed by whom?

A chirping sound came from her pocket. Reaching in, I pulled out her phone and looked at the screen. It said Raf with a smiley face beside it. Maybe they could help shed some light. I hit the call button.

"Hello?"

"Crissy?" A deep male voice asked.

I looked at the woman again. "Is Crissy petite, bright red hair and a little nuts in the head?"

"Who is this?" A woman asked.

"She grabbed me and said we had to hurry, so we rushed out of the club and ran down the alley. Then she just sat down and," I looked at her again, "I think she passed out."

"Where are you?" The male demanded.

"In an alley…"

"What alley?" The woman asked.

I looked around for a moment, seeing which dark alley we'd stupidly run into. "The one across from the perv club…"

"I know where that is. Stay with her, I'm on my way." The woman said and then the line went quiet.

I hung up the phone, looking at it before tucking it back into her pocket. Well, one question answered. Someone was coming to get Crissy. I studied her, she looked like a Crissy.

The sound of boots on the pavement had me backing deeper into the shadows, reaching up under the back of my jacket, I squatted, ready to spring into action if needed.

"Crissy?" Someone whispered.

They must have been around the corner when they called. I stood slowly, silently, then stepped away from her. "She's here." I said as I stared down into the darkness.

A woman stepped into view, gave me the once over, then dropped down beside Crissy. "Was she hurt?" She asked, as she checked her.

I shook my head. "Not that I know of. She grabbed me in the club and said we had to hurry, then we ran out the back exit." Two very large males moved into sight. I wrapped my hand around the dagger strapped to my back.

One dropped down beside Crissy, worry and concern written on his face. He must be the Raf with the smiley face. The other stood stiffly, assessing me with cold, flat eyes. There was something about him that set off alarms inside me. Not entirely bad, but not good either. There was more about these people than the eye could see. I knew better than most could ever imagine. Things were not always as they appeared.

I couldn't sense their emotions, other than seeing their concern for Crissy. Something was not right. The sooner I got out of here, the better off I'd be.

"I need to get her back to my place." The woman said.

"I got her." The man beside her said as he scooped the little redhead up in his arms.

Standing up, the blonde woman looked at me. "Thank you for staying with her." She glanced at the stiff one standing behind her, then back to me. "What was Crissy trying to get you away from?"

I shook my head. "I don't know." I took a step in the direction of the narrow alley between the two buildings. "I hope she's alright. I'll get going now."

"Wait," She held up her hand. "You should come back to my place until Crissy wakes up so we can find out. You could be in danger."

Danger wasn't anything new to me. I looked at the drooping redhead in the big guy's arms and debated on it for a brief moment. The entire scenario screamed of attachments, and I knew too well how that always ended. Shaking my head, I glanced from her to the one with the strange vibes. "I'm going to pass. I need to be somewhere." It wasn't a complete lie, I needed to be anywhere but here.

Not giving them a chance to stall me any longer with chitchat, I backed up a few more steps and then gave them an abrupt nod. Turning, I hit a full run in a few short seconds and took off away from the dark alley.

Chapter One

Two things registered—well, three did, but the last one didn't count because it was only my stomach telling me I hadn't eaten recently. I was laying on a bed, so that confirmed I'd blacked out, and the bed moving meant I wasn't alone.

"Crissy, open your eyes for me."

I didn't open them. I knew if Daxx was talking to me, I was safe. Her watching over me meant I had a few moments to assess the chatter inside my head. So many still, which was not a surprise… none were demanding I needed to really see them, so I didn't. A sound from beside the bed told me she wasn't alone… that was the second thing I noticed.

"Crissy, you gave me a heart attack." Rafael was with her.

Opening my eyes, I looked up at him. He smiled. I liked him, he always smiled at me. Too bad his teeth were normal right now, I liked his fangs better. It was an odd thing, but that confirmed my whole life wasn't just me losing my mind, seeing stuff in my head, and knowing there were things out there that everyone didn't know about. I looked around to see where we were, and recognized Daxx's apartment.

"Next time you text 'help', try to give me a hint about what is going on."

I *had* sent him a message. I bolted up and looked around. "Where's Alona?" I crawled off the bed and went out into the other room. She wasn't here. A large man with red hair was, but no one else. "No, no, no, no." I spun around and went to the window to see if it was still night time. My blackouts weren't always short. "We have to go find her." I went quickly into the kitchen and turned on the tap. Leaning down I took a quick sip, then shut it off and turned, running into Rafael's chest. He reached out to steady me, so I wouldn't fall backward. I looked up into his blue eyes. "We have to go get her. They found her." I ducked around him and went to go get my pack. I'd been staying here for weeks now, but I went nowhere without it. You never knew when you would have to run and hide, or disappear, so keeping what you'd want to take with you was very important.

"Criss." Daxx stepped in front of me and put her hands on my shoulders. "Slow down. We found you passed out in an alley with some strange woman."

I nodded. "That's Alona." I went to go by her, but she blocked me. She had that look, the 'we have to talk' look. I would have to talk before I was going to be able to do anything else.

"We'll get to Alona in a second. Are you okay?" Her eyes searched my face.

I frowned at the odd question, but the way she stared at me demanded an answer. She was very determined. "Why wouldn't I be?"

"You were unconscious when we got there." Rafael said coming to stand beside me.

I shrugged, "I'm fine. I knew it was coming, I tried to hurry…"

"Wait." Daxx stopped me with the look that said she wasn't happy.

I loved her, she had so many looks, the fact I recognized them always made me feel like we could have been family in another life.

"You knew you were going to pass out?"

I nodded again, it was too complicated to explain, we didn't have time for this. "Yes. It happens when there's too much filling my head at once." Glancing to the redheaded man standing on the other side of the room, I wondered who he was. He was as big as Raf, but nowhere near as nice. He hadn't moved or smiled. Waving my hand, I decided I'd figure out who he was later. Snapping my head around, I looked back to Daxx. "We have to go find Alona. They found her and she isn't safe now."

"Is she a friend of yours?" Rafael asked.

"No," I shook my head, "I've never met her, but I saw her before and that didn't make sense, until it did." Daxx rubbed a hand across her forehead, the way she always did when she listened to me. I know she didn't understand me most of the time, but she always listens to me, and that was more important than anything. I needed them to help me find Alona. "We have to find her. She doesn't know, but she just carries on…" I glanced at Raf, he was nodding, but his expression said he had no idea what I was saying either. "if they know her, that's bad."

"Okay." Daxx put her hand on my shoulder so I would look at her. "First, you passing out is a normal thing?"

I could see the worry in her eyes and it upset me to see that. "Yes. It's like…" I paused and looked at the floor trying to figure out how to explain it, and be clear with all the things in my mind right now, "a system reboot. When I get over-loaded *seeing*, I just shut down for a few minutes then I'm good to go." I nodded.

"Does it happen often?" Rafael leaned down and looked at me. He was so sweet and good inside.

"No. Lately though, with so much going on here, it's been more frequent." Hundreds of visions a day would be taxing on anyone, if there was another person that went through it. I doubted what I had was common at all.

"You feel okay now though?" Daxx asked with her eyes searching mine again.

"Yes." I hoped that explanation would clear it up so we could go. "Can we go find her now?"

"I don't think she wants to be found." The redhead said.

I rolled my eyes at him, "I know she doesn't *want* to be found, but she has to be." I looked back to Daxx, she would understand. "The man with the yellow eyes found her, so she's not safe, but doesn't know she's not. We have to help her."

"You had a vision of a man with yellow eyes?" Daxx

asked.

"What? No. I saw him at the club talking to Alona." I sighed, why were they making this so complicated? "Alona doesn't know. When I saw her, before I actually *seen* her…" I looked back to the redhead man, "her own eyes were red." I spun to Rafael, "like yours."

He frowned, "She's from my side?" Raf looked at the redheaded man, an odd look on his face.

Now they were getting it. "Yes, but she doesn't know because she's never been there." I frowned, "I don't think." I was almost sure, but sometimes I missed things with so much to sort through. I stepped around his large body and went to grab my pack, digging in it for my notebook as I explained. "When I was looking for your lost brother," I stopped and thought for a second, "no, maybe before that, then I saw her and she's quite old…" I pulled out the notebook and dropped the bag. "I mean the cars were old when I saw her…" I flipped through the notebook, I know I'd written it down when it happened.

"That woman with you tonight was not old, nor did she have red eyes. I would have sensed it if she were from our side." The stiff man informed me.

I stopped and examined him. There was something hard about him, not bad, but he was definitely not a soft-hearted person. "Maybe your radar is broken." I tilted my head and studied him some more, or the space around him, more than his actual body. "And sometimes people are *much* older than they appear." As he was.

"Okay." Daxx came over and lightly grasped my hands before I could open the book again. "Just give me a second." She looked over to the man. "Victor, is it possible that someone got lost or trapped over here years ago?"

He rubbed the back of his neck and stared at the floor for a moment. "I suppose it could happen."

"Before cellphones communicating was hard." Rafael added. "It's not like we could use landlines or telegraph."

Victor took a deep breath and then nodded slowly. "I can check the records and see…"

I was happy they were listening and seemed to believe me,

a rare thing in my life, but they still weren't getting it. Did I tell them she'd never been anywhere but here? That she didn't know she was like them? Or did I let them look for her their way? I hated decisions like this. *A rainbow. Why is there a rainbow in my head?* It didn't last, so it couldn't be important.

"Can you tell us more?" Victor asked me, making me focus on him and not my own thoughts.

I shook my head and then tapped the side of it with my finger. "This doesn't come with instructions. Its more like movie clips, you know short YouTube videos." I shrugged, "sometimes they are longer with sound, but that's rare…" I stopped because his serious, but pretty green eyes locked on me, and made me feel like I'd just said something wrong. I thought back to what I'd just said, there couldn't be anything wrong with it.

He raised his hand slowly, it was a big hand, as far as hands go. "You actually see inside your head?" He glanced to Raf, then Daxx, "I thought, when we were talking, she was seeing," he pointed to one of his eyes. Stiffening, he placed his hands on his hips and looked at me again.

I felt like he was examining me under a microscope now. Not a good feeling at all. I'd never seen him, I didn't like not knowing what was inside a stranger. I shook my head and tried to stay focused on what he was saying.

"When she could see Marcus and his followers I thought that was her *seeing*, but it's not, is it?" He snapped his head to look back to Rafael.

"Right." Raf replied, looking as confused as I felt.

The space around him changed, it was murky, flashing between hot and cold so fast I couldn't possibly understand what it meant.

"I will search the records." He strode across the room and out Daxx's door before any of us could blink.

"That was…" Daxx looked from me to Raf.

He nodded. "Yeah, just a little on the strange side, but Victor can be abrupt like that." He shrugged and then looked at me.

"I don't think we're going to be able to find your Alona

tonight, Crissy. She took off running and will be nowhere to be found by now."

I gnawed on my bottom lip. "You're probably right, she hides very well." I sighed, "It took me weeks to find her this time." I hugged my notebook. "If I see her again, will you help me?"

He nodded. "Yes. If she belongs with us, then we have to find her."

Belongs with us… *Brother.* "Oh." I turned and went into Daxx's room, dropping down, I pulled my other bag from under her bed. When I looked up, they stood there looking at me. "I am getting closer to finding your brother, Raf, he keeps changing his name…" I tried to remember how many times he had, but couldn't. "So, I lose him and have to start tracking the new name… after I narrow down which one is his." I got up and lifted the heavy bag onto the bed and opened it. "It's not easy. The years he spent in another country… that was tricky to follow." I pulled out the thick stack of papers and held them to my chest. "But at least I'm in this century now, so if I can just figure out who he was next, I might be closer to who he is now."

Rafael looked at the papers I was hugging and grinned. "That's amazing. I don't know how you do it."

I shrugged, "I'm used to processing a lot at once…" I nodded and went back into the other room, "I mean, some days I get hundreds of flashes." I thought about that for a second. I'd tried to count a few times, but kept losing track. Sometimes I wished my brain had a remote that I could just hit pause and take a closer look…

"You get hundreds of visions a day?" He asked, following me out. Huffing out a loud breath, he shook his head. "I can barely handle one or two a week."

I froze and stared at him. "You see things too?"

With that smile I liked, he nodded. "I started seeing Daxx about five years ago, that's how I knew she really existed."

I looked at her, of course she existed. What a strange thing to see. "Are they little clips or long movies? Do yours come with sound? Mine rarely do…"

Rubbing her temples, Daxx walked in carrying my bag, she looked at Rafael. "My king wants me to get back ASAP."

Raf chuckled, "I've been ignoring his *requests*."

She gave him a stern look. "I don't think that's an option with the mating bond."

Her King? She had a king. That was a kind of cool.

Daxx stopped and looked at me, her eyes locked with mine and I knew what that meant, she was going to make a request that I stay put or laid low, like she always did.

"I want Crissy to come back with us." She turned and looked at Raf. "Do you think she'll need a device? A legal one."

I frowned and looked from one to the other.

Rafael rubbed his jaw as he thought, "With the way she can see through magic and spells, I don't think she will, but to be on the safe side, I'll get Quint to meet us when we land and bring one." He pulled out his phone and walked over by the window.

Daxx nodded, then turned those blue eyes of hers back to me. I hugged the papers tighter, going to new places never worked out well for me. My mind would explode with the new onslaught of visions popping in.

"Crissy, we'd like you to come home with us for a few days." She smiled and motioned to the papers I held. "You can work on finding the brother, and not have to worry about being caught, chased or..." she smirked, "everything else."

I looked at Rafael as he talked quietly into his phone, then back to her. "I don't know. Its cool that there's a *place* from inside my head that really exists, but I don't know if my head can handle it." I glanced to the window. *Maybe the rainbow means its going to rain.* "It's used to here, sometimes the hundreds can turn into so much more if I go to a new place." I wouldn't mind seeing where Quinton and Rafael lived though. I chewed on my bottom lip, trying to decide if I should chance it. "What is this device? Is it like the ones you're trying to track down here?"

"Sort of, only it would be a legal version of it." She shrugged, "I don't need one, and I don't think you would to stay there, but we'd like to be sure."

"What happens if I do need one and I don't have it?" Losing things was something I did a little too well.

Daxx glanced at Raf, then gave her a nervous look. "We don't want to find out."

Wide-eyed I looked at her. "If it's too much for my head to cope with, can I come back?" It would be nice to not have to look over my shoulder for a few days, something I hadn't had in… well, ever.

"Yes." She smiled. "Just say the word and one of us will bring you right back here."

My heart started beating so fast in my chest, I felt like my whole body was pulsing with it. "Okay." Taking back the bag she held, I stuffed the papers in it and turned to get my other things.

Chapter Two

I opened my eyes slowly and looked around. I hadn't thought to ask how we 'crossed over', my mind pictured us walking over an invisible line. We hadn't. They teleported me or something like that. Whatever they'd done to bring me here, my stomach wasn't happy about it. Taking a deep breath, I let it out slowly and looked around. We were in a room with a long shiny wooden table and many chairs. Portraits of couples with loving eyes looked over it.

"Crissy," Quinton came dashing through a door. "How are you feeling? Any pains?" His big brown eyes were searching me from my feet up.

I smiled at him and did a quick check. "No. My stomach is a bit wishy-washy, but I don't hurt." I touched my forehead and closed my eyes briefly. They were still there, not as many but at least it wasn't overwhelming. Quinton was right in front of me when I opened them. "I'm okay." I smiled and hugged him tightly.

"Interesting." A deep voice came from behind me.

I let go of Quinton and turned to see a big man with long blond hair pulled neatly behind his head. His hazel eyes moved over Daxx for a moment before he looked back to me. I'd seen him before. Going over, I looked up at him. "I know you." I looked at Daxx. "Your Daxx's king." Something was different though. "You shaved your little beard off."

Rafael laughed. "I think you've seen Chase ... this is his

twin, Troy.”

I smiled up at him. “Oh. But you are the one Daxx chose?”

“I am.” His brows were creased as he studied me, a strange look in his eyes.

I looked at his mouth. “Do you have fangs?”

He raised one eyebrow at me and glanced at Quinton over my head before nodding slowly. “I do.”

“I like fangs.” I told him and then turned to look at one of the portraits. “When I saw Rafael’s fangs, it was the first time I knew I wasn’t insane and that other stuff out of my head was real.” I didn’t know the couple in the portrait, which was comforting in an odd way.

“She has hundreds’ of visions a day, Troy.” Rafael told him.

I moved to the next portrait, the man seemed familiar, but then again, his relation was standing across the room with the same brown eyes, most likely watching me. Quinton was a silent observer, despite the front he let everyone see. The pretty lady in the portrait was looking at me with soft eyes, she must have been a loving mom.

“Really?” Troy asked, I didn’t bother to turn around and clarify, I stopped trying to validate what happened in my head to strangers a long time ago. It was safer that way.

“Glad you’re back. I don’t know what happened over there, but Victor came back in a mood.”

I turned around to see who the new voice belonged to. It was him. Or was it? It could be, but if it was him, then he wasn’t lost at all. I went over to the man and looked into his grey eyes. They weren’t the same, but close enough that they could have been twins. “Your brother looks just like you.” I told him.

He looked over to Troy slowly and then back to me. “*Which* brother?”

Standing on my toes, I searched his face carefully. “The one you’ve never seen.”

He leaned down, closing the space between our faces, his long black hair framing us. “You’ve seen him?” I watched the pupils of his eyes redden slightly, and nodded. “Where?”

Reaching up, I touched his mouth so he would open it, smiled on seeing his fangs when he reluctantly did. Dropping my hand, I stepped away. "In my head." I looked at Daxx and nodded, she knew it was true, and that's all that mattered to me.

Daxx smiled at me. "Arius, this is Crissy, my friend."

He straightened and looked me up and down.

I went over to my bags and opened the big one to pull out the pages and held them out to him. "I haven't found him yet, but I'm in this century now, so soon you can see him too."

Hesitantly he came over and took the pages and flipped through a few. "You've tracked him through these name changes?"

"Yes." I clapped my hands together lightly. "He's not easy to find."

Looking up from the papers, he searched my face. "Do you know who he is now?"

I shook my head. "No," then frowned, "I'm at eighty years ago right now, so that will probably mean two more names to find and track before I'll know who he is today." I took the papers out of his hand and went over to the table to spread them out. "Other than when he tried living in a different country for forty years, he seems to stick to a pattern, always going back to the same areas..." I pushed the pages around until I found the one I'd written that on, then tapped it. "It's sad really, it's like he can't be away from them." I glanced to Daxx, "his wives are buried here though, so I think that might be why." I remembered the others and leaned down to dig out those pages. "Or it could be his children..." I shook my head, "No they'd be dead now, but he has grand and great grand children..."

"What?" Troy came over and pulled the page from my hands.

"How is that possible? I thought only true mates could have children." Daxx looked from one man to the other that were in the room.

Arius with the pretty hair, rubbed the back of his neck. "He's technically not true-blood, his mother wasn't one of us."

"I don't know what you just said, but I love your voice, so

please keep talking." I told him. He grinned at me.

"How many children?" Quinton came over and looked down at me.

I bit my lip and thought. "Five, which if you look at how long he's lived, that's not a lot." I rubbed a hand over my throat, it always made me feel sad to think about him. "Three of them are still alive, I mean he had them with his first few wives and that was…" I blew out a breath as I did the math, "between two hundred and fifty and one hundred and fifty years ago." I glanced to Daxx and frowned, "He's never married again, that I've found, for the last one hundred and fifty years. He's just been alone. It's very sad." It was, I knew better than most how hard alone could be.

"If the children died, they weren't of our blood then. Or they didn't know enough to sustain their lives properly. Do you know where the great grandchildren are?" Rafael asked as he sat on the corner of the table.

"I don't…" I looked at Daxx then back to him, "I only follow him. I didn't know you'd want to know about the others." I shrugged, "I don't think he has been able to stay with his wives for long, because they'd sort of notice he wasn't aging, wouldn't they?" How long would I live, I'd always questioned that. I loved life and seeing new things, learning unknown pieces, but to live too long I would grow tired of the constant flashes inside my head. I would never know peace, that I knew for sure. Shaking my head, I remembered they were talking.

Troy hissed out a loud breath. "We're going to have to find them. All of them, to be sure."

"Find who?"

I looked to see Troy's twin come through the door. It was quite clear, now that I was seeing him, that they were nothing alike. He stopped and looked me up and down then gave me a charming smile.

"Ah, the infamous Crissy has finally joined us." He grinned. "Love the hair color."

My eyes widened and I felt my cheeks flush, he knew of me. Moving over, I stopped and looked up at him for a moment. "Your eyes don't go red." I found that interesting.

He shook his head, looking amused.

"Do you have fangs?" I looked at him mouth.

"No cutie, I'm afraid I was left out of the gene pool on that one."

I studied him for a moment longer. "Hmm, that's okay, I think you got something the rest of them didn't."

He exhaled and held his hand over his chest then glanced to his look-alike brother. "Can we keep her?"

Daxx laughed, "She's not a puppy, Chase."

He chuckled, "Good thing, kitten, or you two might not get along." He touched my hair and smiled again. "I do love this color."

I blushed again. "I wanted to feel bold and daring when I did it."

"I don't know about that, but it takes a daring person to try it." He smiled down at me for a moment, then looked around at the others. "Who are we finding?"

I remembered what we were talking about before he came in. "Your lost brother... who looks like Arius and his great grand children." I bit my lip, "Or maybe they're great, great," I shook my head, "I'm not sure, I didn't know I should trace those branches of the family trees with his wives." Turning, I went back to the pages and started to flip through them to find the dates he'd been married. "I don't know if any of them lived a longer than normal life span, but those that didn't wouldn't be hard to track..." I frowned, "if any of them did though, that takes hours of reading and searching to find who they became next, or are now..." I looked at the papers. "I'm going to need more pens and paper too." I nodded.

"I don't know who pissed off Victor, but they can go fix him. He just fired one of *my* constables."

A man with short black hair and blue eyes came in and then stopped and looked at me. I'd seen him before too. I was sure this time, his scar on his face confirmed that it could only be him.

I had to pause for a second and wonder if all people were this large in this world we were in. I wasn't tall, just five foot five, which worked out fine for me, easier to hide in small places, but everyone I'd met here so far had to be well over six feet tall.

He glanced around at everyone else then walked toward me. I could feel he was safe, knew it matched what I'd seen of him. When he stopped in front of me and held out his hand, I looked at it and then reached up and ran my finger over the faded scar that ran down the right side of his face. "It's sad, how you got this." I looked to see surprise in his blue eyes. "You shouldn't have kept it as a reminder." I offered him a little smile, "you'll never forget."

He pulled his hand back and frowned at me.

"This is Crissy." Daxx offered, "Criss, this is Michael."

His eyes searched my face.

"Michael, call everyone now." Troy said as he tossed the papers on the table. "We need to discuss what Crissy has found out."

Straightening, he suddenly looked like a warrior, on alert. "Regarding?"

"Our lost brother," Arius said without looking up from the papers, "and his children."

Michael's head snapped toward him so fast, I was sure it must have hurt. He nodded abruptly and pulled out his phone.

I needed my notebook, many things I'd put in it were standing right in front of me, for real. I couldn't write down everything that came to me, some were so brief I didn't even see them, but the ones that last long enough to note, or those that played on repeat, I did write down. Turning, I went back to my pack and squatted down to dig through it. Someday I'd empty this and see what long forgotten treasures were in it.

"I was just going to put coffee on, does anyone else want some?"

I glanced around the chair I was behind to see a normal sized lady coming out the door Quinton had run through. Her aura had such warm vibes, I could feel them from this far away. She had a sweet smile, understanding eyes and her pretty strawberry blonde hair was twisted up like she was going to a party.

"Oh. Hello, dear." She started walking toward me. "Aren't

you just too cute for words."

I stood up slowly and glanced to Daxx quickly, she nodded. "Mitz, this is my friend Crissy."

She stopped in front of me and gave me a fast hug, then clasped my face between her hands. "I've heard a lot about you, dear. Are you hungry?" She let go of my face when I nodded.

"I'd like toast and marmalade, please." I nodded again, "three pieces, white bread if you have it." She smiled at me. "Two always feel like I need more, but four is too sweet and makes me feel ill."

"I'll go get that. Would you like some juice with it?"

Quinton and Rafael had both told me all about Mitz, and brought her food often. It was no wonder they were all so large, her cooking was so tasty. "Cranberry if you have it."

"I'm sure we do." She smiled at me again then turned and walked back through the door.

I looked to see everyone there going through the papers I'd set on the table. Grabbing my pack, I turned slowly until I spotted a corner with a small table in it. Going over, I sat under the table and pulled out my notebook. It took me longer than I'd like to find a pencil, confirming I needed to clean out my pack soon. Flipping through the pages of writing and sketches, I tried to find the one that kept playing through my head.

New voices had me looking up. The man with the red hair, Victor, was back, and with him was another man with short, spiked red hair. It may have just been my view from the floor, but they looked as large as the others.

"What do you mean children?" Victor asked.

"Is that possible?" The man I didn't know asked.

Troy shrugged, "Our lost brother..."

"Would you like to know his name? I mean, I don't know who he is now, but I know what his name was when he was born." I frowned, "so you can call him something other than lost brother. He's not lost to him, only to you."

Everyone looked around, then Rafael turned and tilted his head at me and smiled. I smiled back, you had to with him, even if you didn't feel like smiling. Coming over, he squatted down and looked under the table at me. "You don't have to hide here." He held out his hand.

I took his hand and grabbed my pack, clutching it and my book to my chest as he helped me out. "I feel better in little spots." He didn't let go of my hand. "I feel safe then."

Pulling my hand gently, he went over to the table. "You're safe here. I promise."

He didn't let go of my hand until I stood by the table again, surrounded by so many tall men it was like land of the giants. I looked at the new one, him I didn't know. He looked more scared of me than I did of him, which was completely silly. Hesitantly, I held out my hand to him. "Crissy." I said with a soft voice, knowing that tone always made me feel better when I wanted to run the other way. His eyes flicked to my hand then back to my face. He took it and squeezed once, then dropped it.

"Leone."

I smiled at him and then remembered. "Oh. Emil." I nodded and looked up at them. "That was your brother's name when he was born." I exhaled like I just told a secret held for too long. "He always changes it to another one that starts with an E, which took me a hundred years to realize, but that's who he was when he was born."

"Emil." Victor said quietly. "Wasn't our great grandfather's middle name Emil?" He looked to Quinton who nodded. Exhaling slowly, he glanced around at the others. "That confirms it then, father had a hand in naming him."

Chase snorted, "and making him, then leaving him to live on the other side with no clue."

"You've found him?"

I looked around Raf to see Mitz coming back with my toast, her brows were knit together with worry. "No, but I'm close." I told her. "I promised to find Emil, and I will." I nodded, hoping to make her feel better.

The plate in her hand started to shake, so she set it on the table with a clank. "Emil?" A soft smile appeared on her face. "Emil," she repeated with more reflection as she set my juice beside it. With hurried steps, she brushed through the tall bodies and hugged me tight. "I can't thank you enough for trying to find him.”

I looked to Quinton for help. I wasn't big on being touched and her emotions were enough to drown me right now. He understood my silent plea and came over and gently peeled the lady off me.

“We'll find him, Mitz.” He wrapped his arms around her small body.

She sniffled, “he needs to come home. He's been out there alone for so long…”

“Not as alone as you'd think.” Arius said with a smirk.

Quinton grasped her shoulders and leaned back to look down at her. “You need to sit down, Mitz. Everyone does, we have some interesting news to share.”

I wandered around the room as the ten sat at the long table, going through my notes. I didn't know much about what they talked about. Their father—and yes, they were all brothers, which explained how they lost one in the first place, with so many to watch over. I back-tracked, they didn't know how dad had managed to have a child with someone not his wife, or how Emil had had children. It was all very strange and mysterious to me, and I couldn't get too bogged down with figuring it out because my brain already had more than enough to process, I didn't need to add to it right now.

I found the tattoo on Daxx's arm intriguing though, and the fact her king had one to match was something I made a note to inquire about later. Nibbling on the second piece of toast, I stood back and looked at them. Never having had family that I knew of, it was so clear the connection they had by how they interacted, *that* I'd missed out on something became quite obvious. Then again, with my tendencies, I doubt a family would have wanted me.

My eyes stopped on Victor, I still couldn't figure him out. The way he held himself, I was fairly sure he was the eldest, he just had that watchful way about him that told me he'd been looking out for all of them the longest. He wasn't a bad man, but there was something hard and unmovable about him. I may have to ask Rafael or Quinton about him, not knowing always bugged me. It was better to ask and get answers, so not to tax my mind with things I didn't have space for.

Chewing the last bite, I glanced at my plate at the other end of the table, then decided not rushing to eat the last piece was a better idea. Meals weren't always guaranteed in my life, so when I could, I took my time. I did.

Hands tucked into my pockets, I wandered closer to the end of the table where Victor sat. His dark red hair was brushed carefully back from his face, and I swear there wasn't a hair out of place. How did one manage such a thing? My hair did not follow instruction at all, but hung to my shoulders in every direction possible, some wavy, some straight.

I didn't miss how his green eyes tracked my every move, and that was fascinating to realize. When I watched him watch me, I felt… I wasn't sure, warmer didn't quite cover it but I didn't know how else to describe the feeling. Normally, when someone looked at me too closely I felt uncomfortable, with him it was kind of like a fever, but without the germs and sickness.

Deciding I needed to study him closer, maybe to get some answers, I went and hopped up and sat on the table right where he was sitting and leaned in closer to look into his green eyes. So many emotions went through them I didn't catch one long enough to be sure of anything, they changed that fast. "You feel like an allergic reaction, minus the sickness." I told him.

His eyes widened and then he scowled at me. I realized everyone had stopped talking then and was glad my back was to all of them. I didn't like being watched.

"Are you demented?" he asked me in a quiet tone, then glanced beside him to where Daxx sat, "Is she crazy?"

"Do I need to be?" I asked him, I tilted my head and continued to watch him, "I can do it if there's a need…" He didn't answer, just sat there and held my stare. His eyes started to change and I knew there would be fangs to go with it, but I didn't want to touch him to see. A cool hand touched my shoulder and I scrambled across the table off the other side. Hitting the floor, I turned and backed into the corner.

Victor jumped up and knocked the chair back, but didn't move any closer.

Troy stood there beside him and held his hands up. "I'm sorry. I didn't mean to startle you."

My heart was in my throat and beating too fast. "I don't like…" I exhaled slowly, "being touched." I told him quietly. "Unless I know, then it's okay, but not before." I nodded, hoping he understood.

Victor took a step toward me, then stopped and jammed his hands into his pockets and just stared at me.

Quinton got up and came around the table to me. I almost jumped into his arms, needing to feel the steady calm he always projected when I was near him. "It's okay." He said hugging me back. "Troy wouldn't hurt you." I looked up into his brown eyes and he nodded.

Letting go of him, I turned so I was facing the others again. Uncomfortable didn't begin to describe how I felt, every single one of them was looking at me.

"How is it, Quint that women new to Alterealm throw themselves in your arms?" Chase drawled with a smirk on his face.

Quinton looked down at me and winked, then back to his brother. "Its my irresistible charm."

Chase snorted, "It's your something."

Troy moved around the table slowly. "I didn't mean to frighten you, I only wanted to ask if I could take a look."

My eyes darted from him to Daxx, then back. "A look?"

He stopped and nodded. "I can read people's minds, see their thoughts…" he glanced to Daxx and smirked, "mostly. I just wanted to see if I could see yours. Maybe see our brother for myself?"

I crossed my arms over my chest and frowned. "You want to look inside *my* head?" He nodded again. "I don't think you're going to enjoy that." It was fascinating though, that he could do something like that.

"I'll take my chances." Troy said motioning to the chair beside him.

I looked at it then back to him. "Do you have to touch me?"

He shook his head. "I don't think so."

I clutched the book to my chest. "Will it hurt?" I shrugged, "I'm not a fan of pain."

Troy smirked, "I don't think anyone is." He tucked his hands behind his back. "It won't cause you pain."

Did I want to do this? It would be something new, that was for sure, but what was in my head, might not be what he thought it would be. "Okay." I walked over and hopped up on the table beside the chair he'd motioned too.

Chuckling quietly, he pulled the chair out and sat down, putting us at eye level. I held the notebook in my lap and tried not to show how nervous I was. Who wouldn't be, when someone was going to look inside your head? His eyes turned red and I smiled, and knew I needed to look. Leaning down, I touched his bottom lip hoping he'd open his mouth, he did. Sure enough, there they were, fangs. I touched the tip of one and he grinned and sat back.

"Sorry." I whispered.

"Criss," Daxx stepped beside him, with that look on her face letting me know I was doing something that wasn't sociably acceptable, again.

I shrugged. "Rafael doesn't mind me touching his fangs."

She shook her head. "Raf doesn't have a mate."

"No, he's just a manwhore." Chase snickered behind me.

"Kettle, pot." Rafael retorted.

"If you're finished…" Troy interrupted.

Everyone went silent. He took a deep breath and looked back at me. "Okay?" he asked with his mouthful of fangs.

I nodded. "I'll behave this time."

He grinned and gave me a quick nod, then leaned closer, his red eyes locked on mine. It was a bit weird, but then again, I wasn't one to judge what was normal. I didn't feel anything, which was disappointing, and was just about to say it wasn't working, when he grabbed his temples and fell back against the chair.

"Troy?" Daxx leaned over him.

He held up a hand to silence her, then opened his eyes, hazel again and looked at me. "How do you function with all of that happening at once?"

I shrugged. "It's always been like that." I glanced around to see everyone looking at me like I was a bug under a microscope. "I told you that you weren't going to enjoy it." The closer everyone moved, with those looks on their faces, the more the walls seemed to close in on me. I Jumped off the table and went over to grab my pack. *Butterflies, so many of them fluttering about.* Turning, I looked around at them and stopped to focus on Victor. "I don't like being inside. There are no butterflies. I like butterflies." I backed up and then turned and ran out the nearest door.

Chapter Three

I squatted down in the big closet and then sat and pulled my legs against my chest. I didn't know whose closet I was in, but with the number of doors I'd run past, it would take them a while to find me. Later, I'd stop and examine the fact that I knew the halls I'd just run through. I'd seen them for years. These halls had been the magical place I escaped to when I was young and needed some solace from reality. Now, here I was and they were real after all.

Looking out the closet door that was open a crack, I noticed I'd left the door to the room open. Stupid move, may as well have left them bread crumbs to follow. I was just about to rush out and close it when two large men walked in. Troy and Victor. I lowered my head to my knees and stayed as still as I could. This was something I could do. I'd practiced it all my life, being small and invisible.

"She came in here." Victor said with no hesitation.

"Anyone could have left the door open." Troy told him.

Victor shook his head, "No. I can smell her essence."

Frowning, I lifted my arm and sniffed. I didn't smell that bad. A little dirty maybe, but after running through the club anyone would have a bad odor.

"Oh." Troy rubbed his arm with the tattoo. "I'm afraid all I smell and taste is my mate at this point."

Victor stood with his hands on his hips and looked around the dark room. "Not surprising, you've only been bonded a little over a day." He looked at his brother. "Are you all right? I've never seen you have pain while looking inside a mind."

Troy exhaled loudly, "there's never been pain before. I don't know how she does it. If I had that much crammed in my head, like she does, I'd be a vegetable, unable to form a coherent sentence."

Victor snorted, "That's questionable with her as well." He ran a hand through his hair, "when we crossed to the other side, we found her passed out in a... less than favorable neighborhood alleyway, with a woman watching over her."

"Passed out?" Troy moved back to the door and shook his head at whoever was out there.

"Yes, she told Daxx it happens when her mind can't cope with so many visions at once. She said it was like a reboot." His voice was quiet, I thought I heard a touch of concern in it.

"So, she just crashes basically?" Troy came back into the room.

Victor nodded, "Yes, I'm wondering if her health is at risk."

I frowned, I'd never thought about that. I'd always been this way and losing pieces of time when I blackout was a normal thing for me. Other than inside my head, I felt fine, the odd hunger pang probably wasn't a risk.

"We can have doc take a look if she agrees. We owe her a lot. Not only has she helped with finding Marcus, but also Emil."

Victor turned and looked around the darkened room again. "Not to mention Daxx, Rafael and Quinton's attachment to her." He mused quietly. "There's more, but she took off before I could mention it."

I hugged my knees and made sure my pack was right beside me in case I needed to bolt out of here. I should have asked Daxx how I could get back to her apartment. Another classic dumb moment on my part, not getting all the facts first.

"More?" Troy pulled his phone out and glanced at it.

"Yes. The woman that was watching over her, she says she is one of us. Rafael and your huntress thought perhaps she'd crossed over years ago and somehow gotten stuck there, but I have no records of any female in the last hundred years matching her description."

I bit my lip, to stop from blurting out that they weren't listening when I said she hadn't been here. Did I say it? I closed my eyes and tried to remember. I spent so much time alone and talking inside my head, or out loud to myself, that I could hardly remember what had happened and what had yet to happen.

"People can change their appearance. Did you get a read off her? Is she one of us?" Troy ran a hand over his jaw. "This day is just filled with missing people, isn't it?"

Victor made a sound of exasperation. "It is. I'm not certain if she's one of us or not, I was more concerned with the woman unconscious on the pavement. While I'm concerned about Emil's lineage, this Alona is in danger. A yellow eyed man approached her, according to Crissy."

The way he said my name struck me strangely, sending shivers up my back. He pronounced it like it had several s's and not just a few. *Crisssy.* It wasn't bad, just different.

"Fuck. Okay, priority one will be finding this woman then. Was the yellow eyed man one of Marcus' people?" Troy asked.

"I don't know. Getting details is more than a little exasperating with her, but if Alona has been trapped on the wrong side for many years, we should…"

I lunged forward, gripping my pack tightly. "She's never been *here*." I gave him a stern look. "I said that… I think I did… out loud." I shook my head to clear and focus. "She was born on… my side, space, whatever and has no idea why she's as old as she is or different." I nodded abruptly, having cleared all that up and then realized I was no longer hidden. Both men were just standing there looking at me.

Troy raised his hand, "First, you don't need to hide here." He waved a hand around. "This was Daxx's room, you can stay here."

I looked around, taking in how big it was. "What would I do with all this space?" Looking back at the closet briefly, I shrugged, "The closet is more than enough space for me."

He sighed and lifted his hands for a second before dropping them. "Then stay in her closet, but you are perfectly safe here."

I wanted to believe him, I really did, but I had trust issues… to add to all my other issues. Looking at Victor, I was surprised to see his eyes were red and in the dim light they almost glowed. "The rats' eyes in the alley are almost like that if light hits them a certain way."

Troy snorted.

"Did she just compare me to vermin?" Victor asked quietly.

"I don't think she meant it quite like that." Troy said with a big grin on his face.

I remembered. "Do you really think there might be something wrong with me?" I waved my hand at them. "I heard what you said about when I blackout." I hadn't been to a doctor since I was young, when the caretakers of the group home had dragged me there to get the drugs to keep me quiet and docile. "Maybe I'm broken after all?"

Victor exhaled and looked at the floor, when he lifted his head the red eyes were replaced with his normal ones that didn't glow in the dark. "It could be possible."

"There's no harm in making sure, Crissy." Troy added.

Biting my lip, I paced over and looked down at the bed. It was big enough for a whole family. Distracted by the door across from it, I went over and peeked in. Feeling along the wall I flicked on the light. It was a huge. shiny bathroom. I wasn't certain, but it looked like it was bigger than Daxx's whole apartment. I looked down into the tub, which could have easily been mistaken for a small swimming pool. Stepping over the side, that came almost to my hip, I sat down, when I looked up the men were standing there giving me a strange look. "I'll see your doctor," I pointed at them, "but no needles and I won't take pills *ever* again." I shook my head. "Been there, done that, and all it did was make me go crazy inside my head." I looked at Troy for a moment, feeling like I needed to justify I wasn't crazy. "They never stop." I pointed to my head, "What you've seen. That's how it is, when I sleep, when I wake… they never stop."

His expression changed and I could see why Daxx had chosen him, he had a compassionate heart. "I'll set something up for you." Troy told me and then looked at his phone again. "I need to go take care of something." He smiled at me. "Daxx will be here shortly. I'll see you at dinner."

When he left my sight, I sat there and looked at Victor, he didn't look like he was trying to dissect me, but he still had a weird expression on his face. I liked to learn new faces and what all their expressions could mean, I just wasn't sure if this was something I should do with him.

He cleared his throat, "If you'd like an actual bath, I can come back later to talk about Alona." He motioned out into the room. "I'm sure there will be something in the closet you could change into. Daxx's clothes have already been moved to the King's chamber."

"She is a queen now." I stood up, debating on if I did want to have a bath.

"She is our Huntress Queen." He nodded abruptly.

I stepped out and looked back down into the tub. Maybe a bath wouldn't be a bad thing. I wasn't even sure if I remembered the last time I had one. Falling in the river probably didn't count. He still watched me. "Do you have a title or job?" Going to the mirror I looked at my bright red hair, it was a mess, but that wasn't new. My roots were starting to show already. I wondered if I could combine dyes and make the purple shade I wanted. My eyes, with the dark circles underneath were just a normal, washed out brown. Maybe I could get colored contacts. Glancing up, I saw he watched me in the mirror.

"I'm the justice here." He finally said.

I studied his reflection in the mirror, somehow feeling less analyzed then if I just turned around to look at him. "I sensed there was something unbendable about you." I smiled, "I guess you always tell the truth?" That must be why he felt so cold, the decisions he made couldn't be easy.

He straightened, but still held my eyes in the glass. "Yes, which doesn't always suit others agendas."

Turning, I leaned back against the counter and hugged my bag. "So much tragedy could be avoided if people stuck to the truth."

"Indeed." Victor said softly.

"You don't like me." I observed out loud.

His green eyes moved over my face for a tense minute. "I'm not well enough acquainted with you to like or dislike you." He stated in a low voice.

"There's something though, that makes you *want* to dislike me." I realized I was standing in a bathroom with a strange, large man. That was something I never did, allow myself to be boxed into a space I couldn't get out of. Quickly I went back out into the room and started looking for a light switch.

"That may be so, it's too soon to know for certain." He answered quietly.

He wasn't following me around the room, which made me feel better. I went over by the door and felt along the wall, but still didn't find a switch. I glanced to see he was moving in my direction, "When will you know for certain?" He moved by me and flicked on the lights. I had looked in the right spot, just not high enough. I looked at the room now that I could see it. "Holy." I whispered. "A whole family could live in here." It was huge. The decorating was wonderful, all shiny wood and pretty carpet, but still it was so much space.

He chuckled and stood beside me. "You may not have noticed, but we are a fairly large breed on this side."

I looked up at him and nodded, "I noticed." Shrugging, I went over to look at the closet now that I could see. "I like my size." I shrugged. "It has saved my life more times than I can remember." The closet was filed with clothes of every kind. Someone had put a clothing store in a closet. I remembered I was talking. "Being able to hide and not being found is very important in my world."

"And why is that?"

He spoke from right behind me and I almost jumped out of my skin. Turning, I glared at him.

"I apologize I didn't mean to startle you." He bowed his head like they did in movies when he said it.

"Your kind of stuffy." I told him, "but I like it and some of the words you use too." I turned back and went over to the line of shoes on the floor. Shoes, boots of any and every kind. I looked down at my worn out running shoes, the one side of my left one was worn right through. Squatting down I picked up a pair of black boots, they felt like real leather. I set it beside my foot and it looked like the same size. I remembered he was there. "I like these." I held up the boot.

"Take anything you wish from this closet." He said with a strange tone in his voice. "All of this was for the huntress, and as we had no idea her size, Mitz made certain all sizes and styles were covered."

I stood up holding the boots and my pack to my chest. "Really?" Turning I looked at him to see his eyes were red again. Frowning, I went over. "Why do you keep looking at me with red eyes?" I didn't know much about his kind, but knew that I had to ask Raf and Quinton to change their eyes and let me see their fangs.

"I'm uncertain about my reaction to you." He said quietly, but continued to stand there stiffly with red eyes.

I set the boots down and went to stand in front of him. "Are you mated?" I'd learned one thing today at least.

One eyebrow raised. "I am not."

I smiled, "Can I see your fangs?"

His mouth twitched like he wanted to smile, but wasn't sure if he should. "What is your fascination with our fangs?" He opened his mouth and showed me his.

Reaching up slowly, I touched the end of one of them. They were quite sharp. "For as long as I can remember," I touched the incisor on the other side of his mouth and smiled, then pulled my hand away. "I could see things and thought for sure I was stuck in some fantasy…" I shrugged, and decided to use his words, "that I was crazy." I touched a finger to his lip because he'd closed his mouth, "when I first saw Rafael's fangs, I knew all those things were real and I wasn't a lunatic." I shrugged and picked up the boots again.

He reached out and took them from my hand and then gently tugged on my pack. "I will hold these if you'd like to look through the clothes."

I released my hold on the pack and spun around. "I never keep more than I can carry in my…" I'd left my bag in the dinning room. I had to go get it.

He put his hand out and stopped me from running from the room. "Your bag will be fine, I'm sure Daxx will bring it with her and you can put it somewhere safe."

I looked up and nodded slowly. He had to tell the truth, so I could trust that. Glancing down at his hand still resting against my stomach, I looked back to him quickly. His eyes were red. Backing up, I studied him, trying to see the space around him. The cool aura I usually sensed with him was gone, or had warmed, I wasn't sure. "I don't know why you have fangs, I never asked Quinton, but someday," I glanced at the floor, away from his red eyes. "I will."

He moved closer, or maybe just leaned down, I wasn't sure exactly. He held my chin lightly with two large fingers. "Have Daxx put my number in your phone and if you ever feel the need to hide, call me, I *will* come and get you."

I nodded, not even able to find words to say, which was something I don't think had ever happened in my life. He didn't release my chin and I didn't move. His red eyes were searching mine for something. If I were normal I'd be running and screaming *demon,* but I was so far from normal that even I didn't understand me.

My head suddenly felt cloudy. I backed up. "No, no, no." I put my hand against my forehead and pressed on it like I was going to be able to stop them from flooding my mind with too many. I squeezed my eyes shut and tried to focus on them, to see if I needed any of them before they were lost.

"Crissy?"

I felt him grasp my shoulders and my last thought was 'oh good I won't do a faceplant on the floor' right as the darkness rolled over me.

Chapter Four

"I don't care if the arm is hanging on by a vein, tell him to get here *now*."

Victor sounded really angry and I realized he was holding me, because when he spoke it vibrated through me. I didn't open my eyes, not sure if I was going to like what I saw when I did. What I needed to figure out was why I'd blacked out again so soon. Normally, it didn't happen this close together.

"He's on his way, his assistant is finishing with the arm." Troy said from some distance away.

Someone touched my wrist, and I could tell by the gentle touch is was Daxx.

"Her pulse is steady. Her breathing is fine." She said in a shaky voice. "You can probably set her down on the bed."

He must have been standing there holding me, because we were now moving. As soon as I felt the soft surface underneath me, I opened my eyes slowly. Hovering above me was Victor and Quinton.

"Hi." I offered a smile, not sure which of Daxx's social etiquette rules would apply in this situation.

"Are you okay?" Quinton asked, his brown eyes almost bleeding with worry.

"I'm okay." I moved up so I was sitting, then realized all of them were in the room. I looked at Victor, who stood above me, his arms crossed over his big chest looking like a statue. "Thanks for making sure I didn't faceplant. I usually have enough warning to at least sit down." Why had did they flood back so fast? I needed to think about that.

"That's twice in less than twenty-four hours this has happened. Is it like this all the time?" He sounded so very unhappy right now.

I shook my head, "No. I don't know why. I can go days, or weeks, without it happening." I frowned, why was it so bad lately? It came to me. "Ever since that Marcus guy… with the purple eyes started stirring things up, they just won't pause." I glanced to Daxx, "When we came here they seemed less urgent, then all of sudden they rushed back." I looked to Rafael. "I can't even single one out right now."

Raf moved to the end of the bed. "Honestly, I don't know how you cope with it. I'm a mess after the occasional one."

I lifted my hands and shrugged. "I don't know any different." I thought back for a second. "There has never been a quiet minute in my head."

"Unbelievable." Troy said softly. "Thirty seconds was all I could handle."

"Where is the doctor?" Victor demanded loudly. Several surprised looked landed on him.

Getting up onto my knees, I touched his arm lightly. "I'm okay." The anger was just pouring off him.

"Blacking out for any reason is not… *okay*." He rested his hand over the top of mine on his arm.

"Sorry it took me so long." A man carrying a leather bag came through the door. Troy went over to him and started talking quietly to him.

"Do you want something to drink?" Quinton asked me and stood up.

"Some of my tea?"

He nodded and looked around for my pack. Victor frowned and watched him go pick it up and reach inside to get my little container.

"Only one left, Crissy. I can see if Mitz has the herbs to make you more."

"Oh, thank you." Quinton turned to leave. "Quint?" He stopped and looked back at me. "I wouldn't say no to those cookies Raf always brings me." I bit my lip so I wouldn't beg.

Quinton glanced at his brother.

"The ginger ones," Rafael said with a grin.

Quinton smiled at me. "I'll be back with cookies and tea."

Victor sat down on the bed and looked at me. "What herbs are in the tea?"

I looked back at him for a moment, there was something different in his eyes, I didn't understand it. "Just peppermint and a few others. It's not magical." I smiled. "I wished it was. I just can't drink coffee or regular tea. The caffeine makes me jittery."

He grinned. "You don't need that."

"Right." I smiled at him again then froze when I saw the doctor walking toward me.

"Well my dear, you've managed to stir up some excitement."

I nodded, not sure what he meant, but I'd learned long ago agreeing with doctors made them go away faster.

He stopped at the end of the bed and looked at Victor, then went to the opposite side and sat down. Reaching over, he took my wrist and checked my pulse. I realized I was squeezing Victor's arm with my other hand, but he didn't remove it or say a word, just kept his hand over mine. It made me feel a little bit better, but there would never be a time I trusted a doctor.

"Nothing weak about that pulse." The doctor said with a smile.

I'm sure he was a nice man, but he was a doctor.

He gave his best doctorish smile. "Is there any pain involved, before or after?"

I shook my head. "I get a cloudy feeling before it happens, sometimes I can stop and breathe through it and sort through to slow it down, but no pains."

I watched his face as he thought about that. He turned and looked a Troy then back to me. "Our night king told me it's like flash photography in there, how do you manage to sleep?"

I wasn't sure what flash photography was, but if Troy told him, he must be right, he'd seen it. "I sleep." I answered, not sure how he wanted me to.

"I could give you some sleeping pills if…"

"No pills." I said quickly hoping he'd move beyond that.

He looked to Victor, "Short of doing a scan, I can't see what is going on from a medical standpoint…"

"No, no." I shook my head and looked at Victor, "I can't be trapped in that tube again." I inched away from the doctor.

Victor squeezed my hand that was a like a vice on his arm now. "We're not going to put you in a tube, he's only talking it through."

I looked at his eyes for a moment and then nodded slowly and looked back at the doctor.

"Your definitely not short on energy." He said with a smirk. Reaching over he pulled his bag over and opened it. "It could be a nervous reaction," he said as he went through his bag. "I could give you a shot to help you settle your nerves and relax…" he pulled out a needle.

"No, no, no." Letting go of Victor's arm, I pulled my legs up to my chest and tried to back away as far as I could. "Relaxing makes them worse," I pleaded, "this *is* me controlling them." I tapped the side of my head.

Victor reached over and grabbed the doctor's hand with a smack as their flesh connected. "No pills. No needles. No drugs." His voice sounded almost lethal, and a chill went up my spine. "If you can't find a physical, or medical reason then you need to go and dig up some history books and find something. We've existed for thousands of years and have had many seers, surely this isn't the first one with a coping problem." He looked at me, his eyes softening a bit, then back to the doctor. "She's absolutely petrified by your very presence." He held out his arm with the bloody welts that I'd left in his arm. I felt bad for that, but they looked like they were healing right before my eyes. "The other side has medically abused her enough in her short life, we will *not* add to that."

The doctor was nodding his head so fast I was sure he must be getting dizzy. He glanced at me, then right back to Victor. "I will call and talk to the elders."

With an abrupt nod, Victor slowly released his hold and straightened up. The doctor got up so fast, I'm sure he got a head rush from it. I watched him leave then grabbed Victor's arm and looked at it. "I'm sorry. I'm sorry." My hands were shaking.

"It's fine," he said softly.

I looked back up at him and wanted to cry. I don't know why, I just did. I sprung toward him and wrapped my arms around him. "Thank you. I wouldn't have survived more drugs and poking." My whole body was shaking. "I want to go home now. Can I go home now?" I hated begging, sounding weak, but I wanted my streets back, the comfort of wandering them to forget.

His big arm wrapped around me and cradled my head into his chest. "You are safe. No one is going to abuse you here. We'll get answers and find a way." He other hand moved up and down my back slowly.

"Who scared the doc, he is almost running down the…"

I turned my head to see Quinton standing in the doorway.

"What the hell happened?" He looked around at everyone. "Crissy?"

Still hidden in Victor's arms, I glanced to see all of the big men looking very unhappy, even Daxx had that look she got before someone got beat on. I didn't like being the cause of drama. Straightening, I nodded in response to the inquiring look Victor gave me. "I'm sorry. I'm okay now." I leaned back and looked down at his arm. "I'm sorry about your arm." It was just red now, with a few spots of blood from my nails.

"I heal very fast." He offered me a little smile.

Quinton came over and set the cup and plate on the table beside us. "What's going on?"

Shaking my head, I backed up and sat with my legs pulled up to my chest. "He wanted to drug me and your brother stopped him."

"Drug you why?" He demanded.

Victor stood up and gave a quick shake of his head to stop Quinton's inquiry. "Enjoy your tea and cookies." He said quietly then walked to the end of the bed.

I looked at the plate of cookies and smiled up at Quinton. "Thank you. I love these." I picked up the cup and a cookie and watched the others gather near the end of the bed. Daxx sat on the end of it and gave me a quick smile before she turned to look up at the men.

Quinton moved to stand with them. "Someone want to fill me in?"

Victor stood there with his arms crossed, his jaw very tense. "As best as I can tell she was put through many unnecessary medical procedures and tests on the other side…"

"That's not unheard of," Michael said, "what they don't understand tends to scare them into stupid."

Chase snorted, "That's a polite summary."

"Is one way to say it." Arius said quietly.

Chase glanced at me, and winked, then gave Victor a serious look. "Something you want to share with the rest of the class, big brother?"

Rubbing a hand along his jaw, Victor turned to look at me for a moment then cleared his throat. "Not at this present time, no."

I didn't know what that was about, so I just picked up another cookie and took a sip of my tea.

"What about some blood? For the connection, could one of us help her control it?" Leone asked and everyone turned to give him a strange look. He held up his hands. "Oh, it wouldn't be me doing it, trust me on that, I just thought maybe Arius, or even Victor, your minds are rock solid."

I chewed slowly and wondered what they were talking about. They could connect through their blood. That was something that sounded like a vampire would do. They weren't vampires though, I'd seen those before and they were definitely not that. I didn't know the purpose of their fangs yet, or why the flirty twin didn't have them while his siblings did, but I knew they weren't for evil purposes.

"Do we know anyone else with seer capabilities? Personally, not just hearsay?" Troy asked, "Aside from Raf, who only has the odd one?" He looked at his brother, "You've never had to control them, have you?"

Rafael shook his head. "No. Mine aren't like that. I only get one here and there. It happens then it's over. I'm always shaky as fuck after, but I think that's more from my system's shock at having something jammed into your head without warning." He gave me a sweet look. "I don't know how she does it."

"Mmm." Troy responded. "What about you, brother king? Is there any way you could take some of the burden from her?"

Brother king. Hadn't the doctor called Troy *night* king? So, Chase was the day king? "You're both kings!" I blurted out. "That's fascinating." I nodded and took a sip of my tea.

Chase chuckled and then looked back at his brother. "Emotions I can take on, but the little cutie?" He shook his head, "her emotions move faster than the speed of sound. Unless you want me parasailing off the tree tops, wearing a toga and screaming Geronimo, I can't do much there."

"I've always wanted to fly." I mumbled with a mouthful of cookie. "Can any of you fly?" I checked to see all of them shake their heads. "Oh, that's too bad then." Setting the cup down I got up off the bed and wandered over to look in the closet. Nothing they said was making any sense to me, so I thought I'd check out the clothes. Victor had said I could take some.

Daxx came over and leaned against the doorframe as I looked through the pants hanging there. Victor hadn't been kidding when he'd said all sizes. I held up a pair of jeans and looked at her. The hem was on the floor and the waist was beside my shoulder.

She nodded. "I know, apparently, there was a chance I was a giant." Glancing back over at the men, she grinned at me. "They'll mull that over for hours. I'm glad you're here."

I looked through a few more pairs of jeans, seeing if any of them were close to my size. "It's all very bizarre," I gave her a wide-eyed look, "I've been seeing the halls here since I was only small." Moving over to the dresses, I started looking through them, "To run through them, for real and not just in my head is…" I looked at the floor trying to find the word I should use. "A relief." I looked back to her. "To know I'm not crazy."

"A little crazy is okay." She smirked at me and then jerked her head toward the men.

I laughed. "I guess the definition of crazy is in the eye of the beholder." I frowned. "That is the saying, right?" Pulling a black denim dress off the rack, I held it up. It was cute, black straps and pockets. I held it against me and looked up at her, she nodded. "I was thinking of having a bath in that tub."

"It's huge, right?"

I nodded, "It would make a great home for a penguin or baby seal."

She chuckled.

"I don't think Mitz would be all that pleased with a seal in the bath tub, baby or otherwise." Victor stood behind Daxx now. He smirked. "Rafael tried a small shark once, it did not end well."

My jaw dropped. "Why would someone want a pet shark?"

"In his defense, he was only fifteen at the time." He shrugged.

I folded the dress and set it with the boots I'd picked earlier. "How old were you when he was fifteen?" I stood up and watched while he thought about it. "I know your older than anyone I've ever met." I confessed.

"I was three hundred and twenty-five." He said quietly while he watched for my reaction.

Clasping my hands together, I nodded, "That's pretty fantastic. The changes you've seen." Turning I went to look through the clothes some more. "I've seen a lot but not physically been there."

"You've probably seen more than I have." He stated in a matter of fact way.

I held up a black t-shirt to see if it was my size. "I don't think I want to see for as many years as you have lived. It's exhausting just living the years I have."

"How old are you, Crissy?" Daxx asked. "I don't think it's ever come up in our conversations before."

I grinned at her. "No, you are always too busy saving me from the trouble I seem to fall into." Deciding I liked that black t-shirt and a tank top beside it I set them with my boots also. "I don't look for it." I touched another shirt, but it felt funny, so I moved on. "I'm twenty-five." I rolled my eyes at her. "People always ask if I'm a child, because I'm so small." Shaking my head, I turned back to the clothes. "I think the drugs the foster homes gave me when I was little stopped me from growing more," I waved my hand, "I looked some of them up once and found out I was better off not knowing the side effects."

"They drugged you?" She came over and pulled a jacket off the rack and held it out to me.

It looked warm, that would come in handy. "For behavioral problems." I folded it up and set it on the floor. "But they weren't behavioral problems, they were just me." I looked at my hands, and twisted the black bracelet I wore. "No one has ever liked me just as I am." Glancing at her I tilted my head and smiled, "until you found me that day." Nodding, I turned back to look at the pile of clothes and then to them.

"I have to go take care of a few things before dinner." Victor said while looking at his phone. "Will you be all right in the bath alone?" He looked to Daxx. "I'm sure Daxx or Mitz would sit with you if you're not."

His concern was nice. "I'm okay now. The reboot worked, I have a handle on the speed the visions are hitting me."

"You've been getting them since you woke up?" He green eyes searched my face.

I had to smile. How had I been wrong about him seeming cold? "Yes. None of them are worth pausing for, just flashes." He kept looking at me, such a serious expression on his face, so I smiled again just to make him feel better.

He didn't return the smile but he stopped frowning so hard. "I will see you at dinner."

We watched him leave.

"I think you broke our Victor." Chase said as he came over.

"He's broken?" I asked

Chase snorted. "Or maybe he's fixed, who knows." He bowed his head. "I won't be at dinner. I need a nap before my day starts, as I've been up far too long already." He nudged Daxx with his shoulder. "See you at practice tomorrow, kitten."

"I'll be there." She answered.

I might like being here. For once it wasn't me saying things that made no sense. If his day was just starting, how was ours ending? And what did they practice?

Chapter Five

I hadn't really slept, but that wasn't a new thing for me. For hours and hours, I'd walked this room. At home I'd go walk the street, or the odd roof top, but in this room I could almost get up to a full run around it without getting dizzy. It was quite fun, I decided.

Mitz had come to see me early, or was it late, being that it was close to night time now? How did they tell the time here? Was there a clock to label whose day was when? I would have to find out. She'd taken me to the kitchen and made me breakfast. Imagine that. She had even remembered three pieces of toast. I could like being here, I decided. We'd talked about hair and clothes. She agreed to help me find a new color, once we decided how to remove the red. That hadn't been in my head when I'd dyed it, the thought of removing it.

Since I'd wandered from the kitchen, I'd come to my room and stayed. I knew the halls, from inside my head, but not what was behind doors. Daxx had always told me not to look behind closed doors, so I didn't.

Mitz had given me a box of hair clips, there were so many, every shape and size. I tried all of them and when I couldn't decide on one, so I put all the little ones in my hair, now my hair was pulled up and it was like a tiny story was being told. Butterflies and small flowers all over my head.

When someone knocked on the door, I almost ran to hide in the closet, but forced my feet to go see who it was instead. I opened it a crack and then flung the door wide. "Daxx." She smiled at me and held up a black leather backpack.

"This was sitting outside your door." She smirked.

I took the bag from her and closed the door. "Did someone drop it?"

"I don't think so, there's a bow and a tag on it." She went into the closet.

I looked at the bag and there was a little rainbow colored bow. *The rainbow.* Flipping the tag that hung from it over, I read 'from Victor' in neat handwriting. Victor had gotten me a new pack. First the hair clips and now a pack. I'd never gotten this many gifts before in my life. I hurried over to my worn denim pack sitting on the bed. It had seen a lot of life, I'd had it for many years now. Smiling, I pulled off the pretty bow and tucked it into the little pocket on the side of the new pack. Opening it, I debated whether to sort through my old one now or…

"We have to get you changed to go to practice."

I looked at Daxx, coming out of the closet holding up some clothes. I looked down at my new boots and the black dress I was wearing. "What do you practice?" Picking up my old pack, I put it into the new one and closed it quickly.

"Fighting skills." She held up some bright red yoga pants and a black tank top. "These should work. There's a pair of running shoes in there that might fit, too."

I took the clothes she held out and then looked at her. "I don't have fighting skills. I'm more of a run and vanish person."

She smiled. "I know, and for you that's probably the best thing, but we could work on a few moves that can help you to get away and vanish."

I chewed on my lip for a moment and thought about how I felt about that. It wouldn't hurt to know things like that. "I'm not very strong." I confessed.

She shook her head and motioned to the bathroom. "You don't need to be. Go change."

When we stepped into the room, I clutched my new pack to my chest. It was a gymnasium, only much bigger. I shouldn't have been surprised, nothing here was of a normal size. Turning, I saw that all of the men were here and, if it were possible, they looked bigger than they had the last time I'd seen them.

Daxx gave me a nudge, so I wouldn't stand in the doorway, although I wasn't sure I wanted to move, but did. Quinton smiled at me and turned to say something to Rafael who then looked over at me and gave me a smile I couldn't resist returning. He started walking over. I don't know why he was carrying a big stick with him, but it was taller than I was.

He held out his hand and I took it, I trusted him. Pausing, he grinned as he looked at the little fingerless leather gloves I had on. I don't know why I put them on, but they matched the black shoes, so I decided I had to wear them.

"Come on, we'll see if anything here will work for you."

I followed along behind him, trying not to feel nervous, but I did anyway. When he stopped, I looked past him to see a wall of weapons. So many, all lethal looking. "Are we going to war?" I asked him.

He chuckled, "It doesn't hurt to stay in shape."

I looked at the swords and blades in front of me. "I guess you could carve any shape you like with those."

"Too bloody for you, cutie?"

I glanced beside me to see Chase standing there. "I'm not really the fighting type." I told him. "I prefer to vanish instead."

He nodded. "I can see that about you, but what if you need to get away first, so you can vanish?"

Quinton and Troy came over to stand beside him. Here I was again, being looked at by too many eyes.

"The eyes," I nodded and set down my new pack and opened it. "if they can't see me vanishing it's easy." Reaching into my old pack inside, I pulled out my little spray bottle and held it up smiling, surely, they'd understand that.

With a curious expression, Quinton held out his hand for it. I handed it to him.

"Pepper spray?" Rafael asked.

I shook my head. "No, I've never tried that, is it effective?"

Quinton sprayed some on his hand and then sniffed it. He

coughed. "Vinegar." He said smirking at me.

I nodded. "I got some in my eyes once and then realized the perfect use for it."

Victor came over and looked down at me. "You spray vinegar in their eyes to get away?" He glanced at my new pack and his mouth twitched like he had to suppress a smile.

I grinned, wondering if his gift was to remain a secret. Not knowing I didn't say a word about it. "Yes."

"That would do it," Chase snorted.

Shaking his head, Rafael took the bottle from his brother and gave it back to me. "It's a good one, but a little awkward to stop and get it out to spray someone." I watched the others nod. "After we warm up a bit, maybe we can come up with a few moves that will make sure you're never caught."

I nodded. There had been times I would have been thankful to know something like that.

"Talk, talk, talk people. Too much talk. Who's feeling brave today?" Daxx said, twirling two small wooden swords.

Michael pushed between the others and grabbed a large wooden sword. "I guess it's my turn to take on the huntress."

Troy chuckled, "I'd love to watch my mate flatten you."

Quinton laughed, "like she did you?"

Arius appeared beside him, his long pretty hair pulled back in a braid today. "As she did you if I recall correctly, Quint."

Faking a growl, Quinton pointed a large wooden sword at him. "Like I'm going to do to *you*."

Even though they were talking about fighting, I couldn't help but be warmed by those vibes again, that connection they had.

As the others moved over onto the large mats, Victor looked down at me. "Take a look," he motioned the weapons, "and see if anything feels like you may want to try it." He rolled his shoulders and glanced at his siblings, "after I warm up, we'll see about showing you some moves."

I looked at the assortment of weapons and then back to him. "I will look." I smiled at him, and gave the others a nervous glance. "Thank you…" I motioned to the new pack by my feet, "for the new pack."

He inclined his head in that fancy way of his, "You're very welcome. The other one looked tired."

Nodding, I bent down and picked it up. "It was *tired*."

"Victor, come! Let me kick your ass." Chase called out.

Smirking, he glanced at him over his shoulder before he looked back to me. "Later, I'd like to sit down and speak with you. We have much to discuss."

I didn't know what *much* he was referring to, but I loved the way he said it. "Yes, let's." I told him trying to sound as stuffy as he did.

He grinned at me and then gave me that little nod of his before turning to go to his brother.

I stood there, watching. So much movement all at the same time. I knew they loved each other, as families should, but the sounds of wood hitting wood was jarring. It would be something to see if I could take in all of it at once. Turning, I looked back at the massive wall of weapons, nothing there felt like I had any inkling to try them. I didn't like violence, I know there was a need for it under certain circumstances, but that didn't mean I had to be part of it.

Sighing, I hugged the bag and looked around. Off to the side, away from the commotion were three large knotted ropes hanging from a beam near the ceiling. I smiled and swung the pack around to put on my back. I may not be a fighter, but climbing was something that I loved so much, even the chaos inside my head didn't interfere while I did it.

Moving over, I looked down at my new gloves and then rubbed them together. Fate had told me I needed these today, and now I knew it was more than they matched my shoes. I grabbed the middle rope and did what any sane person would do and tugged on it. Of course, it was almost as large as my hand and even if it were loosely secured I didn't have the strength to pull it down.

Grasping it, I looked at the first knot and decided it was going to be a bit of stretch with my lack of height, but I knew I could do it. I closed my eyes and thought back to a time I was being chased, there was nothing like that fear to inspire some nimble moves. Huffing out a breath, I pulled myself up so I could get my feet to that first knot. After that it was as easy as running up stairs.

As I reached the top, I kept going until I was sitting with my feet dangling over each side of the beam it had been secured to. Looking down, this was much better, I could see all of the brothers and Daxx at the same time.

From my new perspective, it was like watching a warrior's dance, their deadly moves were graceful to view. I'd seen Daxx fight before, she'd saved me many times, but to see her now with short swords… I'm sure they had a pretty name, but I didn't know what it was… she was graceful and fearless.

Troy and Rafael were trying to attack each other and the speed and moves they made, even for being so large, was fluent and almost beautiful, although I doubted they'd like that description much.

I moved my eyes to watch Chase and Victor, again both engaged in the smooth movements that looked like a carefully choreographed combatant's ritual. I suppose with the sheer number of years they had lived, they'd had many hours, more than I'd been alive, to polish and practice being graceful giants, but it was still impressive.

I looked over to watch Leone fight, I still didn't know why he had been afraid of me, but to see him fight, I knew he had no fear of battle. His moves, like his brothers were sure and steady.

"Victor! Are you having a stroke? I was in full swing and could have taken your head clean off."

I turned to see why Chase was yelling.

Victor stood there, with his arms at his side looking up at me. I couldn't tell for certain, from this far away, but if I were to guess I'd say he was unhappy with something. As his eyes were stuck on me, I wondered what I could have done to make him unhappy.

Chase turned and looked around and then up at me. He smirked and cocked his head to the side. I realized then that everyone else had paused in their mock battles, and were staring up at me. *Too many eyes.* Feeling nervous and unsure, I gave a little wave, again not sure what the proper response should be.

Maybe if I just sat here quietly, they would all stop looking at me. Daxx dropped her wooden swords and started walking over to the ropes. I don't think they're going to look away, I thought and glanced around me to see where I could hide. There was nowhere to escape their observation.

Looking to the floor beneath me, Daxx gave me an odd smile.

"You know you're supposed to climb up and down, not park at the top." She told me.

I looked at the beam I sat on. "I like it up here." I nodded down to her. "No one ever thinks to look up when they're looking for you, they always look on the ground."

She nodded slowly, "I'm sure you're right."

Rafael came over to stand with her. "Crissy, you know that talk we had about doing things that give me a heart attack?"

I frowned, not sure why he was asking me about it now. "Yes, I do."

"This," he motioned to the rope in front of him, "would be one of those things."

I'd never had friends before and I truly treasured his friendship, even though I didn't understand how climbing a rope could do that, I didn't like the idea of causing him stress in any way. "I'm sorry," I called down softly, "I'll come down now." I nodded when he smiled up at me.

I looked at the beam between my legs and then the rope I'd used to reach it, realizing once again I'd done something without stopping to think the ending through. Getting up was easy, down presented me with an obstacle. Not wanting to admit to Daxx I'd done it again, I kept my voice inside my head and leaned over to reach the rope I needed to get a hold of.

I hadn't taken into account the weight of the pack on my back and it tipped with me and caused me to lose my balance. In a complete panic, I reached out for the rope and tried to keep my leg over the beam at the same time. When I stopped, I was upside down holding the rope beside my head and one knee bent over the beam. The weight of the pack was trying to pull me to the floor, so I squeezed my eyes closed and focused on holding on to the rope with all the strength I had, as I moved my leg from the beam to right myself.

It took me a few breathless moments, and I'm certain I stopped breathing when the weight of my body swung around, but I was finally right side up again, hugging the rope between my thighs. I opened my eyes to see the ropes on either side of me moving and looked down, Rafael was coming up one and Victor the other. Chancing a look where Daxx had been standing, I saw everyone there, all eyes on me, again. So much for practicing being invisible was the only thought I had before the two stressed out men were looking me eye to eye.

"I'm okay." I tried to assure them.

"I'm going to take your pack off." Rafael told me in a quiet tone.

I nodded and hugged the knot tighter in one arm as he slipped it off my shoulder. When it was off the other one, I grasped the rope with both hands and stared at my new gloves. I was happy I had them now and could have looked at them all day to avoid turning to look into the green eyes that I knew were on the other side of me, and they wouldn't be happy.

"Go down with Victor, okay?" Rafael said slowly.

I nodded, but continued to look at my gloves. My nails would look pretty if they were purple, I thought. I wondered if Mitz had nail polish. Out of the corner of my eye I looked at Victor, he didn't look mad like I thought he would, he looked scared. Maybe he didn't like heights, and I'd made him come up here. That made me feel bad.

Turning, I looked at him, "I'm sorry." I told him in that soft tone Rafael used with me.

He nodded slightly and I felt his hand on my back, "Grab a hold of my neck, I won't let you fall." His voice was softer than Rafael's had ever been. I looked to his eyes, and in them I saw something I'd never seen before. I wanted to look longer, but figured he'd get impatient if we hung up here while I analyzed the emotions I was seeing.

Letting go with one hand, I reached to wrap it around the back of his neck. I glanced up to see his big hand gripping the rope I was on, it looked small in his. Taking a deep breath, I let go with the other hand and locked it behind his head using my wrist.

"I've got you," he said quietly in my ear. "Swing onto my back and wrap your legs around my waist."

Leaning back a bit, I gave him a wide-eyed look. "I don't think my legs are long enough to fit around you."

Serious green eyes looked back at me. "They will."

Trusting he knew what he was talking about, I did what he said and then paused when I hooked my ankles together, they did fit.

"Hang on." He said abruptly.

I chewed my lip while he climbed down. His soft calmness was gone, I could feel something entirely different as he went down the rope in half the moves it had taken me to climb up. When his feet were on the floor, I released his neck and dropped to the floor.

Rafael was there and held out my pack, I took it and quickly hugged it against my chest while I stared at Victor's heaving, large chest. Quinton mumbled something about grey hair under his breath as he walked away. I turned to see Troy was hugging Daxx, and wondered if she was okay. The others were shaking their heads, but were finally moving away and not staring at me. Without lifting my head, I moved my eyes until I met very upset green ones. "I'm okay," I told him hoping that was all it would take. I doubted it, but it was worth a try.

His jaw clenched a few times as he looked down at me. He opened his mouth and then closed it again. His eyes were now red and somehow the color suited the vibes coming off him. "Why..." His lifted one of those big hands and waved it around, "*What* possessed you to do something as reckless at that?"

I frowned, if he thought that was reckless, he didn't know my life at all, which of course he didn't. "I like climbing. I'm good at it." I nodded.

His big hands grasped my shoulders and gave me a little shake. "You could have fallen to your death." He growled at me.

His fangs did not look as interesting with that tone. Emotions started slamming me and I tried, I really did, to not feel the fear, panic, and anger all at once. Feelings I had promised I'd never feel again. Large fingers tightened on my shoulders.

"It's completely mind-boggling that you have managed to survive this long…"

His voice was too loud. I don't know what happened, I was standing there shaking, fighting to calm down and the next minute I was slapping his hands off me and shoving his chest. He didn't even budge when I did. "I have survived without help since I was old enough to comprehend the words…" I swung my pack and hit him in the chest with it, "Freak. Of. Nature." It dawned on me the voice screaming was my own. Eyes huge, I glanced around to see so many eyes on me. *No, no no.* Covering my mouth with a shaking hand, I back away from him. Turning, I swung the pack to my shoulder and bolted for the nearest door.

I found my way back to the room without a moment's hesitation. Grabbing my other bag, I stuffed my boots and other clothes into it and then pulled the dress over the top of what I was wearing. I had to go. Needed to go. Rushing into the bathroom, I grabbed the little box of clips Mitz had given me and jammed them into the bag too.

When Daxx came running into the room, I stood there facing the door holding my pack in one hand and bag in the other. "I want to go the apartment now." I nodded, trying hard not to cry. I don't know why I would, just that I was scared. I hadn't felt like that in years and so many memories were crowding into my already too full head. "Please. You said when we came if I wanted to go back to say the word." I frowned, "I-I don't know what the word is, but I'm saying it." She was walking toward me slowly. "Just…" Letting go of the bag, I rubbed my hand over my forehead, trying to keep the feelings out, "Just for a while." I nodded. "I'll come back and find Emil, like I promised I would." I took a deep breath, "I will." I nodded again, she had to understand.

"Okay," she finally said quietly.

I was blowing out breaths, trying to stay calm. It was too much. Too much. "Now?"

She came over and rubbed her hands down my arms. "Yes, just take a few deep breaths and calm down. I don't know if it's bad for you to do this when you're this upset."

I swallowed and took a deep breath, releasing it as slowly as I could manage. I nodded. "Okay." Almost gasping, I tried again. I grabbed my bag again, needing to know I had it close.

"I'm going to hug you, just close your eyes and I'll take us there."

Nodding, I rested my head on her shoulder and did as she asked, squeezing my eyes shut.

Chapter Six

I studied the phone, trying to decide if I wanted to turn it on. I knew there would be messages waiting for me as there had been when I'd checked the last few times. Knowing others were upset or worried didn't sit well, but I needed time before I could think of them. It had been three days since Daxx had taken me back to the apartment. She'd left me saying she would be back in a few hours. I wasn't there when she came back. I told myself I hadn't done anything wrong by leaving, she hadn't asked me to *be* there when she came back.

Hugging the phone to my chest, I looked over the part of the city I could see. It was dark, but the lights were pretty from up here, and it was quiet. I needed the quiet right now. Since I came back, I was having one flash that came back many times. I had to figure out what it meant, or I wouldn't get peace. If it weren't for all the other flickers, I may have been able to catch it. It never appeared long enough so I could study it, I just tried to write down as much as I could from memory after it disappeared again. There were three faces in it, and one I knew was Alona and the other that I knew was Emil. For the first few times I thought it might be Arius, but it was definitely his brother. I didn't know the third face, but it held a bad feeling. My mind wouldn't give me a moment's pause so I could be sure, but somehow the lost brother and found woman were part of it.

I don't know what this building used to be or what it was now, but I spent a lot of time up here. It was ten stories high, I knew that from having counted the floors as I navigated the fire escape, even where I had to jump to reach the next section. There were never lights on in the building, so I suppose it was just some old broken space, long forgotten. There was a small awning that could have had a purpose when the structure was younger, but I didn't know what that could have been. I used it when I stayed here to shelter from the rain, or sun.

Getting up, I went back under and sat down, leaning back against my bag. Looking at the phone, I let out a long breath. If there were too many to read or hear this time, I would have to go back to the apartment to charge the phone. I could always go to a laundromat or coffee shop, but I didn't want to be found right now, so the best way to stay hidden was to stay up here.

I held the button to turn on my phone and watched as the colorful screen appeared and while it played its song. I only had eighteen percent battery left, so I hoped for no voice messages. The notifications popped up. I had three messages and one voicemail.

I opened the first message. It was from Daxx. *Call me when your ready*. She understood that I needed time, she always did, even when she wasn't sure she did. I sent her back a smiley face.

The second one was from Quinton telling me to be safe, not just okay. I sent him back a smiley face winking. He would understand that.

Rafael left cookies at the apartment for me. He got a heart sent back to him for that. I would have to go get them in the morning. I had only tried once to climb down this fire escape in the dark and it had almost ended with me in the dumpster in the alley, so I knew not to try it tonight. My grumbling stomach would just have to be happy with the crackers and water that I had now.

I knew the voice message would be Victor again, and not because I had seen it. He had left me one every day for the last few days. I messaged him I was okay after the first one, but his next message had said that was not an answer that assured him I was safe. He even talked funny in texting, I wonder if he knew that. He had apologized for getting upset with me and explained it wasn't because he was mad at me, but scared that I almost fell. I understood it now, I think I did then too, but I couldn't control my reaction when all of the emotions and memories came back at me. I should tell him I'm sorry about hitting him.

I hit the button to listen to the message and entered my password. *"Crissy,* I'm quite concerned now that you haven't spoken to anyone since you left. I would much rather express my sincerest apologies in person, but as you've made that impossible at this time, I can only reiterate that I will forever regret upsetting you as I did. Please, when you get this message let me know that you are, in fact, well and safe." There was a pause. "I worry." I listened to make sure there was no more, but he hung up. Ending the call to the mailbox, I studied the phone. I had to smile, his voice messages were even funnier than speaking to him face to face. After I charged my phone tomorrow, I may save that message, just to listen to it when I want to smile.

I opened a message to send to him, I just didn't know what to say other than I'm okay and he didn't seem interested in reading that again. I typed, *I am well and safe* with a smiley face, then sent it to him.

Before I could close the screen his reply came back. *Can I call you?* I looked at the little battery symbol at the top.

My battery is 15% Frowny face. Then sent *no power here,* just in case he told me to plug it in.

Can you go to the apartment and charge it?

I thought about the climb down the fire escape and knew he would get mad again if I tried it, so I sent back, *Not safely in the dark.*

Stay where you are until light. Came back very quickly. I smirked when I pictured him with his big hands and fingers typing on the phone. Checking the battery, I made sure I had enough to send another one. I never let my phone completely drain. Ever.

Okay I will. I smiled again remembering this was the man that said so few words when I had first seen him, but now he wanted to talk.

Have you eaten? I can leave food at the apartment for you to get in the morning.

My stomach gurgled when I thought of food. I looked at the crackers and sighed. *I have some crackers.* I told him.

Frowny face *I will leave food at the apartment for you.*

I looked at the battery symbol again and then sent him, *I saw Alona and Emil.*

With your eyes?

That made me laugh, he understood now. *No.*

Were they together?

I frowned, I really didn't know that answer. *I'm not sure. I have to stay until I see it all and know.*

I understand.

I just sat there and stared at those words, to me they meant more than any other words someone could say. They had been words I needed to have said to me all of my life. *Thank you.* Smiley face.

Are they in danger?

I bit my lip, I didn't know how to explain it in words, whether typing or with my voice. *I'm not sure. There is a man I don't think he's good.* My battery was at twelve percent now.

You will figure it out, I have faith in you.

I read that twice. Was this really Victor on the other end? *Thank you.*

Crissy, are you honestly safe where you are right now?

I looked around and listened for a moment before answering. *I am. My head feels at peace when I am here. I can focus best to control them.*

What do you need to feel peace when you are here in Alterealm?

I smiled at the phone, even though he couldn't see me smile at it. *Someplace up high with quiet and no people.*

Tell me you are on more than a beam right now!

I laughed and shook my head. It was Victor texting back. *I am on a* BIG FLAT ROOF.

Thank you. I will find you someplace high, quiet and SAFE for when you are here.

Smiley face *my battery is down to 10% I have to go.*

What food do you want left at the apartment?

I looked at my crackers again. *Anything but crackers. Thank you.*

Very well. Turn off your phone and get some rest.

Okay. I held the button so it would go off. Tucking it into the pocket of my jacket, I picked up my crackers. They were going to taste drier than before, now that my taste buds knew there were cookies and food waiting for me.

I had to keep reminding myself to go slow when I went to the apartment just after dawn. I was excited and didn't want to make a mistake and fall as I went down the broken fire escape and then up the one at Daxx's building. I rarely used the entrance unless someone else was with me. It was too easy to get trapped in stairwells and dark corners when you were alone.

Closing the window, I turned around to see the wrapped cookies and a small box on Daxx's bed. Dropping my pack by the window, in case I had to leave in a hurry, I went over and sat on the bed. Rafael's note of a happy face was taped to the wrapping on the cookies. I took it off and folded it to add to the other faces he'd left me.

Pulling the box over, I opened it and peeked inside. There was an apple and an orange, those would be put in my pack for later. He had left me two boxes of juice as well, cranberry. A note was taped to three pieces of wrapped up white bread.

Toaster is in the kitchen.

Call me when your phone is charged.

Please

Victor

He brought me a toaster. I opened a small container to find marmalade and had to smile. At least he remembered things I said. Setting it on the bed, I picked up the other small containers in the box. It was smart of him to leave containers, then I could put them in my pack without getting crushed or making a mess, maybe he knew that and it's why he did. Inside one was protein bars, I wasn't sure what those were, but they weren't crackers, so I'm sure they would do just fine. Inside the other was little packets, I had to read what they were. Apparently, I could put them in water for something called a protein juice. Victor liked protein things I surmised.

At the bottom of the box was a strap. I took it out and looked at it, but couldn't think what it was for. There was a big clip on one end and a loop on the other. I would have to think about that while I made my toast.

Grabbing my pack, I found the cord for my phone and plugged it in, then spun around back to the bed.

Picking up the bread, I rushed out to the kitchen to see the shiny toaster sitting on the counter. Plugging it in, I put the bread in and turned to go get the marmalade. As I went around the corner Quinton just appeared in front of me. With a screech, I turned and ran back into the kitchen.

"Crissy," He came in after me, "I'm sorry. I didn't know you would be here."

Huffing out a breath, I glared at him. My heart was bouncing around inside my chest. "You scared me." He held a wrapped plate in his hand. Quinton had brought me food too. I'd never had so much food at once before.

Holding it out, he shrugged, "I thought you might be hungry. I was going to leave it here."

I took the plate and looked at it. I wasn't sure, but it looked like bacon and potatoes on it. "Thank you. I will eat it with my toast." As if on cue the bread popped. "Oh, my marmalade." I set the plate down and rushed to go get it.

"Toast?" He followed along behind me.

I grabbed in and rushed out by him. "Victor brought it for me." I paused, "he brought me bread, I have to make the toast."

"Oh?"

I didn't stop to talk, I wanted to put it on the toast while it was still warm. Getting a knife, I put it on each piece, making sure it was spread evenly so each bite would be the same. Taking the plastic off the plate, I set it on top and got a fork.

When I went back out, Quinton was standing in the bedroom doorway, he held up the mysterious strap from Victor. Kneeling on the couch, I nodded. "I don't know what it is, but Victor wanted me to have it, so I'm sure there is a purpose for it."

Smirking, he came over and sat on the table in front of me.

I took a bite of the toast. Perfect.

He held up the strap, "It's so you can hook onto something when you're up high so you won't fall." He opened and closed the big clip a few times and then held it with one hand and put his other through the loop and grasped the strap together.

I know my mouth dropped open, but it was such a surprise. "That is amazing." Balancing the plate on my knees, I reached out and took the strap from him. "Your brother is very sweet to think of something like this for me. He knows I like to climb and be up high."

He snorted, "Victor is sweet." He chuckled, "that's a first." Getting up, he dropped down into the chair. "He's been on a rampage since you left. I'm pretty sure he's found and brought to justice every criminal in Alterealm in a few days' time."

I took a bite of the toast and looked at him. "That's his job." I nodded.

He laughed, "Yeah, he's just not usually so zealous when he does it." Rubbing the back of his neck, he huffed out a breath, "Last night he came back with so much blood on him, we weren't sure if he was injured or…"

I set the plate on the table with a clatter and scrambled off the couch. "Is he okay? What happened?" A tight feeling crushed my chest to think of Victor being hurt. I rubbed my hand over it, trying to ease the feeling.

He stood up and grabbed my hand softly so I would look at him. "He's fine. It wasn't his blood."

I stared at him for a moment, then nodded slowly and sat back down. Picking up the plate I took another bite of my toast. "Whose blood was it? Someone else was hurt?"

Quinton sat down and frowned for a minute, I knew he was thinking, because he did it a lot. "Listen," he gave me a soft look, "you need to understand that sometimes," he shook his head, "most of the time, Victor has to be quite violent." Rubbing his hand over his face, he glanced at the floor then back to me. "He can't afford to be…soft."

I nodded as I nibbled on a piece of the bacon. It was good. "He is the justice keeper." I stopped, hoping I'd remembered the name right. I waved my hand in a circle while holding the bacon. "Sometimes being around him is very cold, but not evil."

I took another bite and watched him. There was something in his eyes, like he didn't want to say it out loud. I set the bacon down and tilted my head to focus around him. "Does he *kill* others?" I didn't want to believe it, but it was in my head now and I had to know.

"Sometimes there is no other way." Quinton told me in a quiet voice, his eyes searching my face as he did.

"Oh." I looked down at the plate, assessing how I felt about that. Violence was so dark, it hurt when I felt it, inside and out. I knew there was a hard side to Victor, but there was a gentleness there too, he just didn't show it often. Glancing back to him, I took a breath and let it out quietly. "I don't think he likes doing it." I shook my head, "but he needs to feel everyone is safe." I nodded and picked up a piece of toast.

"Yes, he does. All of us do. Michael and Leone work with him the most, helping him," he shrugged, "Arius and myself as well, it keeps everyone safer." His brown eyes searched my face again, "but in the end, it's Victor's call, and his decision to make."

That felt sad to me. "That must be hard for him." I jumped up to get my juice. Grabbing it, I came back quickly and stabbed the straw into the little hole. "To be alone to make such important decisions." I took a drink of the juice and it was good. I would have to thank Victor for bringing it.

"I've never thought of it that way." Quinton said in a thoughtful voice.

"Why is he on a rampage now?" Had he said that, I couldn't remember. "Is something bad going on?" I shook my head, "besides all the bad I know about." There was so much bad, the people with those devices they weren't supposed to have. The scary man with the purple eyes. That bad one I kept seeing…I realized he was talking to me again.

"He's beating himself up because he upset you."

Stepping onto the couch, I squatted down and set my juice on the table so I could take another piece of bacon. "How is he beating himself up?" I frowned, "I don't see how a person could do that."

He snorted, "It's a figure of speech, he's not really beating himself. He's just angry with himself."

Chewing slowly, I thought that over. "Okay," I nodded. It made more sense now, why he didn't just say that, then again sometimes things didn't work that way. "He was okay when I messaged him."

"You've been messaging him, huh?" He smirked.

I nodded. "Yes, he's going to find me a high, quiet, *safe* place in Alterealm, so my head can feel peace there." Taking another bite, I watched him grin at me.

"That's something." Shaking his head, he smiled for a few more seconds and then his expression softened and he looked at me. "When *are* you coming back? Michael tried to pick up where you left off with searching for Emil, even backtracking to find some of the children, but he's lost in it."

I remembered. "Oh. Emil. I saw him." I set the plate down and jumped up to run and get my pack. "Alona too." When I turned back I almost ran into him. "Oh."

"Slow down. You had a vision of them? Together?" He leaned down so our faces were closer.

I shook my head. "No," I bit my lip, "I don't think they were together, or at least know they were together." I pulled out my notebook and flipped it open so I could see the sketch and remember. "I keep seeing it on repeat," I looked up at him, "it's why I'm staying for now. Victor understands." Frowning, I remembered the other man. "I need to see why the other man is there in my head, too."

Putting his hand behind my back Quinton guided me toward the couch again. "Come and eat, and then tell me about it."

I clutched the book to my chest and nodded as I walked. "Okay."

Quinton sat there while I ate and we talked about what I'd been seeing. I told him I was going to go to some of the clubs that night to see if I could find Alona, and he told me I shouldn't go alone. I agreed with this, he didn't say I couldn't go though, so tonight I was going.

When he decided to go get some sleep, I packed up the

food that had been left for me and clipped my safety strap to the handle on my pack as I waited for the phone to charge. That's what I was telling myself inside my head, that it had to finish charging. It was a small fib, because I was really trying to decide if I wanted to call Victor. He had said please, so it would be rude not to, and I needed to thank him for the food and my strap.

I unplugged the phone when the charge reached one hundred percent and tucked the cord into my pack. Sitting on the bed holding the phone, I stared at it for a minute before I brought up Victor's name and hit the green call button on the screen.

It rang twice and the thought hit me that he might be sleeping. I had just decided to hang up when his voice came through the speaker.

"Crissy."

I smiled of course it was me. "Yes… hi." I nodded, which I thought was silly because he couldn't see me.

"Hello."

"Were you sleeping? I can call after you wake up…"

"No." I heard a door close. "I was just taking a shower."

"To wash off the blood?" He may have been rampaging again.

"I-what blood?" He cleared his throat.

I picked at the strap on my pack. "Quinton told me you've been rampaging and get covered in other people's blood a lot."

"I see." His voice was softer. "I will have to speak with him about his loose mouth."

I frowned, how could Quinton's mouth be loose?

"There was no blood."

"It's okay if there is…" I scrunched up my nose, thinking of the words, "well, not okay for the violence, but I know it has to be that way sometimes. Violence is so dark it makes me sick." I nodded quickly, not wanting him to think I would judge what he was required to do. "I understand."

He exhaled loudly enough I heard it in the speaker. "Yes, I know it does, and I wish there was a way I didn't have to expose you to such a thing. Sadly, there is not." He cleared his throat.

"I am very much filled with regret for upsetting you…"

"I'm okay." I wanted to reassure him.

He made a soft sound like a laugh, "Of course you are." There was a long pause and I wondered if he was as unsure of what to say as I was.

I wanted to make him feel better, so I blurted out the first thing that popped into my head. "My real name is Cristy, but I don't think I'm a Cristy type."

He was silent for a moment. "I think Cristy is as unique and lovely a name as you are."

I felt my cheeks get hot. No one had ever said anything about my name. I didn't know what to say.

"Did you get what I left for you?"

I smiled. "I did. The toast was good. Thank you." I studied the strap clipped to my pack. "And for the strap. Quinton explained what it was for." I smiled, "It's very sweet of you to know I have to climb, but want me safe when I do."

"Is Quinton still there with you?" His voice had that hardness to it.

I looked around. "No. He went to sleep." I looked out to see the sun outside. "I can hang up so you can sleep."

"No." he said abruptly. "That's fine, I will shortly. I wish to talk to you more."

I felt my face get warmer. "What do you want to talk about?"

He snorted, "The topics are so vast I may have to start a list soon."

I didn't know what that meant, at all. "Okay?"

"Can you explain this vision with Emil and Alona in it? You said there was another man?"

I turned to sit facing the window and stared out. Sometimes, if I emptied my mind, I could see it again even with the other flashes filling in the spaces.

"Cristy?"

"Yes?"

"I thought I lost you there."

I looked around the room. "No. I haven't moved."

He exhaled loudly again. "Did you hear my questions?"

I nodded. "Yes. I can't say the words I need to show you what I see." I bit my lip, trying to find them. "I don't think Alona and Emil are together…" I frowned, "or they don't know they are."

"So, they may be in the same place, but not there together?"

"Yes." I smiled. He was a very smart man. "The other man is there too." I closed my eyes to see if I could see what I'd saw. "I'm not sure if he's there for them, or just there at the same time."

"Does staying where you have been help the visions to be clearer?"

I couldn't explain to him how it worked, it just did. "It makes the others slow down." I nodded, "and then…then I can see more of what I need to."

"Mmm," he made a thoughtful noise, "when you know where they are, please call me. I don't want you to go walking into danger."

That was a strange thing to tell me. Why would I walk into danger on purpose? "I will. I won't walk into danger."

"That is to say, *it* finding you is also a valid reason to call me. I don't care what time of day or night it is."

I nodded. "Okay." I hoped danger didn't find me, I'm pretty sure I wouldn't enjoy that.

I heard a door close again. "Cristy, are you certain you are alright?"

I smiled. "I am. My stomach is very happy right now, too."

He sighed, "I'm pleased it is." I heard another voice. "I need to go…" he cleared his throat. "It was a long, trying night and I have to…" He cleared his throat again, I wonder if he was getting a cold. "Please call or message me later and let me know you are well."

I huffed out a breath. I kept forgetting about the strange time when some were awake and some were not. "Okay. I am going to go sit and watch, to see if I can find the place I see."

"Please. Please, be careful. I know you need to do this alone, but accepting that has been *very* difficult for me." He paused, "when you are back here, we really need to discuss a few matters."

It sounded quite serious and important. "Okay. I will be safe. I promise."

He exhaled a long breath, "I pray it is so."

I stood up and picked up my pack. "Good bye, Victor."

"Take care of yourself, Cristy." His voice was soft.

I hung up wanting to keep that softness he hid so well, inside my head. He said Cristy like he did Crissy, making is sound prettier than it was. Putting the phone in my jacket pocket, I zipped it up so I wouldn't lose it. Daxx got upset whenever that happened.

Chapter Seven

I looked at the strap and gave it a little squeeze in my hand. I would have to thank Victor again, without it I never stayed up here this long before. My legs were getting tired though, staying in this position for so long. Looking down, I watched people leaving the club. I had seen many go in and out since night had come, but I knew what I saw, and here was where I needed to be. I wandered most of the day, looking, then remembering a symbol that I knew, but wasn't sure from where.

It finally came to me that it was on the one wall of the club so many liked to go to. I don't know why anyone would, it was smelly, and the vibes were just wrong, but if I saw it, then was true.

I looked around, it was dark enough now that I could go down and find a hidden corner inside the club to watch from. I didn't know if Alona and Emil would be in there, but I had to watch and find the time I had seen inside my head.

Checking that my pack was closed, I put it on my back and stood up. My head was a little dizzy, and legs were shaky, but I knew I was safe and wouldn't fall from the ledge because Victor's gift made sure of that.

When my legs felt right, I unclipped the strap and slowly worked my way along until I was at the roof's edge. Once there, I could go down the fire escape at the back and slip in the door, as I had many times before.

The flash in my mind had finally shown me that the man

was watching Emil and Alona, I didn't know if it was at the same time, but he saw them. I wasn't sure what the image of the snake I kept seeing had to do with any of it, but I was hoping to think more on that, later.

Once inside I went and squatted down in a dark corner I had used before. I took my pack and looped it on the front of me, knowing that someone couldn't take it then. No one saw me here, but how could they, when they weren't looking for me? I looked at all the people moving around and tried really hard not to smell the awful scent this place always had.

It was so loud here, the music and people talking over the music, all to be heard at once. I wondered if any of them ever thought to listen to the silence.

A tall woman came out of one of the corners and walked up to the bar. I got up to move closer, she looked like Alona, but I needed her to turn so I could make sure. Grabbing onto someone, only to find out they weren't who you thought they were never ended well. When she did turn, I went quickly over to her and grasped her wrist, tugging on it so she'd follow me back to the corner.

When we got there, I smiled at her. "You're here." I nodded. "Why are you here again?" Didn't she know they watched for her?

"Crissy?" She frowned at me and leaned down. "Do not tell me we have to hurry, then pass out on me again."

I checked inside my head. "No, I'm good today, there aren't too many"

"I don't even want to know." She said and then looked over her shoulder, "What do you want with me?"

I had forgot she didn't know. "You can't come here. They know."

"Who knows what?" She straightened and turned so her back wasn't to the rest of the room. "I come here to…" she shook her head. "I just need to."

I looked around seeing if Emil was here. "Have you seen a man with black hair…" I touched my shoulder. "To here, with serious grey eyes?"

She gave me a strange look. "Is that who you're here with?

You've lost him in the crowd?"

Her black hair was so shiny in the lights. I shook my head. "No, I didn't lose him, I saw him, but now I'm trying to find him." I nodded.

With wide eyes, she continued to just look down at me. She wasn't as tall as Rafael or Victor, but I still had to look up at her.

"I know you're old. My friends are too." I paused and thought. "Not Daxx though, but she may be now, I never got to ask her what happens now that she has a king." I gave her an abrupt nod. "Their eyes go red... not Chase though, he's different." I looked at her mouth. "Do you have fangs?" I wondered if girl fangs looked different.

She gave me a gentle push, so we were right in the corner. "Have you been following me?"

Slowly shaking my head, I looked up at her. "No. I could only *see* you and it took forever to find you."

Heaving an exasperated sigh, she glared at me. "I really have no idea what to make of you."

I frowned, how could she make anything with me? I wasn't an ingredient. "You should meet my friends, you're not safe." I looked around the room, watching for Emil.

"I'm not as harmless as you'd think." She told me quietly.

A shiver went up my spine, I grabbed her arm and looked around again. The man I'd seen was here. "He's here."

"The man with the black hair?" She turned and looked.

"No. The bad one watching you."

She backed up into the wall and turned her head slowly. "Where?"

"His eyes go yellow and he's bad." I glanced and seen the symbol on the wall. "I don't see Emil," I mumbled quietly.

"Where is the bad man?" she asked leaning down to look in my eyes.

"Over by the end of the bar. He is very tall and has no hair." I didn't look away from him as I told her.

"I see him." She nodded. "Why is he watching me?"

"He knows what you are, and they want you on their side." I whispered. Another man walked over to the bad one, then they both started looking around. I dropped down to squat when I saw his eyes. They were purple. When he turned, the light shone on him and I saw a snake tattoo on his throat. I pulled Alona's hand down, so she would make herself small too. "Purple eyes. Stay away from purple eyes." I said quietly.

"I'll take your word for it."

They started walking toward us. "I have to go. You have to go. We have to hurry." I grabbed her hand and tried to decide which way to go. Then I remembered. "If you need help." She wasn't looking at me, I tugged on her hand. "If you're not safe. Go to the fish factory and paint an x on the wall. My friends will help you."

"Fine." She nodded and started to get up. "Let's get out of here."

I was so happy she saw now. We started to move along the wall. There were so many people and so much sound, we should have been invisible, but the bad one with yellow eyes saw us and started pushing through the crowd. I lost my grip on Alona's arm.

"Go." She told me when I turned around to take her hand. "They can't follow both of us if we split up."

I nodded. It made sense. "The factory."

She pushed me in the other direction. "Yes, yes an x."

I paused long enough to see the yellow-eyed man spot her and followed her. When I turned to go the other way, the new man with the purple eyes blocked my way. Now what? Huffing out a breath, I spun around and pushed into the crowd of people. I had to be careful, I was much smaller than most of them. I knew if I could get to the back hall again I would be able to slip out the same door I came in. I hurried as much as a body could with all these people in my way.

Turning, I darted down the hall and reached the door. I wanted to look behind me to see if he followed, but I was afraid to know. Shoving the door, I ran out into the alley and kept my legs moving as fast as I could. My new boots were very good, my feet didn't slip at all. I was almost to the end, where I knew I could vanish when something hit my back. It was so forceful I stumbled several steps and almost fell. My back burned like it was on fire, but I kept running, I had to keep going until I could hide.

My legs hurt, and I was shaking by the time I reached the building site. Stopping, I gasped to breathe and looked behind me. No one was there. My body was shaking and the pain was getting worse. I should check why, but I didn't feel safe, so I turned and looked up at the beams that were like the building's skeleton. I needed to go higher.

As I climbed up the ladder, and went across a beam, my knees started to shake more. The burning was so bad I needed to stop. If I fell, Victor would be very upset with me. Crawling across the last few feet, I looked down. No one would look up here. Taking the strap off my pack, I looked around and saw a small metal bar I could clip on to. My hands were vibrating, and it took a lot of talking to myself to get it hooked on. I leaned over the bar and put my head down, trying to catch my breath.

I had to check my back, maybe I did get burned or cut. I took off my pack and hooked it through my one arm so it wouldn't fall to the ground. It was a long way down. My head was dizzy now and I didn't like how that felt. It took me three tries to unzip my pocket and get my phone. Turning it on, I watched the colors on the screen, then my eyes fogged and they weren't clear.

Hearing the sound that told me it was on, I squeezed my eyes shut and then opened them so I could try to see the buttons to push. I wasn't sure, but I think I called Victor. It didn't matter, the only people in my phone were my friends from Alterealm and Daxx. Leaning down to the phone, because I couldn't move my arms without the burning hurting more, I rested my forehead against the bar.

"Cristy, I was just about to explain to everyone…"

"Victor…" I closed my eyes and took another breath, "I'm not okay."

"Where are you? Are you injured?" His voice was very loud now.

I opened my eyes but everything was blurry. "He had purple eyes…" I panted out a few breaths, why was it so hard to breathe? "My back is burning…"

"Criss, it's Daxx, where are you. Talk to me."

"Daxx." I smiled, she would find me, she always found me. "I don't know." I could hear other voices.

"Crissy, stay with me. What do you see?"

"It's blurry," I told her. "I ran." I couldn't even move my head to nod. "From the gross club…"

"Which way, Crissy? Tell me." Her voice was very loud or maybe I had hit the volume button on my phone.

"Out the back." My arm dropped and heard my pack hit the ground below. I tried to see where it fell but it seemed to be getting darker and darker out.

"Are you in the ally?" Someone else said something but I couldn't hear it. "Crissy!"

"No. Daxx?"

"I'm here." Her voice made me feel better.

"I'm not okay." I told her, she would know to come and get me.

"Crissy…"

It was Rafael. "Raf, I dropped the cookies."

"I'll get you more. Where are you, we'll come and get you."

"My back hurts, I feel sick…" I tried to take a deep breath and it hurt more. "I ran…" My other arm started to go numb which was very bad, it was the one through Victor's strap and holding the phone. "to the new building, they're making…"

"You're at a construction site?"

"Yes." I smiled, at least I think I did.

"I think I know where she is." Daxx said sounding far away.

"I'm coming to get you, Cristy." Victor said in hard voice.

I closed my eyes. "Okay. I'll wait." I don't know if they hung up or I dropped my phone, but there were no more voices. My whole body felt like it was floating, which I knew it couldn't do.

I heard people running and hoped the man hadn't found me.

"Here's her backpack."

Was that Rafael?

"And what's left of her phone."

Daxx was going to be mad, I needed a new phone, again.

"Do you think they got her?" Daxx's asked.

"No." It was Victor. "She's up there somewhere."

"Holy hell, Victor there's a hundred beams up there." It was Quinton.

All of them had come to get me. If I didn't think I would throw up, I would call down to them so they could find me.

"Get some kind of light so we can see." Victor said, not sounding happy at all.

I tried to focus and listen, but my head felt like it was swaying, like a swing would when someone jumps out of it.

"Cristy…" Victor sounded so close now, his voice softer. I felt someone touch my face and wanted to cry, they found me.

"Victor. My back…" I swallowed and even that hurt. "I feel wrong."

"Get some rope up here, it's the only way we'll get her down." He said to someone.

I felt bad to create such a problem. "I'm sorry."

"Don't be. You got away and hid, that's all that matters right now." I could feel his hand brushing my hair out of my face.

"I used the strap."

"I see that. I don't want to think what would have happened if you hadn't."

I heard someone on the other side of me.

"It looks like backlash from a spell gone wrong."

It was Rafael, but I didn't know what he was saying.

"She's not as impervious to magic as Daxx is, but still has a resistance." Victor told him, but I didn't understand.

"I can't feel…" I swallowed the sick feeling down, "my body." I closed my eyes, hoping the strange feeling would end.

"I've got you." Victor said close to my ear.

"Okay."

I didn't know where I was, but there were voices all around me.

"You can't ingest it, Victor! We don't know if it's magic or poison." Troy said from behind me.

"Get me that idiot mage, Romulus. *Now!* And find me a witch and that useless doctor." Victor yelled. He was very angry with someone.

I didn't like knowing that. "Vic..." talking was so hard, I wasn't sure if I said that in my head or out of it.

"I'm here." I could feel his breath on my face and it made me feel better with him close.

"I need more bars," I told him, so I wouldn't forget.

He brushed the hair off my face, and his palm felt cool against my skin. It felt good. "Did you like them?"

I hadn't thought to eat one myself. "I gave them..." I swallowed that sick feeling again, "to others with no food."

He made a strange sound and rested his head against mine. "Of course, you did." I felt him kiss my forehead and thought that was a nice thing to do. "When you're well, you can hand out cases of them if you must. I will even carry them for you."

He sounded calmer now. "Okay." I closed my eyes again. "Is Daxx mad?" I tried to keep thinking, so this feeling didn't scare me. "I lost my phone again."

"We found it," he told me quietly, "we'll get you new one."

I wanted to nod, but I had no strength to do it. "Okay."

"Romulus is here." Quinton said.

I remembered. "Quinton..."

"He's right behind you," Victor said to me.

"The fish factory..." I tried to focus to say the words. "If Alona is in trouble..." I panted out a breath. Why was it so hard to breathe? "she will paint an x on wall."

"You were with Alona tonight?" Victor's breath brushed against my face.

"Yes."

"I need to test to see what type of spell was used." A strange voice said from behind me.

"Get on with it." Victor growled. I wondered if he had fangs right now. "Did they get Alona?" His voice was softer again.

I hoped not. "We went two different ways." I tried exhaling slowly to see if talking was easier. "Yellow eyed man went after her…"

"Quinton, get Tim a device and take him to this place." Troy's voice said roughly. "Have him stay there and watch in case she makes it there. We'll set up a few shifts to watch for her."

"I'm on it." Quinton said. "What does Alona look like."

"Tall, long black hair, sexy green eyes." Rafael said from behind Victor.

"Of course, you'd take the time notice that," Chase drawled from somewhere in the room.

"I observe things." Rafael told him.

"I'm sure you do." Chase snorted.

"I'll go wait for her, Crissy." Quinton sounded like he was over my head when he said it.

"Okay. Thank you." I felt cool flesh against my face and tried to move into it. Victor's hand held the back of my head in a soothing way. Later, when I wasn't feeling so wrong, I would think how I knew it was his hand. "I told her you were… like she is… and would help."

"We'll find her, little one." Victor kissed my forehead again.

"I'm going to need a salve to counteract this. It's very strong." The strange voice said. "I don't know how she survived. They probably gave up thinking she'd be dead in a few minutes' time."

I felt Victor stiffen, but he didn't say anything. I didn't know how long it had been, but knew it had been longer than a few minutes. Someone would tell me if I was dying, wouldn't they?

"Clairee is on her way here." Daxx told him.

"I'll go tell her what we need." He answered, sounding like he was walking out of the room.

"Romulus," Victor's voice boomed in my ear, "will blood help her?"

"Not until I stop the magic trace bubbling in the wound. If you heal it shut, I will never get it out of her. After that, blood will take care of closing it, and the side effects." There was a pause. "A cool bath will slow absorption further though."

"Thank you." I heard Daxx answer. "Mitz can you turn on

the tub?"

"Yes, love. All of you men get out so we can make her decent."

I realized they were talking about me. I was thankful Daxx and Mitz were here.

I had to know. "Am I dying?" I asked when I felt Victor moving away from me. "I have more living to do." I told him.

"You are not dying." He told me in a very firm way.

I believed him. Victor told the truth. "Good."

"Victor, you can come back in and hold her in the water." Mitz assured him.

"I'm going."

I felt him kiss my forehead once more. It was very sweet of him.

"Cristy, did you see who did this to you?" His voice was soft but quite serious sounding.

"I just need a description." I thought I heard Michael say.

"Snake." I said as loud as I could. "On neck."

"A snake tattoo on his neck." Victor repeated.

"I'll go get Wanda to do a search for me." Michael said. "Using a sample Romulus took of the magic."

"Michael, if you find him. He is *mine*." Victor said in a voice I was sure I never wanted directed at me.

"Understood."

I didn't know what that meant, but if I was the man with the purple eyes and snake tattoo, I would hide. Forever.

"Now get out, Victor, so we can get her ready for the bath."

He kissed me again. I had never been kissed this much ever. It would have been nice if I wasn't feeling this way, but maybe sometime he might kiss me again when I felt better.

I heard Daxx behind me. "We'll have to cut the tank top."

"Daxx?"

"I'm here." She said near my ear.

"Is my new jacket ruined?"

She snorted. "We'll get you ten more later."

"Only need one."

"We're going to change you, love, so you are covered and

can soak with Victor." Mitz told me softly.

"Okay." I closed my eyes feeling like I just needed to rest for a minute.

Chapter Eight

I felt cooler, and was thankful for that, then realized I was in water. Opening my eyes, I saw green eyes I knew very well. "Hi." I said to Victor.

He searched my face, worry filling his. "You had me worried when you passed out after we got in."

"I don't feel so wrong now." I assured him. My arms still felt heavy and my back still hurt, but I could see clearly again, and that was a nice start. He was holding me in the big tub so I was almost leaning back in the water, but not touching it at the same time. I don't know how he fit all of him in here too, but he was leaning over me, watching me.

"They're working on a salve that will stop the burning." His green eyes looked so stressed.

"I'll be okay." I told him.

He smiled. "When you are, we are going to work on expanding your vocabulary. Hearing 'I am not okay' coming from your mouth gave me grey hair."

I looked up at his hair, but didn't see any. "It doesn't look grey."

He leaned down and touched my forehead with his lips. "What am I going to do with you?"

"I don't know," I answered, unsure of what he meant.

Someone cleared their throat from the other side of the big bathroom. "How is she?" It was Daxx.

"Awake now." He sounded relieved. "And far too thin."

He looked down at my body.

Daxx snorted, "Oh I know, I've tried for five years to fatten her up. Clairee and Romulus are back. I sent the doctor away, figuring after the last time his help wouldn't be of much use."

Daxx was so smart, I don't know why she wanted me fat though, but no doctor was a good thing.

"Get me a towel, please." Victor told her. In one move he stood up, while holding me. I wrapped my arm around his neck and was very happy I could move again.

Victor took the towel from Daxx and wrapped me in it without my feet ever touching the floor. Carefully, he set me on the counter and took another towel from her and wrapped it around his waist. I was happy I could sit here without sliding off. Victor had been right, I wasn't dying. My head was also clear enough to notice he was only wearing his underwear. I hadn't seen a lot of men without their clothes, but I was quite certain he was in very good shape. He tipped my chin up with a light touch and smiled at me when he caught me staring at him. I felt my cheeks warm.

"My head." I couldn't believe it.

"Dizzy?" He asked with worry in his eyes.

"No." I paused. "Yes, but there are no flashes." I had never felt that before.

He frowned. "We'll ask Clairee about that if you're concerned, could be your body knows you needed a break right now."

"I've never felt without them." I told him. "It's very… strange to feel."

He lifted me up and cradled me against his chest. "I'm just going to take it as a small win, that you don't have that to cope with on top of the rest." His green eyes locked with mine briefly. "I honestly don't know if I can cope with any more at this moment."

I wasn't completely sure what that meant, but it seemed like yet another sweet thing he was saying.

He walked out and I saw all the people that were there. Turning my head, I pushed my face into his neck so I wouldn't have to see them. I know they came and found me, and were only here to help me, but it still made me panic. "Too many eyes." I whispered.

"I can tell them to leave," he said as he lowered me to the bed.

I kept holding his neck, even after he set me down. It made me feel better. "I don't like being watched." I told him quietly.

"They're here because they are worried." His green eyes searched mine as he straightened. "Everyone back up and give her a little space, please, being stared at is bothering her."

I released his neck and gave him a little nod. "Thank you."

He pulled the blanket up to my neck and helped me lay on my side so they could look at my back.

"Victor, go put your pants on so my mate doesn't have to see your bare ass." Troy growled.

Exhaling loudly, Victor looked over his shoulder sending his brother a cold look. Getting up off the bed, he looked at the strange man standing at the end of it. "Clairee can do what needs to be done. I don't want your hands on her, she doesn't like to be touched."

I watched Victor walk into the bathroom and close the door. He was remembering everything today, and I would have to thank him later. My mind was so strange right now I was having problems keeping things clear.

A small lady with dark brown hair stepped up to the side of the bed where I could see her without looking around. "I'm Clairee, I've brought something to help your back." She smiled at me. It was a very pretty smile. "I love the red of your hair."

"Thank you." I remembered. "I will have to change it now." I frowned. "They saw me."

"That's too bad." She shrugged. "When you pick a new color, have Daxx call me, I'd love to help you color it." She motioned to her head. "I have plain hair, but..." She moved her hand over her face with her eyes closed and it changed to blonde, opening her eyes she looked at me. "I can do a glamour for a short time to try on new shades."

My mouth dropped open. "I wish I could do that. I would try a new color every day." The coolness was leaving as the burning came back. I hissed and squeezed my eyes shut through it. "I'm sorry. I'm not feeling good right now."

"I'm going to put this on your back now," her voice was behind me, "it might sting a bit, but it will pull out the magic poisoning your system."

I opened my eyes as Victor came out of the bathroom with his clothes on again. "Okay." I told her. I didn't have to ask him to come and sit with me, he just did.

"Is it going to cause her a lot of discomfort?" He asked as he moved me to be more in his arms then out of them.

"We're not one hundred percent sure about that. This is a very rare occurrence, and difficult to know if one body reacts differently than another." Romulus said from the end of the bed. He looked very uncomfortable. "It may, in fact, hurt as much drawing out as it did when she was first poisoned."

Victor didn't look happy, again. I reached up and touched his chin so he'd look at me. I nodded when he did. "I'll be okay." I told him, even though I didn't know if it was true.

He clenched his jaw and pulled me closer. "Are you ready?" He asked.

I nodded, hoping it wouldn't hurt the same, or worse. I felt her put something cold on my back, and, for a second, I thought it was going to be fine, it felt cool and that was about it. Before I could say that, it started to get hot. *Really* hot. It burned even more than when it hit me while I was running. I must have made a sound or something because Victor pulled me tight against his chest and growled.

"I need towels to soak this up." Clairee said.

I didn't want to know what she was soaking up. I was shaking and it hurt so much. The burning got worse and I squealed against Victor's chest and tried to breathe through the pain.

His whole body was hard with tension, shaking as much as I was. I wrapped my arms around him and squeezed tight. The pain kept growing and I didn't know how much more I could take. I cried out only when I couldn't keep it inside any longer.

"Go see if Michael has found *him*." He said in a very scary tone. "Now!" He roared.

"I'm sorry," I cried against his chest. He was so upset. "I'll be okay," I gasped between panting.

"There is nothing okay about this. Scream if you must, I've got you." He told me against my ear.

I nodded, feeling too tired to make a sound. I felt sick from the pain but had to believe it would end soon, or I would cry. Squeezing my eyes shut, I realized my eyes were already wet, and I hadn't even known I was crying.

I don't know how long it lasted, it felt like forever, but it finally started to hurt less. The burning was slowly going away with each breath.

"Get rid of that." Victor said in a low voice.

"I'll take them." Romulus answered. "I want to see how he did that."

"I'm so sorry." Clairee said softly behind me. "Most people would have passed out during the worst of that." I felt a cool hand on my shoulder. "You're a very strong woman." She took her hand off me. "I'll just rinse away any traces, and then you can give her some blood to heal her, Victor."

"Thank you, Clairee." Victor responded, sounding void.

I wasn't ready to move yet. I couldn't remember feeling this tired before. Ever. His hold gentled, but his muscles were still hard. I felt cool water run over my back and I can honestly say it was the best thing I had felt all day. Well, maybe not the best, Victor kissing me was the best thing, but the water was a close second.

"Daxx," he said quietly, "We're going to need a few minutes of privacy."

"Okay," she answered him. She sounded so upset.

I lifted my head off his chest to look around. Everyone looked sad and angry, all at the same time. "I'm okay." I told them.

"Out!" Victor barked.

Turning, I looked up to see he had tears on his face as his red eyes looked back down at me. I heard the door close but didn't look to see if everyone had gone. Leaning back, he wiped a tear off my cheek. I wanted to tell him I was okay, but somehow knew he didn't want to hear me say that again.

"I will find him," he said in a low voice, "and he will pay for putting you through that."

A shiver went over my skin, it wasn't a bad one, but it was something I'd never felt before. I didn't know what to say to make him feel better, so I said nothing at all.

"I want to give you some of my blood, little one, it will help heal your back and make you feel better." His eyes were green again as he watched me carefully.

"Then there will be a bond?" I remembered what they had said after I blacked out.

"Yes." He nodded slowly, "it won't be intrusive. I can shield you from my emotions, so it won't add to your already overtaxed mind." He kissed my forehead softly. "I've never felt as helpless as I did just now. Please, let me help you."

I thought about how that made me feel. His words were sweet and I could sense his good intentions. Biting my lip, I looked back to him. "I don't know if I like the taste of blood."

He smiled. "I suppose we'll find out then."

I nodded. "Okay." He kissed me again. I had lost count how many times he had done that today. As he sat up, opened his shirt and reached over to the table. I wondered if there was a way to get him to kiss me like that on a day he didn't have to rescue me.

When he turned back, he held a short, very sharp blade in his hand. I know my eyes were huge.

"It's to make a small cut on me." He paused watching me.

"I'm not watching." I informed him.

He grinned. "You don't need to." Raising the blade to his chest, he paused, "I heal very fast, so I will need you to try to take as much as you can, or I will have to keep cutting myself."

My eyes widened again. I didn't want that. I nodded and covered my eyes with one hand as he put the blade against his chest near where his heart beat.

"Come here." He touched the back of my head.

Opening my eyes, I saw the blood dripping down his chest and didn't want him to cut himself again, so I leaned down and licked it. I stopped and tasted it on my tongue. It wasn't a bad taste at all. Not what I thought blood would be like. He pulled me closer, so I put my lips against his skin and sucked gently.

After I swallowed a few times, I moved so more of me was close to him. I didn't know if it was the blood doing what he said it was, but I felt different, in a good way, and wanted more of that. I'd had a feeling kind of like this with a boy once when I was younger, but he'd vanished, so I never got closer to another again. Victor, I was fairly sure, wouldn't just disappear.

Licking one more time, until there was no blood on his skin, I lifted my head and then touched where he'd cut himself. There was only a red mark remaining.

"How do you feel?" He asked me, his face in my hair.

"Better inside." I told him and then looked up at him. His eyes were red and I smiled. Reaching up, I touched his bottom lip so he would open his mouth. I wanted to see his fangs. He did. I ran my finger carefully over them, he closed his lips and sucked gently on it. Before I could over think it, as I tended to do, I stretched up and did the same with the tip of my tongue over his sharp teeth.

He sucked in a breath and stayed very still, but his hand on my hip pulled me closer, so I didn't think he was unhappy. Closing my mouth, I looked up at him.

"Have you ever been kissed, Cristy?" He held himself very still again, watching me with his red eyes.

I nodded. "When I was seventeen, I had a boyfriend." I frowned. "Well, he was a boy and a friend." I wasn't sure what the meaning of a real boyfriend was exactly.

"I want to kiss you." He told me in that soft voice he used.

Butterflies started to fly around inside my stomach. "Okay." I nodded.

He touched under my chin lightly and tipped my face up to his, while his other arm pulled me tight into his body. Slowly, as if he was waiting for me to change my mind, he touched his mouth against mine.

It made me smile, that feeling. His lips moved against my mouth and I did just what he did to me. It wasn't hard, but it made me feel dizzy, in a very good way. When he opened his mouth more, I put my tongue in his and touched it against his teeth again. He made a soft growling noise and goosebumps covered my whole body.

Someone knocked loudly on the door. "Victor." It was Michael on the other side.

Lifting his head, he glanced at the door. "I'll be out in a minute." Then looked back to me. "You tempt me far too much."

My head was still feeling light from his kiss. "Is that bad?"

He grinned. "I don't know." Kissing my forehead, he sat up and picked up the knife. "I may have to go out for a little while. I'll leave Daxx here with you to help you get changed, and the bed cleaned up."

I nodded and watched him get up and look at my back.

"It will leave a scar, but I want to try more blood when I return."

I felt my cheeks grow warm. "Okay."

He stood there, looking down at me smiling. "Okay." He winked and went over to the door.

Daxx and Mitz helped me change into something that wasn't wet and felt comfortable against my back. I'd made them let me look in the mirror: between my shoulders was a long scar down my spine. I was okay with it. From what I'd overheard, now that my thoughts were clearer, I shouldn't be alive right now.

My head still wasn't filled with flashes. There were some, but not too many to see. Daxx had phoned Clairee and she told her it was probably just temporary from the magic used to heal me. I honestly wasn't sure if that was a good or bad thing.

Troy, Rafael and Daxx were sitting talking to me when Victor came walking in. Only this was not the same man that had walked out before. He was dressed in black leather from his neck down, wore a long coat that went to his knees, and had two long narrow swords in an x on his back. There were more knives on his hip. He looked more dangerous than anything I had ever seen.

I looked at him with my eyes huge, surprised this was the same man. I knew I was looking at the man of justice right now and not just Victor. The cold aura surrounded him, all except his eyes that looked at me with warmth. I looked at the door and Michael and Leone stood there quietly.

"How are you doing?" He glanced at my pack beside me, then back to me. "Should you be sitting up?"

I smiled. "I had a shower and changed." I nodded. "Mitz is bringing me food."

He sat on the edge of the bed. "Food is good."

"Yes, it is." I watched his eyes, to see if they were different when he was dressed like this, but it was the same soft look he had when he'd walked out earlier. "My back," I said quietly, "it's like I was a butterfly and I lost my wings." He frowned. "The scar, I mean." I nodded. "Everything else with wings has two, but can lose one or the other." I gave him a serious look. "A butterfly's wings, are attached so close together it looks like they're one, so I have a scar from my wings."

He watched me for a moment and then leaned forward and kissed my forehead. "Or maybe," he whispered, "they're invisible now, like the wings of an angel."

I smiled, because I had no choice. It was the best thing anyone had ever said to me. "Maybe."

Taking a deep breath, he stood up. "I have to go out. I will return later and check on you."

I looked over to Michael and Leone, they looked like they were going into battle too. I nodded up at him. "Come back with no blood on you."

He smirked. "I will try." With that he turned and headed toward the door.

Rafael stood up to follow. "Guess you're going to be taking a lot of showers to get clean from now on." Victor looked at him then smacked him in the back of the head as he went past.

When the door closed, I looked at Daxx and Troy.

Daxx smiled. "Don't be frightened of Victor when he's that way. You know his job?"

I nodded.

Her smile was warm. "But you know he has another side, the soft, gentle one you've seen."

I nodded again. "I know. He has to be cold to do it."

Troy hissed out a breath. "Another side?" He pointed to

the door. "I don't even know *who* that man is right now." He shook his head. "Not in two hundred and sixty years have I seen that!" He got up and rubbed the back of his neck. "I'll be back, I need to go read a book," he looked at me then to his mate. "with leaves on it."

Daxx smiled up at him. "I already did and it is what you're thinking."

He sat back down and huffed out a loud breath. "I'll be damned. I never thought this day would come."

She nudged him with her shoulder. "Its not here yet." She smiled at me nicely, then back at him. "We both know this isn't simply going to be plain black and white."

He laughed, "Yeah, because we were so plain and simple."

"What is the book with leaves on it?" I asked.

Troy turned and looked at me for a moment. "Ask Victor, I'm sure he can explain it better then I can."

I smiled. "Okay. I will."

Mitz walked in carrying a tray. I was so happy, I couldn't remember being as hungry as I was right now.

Chapter Nine

I was alone when Victor did return. Everyone was needed to be somewhere else doing something else. I didn't mind. Too many people around all the time stressed me out. I was okay with quiet. I wasn't feeling like moving around much still, and wasn't sure if it was from the magic, the healing, or if my body was just tired. Then again it might be a food coma, as Daxx suggested. Mitz had fed me three times.

Victor knocked quietly and then opened the door and looked in.

"Hi." I watched him smile and come in. He wasn't in his justice clothes now and I had to wonder if that meant there was blood on them that he didn't want me to see.

He came over and sat on the bed. "You're still in bed. Should I worry?"

I smiled, "I am tired. Daxx says it's a food coma."

He laughed. "As comas go, that's the best kind."

"Rafael went and got my other bag. I keep it under the bed at Daxx's." I don't know why I blurted that out. I noticed his hair was wet. "Did you have to wash off blood?"

His eyes jumped to mine. "There was some blood. Not as much as I would have liked, but Leone and Michael stopped me."

"You found the man that did that to me?"

Victor nodded. "Yes. He is in a cell now that he can't get out of or use magic. Troy was able to see inside his mind and confirmed it was him. We have two others that were with him as well."

Taking my time, I studied him, he didn't look relieved. "You don't seem happy that you caught him."

"I am." He reached over and brushed my hair back from my face, his touch was gentle. "He needs to be punished for what he did to you."

"You are the justice." He nodded, but gave me an odd look. "Not the punisher." I finished.

He smirked briefly, "Sometimes there is no difference."

"Maybe this man is just following orders." I nodded, when he continued to look at me. "We know he is not the one with the purple eyes, the one that is the leader." I offered him a little smile. "You can't find out what he knows if he's dead."

"Mmm," his jaw clenched a few times. "I know you're right, but that doesn't mean I have to like that he still breathes." He looked at me, then to the bed and shook his head. Standing up, he reached down and scooped me up into his arms, blankets and all and carried me over to the couch and sat down with me in his lap. "I am not used to you sitting still, so I'm going to enjoy it while it lasts."

I laughed. "I can walk. I'm okay."

He snorted, "You are always okay, even when you're not." He tucked the blanket around my legs. "Quinton stopped to see me, there is still no sign of Alona. We'll leave someone there the next few days to watch for her." He tucked the hair behind my ear. "Troy is going to see if there is anything useful inside the other men's heads in regard to her."

"Can I go see them?"

"The men we brought in?" His brows drew together. "No."

I bit my lip. "I wanted to see if the one that chased after her was one of them."

Turning his head, he looked at the floor for a moment and then sighed. "I'll get Arius to send photos."

I nodded. "Okay." I was happy with that, the idea of seeing them in person hadn't seemed like a good idea after I said it.

Shifting, he pulled his phone out of his pocket and tapped the screen a few times before putting it to his ear. "Send me pictures of them." His green eyes moved over my face as he spoke. "Cristy wants to confirm their identity." He smirked and looked at the floor. "Just do it." He hung up. "He's going to go take them and send them to me."

I clasped my hands in my lap. "I don't know if Emil went to the club."

"And that's going to worry you." Rubbing a hand over his face, he exhaled loudly. He looked tired. "I can send Raf there to keep checking, maybe a few of the guards we trust. He looks like Arius?"

I nodded. "His hair is shorter." I held my hand to my neck, near my shoulder. "To there, but if you didn't know Arius you would think it was the same person."

Lifting the hand with his phone in it, he hit a few buttons again and put it to his ear. "Can you come to Cristy's room?"

Someone tapped on the door, it opened, and it was Rafael with his phone against his ear. "Sure can." He grinned and hung up, then came over and looked down at us and raised an eyebrow.

I realized it was because I was sitting on his brother and wondered if that would be one of those socially unacceptable things Daxx talked about. But Victor was proper in so many ways, so he wouldn't have done something that was wrong. I saw the plate in his Rafael's hand.

"I promised her more cookies." He set them on the table and sat in the chair. "What's up?"

"When I saw Alona, and the man watching her," I focused to remember it all, "the one that chased her tonight," I looked at Victor to see him watching me, then back to Rafael. "Emil was there too in my head." I shook my head. "But I didn't have time to see him before I had to run."

Rafael glanced at his brother. "You want me to go hang out and see if he shows up?" He glanced at his phone. "It will still be open for a few more hours tonight."

Victor nodded. "We'll set up a rotation, keep an eye out for him and possibly Alona for the next few days. Emil looks like Arius, with shoulder length hair, so he shouldn't be to hard to spot."

"And if I see either? What am I supposed to do?"

I bit my lip. "I told Alona my friends could help her."

"So, just tell her I'm a friend of Crissy's?" He glanced to his brother briefly than back to me.

I nodded. "I don't know about Emil though." I frowned. "He doesn't know he's not alone."

Rafael shrugged, "Alright, we will play it by ear with him."

I started to nod then stopped. "I don't know what that means."

He smirked, "I will see how he is, and if I can find a way to talk to him."

"Yes. Okay." I looked at the cookies. "Thank you for the cookies. I can't eat anything else right now, but I will save them for later."

He laughed. "Mitz consoles herself by feeding us whenever something happens."

"She does it very well."

He got up. "I'll go now. Call if I'm needed back here."

Victor nodded. "Of course. We're just waiting on pictures of the men we brought in for Cristy to confirm."

"Confirmed or not, they're not going anywhere for a long time. If ever." He turned to the door, then looked back at me. "No more heart attacks today, please."

I smiled. "I promise. None."

When the door closed, Victor started to say something and then his phone made a sound. Sighing, he held it up and looked at it, then turned it toward me. "This one?"

I looked at it, he seemed familiar, but it wasn't from tonight. "I've seen him before. Outside my head, but I don't know where."

He flipped it to the next picture and held it up.

It was the man with the purple eyes, the one that had hurt me. I looked at it longer then the other one, trying to see if I had any good feelings toward him. I could find none and that upset me a little. Daxx always said I was too soft and tried to find the good where there wasn't any. I realized Victor was still waiting for an answer. "He's the man that chased after me."

His jaw clenched, but he didn't say a word as he flipped to

the last photo. It wasn't the man that went after Alona. I sat taller and looked at him. "It's not him." My heart sped up. "The one that went after her is still out there."

Turning the phone around he hit some buttons on it then put it to his ear again. "The one that went after Alona is not any of the ones we brought in. Hold on." He looked back to me. "What does he look like?"

I bit my lip for a second trying to remember if he had any tattoos or something helpful. "He's big like Raf and has no hair. His eyes go yellow."

He nodded, then spoke into the phone again. "Did you hear that? Yes. Emotion feeder. You see him, call. I want him." Nodding again, he hung up. "I'm going to text Troy so he can go see what he can find out from them." He smirked. "I'd call, but I have orders to not disturb him while he spends some time with his queen."

"Won't the text disturb him?"

Victor smiled. "Yes, it will."

"Oh." I smiled back. I remembered. "Troy told me to ask you about a book with leaves on it."

He stopped typing and looked at me. "Oh, did he?"

"Yes."

"On second thought, I better call him. Finding out if those men know anything about the bald one or Alona is of the utmost importance."

I agreed with that. "I'm going to put my cookies away." I got up, dragging the blankets along with me and picked up the plate. I wanted to wrap them and put them in my pack for tomorrow.

"Sorry to disturb. Cristy looked at photos of the men in the cells and none of them are the one that went after Alona. I need you to get in their heads and see if you can find anything, now. Raf is going to the club to watch for Emil, because Cristy saw him there in the vision with Alona and the one that chased her." He snorted. "I'm sure your queen will understand the importance of this, brother."

I turned around to see him laughing quietly and holding the phone against his chest. He stopped and put it in his pocket and then got up. "You know you don't have to hide your cookies in your pack here."

I stood there with the plate and looked at him. How did he know what I was going to do? "I just, always have."

Coming over, he took the plate from my hand gently and set it on the table. "I know I upset you and you left abruptly the last time, but I do hope your exit, when you do, will be more planned from now on."

I forgot how tall he was, but now standing and looking up at him I felt small. I didn't have a way to measure or anything, but he had to be a foot taller than me.

"Now, as for the book with leaves on it. *That* is a very long and complicated conversation and I think you have been through enough for one day." He smiled down at me. "I have been through enough for one day." Leaning down he kissed my forehead. "If you are feeling one hundred percent tomorrow, we can have that discussion. Agreed?"

If he thought it was complicated, I was very interested to find out, but I had to agree. I was tired, both my body and my head, so tomorrow would be better. "Yes." I remembered. "What is an emotion feeder?"

He sighed. "That one is a little easier to explain but could be a long explanation as well." Sitting down on the bed, he held my hand. "I will explain, but first, how is your back?" Turning me slowly, he wrapped the blankets around my waist and lifted up the big t-shirt I was wearing. "It's still very red. Does it hurt."

"Not painfully. It's sort of numb." I told him. "When I was so sick, I heard some things." I thought back, "I think I did. Troy told you not to ingest it. What did he mean?"

"Mmm, that's an easier one." He ran his finger along the scar. "Those of us with red eyes, have healing saliva, I will explain why shortly, but I was going to use that on your back and he stopped me."

"Would you have gotten hurt or sick?" I clutched the blanket to my chest.

"Quite likely, yes."

"I'm glad he stopped you then. I wouldn't want to see you hurt." I glanced over my shoulder at him, he had a strange look on his face.

"I can honestly say that was the hardest thing I have ever done. To watch you in pain the way you were today."

I felt his breath on my back.

"It's probably too late to help, but I can hope."

I know my eyes went wide when I felt his tongue swipe along the mark that had caused me so much discomfort earlier. I didn't know if it would help it at all, but it did wipe away the feelings that it had caused me. When he stopped, he rested his forehead against my spine, his breath brushing over my skin.

"I want you take more blood. Make sure everything inside is healed as it should be." He turned me slowly and looked up at me. "I have a confession before we do though."

"You do?"

He sighed, "Yes. Since the first time I have been concentrating, as hard as I am able to help give your mind peace from the usual chaos." His eyes searched mine. "I can't do it indefinitely, but I can to allow you to get some rest today." Shaking his head, his eyes serious, "I don't know how you have managed to live with it like that for so long. It would drive me insane, the constant motion."

I reached out and played with the hair that had fallen on his forehead, it was softer than I had thought it would be. "Most think I am insane." I raised an eyebrow at him, remembering he had asked me that. Shame filled his eyes. "My fourth," I looked down trying to remember, "It might have been the fifth foster home, had me locked up in a place with a lot of sick, and sometimes scary, people. They did horrible things to me, trying to pick me apart and figure me out." I bit my lip, not sure how much to tell him. I had never shared this with anyone, but something inside me told me I should. "I broke for a little while after that. So many emotions to avoid, I couldn't sense people well there, and I felt like I was wandering around lost every second I had to stay inside those walls." I took a deep breath and then continued. "I'm not crazy. I just have to sort through the never-ending flashes in my mind, and my own thoughts sometimes get mixed up with them." I shrugged, "or I think I'm thinking something but then say it out loud." I touched his hair again, not wanting to look at his eyes yet. I don't know what I would have done if he'd judged me now, like most did. "I couldn't stay in school, the teachers thought I tried to be bad, but I didn't." I shook my head. "So maybe I'm not as smart as I could be, but I never forget once I've read something or I've seen it..." I finally looked at his eyes, they weren't cold or judging. "I just..." I wasn't sure of the word, "*misplace* things inside my head sometimes and have to find them again." He was completely focused on every word I was saying, it made me feel good. "Because I pick up on so much around me, in addition to the noise in my head, I haven't been around a lot of people." I shrugged slightly, "so I don't always know what I should, or shouldn't, do." I gave him a little smile. "And if you weren't helping control the flashes right now, I wouldn't have been able to say all of that and have it make sense the first time." I leaned down and kissed his forehead, like he had mine.

His fingers squeezed my waist tightly, and his jaw clenched a few times. "I have talked to the elders and many others to see if there is anyone that can help you learn control." He gave me a soft look, one that I'd never seen before, but it gave me warm feelings, so I would remember it always. "I think my heart just grew inside my chest." He said quietly. "To survive what you have and cope with so much all the time. Yet, here you are, so gentle and full of goodness. You look after everyone, but yourself. I believe you may be the strongest, bravest person I have ever had the pleasure to know."

I tilted my head and looked down at him, trying to sort through what he said. "I'm not very strong at all," I smirked, "and I am much better at hiding then being brave."

He stretched up so our eyes were closer. "You don't even know it."

I studied his eyes, they were a very pretty green, but he looked tired. I remembered. "With you helping me," I tapped my head lightly with my hand, "with my head, is that why you look so tired?"

He smirked, like you would if you were caught doing something. "Yes. That and I haven't fed..." He sighed, "which brings us to the explanation regarding emotion feeder, or in my case essence feeder."

I grinned, "and your sexy fangs?"

His eyebrows rose as he looked at me. "Yes." Tapping my hip with his hand, he slid back further on the bed. "First I want to give you more blood. I will help keep your mind at ease tonight so you can rest, and then we will see how you are feeling tomorrow."

"Can I be in your mind too?" The idea of someone else's for a change, did hold some appeal.

"I don't think my mind is a place for someone like you." He told me.

I frowned, not sure why he would say that.

"For the last four hundred and fifty years, I have been *the* justice for all of Alterealm. I have seen a lot of evil. Had to be violent. I fear you would not cope with it well, due to your sensitivity."

I sighed, "You are so sweet, Victor."

He snorted and shook his head. "No. I am not."

I nodded. "You are. You help quiet my mind. Protect me from violence, even though I know you have to have a darker side, to do what you have to do to protect everyone else at the same time."

The look on his face changed, but before I could figure out what it meant, he gently pulled my head down to his. His lips brushed over mine so softly, I wondered if I imagined it and it hadn't really happened. When he moved away, he patted the bed. "Come. Take more blood and then I will explain what my fangs are for."

I smiled, I was finally going to know. "Okay."

He reached down and lifted his pant leg and pulled out a small, very sharp looking knife.

I paused. "Do you always have a knife strapped to your ankle?"

He grinned. "Yes."

Nodding, I got on the bed. I would have to remember that. Turning, he gently pulled me closer so I was sitting next to him.

"I don't trust myself to lay on the bed with you." When I was going to ask why he shook his head at me. "I will explain it all tomorrow."

I bit my lip and tried to be as brave he said I was, when he raised the blade to the skin on his chest, but I squeezed my eyes shut when he started to cut himself.

I heard him chuckle softly, "Come here."

Opening my eyes, I looked to see the blood dripping down his chest. "You don't even act like it hurts." I told him quietly as he pulled my head closer. I licked the blood with my tongue and he hissed out a breath, but put he pushed on the back of my head so I would continue.

By the time the gash healed closed, something I still found fascinating, I was in his lap, my body against his warm one. Lifting my head, I looked up into his red eyes and wondered if he was going to kiss me again. His hand continued to stroke down the back of my head gently, his eyes searching my face.

"I want to kiss you again…" He looked at my mouth, "but I am too tired, you are too tempting, and because I haven't fed, I'm finding it very difficult right now."

I looked at him mouth, and thought of his fangs, a warmth spread through me.

He growled softly. "Your emotions and mine… both wanting the same, is not helping. I know what you are thinking."

Biting my lip, I felt my face flush. "I can't help it."

Heaving out a heavy sigh, he straightened and set me further from him, then slid up on the bed and leaned back against the headboard.

I moved closer, so I was facing him and pulled my knees up to my chest. "Tell me about emotion feeders."

His eyes were slowly turning back to green as he looked at me. "Those with yellow eyes, never let them stare into yours. They live off emotions and I'm told human emotions are the most appealing. There are more colors, but I am too tired to go into that tedious details, tonight."

I nodded slowly while I fit the pieces together. "So, purple is magic?"

"Yes. Witches are more inclined to be paler, lighter hues, and mages a darker shade."

I had wanted my hair to be the darker purple I'd seen the

leader of the bad ones, Marcus, have, but had since decided I didn't like that color. "Yellow eyes are emotions," I mused quietly filing away the information, "Red is blood then?"

"Mmm," he studied me for a moment. "Essence is in the blood, so in a way you are correct."

"You don't drink blood?" I had seen vampires in my head before and it was a scary, upsetting thing.

He shrugged, "A little may be swallowed, but our fangs," he frowned, "you would have to speak to someone more scholarly then I for all the details I am sure your mind seeks," he smiled at me. "Our fangs are designed to draw out the essence from your veins."

I wanted to look more closely at his fangs, but as he was too tempted by me… whatever that meant, I didn't want to upset him by asking. I remembered. "Your healing tongue heals the bite."

He smiled. "Yes."

I moved closer, finding that whole of that very interesting. "Can you feed from me?" I turned my head, and brushed my hair back so my neck was bare to him.

He made a soft noise, like a growl, I wasn't sure if it was good or bad, but he did lean closer. His breath brushed against the skin on my neck and warmth spread through my body. When he inhaled right next to my ear, and licked my skin slowly, I held my breath waiting to see what came next.

He moved away from me again, his eyes red. "I can, but I won't… yet."

Letting out a shaky breath, I frowned. "Why?"

"*That* is part of the long conversation regarding the book my brother mentioned to you." He leaned his head back against the wall and watched me.

"The book with leaves on it." I had to know more. "What is that book?"

"It is the book of prophecy for the nine sons of the king." He smirked. "I used to think it was hog spittle." He chuckled.

"I don't know what hog spittle is…" I thought through it more, "but you are number one in the nine sons?"

He inclined his head to me. "I am."

"I find that fascinating." I nodded.

He grinned, and then sobered just as quickly. "Until I stood in Daxx's apartment, if that can ever be considered a dwelling, I am uncertain…" Serious green eyes connected with mine, "when we found you unconscious in that alley, I thought the prophecy was just ramblings of someone's fantasy."

I thought back to the cold, motionless man that had stood there that day. I knew now that wasn't this Victor, but the man of justice instead. "As someone who has lived with seeing inside her head, for all of my life, I believe all things are possible." I smirked. "Even ramblings of fantasy."

Reaching out, he tucked the hair behind my ear with a soft touch. "Yes. You have in a short time educated me on many things." He shrugged. "I had thought I was beyond finding newness in anything, having seen so much these five hundred years, *but* I have been proven wrong and find, oddly enough, that I am quite pleased. Knowing that something I thought meant things that were entirely different and change my world in ways I was not very receptive to."

I nodded, slowly, I had no idea what he was talking about, but I loved to listen to him talk. Even when he used that stiff funny way of his. Then I shook my head and smiled at him. "I don't know what you just said, but I like listening to you."

He laughed. "Let's just say it has been messier in my mind than in yours, since the day we picked you up in that alley." Leaning forward, he kissed my forehead lightly and then got off the bed. "I must go."

I scrambled up off the bed. "To feed?" I did want to know more about that.

His big hand rested against my cheek with a light touch. "Yes. I find my restraint at its absolute end."

"Who do you…" I frowned, "feed from?"

Victor stood there looking down at me, many emotions going through his eyes as he thought of his answer. "That, I am not ready to discuss with you."

I nodded. I understood that, sometimes things needed to be kept to yourself. "Are they good?" I blushed, "I don't mean tasty good," I put my hand on my chest. "I mean in their heart, good."

He cleared his throat. "Not always, no."

A realization came to me that when he didn't want to answer, he would clear his throat. What a funny little quirk, I thought. "I'm sure you do what you have had to… to be how you are." I tried to assure him.

"Indeed." He leaned down and kissed my mouth softly. "You may unravel me entirely if given the chance, my dear. That may be bad for my ego." He straightened. "Please rest, I will see you at breakfast."

I looked up into his eyes, trying to figure out what he meant, but couldn't. Nodding, I touched my stomach. "I don't know if I'll be hungry by then." It was true, Mitz liked feeding me too much.

He laughed. "I'm sure you will be." With that his long strides took hm to the door and he left.

I looked back at the big bed and then down at the blankets I was still hugging around me. Going over I grabbed a pillow off the bed and my pack from beside it and went into the closet to get some sleep. I must ask about the outside here, I thought, I couldn't stay indoors all the time, it made me feel like an animal in a cage, with no way out.

Chapter Ten

I found my way to the kitchen to see Mitz already there.

"Oh, love, you look so much better today." She smiled and patted one of the stools by the counter. "I'm afraid you're up before anyone else, but you can keep me company while I get things under way here."

I went over and sat on the stool, holding my pack in my lap and watched her make a tea. "Do you do all the cooking by yourself?" That was a lot of cooking. She fed a lot of very big people.

She gave me one of those smiles that just made you feel special. "No, love," she pointed to a door on the other side of the room, "there's another much larger kitchen through there… this is the royal family's kitchen." She winked. "I cheat more often then not by having them whip things up then bring them through." Coming over to me she set a steaming cup in front of me.

I leaned down and sniffed it. It was the tea mix I liked. "Thank you."

She nodded and went over and to the fridge and pulled out some eggs. "How are you feeling?" Glancing my way, she opened the top of the fridge to get something out. "It broke my heart yesterday seeing you go through that." She closed it and set something on the counter, a very stern look on her face. "I have a mind to go stab the man responsible."

With my eyes wide, I wondered if she would. I sensed no

violence coming from her. "I don't think Victor would let you."

Smiling, Mitz shook her head. "From what I hear, the boys had a hard time keeping him from doing it himself."

I nodded. "He wasn't happy that I didn't think it was right to punish him." I sipped the tea. It was perfect. "I told him he was the justice, not the punisher."

She stopped what she was doing and gave me a funny look. "I'm glad you spoke your mind." She shook her head. "He's a bit headstrong and always taken on the responsibility for his siblings' well-being onto his shoulders." She made a strange little tsking noise, "a man can only take on so much." Nodding her head, she kept going. "You are good for him."

I tried to process what she said, but some of it made no sense to me. "I would like to be good for him, but he says I am bad for his ego."

Mitz stopped what she was doing and laughed. "Then that confirms it, you are just what he needs."

I didn't know how being bad for him was just what he needed, but I didn't want to argue with her, she was very nice to me and I felt love every time she was near. So, I just sat here and drank my tea.

The breakfast with all of them was an experience I had so many feelings about, I wasn't sure where to start sorting through them. I had been afraid there would be awkwardness as they had all started coming in. I mean, I wasn't at my best when most of them saw me the day before. But there was no sense of tense emotions coming from any of them. Victor was the last to arrive, and he smiled at me with one of his funny little nods that I liked, but didn't stop to speak to me because Mitz had come in right behind him, telling them all to stop hovering about and sit. I found it amusing as they listened to her immediately.

No one seemed bothered that I sat closer to the empty end of the table either, which I was thankful for. I felt a connection to all of them, they were compassionate people, but I still wasn't ready to be surrounded by them.

The food, so much food, again. I didn't want to seem rude or unappreciative, so I took a little of several things to try. I noticed many things while I sat quietly and observed. I knew nothing of what they were talking about, maps, locations, it was all very busy sounding, but I saw the bonds between them. They finished each other's sentences and seemed to be able to have several conversations at once without losing track. It was all very fascinating. I also noticed how they looked to Victor more often than anyone else, for an answer or response. What Mitz had said made more sense to me now.

Rafael looked down and winked as he reached for something in front of him. Troy cuffed him in the head and then leaned in close to say something. I don't know what it was, but Raf looked to Victor then sat up straighter, with a strange look on his face.

I had always thought it would take violent emotion to hit someone, but since I had met these wonderful people I had noticed quite often they smacked one another in a way that held affection, not ill intent. I was learning so much.

I realized someone was speaking louder and climbed out of my thoughts to focus.

"Victor, did you stay up all night or something?" Michael asked him. "Your answers are so vague today, it's not helpful."

Leone nodded. "You didn't spend all night in the cells, did you?"

Victor picked up his cup and took a sip, his eyes flicking to them briefly. "I did not. I went to check on them briefly and that was all."

"Are you alright?" Daxx asked, a look of concern on her face.

I didn't know why they were all so worried, so I watched him for a few moments. His eyes connected with mine more then once as he tried to assure them he was in fact *well*. Frowning, I focused hard and felt around inside my head, or that's how I thought of it when I was trying to see. It took me a few moments and then I found it. A barrier so hard it may as well have been made of steel. Inside my head. I looked back at Victor. He was draining himself to help me. I had been so preoccupied with everyone and so much motion around me that I hadn't noticed the flashes were but a slow trickle inside my head.

Pushing back, I got up and started walking to the end of the table where he sat. "You need to stop." I told him softly, he would know. The others paused, but I had to push past being watched and get him to understand.

"I'm am fine." He told me in his stiff Victor tone as he set his cup down.

Shaking my head, I leaned down so our faces were close together. "And I'm *okay*." Finally, understanding how he felt when I told him that, even when I wasn't. He lips quirked like he wanted to smile, but didn't. "You are using too much energy to help me, and you need it more than I need the help." I straightened up and nodded at him, feeling I had made my point and he would stop now.

Clearing his throat, he placed his hands on the table and pushed his chair back so he could stand. I didn't have to see his aura to know he didn't understand at all. "You need the rest." He motioned to where I had been sitting. "You've actually sat still for the entire meal thus far."

I glared at him and stepped closer. "I sat still because I've been observing." I motioned to his siblings, not feeling brave enough to look and see all their eyes on me. "The love and connection is unlike I have ever seen." I nodded once. "And I've *seen* much." His eyes softened some, but he still had that immovable air around him. "You need to let it go. Stop using too much for me. What you do is more important than too many flashes in my head."

His jaw muscles flexed. "It is not." He said in a low tone.

"I can see your *justice* aura filling the space around you, but you need to listen to me" I wanted to stomp my foot and wasn't entirely sure why I did. "Everyone here looks to your council, seeks your thoughts on all matters. They respect your opinion and I won't be responsible for getting in the way of that." Why didn't he understand what I was telling him?

He grasped my elbow with a firm but gentle hold and leaned his head down closer to mine. I didn't give him time to try to change my mind. I poked him in the middle of his forehead a few times. "This head is meant for other things." I tapped the same finger against the side of my head, "mine is meant to see." Huffing out a breath, I searched his eyes, hoping he would hear me. "What if something happens I am supposed to *see* and you are holding it back so I can't?"

Victor closed his eyes and clenched his jaw for a moment before his green eyes connected with mine. I could tell by the emotion in them he didn't want to stop helping me, but he now understood. "If it becomes too much for you, you *will* tell me. I will *not* have you blacking out because it becomes so overwhelming you cannot cope." His eyes were red now.

I nodded, and tried to keep my eyes from looking at his mouth where I knew he'd have fangs now, but I failed and stared at it. His lips quirked and then he sighed loud and stepped back from me.

"Go sit and finish your food. I will let go gradually so it's not too much of a shock." His eyes were green again and he looked annoyed, but not, at the same time.

"Okay." I turned around and ran back to my chair and sat down. When I looked up from my plate, all eyes were on me. I felt my cheeks go red.

Victor looked around at them, a hard look on his face. "Do not stare at her." He told them in a rough voice.

"I... right..." Rafael shook his head and looked away.

Michael looked at Leone, "I can't..."

"Yeah." Leone said and picked up his fork.

"I've never..." Troy stopped talking when Daxx swatted his arm.

"Everyone else saw that right? Arius asked.

Quinton nodded but didn't speak.

"Did anyone by chance take a video of that?" Chase poked his own forehead and then looked at me and winked.

I didn't know what any of that was about, but I picked up my own fork and looked down the table to the green eyes watching me. A warmth filled me and I don't know how I could tell, but knew it was Victor using our blood connection to send it to me.

I didn't want to go to the practice, I knew it was some sort of bonding habit they had, but the last time it hadn't ended well. Daxx finally persuaded me that I needed to be there. She told me that together, they were going to help me learn how to protect myself.

The flashes were back, and I found they made me feel more normal. Which, I knew I was so not normal it was pure silliness, but I agreed to go. With the return of my seeing came the energy and drive that made me keep moving. I hated being frightened all the time, so hopefully training could help with that.

Victor seemed to be keeping his distance from me now, but his looks and the small waves of warm emotions he sent me were enough to reassure me that he wasn't upset. It took me several minutes of thinking to realize it may be until we talked about the book with leaves on it, what he needed to do. I accepted his decision to avoid our being close.

I glanced back at Quinton and shook my head. He'd had me try several poles of different sizes to swing around, to see if any of them felt right. None of them felt right at all, and unless someone screamed in my face and startled me into me jumping and accidentally hitting them, these were not the weapon for me.

Rafael said everyone had a weapon that would feel right. Just the word, weapon, felt wrong to me.

Chase had been leaning against the end of the wall of lethal, violent weapons watching me. With a grin, he came over and watched me put the last pole back. "I think you need something compact and easy to hide."

I looked at him. Those were two words I could understand completely. I glanced at the items on their wall and shook my head. "Nothing here is small." I looked up at him, then around at the others that were sparring. "I think they were all designed for big people."

He chuckled. "If you find something that feels right, we will have it made in your size."

I looked back at the wall. "I don't do violence very well." Shrugging, I looked down at my little black gloves and picked at one. "I'm sorry."

Chase stood right beside me now. "Never feel sorry for that." He motioned to the other end, the end where the weapons were not wooden. I followed him. "I think any weapon for you should be only used in a situation to save your, or another's life."

Nodding, I agreed. "I'm not very brave." I told him.

He snorted. "You are and don't even know it, cutie." With a jerk of his head toward Victor he smirked. "No one stands up to Victor. You did, without breaking a sweat."

Turning around I looked to watch Victor was sparring with Leone. He looked so graceful, and sure of himself in the way he moved. "I needed him to stop." I said quietly.

"Yeah, I caught that, and I'm still a little shocked he did." Shaking his head, he looked back to the wall of metal and pointed to some small knives. "What about something small you can hide, and only use if absolutely necessary." He shrugged. "We can work on some evasive moves as well, so you can get out of any situation."

"If she's in a situation *that* dire, people will have to die."

I jumped to hear Victor right behind me. I turned to see him giving his brother a hard look.

"I don't like feeling frightened all the time, Victor." I told him and waited until he looked down at me. "I want to learn." I bit my lip. "Just…I may not be good at it."

His big chest expanded as he took a deep breath and let it out slowly. "Chase will help you with moves, as he did with Daxx." His eyes moved up and down me slowly, almost in a caress. "Your size allows you more freedom than that of a larger opponent." He glanced to Chase, then back to me. "Chase is a better instructor in that than I am." He nodded toward the knives in front of us. "I can show you how to use the blade, if you wish."

I looked at the knives and swallowed. I didn't know if I could ever use one against another person, but I wanted to try to learn. Running away didn't always work. I had the scar on my back now that confirmed that. Releasing a breath, I didn't know I held, I nodded and looked up at him. "Okay." I noticed Leone stood there quietly. He looked scared, the air around him was filled with fear. Moving toward him slowly, I hugged my pack. I tried to focus, there was more around him, I wondered if he knew. "I think everyone has a strength and weakness." I told him. I didn't know how I knew he needed to hear that, I just did.

His brown eyes studied me, his body tense.

I smiled, in that soft way that everyone did to make me feel better. "My weakness is cookies," I nodded, "and, I think, fangs."

I heard Chase laughed from behind me.

He looked at me for several seconds, something going through his head. Leone, glanced over my head to his brother. "I think all of us would feel better if you learned how to rappel."

Victor moved up beside him. "Isn't that encouraging her to climb more?" He rubbed the back of his neck.

I looked from one to the other. "What is rappelling?"

Chase came over and held out his phone. I looked at the video of someone using a rope of some kind to run down the side of a building. My mouth dropped open, I turned to look at Leone, feeling very excited. "Can you teach me to do that?"

He looked over at the video playing on Chase's phone. "Not quite like that but I can show you how to descend a building, or whatever, quickly and *safely*."

I turned and looked at Victor. "I want to rappel." I nodded.

He sighed loudly. "Of course, you do." He looked at Leone. "Get her a retractable cable unit and make sure she knows how to use it." He glanced over at the ropes hanging from the beam. "And how to use ropes."

Leone nodded. "As well as she does walking." He turned around and went over to spar with Quinton.

Chase tucked his phone in his pocket and gave me an odd look. "Did he just consent to teach a *human* girl how to rappel?"

"I think he did." Victor said quietly while looking at me. "Make sure someone volunteers to be on hand in case he can't cope with it."

"Will do."

I frowned, not understanding.

Victor looked at my hair, with the assorted clips in it again, then back to my face with an amused smile. "I have to go tend to some matters, but later I have something I need to show you."

I realized I was watching his mouth again and gave my head a little shake before looking back up at him. "Very well." I told him in a stiff manner and inclined my head like he did.

He chuckled and lifted my chin so I had to look at him. "The visions are under control?"

I nodded, which felt funny with his hand holding my chin up. "Yes. All is normal in there." I grinned. "Well, my version of normal."

"Mmm, good." He released my chin. "Try not to find trouble. I'm not up to any grey hair moments."

I looked at his hair, still not seeing any that weren't red. Then I heard Chase laughing behind me.

"Go Victor, or I will never get this lesson started or get to sleep this day."

I kept forgetting that Chase's day was our night. I must ask if they have a clock that tells both, it would make things simpler in my mind if I could see it.

"Not a scratch on her, brother." Victor said then turned to walk away.

"No worries, brother justice. I like breathing too much." Chase answered and then motioned for me to go out onto the mat with him.

After Chase's instruction, I found myself quite hungry again, so I wandered to the kitchen. I knew I had cookies in my pack, but I wanted to save those in case I needed them later. Chase had shown me so much, and I had to admit, it wasn't violent or scary. I found learning the flips and evasive moves was fun.

Daxx was in the kitchen with Mitz when I walked in. I smiled at both of them. "I'm a little hungry."

Laughing Daxx patted the stool beside her. "That was some workout you had today."

I nodded and set my pack on the floor beside me. "It was

fun." I grinned, "I don't think throwing knives is going to be my *thing* though, Chase agrees."

Mitz gave me a strange look and Daxx laughed again.

"Her throw is a little wild yet." She covered her mouth and then laughed quietly again. "The guys almost got hit a few times."

I nodded, still upset by that. "I didn't feel good about that, even though Chase told me they'd heal so no 'biggie'." I frowned. "I'm not sure what a biggie is."

Both Mitz and Daxx laughed. I sat there and watched them, smiling myself. I couldn't remember laughing and smiling this much before.

"I'll make you a sandwich, love, how does that sound."

"Fantastic, thank you." I told her and then looked back to Daxx. "Leone is going to teach me how to rappel."

"Really?" She had a strange look on her face.

"Leone is?" Mitz asked me, a serious look on her face.

I nodded. "I'm still not sure why he's afraid of me, but he said he would." I watched Mitz put some meat on the bread. "Victor asked Chase to have someone volunteer to be on hand in case he can't cope." I frowned. "Cope with what, Daxx?"

She cleared her throat, not smiling now. "Leone had an addiction years ago…" she glanced briefly to Mitz before continuing, "to human essence."

I understood. "Oh, so I'm probably like the favorite cookie he can't have."

Mitz chuckled. "Exactly that, love." She set the plate in front of me. "You are so refreshing to have here."

I peeked between the bread and nodded to Mitz. "Thank you." I took a bite and chewed it slowly, it was good. "I asked Victor if he could feed off me, but he said not yet."

Daxx coughed. "Really?"

I took another bite and waited until I swallowed it before answering her. "Yes. He won't even kiss me again until after we talk…" I smiled when Mitz set down a glass of milk, "about the book with leaves on it." I took a drink of the milk and noticed a look pass between the other women.

"He seems to be taking great care." Mitz said, with that soft look she got.

Daxx snorted, "you mean unlike my initiation into this life?" She rolled her eyes and looked at me. "I was almost marked by the wrong twin, then accidentally marked by my mate." She waved a hand around. "and no one was telling me anything."

I looked at her arm. "Is the tattoo your mark?"

Mitz sat down beside Daxx. "It's the mate's tattoo, yes, love."

"It just appears?" I shrugged, "I mean it's not done like a regular tattoo?"

Daxx nodded. "Yeah, no needles and ink."

I pulled her arm across the counter and looked at it. "That's fascinating." It was, to have a tattoo just appear, it was very cool. Releasing her arm, I picked up the other half of my sandwich. "Will you live longer now too?"

"That's what they're telling me." She ran her hand lightly across the pattern on her skin.

I paused in eating and looked at her. "That is wonderful. To know you will always have someone and not be alone." I put the sandwich down. So many. No, not many. One with many pieces. I had to focus and try to sort out to make sense of what I saw.

"Crissy?"

Blinking I looked at Daxx.

"Are you okay? Do you need anything?" She was standing beside me now.

"I'm sorry. I didn't hear what you said." They were still there, just flashes in pieces. So many of them, there was danger or was it evil? Many would think them the same thing but they weren't. I looked back at Daxx. "So many pieces, I can't catch them all right now." I leaned down and picked up my pack. "My notebook." I told her.

"Mitz have you seen Cristy? She not answering..." Victor walked in and stopped with his phone in his hand.

"Hi." I smiled at him and tried stay focused and not get lost in my head.

"What's wrong?" He walked over to me with long strides.

I tapped my head. "Just too many pieces right now." I hugged my pack. "I will have to fit them together." I wished I was on my roof top. The quiet there would help.

He held out his hand. "I was just trying to text you to tell you I had time to show you now. Come. It will help fit the pieces together."

I didn't know what he could possibly show me that would help. "It will?" I put my hand in his.

"Yes. I told you I would find you a high, quiet, safe place that was just your own in Alterealm, and I have."

"Oh." I smiled up at him. "You did?"

He nodded, his green eyes moving over my face. "Are you well enough to get there now?"

I paused for a moment to assess. "I'm okay." I grinned. "Really, I am this time."

"Very well." He inclined his head to Daxx and Mitz. "Ladies." And then gently pulled on my hand so I had no choice but to follow.

I glanced back to the two women to see both of them looking shocked, but pleased, at the same time. "I will see you later." I told them, feeling excitement about where Victor was taking me.

Chapter Eleven

Victor led me through hallways and down a tunnel, all I had seen in my head, but was excited to know they were real. He stopped at the end of one and looked down at me. "Would you know your way back from here?"

I nodded. "Yes. I am very good with directions." I smiled, still feeling very excited to see where we were going.

He motioned to a ladder on the wall. "After you." Reaching out, he took my pack and swung it behind his shoulder.

I didn't know what was at the top, but I hurried to find out. I tried to count the rungs, but lost track trying to go faster. It was quite a long climb though, so I was even happier to be climbing. I went through a square hole and then stepped onto a floor. I looked down to see Victor right behind me. When he stepped up behind me, he closed the lid over the hole and then pulled a chain out of his pocket and held it out to me. I took it only to see a key on the end.

"It unlocks the door on the other side." He knelt down and slid a large bolt over the door. "And that from the inside. So, you can feel safe." He straightened up. "The key is yours. This is your spot, no one else's. All I ask is you keep your phone turned on when you are here."

I didn't know what to say. I looked at him, then the key again and put the chain over my head, tucking the key inside my shirt. "Thank you."

Turning, he slid a panel on the wall that revealed something like a window, but with no glass. The panel folded into itself and disappeared into a slot on the wall. I watched him walk around and roll the panels back on all four sides. It was amazing.

"This was an old guard tower, it hasn't been in use for at least a hundred years now." He smiled. "Modern technology has enabled us to replace it."

I went over and leaned on the ledge to look out. I could see open fields, just the sight made me feel more peace than I had in the last day.

"It wasn't always peaceful here, so guards were needed." He touched my arm so I would look at him, then he motioned to the other side. "You can see the bulk of the Nightwalker side of Alterealm from there. It's too far from this tower to see Chase's side, but this was the best I could manage with short notice."

I walked over and looked, so many buildings and homes. I hadn't thought to ask what it was like outside the halls I'd seen in my head. It really was another world here. "I don't know what to say, Victor." I looked back at him. "No one has ever done something like this for me."

"I want you to be happy when you're here." His voice was so soft, so gentle.

I stepped closer and hugged him. "This makes me happy." I looked up at him. "I had fun at practice too."

He smirked, "Yes. I was told you need a little more practice aiming."

I nodded.

"If you keep your eyes open, it might help."

I grinned. "That's what Chase said." He wrapped his arms around me, but not in a way I felt trapped. I liked it.

"It's common practice when throwing a knife to see your target while you try to hit it." He said sounding amused.

When he rested his head gently on top of mine, I leaned into his chest and placed my ear against it so I could hear his heart beating.

"Tell me about the flashes returning, is it too much for you?"

I liked listening to his voice vibrate through his chest. "No. They are better now." I listened to him inhale, then exhale. "I will have to wait for them to return and try to piece them together." Tipping my head back, I looked back up at him. "But having this quiet place now will help."

He smiled down at me, his green eyes searching mine. "I am glad." Glancing over behind me, he sighed. "I haven't yet figured out how to get a comfortable chair up here, but I did bring a big cushion for now."

Turning, I saw a big pillow leaning against the wall. I went over and dropped it flat on the floor and sat down, then smiled up at him. "This is wonderful. Thank you."

Victor looked happy as he came over and sat down beside me. "A part of me wants to ask you to never leave Alterealm again, but I know you must, as it is a part of you to keep moving." He leaned over to kiss my forehead. "I wandered for years before I accepted my role here, so I do understand that need." He shrugged. "I was an only child for fifty years, so I was allowed that freedom."

I leaned back and watched him as he talked. I could listen to him talking forever, there was something about his voice that soothed me. I knew it could be harsh and unmoving as well, when there was a need, but with this Victor here with me, I felt myself growing very attached.

"You're not listening to a word I'm saying, are you?" He smirked.

My mouth dropped open and I sighed. "I am, sorry." I tapped my head. "I am alone so much I sometimes forget and get lost in my own head." I leaned closer so our faces were a few inches apart. "What did you say?"

He brushed the hair back from my face. "I said I didn't bring the book with leaves on it because I have to go back shortly. We may have located more residents with those illegal devices."

"Oh," I nodded. "That's good that you have. That is much more important than explaining the book to me."

Victor sighed, and pulled the cushion I sat on closer to him. "It is important, but not more than you." He tucked the hair behind my ear this time. "I do want to explain all of that to you, I just want to take my time to help you understand."

I found myself watching his mouth as he spoke and had to look back to his eyes when he stopped. "I understand. Daxx says the initiation into this life for me is better than hers."

He laughed. "Yes, hers was a bit of a disaster, to say the least." Tilting his head, he gave me a soft look. "She caught us off guard, completely. As you have me."

"Is that a bad thing?" I studied his expression, but wasn't sure of what I was seeing, and then found myself looking at his mouth again. It made me wonder.

"I don't think it is, but it's complicated and it seems I never quite have enough time to explain it properly." He smirked, "and you must stop staring at my mouth, or I will never be able to focus to speak to you."

I bit my lip and looked back at his eyes. "I can't help it. I was just thinking."

His lips twitched, "About?"

I inhaled and then exhaled slowly. "I've kissed you with your fangs, I was wondering what it was like without them."

His hand moved to rest on the back of my neck. "Therein lies the problem. Just thinking about you, or kissing you, makes it hard to control the change. You would think, after five hundred years I would have better control, but you, my dear, have changed everything."

I glanced up to his eyes, to check if they were still green. They were. "Maybe you should hurry then, before they change." I'm not sure if he pulled my head closer first, or sat up on my knees, but before I could take my next breath, my body was against his and his mouth was on mine.

It wasn't a gentle kiss like before, this one was fast and heated. All at once I felt like I was melting into him, my head dizzy in such a good way that I could have kept doing it forever. I didn't even want to think when his tongue moved into my mouth and rubbed against my own.

His hand covered the back of my head and held me in place so he could keep kissing me. I wanted to be closer, so I climbed right on his lap and wrapped my arms around his neck and grasped his hair. I didn't want to stop.

I could feel his fangs against my tongue now, and heat went through my whole body. He pulled me so our bodies fit together and held me there. Lifting his mouth from mine, he pulled my head back and his lips moved down over my throat. I tried to catch my breath, then lost it again when I felt his sharp fangs glide over the skin on my neck. I gasped, it felt so good.

"Cristy… heart, we have to stop." He licked along my throat.

I moaned softly and moved my head further so my neck was open to his mouth. "I don't want to."

I felt sharp teeth nip the skin softly again. "We have to." Even though he said we were stopping, his lips moved back up my neck and across my jaw until his mouth covered mine again. The kiss was hard and so forceful I thought I was going to burst into flames.

When his lifted his mouth away, he was panting to catch his breath. Mine was no better.

His eyes were red as they moved over my face. "I don't entirely trust myself with you, and at any moment I will have to leave."

"I understand about sex," I blurted out. "I am not experienced, but I know how it works."

Victor's eyes moved over my face for a moment before he spoke. "Telling me that doesn't help me want to stop." He kissed my mouth softly.

"I-I wanted you to know." I felt my cheeks go red. "In case you wanted to."

He chuckled quietly. "Oh, I want to and more, don't doubt that." His hands moved down my back to rest on my hips. Taking a deep breath, he looked at me and let it out slowly. "I am afraid I won't stop and I will mark you…"

"Like Daxx is?" I searched his eyes, there was something in them I hadn't seen from him before, he looked hesitant, vulnerable.

Victor nodded slightly. "I believe…" he shook his head. "I know, you are my mate, Cristy, but we have much to discuss before we take it further."

"How do you know?" I frowned. "What does the book with leaves on it have to do with mates?" I didn't know how I felt. I know I liked Victor and wanted to be close to him, but even he seemed to think there were reasons to hesitate.

"I know," he kissed my cheek softly, "because I've never wanted anyone like I do you." He leaned over and kissed my other cheek. "And your essence has become a craving that won't cease." Pausing close to my mouth, he looked in my eyes and then kissed my lips. "Because I want to kill all of my brothers when they come within five feet of you."

I tried to process what he said, but the enormity of it was a lot to take in. He had lived five centuries and wanted me more than anyone, ever, in that time. That was huge. "You won't hurt your brothers." I said when I realized he had stopped talking.

"No. I won't." His eyes hardened. "But I think about it when they are near you."

"Oh." I licked my lips and went back to where I was. "Would tasting my essence… if that makes sense, I don't know about these things," I reminded him. "would that help?"

Victor's eyes brightened and he shook his head. "No, heart, that would only make me want you more."

"I understand better now." I frowned. "Are we in the prophecies? Is that what is in the book?"

Nodding slowly, Victor leaned to pull out his phone and check it. He must have had it on vibrate, because I didn't hear it ring.

"Yes, we are in the prophecies. I promise we will look at them soon." He looked up from his phone. "I wanted you to understand that I do want you, more then my next breath, but I need you to fully comprehend the meaning." He kissed me gently again. "I will not be part of a forced mating."

I know my eyes went wide, but I couldn't help it. "That's happened in the past?" He nodded. "Thank you for telling me." I searched his eyes. "I need to think about all of this." I didn't want him to think I was turning him away. "It's how I am." I nodded. "I have to work it all out inside my head until I feel it."

He smiled, a soft smile. "I know. I was in that head, remember."

I grinned. "I do and you survived it."

"It was a challenge." He lightly grasped my chin and tipped my face up to his. "I have to go." He kissed me so tenderly my head felt light from it. When he released my chin, his eyes held such caring, I felt like I could look into them forever.

"Can I stay up here and see if the pieces come back?"

"Yes. My offices are just past the practice room. Turn your phone on and call if you need me." Moving slowly, like he really didn't want to, he moved me off his lap so I was sitting on the cushion again. "If I get detained, don't forget to come down for dinner."

I nodded. "Okay." I watched him slide the bolt and open the door. "Victor, thank you for this space." I pulled my knees up to my chest as he climbed down the first few rungs.

"You're welcome. You deserve whatever you need to be happy." With that his head slowly disappeared and he closed the door behind him.

I don't know how long I sat there, I just kept looking at the door he'd gone through. I touched my mouth with my hand and smiled, I could still feel the way he'd kissed me. So much to think about, so much to feel. I couldn't help but smile when I thought of him. He thought I was his mate.

Nervousness was filling me. I jumped up to look out over the fields, realizing dawn was drawing nearer. The night was almost done. Then the start of a new day, or was it a new night for some? I didn't know. I needed a watch: one with a sun and moon so I could remember they had two of each here. Both day and night were not the same as where I came from.

Taking a deep breath, I exhaled slowly and thought again. Victor always told the truth, so if he said I was in that book and his mate then it had to be true. I needed to read that book. To study the prophecies. Did they come to those that wrote them as my flashes did to me? It wasn't what any other would think, but it warmed me inside to know that I wasn't the only one with things in my head. Things I had to see.

Flashes in my head made me pause, there were some there. So many. So fast. I breathed slowly and looked out at the fields, only I wasn't seeing them. I focused to slow my breathing, slow the flashes to let me see. The pieces jumped into focus, a few at a time. Daxx was there and Troy in the dark, but why? I saw red, blinding red.

I frowned and closed my eyes, please let me find the piece that will answer why, I thought. Blood. My eyes popped open. So much of it, pooling, smeared, and splattered all around. The eyes, who they belonged to I didn't know, but they were there.

The pieces kept coming, without pause and I tried, I really did, to catch them all. I knew I should write them down, but I was afraid to move in case they stopped, and important things I needed I wouldn't show themselves.

When they slowed and I could breathe with ease again, I sorted through to look for all the parts. My heart started beating faster when my brain caught up understand to the images that had come.

"I have to warn them." I thought and turned to get my pack.

I dropped my pack in my haste to leave and then froze. My cookies would be broken now. Shaking my head, I went down the ladder. Now was not the time for cookies. Climbing onto the ladder, I cleared the floor then, balanced carefully to lock the door. I had a tower, I grinned with happiness.

I jumped down the last few feet and grabbed my pack. They had to know. I had to tell Victor. I ran through the tunnel, not even needing to think what direction. That was a good discovery, I couldn't pause to think. No time. They're watching.

Running as fast I could, I went around a corner and almost ran into Quinton. My new boots stopped me from hitting him and I ducked around him. "No time. Not now." I told him and kept running. "They're watching." I called back, without looking to see if he listened.

I ran by the door where we practiced and saw more doors. Which door? Left or right? Reaching the first pair, I paused and held my hand over the door on the left. No, no. Right. Victor would prefer the right. I don't know how I knew, I just did. Running the last few feet, I grabbed the handle and ran in.

Victor, Michael and Leone stood there looking at me. "Manners." I nodded and went back out the door and closed it, then knocked loudly, opened the door and went in without waiting. "No time." I told them and nodded my head fast. "They're watching. Blood there was blood, no, no." Shaking my head, I dropped my bag on the floor. I had to write it down. "No time." I didn't have time to find my book. The pencils were never easy to find. I had to pause and wonder could I get one and put it on a chain around my neck.

"Cristy…"

I jerked my head up and looked at Victor, then shook mine and rushed toward him. "No, no. There's no time. They're watching." I tried to think. I tapped my hand on the side of my head. "I know. I see it." Turning, I saw a pen on his desk. I ducked under his arm and grabbed the pen. "Paper, I need paper." There was a folder on his desk, I grabbed it and emptied what was inside.

Nodding I looked at him. "There was blood, too much blood." He looked at me and then held up his hand to someone else and shook his head.

"Leave her be."

I didn't know what he was saying. I couldn't stop to find out. As fast as I could I went to the corner behind his desk. "They're watching." I nodded and knelt on the floor, the folder open in front of me. I bent over it and started to sketch as fast as I could do with a pen. "The symbol." What was the symbol. I didn't know but I had to do it before I didn't see it. I needed a pencil, I really did. It sounded like scribbles with a pen and took more thought to get it to do what I needed. What I could see.

"All of them. No, no my friends." I shook my head. "I can see. The red. Not blood, but red still." I stopped. "Oh." I jumped up and touched my hair. "My hair. It's my hair. They know." I looked at Victor. "They know. My hair has to go…"

His eyes went wide. "Cristy… tell me." He nodded, such understanding in his eyes.

His eyes were so pretty when he saw me that way. I took a deep breath and looked at my hand, then looked back to the folder. Jumping back over, I picked it up and waved it around. Turning back, I nodded and looked at his eyes as they watched me. "You were there. My friends were there." I squeezed my eyes shut and shook my head, then looked back to him. "The blood. Victor the blood was on your face." I went over quickly and touched his cheek softly. "But they *see* and it's my hair." I dropped the pen and folder and put my hands over my mouth. "It's me. The blood is because of me." No, no. I shook my head. "They see my hair. Their eyes are on my back."

Turning, I saw Daxx and Quinton looking at me. I didn't know when they got here. I ran over to Daxx. "I have to go. The blood is because of me." I hugged her quick, then let go. "You were there. I can't let them see." I ducked down and grabbed my pack quickly and pushed between them and ran to the door. "If my back isn't here, their eyes cannot see." I called out.

"Cristy!"

I heard Victor call behind me but I couldn't stop. I couldn't let them see my friends. I ran fast around another corner and had to find the path in my head. The halls, so many halls. I didn't know who made this place, but they liked halls.

"Crissy, stop." It was Daxx.

I could hear feet running behind me and wanted to count the feet, but didn't have time. I had to go so, no one would see. I liked Daxx. I turned my head as I ran, faster, as fast as I could. I should have told her. I never had. My feet still moving, I called back to her. "If I had another life where my mind was free. I would have liked you as a sister." There she would know now.

I saw the halls ahead. Which way to turn? Left. I needed left I thought, but I couldn't see. My boots, I loved my boots, they didn't let me slide. I turned, thinking to run to the end of this one. Large arms grabbed me just before I hit the body they went with.

"Whoa, careful."

I looked up to Arius and his voice my ears liked to hear and shook my head. "I have to go. If my back isn't here they won't see you." I patted his chest and nodded, so he would know.

"Crissy." Is was Quinton's voice and he didn't sound happy. I had no time to see why.

"I think," Arius told me, "the others would like a word with you." He smiled nicely down at me, then he turned me slowly.

So many eyes watched me. Why were they all here in the hallway? Quinton and Leone bent over their knees, breathing so fast. Daxx was shaking her head at me. I'd done something again. Michael stood with a hand against the wall, panting like he needed air, he didn't look happy.

"How can legs... that short, move so fast?" He asked Victor.

Victor stood motionless, not even breathing. His green eyes, so soft and caring looking at me. I had to smile, when he looked at me that way.

"Hi." I told him and hugged my pack to me.

He held out his hand and I felt Arius let go of my shoulders, there was no time to pause, but I didn't want to be rude.

"I have to go." I told him, wanting him to understand.

Victor didn't drop the hand he held toward me. He nodded, understanding in his eyes. "I know. I would just like to know more before you do."

I reached slowly and took his hand. "I don't want blood on your face." I told him.

He nodded and grasped my hand, pulling me until I rested my cheek against his chest. I could hear his heartbeat, jumping fast in his chest. "I broke my cookies when I dropped my pack to get out of the tower." I told him.

"Tower?" Quinton asked but said no more.

"Let's go get more and you can tell us what you saw."

Victor's voice vibrated through is chest against my ear. I nodded. "Okay. Then I have to leave"

Chapter Twelve

I tried to sit at the table like they wanted me to, so I could explain, but I couldn't sit still. I got up and walked, just to keep moving. Victor leaned against the table beside my chair, but I couldn't be still.

"If they can see her back, would it have something to do with the magic that hit her?" Arius asked.

My mouth dropped open and I turned fast to look at him. "Can they do that? Follow me through that?" I looked to Victor than back to Arius.

"Stranger things have happened." His grey eyes tracked me as I moved.

I hurried to Victor, he would know. He knew so much. "Is it inside of me?" I stopped and looked up at him. It made me feel unclean, that their dark magic could be in my body and I didn't even know.

"I don't know." He reached out and tucked my hair behind my ear. "Get Romulus and Clairee to Cristy's room, now." He said without looking away from me.

"Already on it." Quinton got up and headed toward the door with his phone in his hand.

"Can we walk there, please?" Michael asked as he followed Quint out the door.

Victor reached down and took my hand, then bent down, and picked up my pack beside my feet. "Come. We'll go find out."

I nodded. "Okay." Fear was filling me to think we were being watched and followed because of something inside of me. I had to stay. I had to know.

There were so many people here, my nerves were jumpy, but I had to stay. I looked around at them all and had just noticed that Chase was not here, when he walked in the door carrying a cup, his hair all mussed.

He raised his cup to me and winked. "As much as I love action, cutie, the excitement that comes with you is robbing me of sleep." He smiled. "I may have to become a nightwalker if this keeps up."

I didn't know what he meant, exactly, but I did feel bad that he couldn't sleep. "I'm sorry." I said, wishing I had my pack to hug to my chest. I didn't, they said it could only be me, to get the answers they needed. My pack and the chain with my key sat on the bed, as I waited on the couch in a robe, and nothing more.

"Someone fill me in." Chase said loudly and then went over to Troy and Daxx where they were talking quietly.

I watched them for a moment more and then looked back to the man with the purple eyes, Romulus, as he talked to Victor and Michael. When he'd first arrived, I wanted to hide, purple eyes meant more bad than good to me. Victor explained, as he held me safely against him that Romulus was on our side, and to be trusted. I had to remember a long time back, to a talk with Rafael, about people with blue eyes were not all good looking. It was the same with mages, some were good and some were not.

Clairee was here again, I really liked her. She was so nice. She seemed so upset that she may have missed something inside me. I hadn't known, so I don't know how she could have.

A man came in, one I had never seen, with my eyes or in my head. He was big, which, being where I was, no longer surprised me. He had long, white hair that I thought was prettier than Arius' black, or maybe as pretty, just in a different way. I studied him as he went over to Quinton and spoke so quietly I couldn't hear. I didn't need to hear their words to see. The air around him was different than any I'd ever seen.

Getting up, I hugged the robe around me and went over to him. Quinton smiled down at me, but I was focused, no time to pause. I looked up into the man's face and his eyes were something I'd also never seen. They were pale, almost as white as his hair.

"Crissy, this is Welsley." Quinton told me.

I stood on my toes to be certain and then nodded. "Your eyes go green." I looked at Quinton. "I don't know what green means." I would have to find out. Looking back to Welsley I smiled, a bit wistfully. "You have no fangs, that's too bad."

The look he gave me was one of surprise, like he didn't know what to say.

"Then look again!" Victor bellowed.

I spun around, all talking in the room stopped and no one moved. Victor looked upset, very upset. I hurried toward him.

"If she's resistant to magic, then find another way!" He said very loudly and pointed at me. "If she says she saw it. Then it is there. Find it!"

No one had ever believed me the way he did. I know Daxx and my other friends nodded when I spoke, but I don't think they understood me the way Victor did. Ducking around the man, Romulus, I went to Victor and looked up at him. I touched his chest to try to soothe him. I didn't like him being this upset. I touched his chin so he'd look down at me and angry red eyes connected with my own. "It's okay." I told him and then nodded.

He pulled me against his chest and I could feel him taking deep breaths to calm down. "It's not, but it will be." He told me in a tense voice.

"There may be another way." Clairee told him. "We have one in the coven temple that can sense magic, without using any."

Victor let out a long breath. "Bring them here." He sounded tired, and not as angry now.

She nodded quickly and turned, leaving the room at an almost-run.

Squeezing me, Victor then rested his chin on top of my head. "I'm sorry." He said softly. "I'm usually in control of my emotions."

I looked up at him and smiled. "It is almost day." I reminded him. "Maybe you just need to feed?" I searched his face, seeing if he really was just tired.

His mouth quirked, like he was suppressing a smile. Green eyes moved to my throat briefly then he looked back at my eyes. "I think I can manage for a little longer."

"Brother," Chase said from behind me, "as much as I'm sure you would like nothing more than to stand there and hold the nearly naked woman in your arms, I need to ask her some questions." I turned to look at him. He smirked, his eyes on the man holding me. "My emotions and hormones *won't* cloud my judgement."

I wasn't sure what he meant, but I felt I needed to defend Victor to him. "I'm his mate." I told him and nodded.

Chase stopped and tilted his head, a funny little smile on his mouth. "Trust me, cutie, we're all aware of that amazing fact." He waved his hand at Victor. "The gods lay in shock at what you've done to our justice." He grinned wide. "We should all kiss your feet for managing to unhinge him, finally."

I frowned and looked down at my bare feet. I didn't know why they'd kiss them, what would it accomplish to do such a thing. Victor's arm wrapped around my waist. "Ignore him." He whispered against my ear, but I could hear that his voice held less tension, so I supposed whatever his brother had just said worked. I looked around at the others, they all had strange looks in their eyes and smiles on their faces. It seemed everyone did know I was Victor's mate.

Not wanting to see them all looking at me, I turned my head back to Chase. "Questions?"

He nodded and sat on the back of the couch, his eyes focused on me. "Your vision, where did it happen?" He motioned to his head. "Not where you were when you had it, but where did you see?"

I moved out of Victor's arms, realizing that was an important fact I hadn't paused to think about. Frowning, I looked down at the floor, needing to focus. "It wasn't here." I turned and looked back to Victor. "It wasn't here."

Daxx came over and stopped close to me. "On the folder, that symbol you drew…"

I nodded. "It was there. That's where it happened." I clutched the robe against my chest. "So much blood."

She gave me a soft look. "I know. We need to know where it is."

I nodded and huffed out a breath and then paced toward the other side of the room. It was such a big room, even with all the bodies in it, I had enough room to move and focus. I stopped and looked at the wall. The symbol was something already in my head, but where? "I've seen it," I said out loud, then nodded. "With my eyes." I added, so they would know.

Turning around, I walked in another direction, moving my eyes around the room as I went, but not seeing. So much to look through, too many things I knew. "There is a duck." I told them and kept moving. "Only it is blue." I stopped and looked at Daxx. "Which is silly, ducks aren't blue."

I looked away and walked some more. Pausing to look down at my feet, I liked the way the carpet felt against them. And then I thought more. "Hearts." I frowned. "So many hearts are there too."

"Wait." Daxx came over to me. "Is the duck a tattoo?"

I bit my lip and thought. "It may be." I said quietly.

"The tattoo shop, the one near the bridge." She was looking at me so seriously.

"Oh." I closed my eyes and tried to focus. "It is. The symbol, just down the street." I nodded and opened my eyes, then turned and rushed toward Chase. "It's there. Not here at all." And then I remembered and stopped, turning to Victor. "But my back. They can still see. Even though I am here."

He nodded, understanding in his eyes. "We're working on that."

"Welsley," Troy said from across the room, "no one enters our halls or Chase's side that doesn't belong there. Minimal staff, only those we know are absolutely loyal." He paused to look at me. "No one here goes anywhere alone until we know what we're dealing with."

"It will be done." Welsley said and then turned and left.

Victor rubbed his hand over his face and then looked at Troy. "Did you see anything inside his head when you looked? How can they see using his magic, if we have him locked up?"

Troy lifted his hands and then shook his head. "I saw nothing that would lead me to believe they were tracking her."

"He's somehow shielding you from it?" Victor told him.

"Mages are harder to read." Troy informed him.

Victor turned to look at Arius. "Would you be able to *suggest* he tell us?"

Arius shook his head, looking sad. "I tried. Mages' minds aren't receptive to my powers."

Smiling, I went over and looked up at him. "You can do that?" I tapped my head. "Tell others to do things?"

He nodded, a little smile on his.

"Fascinating." I nodded. "Sometime," I smiled. "I would like to see you do that."

He grinned wider. "Anytime you want."

I was happy, that would be something to see for sure. "Not now. No, we don't have time." I had to think. I went over to Troy and looked into his eyes as he silently looked back at me. "I need to understand." I said more to me than him. "He can't do magic in his cage, but his magic may be working inside me for others to watch?"

Troy exhaled a long breath. "It looks like that might be the case."

I bit my lip, wondering if I was brave enough to try. "I have to see him. He has to see me." I nodded and looked at Daxx. "I'll get dressed." Turning I went to run to get my clothes in the bathroom when Victor blocked my way.

"You are not going to the cells."

His voice had that tone. The one that the justice side of him used. I looked up at him, trying to think of the way to explain it. "If he sees me Troy will be able to look." I nodded. His eyes were hard, his thoughts unmoveable. "I was supposed to die. He doesn't know." I told him.

"As much as you're not going to like this, Victor, she's right." Troy told him.

I turned and smiled at him. He was so smart.

"Whether someone outside is tracking her using his spell, or another we can't trace… I don't know." Troy told him as he walked over to us. "But if he thinks she's dead, because no one would have survived that," he stopped and took a deep breath. "They may be trying to trace us here, this is where we brought her, but no one knows she survived." He looked down at me. "I don't think they're tracking you. I think they put something inside you to find our location." He waved his hand around. "Very few have access to our inner chambers."

I tried to process what he was saying. People thought I made no sense, but sometimes what others said was no better. "If he saw me, his mind would be in shock and then you could really *see* to find the ones that are watching."

He gave me an odd look and then nodded. "Something like that."

"We won't let her in his cell, Victor." Arius told him. "She can stay on the outside, just so he can see she still lives."

"It might be the opening we need to get in." Troy said, while looking down at me.

I looked to Victor, his brows were knit together and his eyes watched me. With his big hand, he reached and pulled me gently by my head and leaned so our faces almost touched.

"If it upsets you in the slightest, you are to tell me *immediately*." His voice was harsh.

I nodded as best I could while his hand held me, then patted his chest lightly. "I will get dressed." I ducked under his arm and ran into the bathroom.

We all went to the cells. I wasn't sure why so many followed Victor and I, but each time I glanced over my shoulder they were there. I felt odd without my pack, but was told to leave it in the room, so I did.

I found the cells to be fascinating. They weren't cages as I had pictured when they told me they were locked up. There were no chains either. They seemed like a maze of glass rooms to me. We went through a door and I watched the pad Victor placed his hand on to open it. A light flashed and the door slid away. Twice more he did that when we came to a wall, and I decided I needed to know more about how that worked.

When he stopped and the others came in behind us, he finally released my hand. I looked at the little pad he'd touched beside the door they had followed us through, and then down at my hand. Was it something in his hand that maybe I hadn't seen? While they stood there talking, I pulled off my little black glove and looked at my hand again. Moving over quietly, I stopped beside the pad and placed my hand on it. The door we'd just used opened. Lifting my hand away I watched it close and then did it again, just to be sure. It opened. Feeling quite excited, I turned to see all eyes watching me. I looked to Daxx, and her smile. "I had to know." I told her.

She grinned wide. "I know. So did I."

Victor cleared his throat and looked at the group. He didn't look as happy to know as I had been. Putting my glove back on, I walked over to him.

"Are you ready?" He motioned behind him.

I looked around his large body to see the man with the purple eyes. The one that had chased me. I took a deep breath and tried to be brave. I knew I wasn't, but they needed to see. I nodded.

"Let us get in there, before he sees her." Troy said quietly.

Arius and Troy both walked to my right and went through another door. I realized I would have to avoid touching the pads, so I didn't let someone out that shouldn't be free.

"He can't see through the glass." Victor told me. "Until I turn off the reflectors."

I didn't know what that was, but it was fascinating to know I could see him but he couldn't see out to see me. I nodded. "Okay." I watched as he opened a door and motioned for me to step in.

"We'll be right here with the door open." He told me in a voice that let me know he still didn't agree with this.

I took a deep breath and nodded again. I stepped in and looked at Arius and Troy talking to the purple-eyed man. He didn't look pleased they were there. He had big bracelets on his wrists and I would have to ask later if their color had a meaning. With eye colors and other colored things here, color always had a meaning and wasn't just a color to be decorative.

I couldn't hear what was being said. I glanced to Victor. "Can I hear them?"

He looked hesitant. "If you need to."

I turned and looked again and then nodded. "I think I do." Then I remembered. "Can he hear me if I talk?"

His green eyes searched mine, there was a question in them. "You want to talk to him?"

Shaking my head, I clutched my hands together. "No. I don't…" Then I remembered and went back to stand in front of him. "That time." I smirked. "You thought I was…" I looked for the word. "demented." I saw regret in his eyes and waved my hand. "You know the truth now." I looked back into the place where his brothers were and then back to him. "I told you I could be… if there was need." I nodded. "I think this is that time."

He frowned, a puzzled expression on his face. "I don't understand, but I trust you." He said softly. "Are you ready? I'll turn on the intercom and remove the reflector."

I closed my eyes and took a deep breath. Opening them, I glanced briefly at Daxx and the others watching me silently. Turning, I went and stood close to the glass, so he would have no choice but to see me when Victor made it so. I nodded. "I'm ready."

I knew when the man could see me clearly. He stood up and just stared at me through the glass. I heard Arius say something, but couldn't stop to listen right now. With a smile on my face, I touched the glass with my finger, as if I was writing something and looked to the man.

I saw him push past Troy and come over to the glass, my heart sped up and I had to remember he couldn't reach me. It took all I had to stand on this spot and not run. I was so much better at running.

"Impossible." He spat at the glass.

I moved closer to the glass, making sure he watched my eyes move over his face. "Your eyes." I said quietly. "I saw them see me," I traced a circle around his face on the glass, "but you didn't stop me." I laughed, it was fake, but he didn't know that. I looked at the snake over the skin on his throat. "The snake. The snake." I told him, moving my face closer to the glass. "it fills you with poison." I whispered. "It seeps in slowly, so you can't know, slowly, slowly," I said with a smile. His eyes were locked on mine, he looked so angry, scary too, but I was safe here. I moved closer so my breath touched the glass. "Slowly." I said again and then smacked my hand on the glass over his face and laughed.

"Cristy." Victor said softly.

I glanced into the room with the man to see Arius and Troy leaving. Backing away with careful steps, I watched him and then his expression changed to confusion and I knew Victor had changed the glass so he couldn't see.

Stopping, I dropped to squat close to the floor, taking deep breaths and trying to settle my heart. I didn't know if it worked, but fear rolled over me now, knowing I'd just looked evil in the eye when it was so close.

Strong hands lifted me to stand on my feet and I looked up into Victor's eyes. I saw pride in them. Something I had never truly seen when others looked at me. He smiled softly then hugged me into his chest.

Someone behind me clapped, I turned to see it was Chase. "That," he clapped again, "was one hell of a performance."

I looked to see everyone grinning and felt my face heat.

Arius was smiling and nodding his head. "His mind was complete soup." He laughed quietly. "I could have had him clucking like a chicken if I'd wanted to."

Troy slapped him on the back and then looked at me. "I was able to see everything he'd hidden from me. Well done."

"I was very scared." I confessed and then looked to Daxx.

She smiled. "I know, but you were amazing, and now we have the upper hand and can kick their asses."

I didn't know what that meant exactly, but everyone seemed so happy, I felt better about not being brave. I looked up at Victor. "I need cookies." I told him. "Mine got broke."

He chuckled and looked down at me. "I think we can arrange new, whole cookies." He kissed my forehead.

"Okay." I nodded and hugged him. I closed my eyes, happy

to be here and knowing that was over with. Flashes came in a rush, like they'd been hiding before. I gasped and opened my eyes. People, so many of them, all were afraid. I looked up at Victor. "I was so distracted by my hair I didn't see it all." I told him and then let go to look through the glass at the man with the snake on him. "They have them. So many." I shook my head. "Why?" I spun around and looked at Quinton and then Arius. "Why do they have them?" I waved my hand to the glass. "In cages, not rooms of glass."

Victor moved so he was in my sight again. "They have prisoners?"

I nodded. He understood. "I don't know why, but they all are so scared."

He turned to look at Troy, I did too. Troy rubbed the back of his neck and I could see the understanding in his eyes.

I pointed at him then rushed over. "You saw it too."

"Troy?" Daxx looked at him. "What did you see?"

"I think," Troy said quietly, but not in a nice tone, "they're using civilians to feed."

Daxx covered her mouth, her eyes huge. "How many?"

My heart sped up. "So many eyes, all full of fear." I said.

"At least a dozen, maybe more." He said and looked to Victor. "I was still sorting out what I'd seen when Crissy said it." He took a deep breath and looked at me as he exhaled, "But she's right. They're holding human civilians to feed from."

"We have to get them out." I said and looked around at everyone else. "They were so scared."

Victor wrapped his arm around my shoulder and pulled me closer to him. "We will." He looked to Chase for a moment and then nodded, like they were talking without words. "It's too close to daylight now, but we'll get a plan in place and go in when it's dark." His eyes searched my face, there was something there. He turned and looked at Daxx. "Do you know where she saw this?"

Daxx watched him for a moment and then looked to me. "Not exactly no. I know the area she's talking about, but it could be any one of hundred places nearby."

Quinton stepped closer and started to say something.

Victor held up his hand so he wouldn't speak.

"I know, Quint, I don't like it either."

I wasn't sure what was going on. Victor looked down at me. "Could you show us where on a map?"

I looked at him and then thought. "I don't understand maps", I told him. I bit my lip. "I can show you for real, where I saw." I shook my head. "But I don't want to, there was so much blood to see. I don't know if you were hurt, or wearing other peoples' blood again."

Someone snorted from behind me. I turned to see Michael with an amused look on his face. "I'm pretty sure it wasn't Victor's blood you saw. I don't think anyone has gotten the upper hand on him in four hundred years."

I looked to Victor, to his eyes to see if this were the truth. "If you get hurt I will not be happy."

He smirked. "I will do everything in my power to make sure you are always happy."

I looked around him and then at his eyes. What he said was true. "Okay, I will take you there."

"Brilliant. I'm awake now and hungry, let's go eat." Chase said and then turned to leave.

As I followed the others out, I held Victor's hand. I was beginning to think they spent more time eating in Alterealm then they did anything else.

Chapter Thirteen

I couldn't sleep. I knew the others would be because it was day. Or their night, I really needed to ask about that clock. My sleep didn't have a cycle, I slept when my body wanted it, which wasn't often.

So much was happening, my mind wouldn't stop for a second. During dinner, or perhaps Chase's breakfast, Clairee had brought a woman to join us, her aura was clear, which I found quite interesting. They hadn't been able to see what was inside of me, but gave me a thin bracelet of leather with silver lines on it to wear always. The bracelet, they said, would block any magic left in me from being detected by others. Victor and Daxx both trusted them, so I had no choice but to wear it. It went well with the big leather one I already wore, so there was that too.

Crawling out of the closet, I looked back and wondered if I should leave the blankets there, in case I was tired soon. Deciding to leave them, I went over to my clothes. Maybe if I went and walked around the halls for a little while I would feel tired. So much seemed to be happening, I didn't know how the others were sleeping.

I remembered that I needed to finish my search for Emil and his children, but all of the information had been taken by Michael so he could help. Since I didn't know where it was, I couldn't work on that to pass the time.

Putting my pack on, I stepped out the door. A tall man

stood waiting there. He had dark hair and a beard. I had never seen him before. I looked down the hall, first one way and then the other, there was no one coming or going. Why was he just standing there across from my door?

I saw he was watching me. The air around him was good, cool like Victor's but still good. His dark brown eyes just looked at me, but he didn't speak. I leaned closer, not wanting to talk too loud because others were sleeping... somewhere. "Are you lost?" I didn't know what was behind most of the doors, but I thought I could help him if he needed it. Pulling out my phone, I looked at it, remembering who would be awake. "I can call Chase, if you are." I looked down the hall again. "I don't know what is behind most of the doors." I told him.

"Uh, no. My king, Chase, told me to stand and guard your door. I am from the daywalker kingdom and am used to being awake during these hours, so he thought it was best."

I nodded. I didn't know why he had to guard my door, maybe he was being punished for not listening. When I had been in school a teacher sent me to a corner once. I still didn't understand what I was supposed to see in that corner, but I had stood for as long as I could. I stepped over and stood beside him. Standing here, alone, would get boring. The door to my room wasn't that interesting to look at.

I looked up at him again, noting he watched me with a strange look on his face. "You look like a pirate." I told him. "Rafael and I watched a movie with pirates once." I nodded. "You could be in a movie if you wanted to be."

He smiled down at me. "I'll keep that in mind, but I am loyal to my king."

I smiled. That was a good thing. "I find it fascinating there are two kings." I thought about the time mystery again. "The day and night confuses me, but I'm going to see if there is a clock that would make it more clear to me." I told him.

The expression on his face told me he didn't completely understand what I was saying, but he was listening. "You can set one up on your phone."

I looked at my phone and frowned. "I can?" Would it really do that to make it clearer to me?

He held out his hand. "May I?"

I nodded and let him take my phone. He tapped his big finger on the screen, doing things so fast I couldn't follow. I didn't do much with my phone. I texted and talked on it. The first phone Daxx had given me, I'd tried to see all the things it did, then somehow had made it not work at all. Since then, I didn't try to explore what all the buttons did.

When he handed it back to me, I looked down to see there were two times on the screen. Even though it was the same time he'd labeled it twice and one said Day and the other Night. It was a small thing, but suddenly I understood. I smiled up at him. "Thank you." I waved the phone around. "I was going to find a clock or book to explain it to me, but this is better, I can see it all the time." I paused for a moment to wonder if I stood on the line between the sides of day and night, what time would it be there, then decided that was something I didn't need to know.

He nodded his head, looking pleased I was happy. "Were you going to the library?"

I bit my lip. "I didn't know where I was going." I looked down the hall. "There's a library?" I nodded. "I would like to see that."

He smiled at me. "I'll take you there."

We had only taken two steps when Rafael came out of a door, running his hand down his face. He looked so tired.

"Crissy." He nodded abruptly to the man with me. "Bronx. Chase have you guarding Criss?"

The man nodded. "Yes. I was just taking her to the library."

I looked up at him. Bronx, what a unique name. I liked it. "You're guarding me? I thought you were guarding the door?"

Rafael chuckled and then shook his head in answer to the odd look the man gave him. "We aren't taking any chances *that*," he motioned to my new bracelet, "isn't working properly. You will have a guard if one of us aren't with you. Victor's orders."

I suddenly felt, I wasn't sure... Special, wasn't the right word, but it was close. I felt safe. Victor knew that was something I needed. "That's very nice of him." I smiled at Bronx. "Victor is very sweet."

He raised one dark eyebrow at me. "Victor, our justice? Sweet?"

I wondered if he had problems with his hearing. "Yes." I looked back to see an amused smile on Raf's face. "I couldn't sleep so I think I'll visit the library until I feel tired."

He nodded his head slowly. "Don't read every book there." Sighing loudly, he nodded to me. "I'm going to get some sleep. I'll see you at breakfast."

"Okay." I watched him walk away and then looked at Bronx. "They eat a lot here."

He grinned. "Food is good."

I couldn't argue with that. "Yes, it is."

~

I stood in the bathroom deciding what to do with my hair. I had finally slept, it wasn't for long, then again, it never was. The library was a huge room full of books, maybe two rooms, I'm not sure. They went on forever and ever, everywhere I looked. I met the most mysterious man there, he was old. Older than I'd even known, but filled with nothing but goodness. A form so pure, it took me a long while to figure out what it was. When I'd really seen him as he was, I found it more fascinating than all the books.

He knew who I was, without me telling him. I was quite excited to be known. I don't know how long I stayed there, only that when I had decided what books I needed to answer the questions… so many questions, Bronx had to help me carry them all back to the room.

Then I read, and read more, thoughts filling my mind as all the pieces came together. Some of the pieces I didn't like, but I planned to think about them more before deciding I knew what they meant. I was drooping on the couch when I noticed I was tired, and that's when I decided I needed to sleep for a while.

Pulling up my hair, I decided two pony tails was how I wanted it to be today. I liked the little clips, I really did, but they pulled more hair out when I tried to remove them then they held while on my head. I already had my red pants and black shoes on, so I would be ready to practice after breakfast. I paused, feeling oddly comfortable as part of a routine. That was something rare in my life.

"Cristy?"

I heard Victor in the room and went out. I smiled when I saw him standing over the table of books and looking at the titles. "Hi."

He straightened and looked at me, his green eyes filling with happiness as they moved over me and stopped on my hair. "Doing some light reading?" He tucked his hands in his pockets and watched me walk over.

I nodded and looked down at the books. "I found many answers," I bit my lip, "and more questions." I remembered. "The man, if he even is, at the library gave me the book with the leaves on it." I shook my head. "But I didn't read it yet. You said *we* would, so I thought I should wait." I stopped and looked up at him, wanting him to kiss me and I wasn't sure why, I just did.

"You could have, if you wanted to, but I would like to be with you." He smirked, "there will be more questions, I'm certain."

I smiled, happy that I had waited. "I will wait until you and I both have time." I huffed out a breath. "I don't know when that will be. Things don't pause for long lately."

Taking his hand out of his pocket, he reached over and played with the hair in one of my pony tails. "I've noticed. If I could change that, I would."

I watched his mouth as he spoke. "I do have a question right now." I looked up to see his eyes watching me.

"I will try to answer it." His tone was sincere.

I bit my lip and then smiled. "Will you kiss me?"

His eyes lit and he smiled. "The simplest question I've ever been asked." Tilting my chin up with a single finger, he leaned down and brushed his mouth over mine.

I thought that was going to be *the* kiss, but then he pulled me closer with his other hand on my back and covered my mouth completely. This was the kiss I had wanted, the one that sent heat through me and made my head light.

When he lifted his mouth from mine, I looked up into red eyes and smiled. "That's the best answer I've ever gotten."

He growled softly. "I better be the only one to answer you *that* way."

I sensed tension and rubbed my hand over his chest lightly. "I didn't even think I liked being kissed until you kissed me, Victor." I shook my head. "So, I don't want anyone else to."

His red eyes slowly turned back to green as he looked down at me. "We need to go find a room filled with people and other distractions. Now." He motioned to the couch. "Get your pack."

I turned and picked it up, smiling because he remembered I had to take it with me.

As we were walking through the halls to the dining room, I thought about the man at the library. "I find the man at the library quite mysterious." I told him.

Victor glanced to me as we walked, "He's been there as far back as I can remember. As far back as everyone remembers." He shrugged slightly. "I've never seen him outside the library, ever."

I nodded. "Because he's not."

He turned down the next hall. "He's not?"

"Outside the library. Ever." I told him.

He stopped in the doorway of the dining room and turned so I would look at him. "Are you saying the man has never left the library?" His brows furrowed. "I find that hard to believe that one man…"

I put my hand on his arm to get his attention. "He is not one man, he is many." I nodded. "It took me quite some time to see that, the air around him was so pure it was blinding me at first." I frowned. "They may have had bodies before, the many," I clarified, "but they do not now." I nodded knowing this to be true. "He… they, watch over the library and the prophecies mostly, I imagine."

Victor looked down at me, his eyes searching my face. "You're saying he is the souls of many, there to be a guardian of the library."

I had to think that through for a moment and then nodded. "Yes. That is the easiest way to say it."

"It actually makes sense now." He mused quietly.

"Yes, it does." Troy said from behind me.

I turned to see eyes on us. I had forgotten where we were.

"I always knew there was something about him." Quinton said.

Leone snorted, "Like you've ever read a book in your life."

Everyone smiled, it was funny, the way they always poked at each other, but loved each other fiercely.

Victor took my elbow and guided me toward the table.

"Look," Chase said, "it's cutie and the beast."

Victor stopped walking and looked down at me, then smiled at his brother. "Calling Cristy a beast is uncalled for." He said in a light tone.

Chase put his hand over his heart and then gave me a shocked look. "The gods are in shock, you've given him a sense of humor." He shrugged. "A bad one, but it's a start."

"Ignore him." Victor said close to my ear and then released me to chose where I wanted to sit at the table.

I sat a few seats away from Quinton today, feeling a little more comfortable with everyone, but still not sure if I could be too close to so many people at once. Mitz came in and set a plate in front of me, it had three pieces of toast with marmalade on it. I smiled up at her, she always remembered. "Thank you."

Rafael came in the other door and didn't look happy. He stopped behind the chair he always sat in, but didn't sit down.

Victor paused in what he was doing and looked at him. "What has happened?"

Raf looked at me for a moment and then to Daxx. "I went to check in with Tim and see if Alona has shown up." He shook his head. "She hasn't, so I swung by Daxx's apartment before heading back, and it's been trashed."

Daxx jumped up. "What?" She put her hands on her hips, looking very angry. "There's nothing there of value, why would someone break in?"

Troy stood up and leaned closer to say something, I don't know what it was, but she nodded and didn't look as upset.

Victor glanced at me, something hard in his eyes. "I believe," he cleared his throat, "they may have been looking for another way to find us."

He was right. I looked down at the bracelet Clairee had given to me. It must work. I touched it and then glanced to Daxx. "I'm sorry." Then I thought more about it. "How did they know to look there? No one ever saw me when I went there." I nodded. "I go in the window."

Daxx sighed and then sat back down. "Marcus. He knows. I," she waved her hand around, "have come to be." She said in a strange voice. Looking at me, she gave me a soft look. "It looks like he knows you and I are connected, Crissy, and is trying to find a way to get someone inside the royal chambers here in Alterealm."

I bit my lip and looked around at all those at the table. Each had been nicer to me than every other person I'd met in my life. I didn't want anything bad to happen to any of them. "I guess we better stop him then." I nodded and picked up my toast to take a bite.

"Amen to that." Arius said and lifted his coffee cup in my direction.

Rafael sat down. "We'll find you an apartment, or place over there later, Daxx." He smiled down the table at me. "And a place that you can call home base too, Crissy."

I wasn't sure if I needed a home base, but I nodded anyway.

Rafael started to fill his plate. "So, is practice just a light warm up then?" He glanced to Troy and then Victor, "The guards staying behind, or coming along for some fun?"

I wasn't sure what this fun was he talked about. We were going in a few hours to find those people that were so scared. Thinking about it too much would make me feel sick, there had been so much blood. I took another bite of my toast, but didn't taste it. None of them could get hurt, they just couldn't.

Looking around at each one of them, my eyes moved to Victor and found him watching me. It was like he knew what I was thinking, and that I needed that connection to him right now. I knew if I got up, they would stop eating, and they were going to need their strength more than I would. I was used to running for hours, sometimes days, without eating. They were not. He sat there watching me, motionless in that way he could do so well.

Turning his head slowly, with a look of regret, he glanced to Rafael. "Four of the guards are coming with us. We're not sure of the numbers we'll face."

"Tim is?" Daxx asked.

Victor smirked at Troy who shook his head. "Yes, he is." He gave Troy a strange look. "You know they fight as one."

Daxx nodded and waved her hand around. "While you all do your he-man thing, I have my blocker."

I didn't know what the he-man thing was, or a blocker either. Maybe I was worrying for nothing, but I know what I saw and no matter whose blood, it still meant someone would suffer. I stood up slowly, and all eyes turned to me. I tried to offer a brave smile, but probably failed.

"I'm just going to practice throwing those knives." I nodded. "I'll see you after you eat." Grabbing my pack, I turned and left quickly. I supposed I would have to practice throwing now, even though I had only said it to find a few moments of quiet. I doubted any of them would need quiet the way I did.

I watched the fifth knife hit the floor and heaved out a breath, defeated. I was keeping my eyes open. I *was* looking at the target I wanted to hit. It wasn't my fault none of the knives wanted to stick.

"At least they're going the right way."

I jumped to see Victor leaning near the doorway. "I don't think knives are my *thing*." I looked back to the target. "I was told everyone has one."

He came over and stood beside me. "You need to throw them like you mean it."

I looked at him and then the last knife in my hand. "Of course, I mean to throw them or I would stand here and just hold them."

He chuckled softly and reached to take the knife from my hand. "Get mad at it while you throw it."

"Get mad at the knife?" I raised my eyebrows at him. "And

people say I make no sense."

Victor grinned down at me and then turned his head and looked at the target. "You have to throw with force and at the end there is a jerky motion. It's easier to show than to explain."

I watched him throw. He hit the middle of the target. Glancing down at me, he walked over to the target and pulled out the knife, and then picked up the ones I had thrown off the floor. "I'm sorry I left before breakfast was finished." I watched him walk back with long easy strides. "I needed quiet."

He nodded. "I know." Stopping beside me, he gave me a gentle smile. "I realize this is going to be quite difficult for you. I am not happy we are exposing you, but it can't be helped in this case." He turned to face the target. "I will ensure you are safe before anything begins." Nodding toward the target, his tone changed. "Watch my hand as I throw."

I looked at his face, he looked so focused. It seemed I was developing a bad habit, but I found my eyes wandering to his mouth.

"Cristy?"

"Yes?"

"That's my mouth, which is nowhere near my hand." He grinned.

I shook my head to focus and looked at how he was holding the knife. It was nothing like how I did. With a smooth motion, he flicked his wrist and the knife vanished. I heard a quiet thunk as it hit the target. Turning I looked to see his knife buried in the center again. "Mmm, your good at this."

He chuckled. "I've just had more time to practice."

I laughed. "Only almost five hundred years more." I took a deep breath when he held one of the knives out to me. I held it the way he had and looked at the target, nodding my head more then once. I tried to copy what I had seen him do and then my jaw dropped when the knife stuck in the target. It wasn't near the center, much closer to the floor, but it hadn't bounced off.

"Were you aiming there?" He asked quietly.

I shook my head. "Nowhere close to there."

He chuckled. "At least you hit it." He flipped the knife in his hand and flicked and it hit the center beside the other one. "I think they are weighted wrong for you."

I shook my head. I had no idea what weight he meant.

"The balance and weight of the entire knife." He held another one out to me.

I took it and tried to focus beyond the flashes in my head. "Maybe it's my head." I adjusted how I was holding it. "That isn't balanced right." I used more force this time and it once again stuck in the board, nowhere near where I was looking.

"The fact that you can focus enough to throw with all your mind processes, is in, itself, amazing my dear." He tapped his finger to his temple. "I've been in there, so I know what you're are up against."

"We've decided to bypass practice and leave earlier." Daxx said coming in.

Victor turned and looked at her and gave a slight roll of his shoulders. "As long as all parties are aware, I'm in agreement with that."

Leone ran in the door behind her. "I just have something for Crissy before we go." He jogged over and then stopped a few feet from me and held out a belt.

I looked at it and then to Victor. He reached over and took the belt from his brother.

Daxx came over with a big grin on her face. "They had to have one made in a girl's size." She laughed. "Damn giants."

Victor leaned down and wrapped it around me, securing it low on my waist. The way it fastened looked complicated, but I would figure that out later. It had a big metal ring next to the buckle. It went with my gloves, so I supposed that was a good thing.

"Here." Leone held out a little box. "It's the right weight for her."

Victor nodded and held the box so I could look at it.

"Thank you." I said slowly, not sure exactly what it was.

Daxx laughed. "Showing her *what* it is would be helpful." She looked at me and rolled her eyes. "Men."

Leone grabbed the box out of his brother's hand. He looked around and then ran over to the end wall. The one that looked like a ladder, only several feet wide.

Victor gave me a little nudge, so I followed Leone over.

Leone climbed to the top of the ladder wall and did something with the box. Reaching behind him he pulled a glove out of his pocket and put it on. I most likely would have fallen just doing that, I thought.

I watched, and know my mouth dropped open when he came down so fast it looked like he was running backwards down the wall. When his feet hit the floor, he did something with the box and the cable came zipping down into the box.

He looked over at me and nodded. "It's only fifty feet long, so don't try freefalling any further." He held it out toward me.

I stumbled the first few steps and then almost ran into him to get the amazing little box. He reached out when I got to him and then jerked his hand back and looked behind me. I turned, and saw Victor was coming over.

Leone cleared his throat and held the box so I could see the side. "This button deploys the hook." He pushed it and something popped out of the side of it. "Give it a twist." He did and it turned into a scary little hook. He walked over to the lowest rung and hooked it on. "Make sure it stays taught." He gave it a jerk. "before you're going down." He pointed to another button and then started to back up and cable came out of the box. It was truly amazing. "When you're down, hit this button again." He pushed it and the little hook flattened and the cable zipped back into the box.

I squealed and ran over to him. "That is amazing!" I took it this time when he held it out and turned it in my hands to look at the buttons. I looked at him again and then jumped toward him and hugged him tight. Then I remembered, and let go and stepped back. He had a strange look on his face. I leaned down and whispered. "I am not your favorite flavor." I straightened. "But when you find the one that is yours, you will never crave another." I nodded.

Victor was standing beside me now. He took the box and flipped it over and showed me another hook, one that didn't flatten and then leaned down and hooked it to the ring on my belt. "There." He said and straightened up.

I looked from him to Leone, then back to him again. "It's

mine?" I glanced to Daxx. "I can keep it?"

She grinned and then laughed.

I looked at Victor, not believing.

"It was made for you." He told me with a smile.

I opened my mouth and then closed it again. "I've never…" I looked at the box on my belt. "Can I try it?" Victor motioned to the wall and I turned so fast and started climbing.

"Wait for me." He called up to me.

I know I was smiling all the way up, as fast as I could climb. I went to the very top and then hooked my arm through the last rung and reached down to the amazing little box. He was beside me now, but didn't reach to help me. I got the hook and twisted it and put it over the rung closest to my belt. I tugged on it as Leone had done and then glanced to Victor, he nodded. I took a breath and pushed the next button as Leone had told me to. I leaned back, but still held onto the rung with my other hand, checking, to be sure. It held me there, so I slowly moved down and more cable came out.

"The further you lean back the faster the cable will come out." Victor told me. "It's made for your weight."

I looked from the smart amazing little box to him. "Okay." I nodded. I looked at the cable and went down a few more feet and then let go of the rung and I stayed there. I looked to the floor and smiled at Daxx. "I won't worry about falling off the broken fire escape any more." I thought for a second. "Or the roof ledge over the club." She didn't look as excited as I was.

"After your feet are on the floor, you can explain." Victor told me, a worried expression on his face.

"Okay." I nodded and then started going down. I was so excited how fast I could move. My gloves made this noise against the cable and I now knew why fate made sure I found them. I jumped to the floor and squealed with delight as I pushed the button and the cable zipped into the box. Victor stepped off the last rung and stood in front of me. I launched myself up into his arms and hugged him tight. "Thank you so much."

He wrapped his big arms around me and hugged me back. "It was Leone's idea, but I'll take the credit for it."

I could hear him chuckle against my hair. I jumped down and saw Chase coming in. He was dressed for battle now, and gone was the flirty twin I usually saw. "Ready to get this party started." He called over.

Daxx came over with my pack and put her arm around me, "Lets go get changed."

I nodded and looked over my shoulder at Victor. I could see the justice side of him coming out as he stood there. I swallowed and turned back to watch where we were going.

"I had Mitz make you a vest with a hood." Daxx told me. "It will be in your room. Wear all black and put that on." She paused and looked at me. "Take your phone, leave your pack." She gave me a serious look. "I want you able to move without worrying about it. It will be safe here waiting for you."

I nodded. If she wanted me to leave my pack behind, then I didn't have a choice. Daxx knew more about battle then I did.

Chapter Fourteen

I stood in the corner and watched all the movement around me. Victor and Michael weren't here yet, but the rest of the brothers were. Bronx was here with three other men I didn't know. Daxx kept talking to one and looked pleased, so I surmised that must be her blocker, Tim. I still wasn't sure what a blocker was.

Rafael came over and smiled. It was the first time I could remember that I didn't smile back. My stomach was in knots. He reached behind me and pulled up my hood and smiled again. "Keep that hair covered." He told me with a serious look.

I nodded. "Okay."

He motioned to the little box on my belt. "Heard you were a natural with that."

I did smile then. "It is amazing. I won't fall anymore."

He raised and eyebrow and then shook his head. "I don't want to know."

All the talking and motion in the room stopped when Victor walked in. I only had to look at him briefly to know he was *the* justice man now, dark leather and weapons included. He stopped and handed Daxx a little box and she smiled, looking very pleased to get it. It looked like mine, only had symbols on it. I wondered what those meant. I watched her clip it on and then pull it and a small cable extended, she released it and it snapped back in place. Looking very excited she nodded to him again. I would have to ask later what her little box did.

"It's a transporter," Rafael told me, "They hold it over the offender and it sends them straight to the cells."

"Really?" I looked to see Daxx play with it once more. That was amazing and different from mine, but I had no plans to be near *offenders*, so it was just as well.

He nodded. "It only works for Justice and the Huntress."

I thought about that for a moment. "That is good. Power in the wrong hands would be bad." Victor turned to look at me, and then started walking to me.

"Be safe, little sister." Raf said quietly and then walked away.

I watched him leave, wondering if he knew how special those words were. I had never been a sister. I had never even been a daughter, not that I could remember. When Victor reached me, his eyes softened, the space around him did not, but I felt some relief knowing that he didn't give into the dark part of himself completely.

He stood there and studied me. "I have decided," he said in a voice so soft it seemed almost out of place with the way he looked right now, "that regardless of how you dress or do your hair, I desire you more each time I lay eyes on you."

I felt my cheeks heat at his confession. I glanced around at all the bodies filling the room. "You need to tell me that without a full room." I whispered back.

His smile was wide for a moment. "I don't trust myself to maintain control then."

I looked up at this man, who had come to mean more to me in ways I couldn't explain. With a small smile, I looked him up and down as he had me. "That seems more cowardly than suits you." I told him in his own stuffy way.

Smiling again, he shook his head and then took a hold of my wrist lightly. "This is a pre-programmed transporter device." He secured it around my wrist and flipped the cover open. "Should anything happen, or it becomes more than you are able to cope with, push this button and it will bring you back to this room in an instant." He snapped it closed. "Once we find a way to help you control the flashes and the chaos in your mind, and you can focus on just *one* thought, we will get you a new one."

I looked at the device and touched it with one finger. "Thank you." I knew in my heart he was giving me the ultimate hiding place if I needed one. It meant so much that I didn't have words to explain.

"This." He held up a case with a small knife in it. "is balanced for you, with a gentle touch in mind." He knelt and strapped it to my ankle and then looked seriously. "Just in case you need it. Even if it is to throw away for a distraction."

I took a deep breath and let it out slowly as he stood up. He leaned down and grasped my chin lightly, his green eyes locking on my own.

"Your safety is the most important thing in this, and all, worlds. You hide when told and stay there until I come and get you." He kissed my mouth hard and then quickly released my chin.

Daxx came over, she was still smiling. Would I ever be like her and look forward to something like this? I doubted it, but for all of *their* safety, I could try to be brave.

"Ok, Crissy, where is the closest you can take me?" She glanced to Victor briefly, "and then we'll transport the rest in."

I thought for a moment. "On the ground?"

She smirked. "Preferably to start, at least to get us there."

I frowned and looked at the floor. "I'm not sure of the exact spot near where those people are. I think I know how to find out though." I glanced nervously to Victor. "Most of my flashes show me the area from above." I shrugged. "It's why I learned to climb so well."

His green eyes traveled over my face, almost in a caress. "I find nothing pertaining to you is ever as it seems. The surprises are endless." He turned his head. "Leone."

Leone came over. "Yeah."

Victor glanced at me and then to him, "You are our…" he looked at me once more, "*second* best climber, so you'll go with Daxx and Cristy. I don't want her left alone while Daxx gets the transports started."

Leone nodded and took off the straps holding the weapons on his back. He handed them to Quinton. When he looked at me he grinned. "So, I blend in." He looked down at the weapons still on him and shrugged, "mostly."

"Okay, Crissy, where are we going?" Daxx asked me

"The end of the alley past the tattoo place." I thought for a second. "Below the bridge."

Daxx bobbed her head a few times. "Yep, I know where your talking about." She reached out and grabbed my arm. "Close your eyes."

I closed them and then felt my stomach drop and knew we had crossed back into our world. Opening them slowly, I looked at Leone and Daxx, they didn't even seem bothered.

Daxx was looking up. "Where are we going to end up?"

I knew she wasn't going to like it, and pointed the beams running under the bridge. "If we're up there, we can get to where we need to be." I looked at Leone. "Without being seen and having to go around buildings."

He grinned and shrugged to Daxx. "It makes sense."

She groaned. "It does, but I still don't have to like it." She motioned me forward with her arm. "Lead the way, number one climber."

I smiled and looked around to make sure no one was watching us. Once assured of that, I ran under the bridge to the spot I knew was the fastest to climb. Leone climbed up behind me and Daxx, a little slower, behind him. Checking again to make sure no one watched, I ducked down and started to run along the beam. It was wide enough to sit on, so balance wasn't a problem. A few minutes later, I stopped when it was wide enough for several people to be. I didn't know why they would make a place like this under a bridge so high in the air, but it was one of my favorite places to sit.

Daxx looked at the ground below us, and then at the buildings, then gave me an odd look. "Some day, you and I are going to talk about personal safety."

I smiled and then nodded. "I feel very safe up here."

She snorted. "Figures. Okay, I'll be right back." Then she was gone.

I looked at Leone. "I find transporting quite fascinating. I tried to find more of it the books last night, but wasn't able to." I squatted down and waited, still not certain I could do this.

Reaching down, I touched the case Victor had strapped to my leg. It felt odd and out of place on me.

"May I?" Leone said and motioned to it.

I watched as he took it off and then flipped it to be upside down. It was a little higher on my leg and I couldn't see how that was right.

He moved away again and nodded. "You can drop down into a squat and move twice as fast as the rest of us, at your size." He stood up and then squatted down in slow motion and reached to the side of his leg. "Once down, a jerk on the handle and it's free and flying." He made the motion a few more times. He made it look like a natural motion. "I'm much younger than Victor, so I remember that not all moves are automatic."

I didn't get up, but practiced what he showed me while I was squatting there. It did feel more like something I would be able to do. "Thank you." I nodded. "For the help, but I hope to never need it."

He grinned. "I hope not too."

Quinton, Rafael and Bronx appeared with Daxx. She gave me a nod and then was gone again. Quinton handed Leone back his straps and weapons while Rafael looked around to see where we were.

"You have the craziest ways, little sister." Raf told me softly.

I looked down at the ground. "No one looks up." I told him.

Quinton squatted down beside me. "Where are we going from here?"

I pointed along the bridge to a building. "That's where I saw them. I'm sure." I took a deep breath and let it out slowly, checking for pieces in my head I may have missed. I wished to know how many people were being held, but couldn't see how many eyes there had been looking up at me. I was glad the flashes were less tonight. I had enough to manage with trying to seem braver then I knew I was.

"Is there a way down when we get there?" Rafael asked.

I nodded. "Victor won't like it, but yes."

He laughed. "It's good to keep him guessing."

I wasn't sure that was true, but if the smile he gave me was any sign, I was pretty sure it was something his brother wouldn't find amusing. Before I could comment Chase, Troy and Victor were standing there with Daxx.

"I've got this." Troy said to her and then was gone.

"It always amazes me that man can look at a place for half a second and then get back to it." She said.

Chase shrugged. "Ever noticed he's thick-headed and single-minded? I'm sure that helps."

I watched Victor look down and then all around. He looked down at me. "A favorite location, I imagine."

I nodded. "Yes."

Quinton pointed at the building I had shown them a few minutes before. "We're going there." He winked at me. "And we'll be able to get in close without being spotted."

Victor nodded slowly and looked along the path we would take to get there. "Once we get as far as we can go, we'll decide if witches are needed."

"Witches?" I couldn't think why we would need them.

"They will cast a bubble of invisibility over us, so no one outside can see." Rafael told me. "To protect the innocents."

"Oh." I nodded my head slowly. "That's a good thing." I glanced to Victor. "I would like to see that."

He smiled down at me. "Did Troy stop for tea?" His eyes turned to Daxx.

She shrugged, "Who knows." She checked the knife secured to her leg. "He's probably trying to bring all six of them back at once."

Chase chuckled quietly. "It's good that he flexes his brain from time to time."

Daxx snorted, and then Troy appeared with the six others we were waiting for. She grinned up at him. "Took you long enough."

He gave her a look as if he were offended, but I could see they were playing and not meaning a word of it. Troy looked down at her again slowly, then to his twin. "I don't like our queen being here, brother king, there could be danger."

Chased nodded. "I agree, Brother." He smiled down at

Daxx.

"I have every right to be here you two. Don't start." She said with a smile.

"Kings." Troy said with great emphasis.

She rolled her eyes at him. "Um, Huntress, and we are *hunting* tonight."

Chase nodded, then smirked. "Still, without our queen the royal line is no more."

With her hands on her hip, she glared at him then her mate. "First, you live practically forever, so I don't think you're close to extinction. Second, the queen can't make babies if she's a widow… so where he goes," She pointed to Troy, "I go, to make sure his ass comes back in one piece."

Chase gave his brother a serious look. "She has a point."

Troy shook his head. "You always agree with her."

Daxx laughed and held her hand out to me. "He's a smart man."

I took her hand and smiled. The way they were together was something to see. I wished for something like this, but just witnessing it made me feel better.

"Lead the way, Criss, this is your show." She told me.

I looked to Victor, who gave me a slight nod and then I moved along the beam until we were off the large space. I moved quickly and quietly, knowing the steps like they were flat on the ground and my feet walked them every day.

I went as far as I could under the bridge, glancing behind me to see everyone was following quickly. Checking below, I squatted down near the edge, then pushed off and jumped down to the roof of the building, just five feet away. Landing, I checked my balance, and looked down at my boots, they made landing hurt much less. I really liked my new boots.

Staying low and silent, I went across the roof to the farthest edge. I leaned over and looked below to the small yard in front of the building I had seen, the one with all the scared people inside.

Victor was beside me first, staying low and unmoving, I had to check he was breathing. He was very good at being still. He snapped his fingers and pointed to the other side and both

Quinton and Michael moved over silently to check over that side.

"What are you thinking?" Arius asked from his other side.

"It's too small to be used for training of any kind." Victor said quietly. "We need…"

The door on the building opened and man stepped out. Holding it open he looked inside and spoke to someone. "Same time tomorrow." He laughed to whatever they replied and closed the door.

I watched him and the space around him as he moved away. Then he turned his head and the light shone on his face, revealing his yellow eyes. I moved closer to Victor to tell him.

"I saw." He whispered. Turning, he looked to Daxx and she came over. "You and Tim go dispatch him to the cells while I send Raf and Leone to have a look inside."

Nodding, Daxx moved away and I turned to see her and her blocker silently going down the fire escape after the man.

"Raf." Victor said over his shoulder. "You and Leone see if you can find a way to see inside."

I tapped his shoulder, not sure if I should speak. When he looked to me, I pointed to the ladder that led to a fire escape on the shadowed corner of the building.

"Go take a look in the windows." He said to Rafael.

Raf nodded and he and Leone moved to get off the roof.

"Michael, get the witches here to this roof, then get them to cloak this end of the building and across the yard. We don't know how many wander this area." Victor looked at me and even in the dark I could see indecision on his face. "I want you inside of the barrier, so you can't be seen if others arrive. The witches will cast and then leave." He pointed to the fire escape where Rafael and Leone now stood. "You and Bronx will stay there."

I nodded, feeling nervous in a way I had never felt before. "Okay." I whispered. Turning, I saw that Bronx had heard and was moving toward the other side, just waiting for me. "Be safe." I told Victor and then moved over to Bronx.

Moving as fast as I could down the steps, I ran into the dark corner by the ladder. As Bronx reached me, the door to the building opened and a man came out. Bronx stepped quickly into the shadows around the corner and I moved to follow him. Before I got a single step, I saw Daxx going toward him, but I wasn't sure if she saw the man. I looked back at the man. He was too close to the building, he could call out and warn the others she was there. I looked up to where Victor was and realized he wouldn't know where Daxx was from his view.

Glancing back to Bronx, I bit my lip and left the darkness, and stepped toward the man. I checked my hood was up and my hair unseen, remembering what Rafael had told me.

Daxx had slowed her steps, staying tight to the building edge while the others were still on top. I could see Tim close behind her as they stood there motionless and silent.

I ran toward the man's back. "Hi." I said quite loudly and then stopped to be sure there was enough distance between us, so he couldn't reach my emotions. When he turned, his yellow eyes moved over me slowly. Before I could decide what to do, there was a quiet pop and he vanished right before my eyes. Daxx stood there looking pleased and holding her little transporter in her hand.

"Go." She whispered and ran toward the corner where Bronx stood waiting. "Victor will be having, kittens right now." She grinned at me. "Good distraction."

I turned to follow her up the ladder. "Kittens?" I asked quietly.

She leaned around and looked down at me. "That was a grey hair moment for him."

"Oh." I glanced to where he was, but in the shadows and lights I couldn't see him. "I'm okay." I said and kept climbing the ladder.

"Witches are here." I heard Bronx say below me.

I got up to the steps where Rafael and Leone waited, trying to look and see if I would be able to see this barrier they were to cast.

Rafael leaned down close to my head. "Heart attack." He whispered and then opened the window quietly.

When Bronx and Tim stepped onto the platform, I thought this space was not meant for so many people, but then Leone went in the window without a sound and Raf quickly followed, taking more space again. Daxx nodded to me once and stepped through.

By the time Troy, Victor and Chase came up the stairs the others were inside. Victor looked down at me. "That better be your last heroic move tonight."

I nodded, it hadn't felt heroic, but I had no plans to do it again.

"Fight well, brother." Chase said and went through the window.

"Well enough to kick your ass, brother." Troy whispered and climbed in after him.

Victor paused and looked to the ground where the other guards stood in the shadows near the door. Looking back he nodded once, then maneuvered through the window. I stopped to think how they had all climbed through so quickly, with weapons and not even touching the window frame.

Looking down and then to Bronx, who was doing what I knew he did best, guarding and not moving, I stepped over to the window and stood on my toes to look inside.

My heart jumped in my chest when I saw how many people were down there. There had to be thirty or more. Panicking, I looked around until I saw Victor and the others standing in the shadows. I leaned back to glance at Bronx. "There's too many." I said softly.

With his brows drawn together he came over and looked down at the scene, with a quick shake of his head. With a relaxed expression, he looked down at me. "They can handle that."

I know my eyes were wide as I watched him look back to check for more captors. There were three times the number of bad guys to the people they held below. How was he so calm? I was lost in my head when he nudged my arm gently. I looked back to him and he held a finger over his mouth and pointed down. I leaned in and saw two men walking toward our guards in the shadows below.

He leaned around me and glanced inside the window. Then pointed to the left. "Get on that ledge and stay there, out of sight."

That was something I knew how to do. Nodding quickly, I accepted the boost he gave me to get through the window, again wondering how larger people had managed it so gracefully.

Squatting on the ledge, staying small, I looked below me again. Rafael glanced up to me, I wasn't sure what that expression meant, but I was sure he'd explain later. I pointed out the window and then held up two fingers, thinking they should know more were arriving.

With an abrupt nod, he leaned close to Victor and said something.

Victor nodded and said something back then glanced quickly up to me. I didn't need to be closer to recognize the expression on his face. It told me, without any doubt, to stay where I was until he said otherwise. I had no plans to move, so I don't know why he seemed concerned.

I held my breath when they started to move, pausing for a second to see Bronx standing where he'd been, immobile, like a statue.

"Who wants to dance first?" Daxx shouted.

I looked down to see weapons pulled from straps and Daxx, the two kings and Tim stepping into the light. Without waiting, they went toward the men and the clash of metal on metal rang out, breaking the silence.

The rest went, without ceremony, into the bodies rushing toward them. I watched Victor as he fought three on his own. How was that being safe, I wondered with my heart in my throat. The scene below wasn't like graceful dance they did at practice, this was hard, violent, and far more chaotic than anything I had ever seen. In or out of my head.

I chewed my lip and winced so many times as I watched the ones I cared about clash with the evil below. A thought came to me and I forced my eyes away, where were they? The scared people? Those eyes I had seen? I looked around the false wall that didn't reach the top, trying to see into the dark spaces. I couldn't see. Then, I did. A man came out from a door to a room behind the false wall looking quite happy… until he noticed the commotion a few feet away. I didn't stop to see what he did, I just continued to search for the innocents being held.

The eyes. I gasped and focused inside my head. Standing, I moved to the window and looked out to Bronx. "The eyes." I told him. "They were looking up at me not out at them." I pointed to below where the battle stormed on.

He leaned his head in the window. "The captives?" He asked and I felt like hugging him because he understood, but knew now was not the time.

I nodded and pointed to the room with no roof. "I think they're in there." I looked around to see how I could reach that spot. "When I saw them they were looking *up* at me."

He gave me a very serious look. "Can you get there safely?" With a raised eyebrow, "without going down in that?"

I bit my lip and looked again. "Yes. I think so."

He exhaled loudly and shook his head. "If my king doesn't kill me, the justice will." He started to climb in the window. Then paused half way through. "I'll go down and try to get to the door while you get over to that room."

Nodding, I touched his arm quickly and then moved back to the ledge I had been on to decide on the best way for me to move. When I decided on my path, I turned to see Bronx quickly moving down the ladder.

My heart beat fast as I made my way from beam to beam to get above the room. I couldn't pause to look below, or I would worry too much about my friends. The sounds coming from the fight made me flinch too many times, and I didn't know if I wanted to know if any were injured.

I focused on my footing and the scared eyes I had seen. I had to help them. I knew the horrors of a cage, even without bars, and no innocent soul should have to live that way. As I got close enough to see the frightened people, I saw a man with a sword watching out from the door he had cracked open just enough to see.

I paused and bit my lip, not sure how to free them when they had a guard. I looked around for Bronx and saw he hadn't yet reached the door and was fighting for his own life. Huffing out a breath, I continued to move over the cage.

I didn't stop to count how many, knowing that now was not the right time, when one captive looked up. I put my finger over my lips and moved across the beam. Now all I had to do was figure out how to get down from where I hovered. I looked at the box on my belt and wished I'd asked more about it. Would it let me hook on and just jump down? I didn't know, but was going to try it and see.

With nervous movements, my hands shook as I twisted the flat piece around to make the hook. I put it over the lip of the beam and closed my mind briefly. I'd never prayed before, I didn't understand the process to do such a thing, but I thought if there was any time to try it, now might be *that* time.

Keeping the line taught as Leone had said to do, I lowered my body over the edge and hung there with shaking hands. Huffing out one breath, then another, I released one hand, grasped the cable and then let go with the other. I went down so fast, I barely had time to watch for somewhere to land. I hit the bars and wobbled slightly until I had my balance. Pressing the button to release the hook, I watched the cable rush back inside the box.

Turning, to check, I saw the man standing guard over his prisoners had noticed my arrival. That was bad. I stood above him on the cage, and he had no way to reach me. I stopped for a second, long enough to be happy they didn't use guns or my life would have ended today. Victor would have been very upset with me then.

Shaking my head, I focused and looked down at the eyes looking up at me. They moved to the bars, making noise, arms reaching out to their guard and making him back away. It was the only chance I was going to have, so I squatted down and jumped to the floor, and pulled the knife on my leg free. I stayed low to the floor and looked over at the man, his sword was ready to strike.

With my heart pounding, I flicked the knife as Victor had said to do, squealing when it stuck into his leg above the knee. He made a noise and then growled and raised his sword. I crouched down further making myself small and watched, then he vanished and only Daxx stood where he had been.

I glanced at the floor to see my bloodied knife and a key ring with single key laying beside his sword on the floor.

She picked up my knife, wiped it against her leg and held it out to me. "Get them out." She said in a steady voice and then was out the door again.

My hand was shaking as I looked at the knife, but I decided I would continue to hold it. Grabbing the key, I turned to the cage to open the lock. When the door opened, I watched the people moved out quickly. They looked worn and battered and my heart broke for them. I nodded and moved over to the door, opening it to peek out.

I couldn't see far but thought there were fewer bodies fighting. Bronx appeared and gave me a nod, so I opened the door wide and looked at the scared eyes watching me. "Follow me. Stay down low." I didn't know if they would know that but had always thought it kept you out of sight if you stayed low.

I rushed in the direction of the door that led outside. A large body stepped in my way and I ducked down then watched to see Victor, with his double blades block the swing and knocked the body away, freeing my path. I don't think I was breathing at that point, but started moving again. I looked behind to see Bronx guarding the others as they ran along behind me.

Reaching the door, I started to open it, then saw Arius running toward me. The odd look on his face had me confused, he shook his head "no" quickly. I released the handle and ducked down, not sure why he didn't want me to open the door. When he got there, he put his weapon in the case and leaned down to touch the first prisoner behind me, he nodded his head, without speaking and then motioned them to the door.

I stood again and grabbed the handle, knowing now that he was doing whatever it was he did to tell them inside their heads to forget what they had seen. I watched them as they left, to be guided by the guards we had left outside, pausing to wonder what it would be like to wake up and see bruises and scrapes, but not know why. I turned to see Arius doing it to the last prisoner freed, when he pulled his weapon and grasped my arm.

"They will be alright." He told me, then gave me a gentle

shove in the other direction.

With Bronx almost attached to me, I moved to the furthest corner and crouched down as close to the floor as possible. The sounds of metal against metal had lessened now, so I hoped that meant it was over and we had done well enough.

When I realized all I could hear were gasps and heavy breaths, I understood I was safe now and it was over. I straightened up and then stepped beside Bronx, who was still stiff with fear. I thought that odd for a warrior to feel and then I saw why. Victor was walking toward us looking angrier then I had ever seen. More than I thought possible. He had blood on his face and across his clothes, but with the way he moved I knew it wasn't his. I looked quickly to see all that had come with me were standing and whole.

When he reached us, he stood face to face with Bronx. His big chest was heaving as he caught his breath. "I told you to keep her safe." He growled and pointed to the room the prisoners had been in. "How is *that* keeping her safe?"

I jumped quickly between the two and pushed against Victor's chest so he would step back, and calm down. His red eyes looked at me. "It was up to me." I told him in a loud voice, not sure if he was focused enough to hear me. "The eyes." I nodded. "When I saw them they were looking *up* at me, not out to you."

All I could hear was his heavy breathing as his eyes searched my face. They were still red, and for a second I thought to look at his fangs, but knew this was most likely not the time for my obsession with fangs.

"Victor." Troy came over. "She did well. She outranks Bronx, so if she said she was going… he did as he should have and aided her." He looked down at my hand and I realized I still held the knife.

Daxx came over, looking exhilarated. "When I got in there to dispatch bozo the clown, she'd flung that blade of hers into his leg. It was the stall I needed to zap him." She stepped over and looked up at the red-eyed justice. "She saved us all by distracting that guy from giving them a heads up too." She patted his chest so he'd look down at her. "She did damn good tonight."

With a shaking hand, I knelt down and put the knife back in the sheath on my leg. Later, I would stop to think how I had done that without feeling sick. I stood slowly and stepped into Victor's personal space, as Daxx called it. "Don't be mad at Bronx. He knew I was going, whether he did or not." I looked behind at the big man. "And he would have fallen off the beams."

Bronx snorted. "I would have puked, I hate heights."

I grinned and nodded, then looked back to Victor. "I'm okay."

With a loud sigh, he grasped the back of my head and pulled me against his blood covered chest and hugged me.

"I don't know about you all, but I have evil slobber on me I need to wash off. Can we go back now?" Daxx said, still sounding very happy.

"Oh." I held out my arm with my transporter on it and flipped the cover open. "Can I push it now?" I asked looking up at Victor. His lips twitched but gave me a little nod.

Chapter Fifteen

After washing and changing, I needed some quiet, so I went to my tower. It was still odd to think I had a tower. The others were busy doing whatever it was they all did, and I had to find some silence to sort through all the thoughts in my head.

I glanced from the lights of the night realm down to my pack and realized I hadn't once missed it when we'd gone to free the captives. I would have to think about that when my mind wasn't full of too much else to sort out.

My phone dinged, so I pulled it out of my pocket to see Daxx was calling me. I hoped nothing new was wrong.

"Hello?"

"Hey, Crissy. The guys are doing their interrogations with the new prisoners, so I thought us girls could hang for a while."

I liked that idea. At least I knew what hang meant, Daxx had explained it to me once when I asked her how we did that, and from where. "Okay." I answered, remembering she would be waiting for me to answer.

"So, you're not in your room or the kitchen… where are you?"

"Oh." I forgot she couldn't just see me. "In my tower."

She chuckled. "Alright, Rapunzel, where is your tower?"

I almost corrected her and then remembered a fairy tale story I had once seen. It was funny to call me that. "Um, you know the tunnels that go past the library?" I focused trying to find the easiest way to explain.

"Yep, I'm heading that way. Where do I turn off?"

I shook my head. "You don't. Go right to the very end then up the ladder. That's where my tower is."

"Okay, see you in a couple."

I wasn't sure what a couple meant, but didn't get to ask because she hung up. I unbolted the door and opened it, looking down to the floor of the tunnel. A few minutes later, I watched Daxx climb up. When she was on the floor of the tower, I closed the little door again and bolted it.

Daxx moved around and looked out in every direction. "Damn. Victor *is* the man to get you a great place like this."

I frowned of course Victor was a man. "He knows I need the quiet to settle my flashes and sort through them."

She nodded and looked out to the town. "I use the gym, but I can see how this would be a great spot." She grinned at me. "I do believe our justice is very smitten with you." She winked at me.

I knew what smitten meant, and thought that was a nice way to say it. "I am very smitten with him too." I nodded. "I guess I have to be, to be his mate."

She snorted. "It helps, yes." Standing there, she looked me up and down a few times. "How are you doing?" She waved her hand behind her. "After all the action tonight."

I bit my lip and sat down on my cushion. "I still can't believe I threw the knife at that man." I watched her lean back against the short wall and squat down. "But I just had to free those people." I shook my head. "It wasn't right to hold them there."

She sighed. "I know. You did so good though." She smiled at me. "I'm proud of you."

"Oh." I wasn't sure anyone had ever been proud of me before, and couldn't find the words to tell her how much it meant that she had.

"You are handling all of this giant-man-alternate-realm stuff so much better than I did." She chuckled. "I still can't believe it's all real sometimes."

I blinked and looked at her. "Why wouldn't it be real?"

Shaking her head, she sighed again. "I forget you've been

seeing it for a long time. I had no clue any of it existed until Wanda sent me here unannounced."

I remembered the flashes I'd seen before all of that had happened. "I guess it was a surprise for you."

Daxx snorted. "Surprise is an understatement, but yeah it was." Her face grew serious as she studied me. "How are you and Victor?" I saw her eyes go to my arm and realized she was thinking of the mating tattoo.

I ran my hand down my arm and looked at it, wondering what it would look like with a tattoo. I once thought I wanted one, until I found out they used needles to mark the skin. After that, I knew the only way I could change my appearance, without pain and terror, was to dye my hair. I stopped, remembering she was waiting for an answer. "He doesn't trust himself with me alone." I bit my lip. "I told him I know about sex and it's okay…"

She made a strange sound, I didn't understand. "You told him that?" She giggled in a way I'd never heard. "I should have tried being straight forward like that. Instead of walking around…" She waved a hand at me, "Sorry. You were saying?"

"I don't know why he won't." I searched her face to see if she understood. "I said it was okay and he is tempted but won't." I shook my head. "I don't understand. I wanted him to feed from me too…" I looked own at my hands, thinking. "I wanted to do that for him," I shrugged and then smirked, "and was quite curious about it too, I admit. I like fangs." I shook my head. "But he won't do that either." I sighed loudly and looked up at the small roof covering my tower. "I have thought about what it must be like to live so long." I waved my hands around feeling the excitement of it. "To see and experience so much, many years beyond my understanding." I looked back at her. "I can't even feel what it would be like." I tapped my head. "In here. It's amazing and more than fascinating…" I frowned. "I don't even know the words to explain it."

She nodded. "I get what you mean. It is something though, to know a hundred years from now you'll still be the same as you are now."

"Yes. Exactly." I told her. I bit my lip and looked down to

pick at the material on the cushion. "I don't know if I can, Daxx." I flicked my eyes to hers then looked away just as fast. "Live that long." I said softly. "In my mind, so busy without end…" I shook my head and took a short breath, feeling my emotions crushing me. "I don't know if I can do it that long." I felt a tear in my eye, but left it to fall. "I couldn't sleep, the excitement and nerves, knowing of the battle to be," I nodded so she knew, "the one we did to free the scared eyes." I took a deep breath and it shook with the release. "So, I read," I smiled briefly when I remembered the look on Bronx's face when I said I was taking all the books I had selected, 'to pass the time.' I bit my lip and felt another tear fall. "I read of others, those that are like me." I still couldn't believe that was true. "Seers." I nodded and looked at her. "I am a seer. That is my skill." I puffed out my cheeks and blew out a breath to control the emotions. "Even about those who learned to control the things forced in their head," I paused to look at her again, her blue eyes hadn't strayed. Daxx always listened. "After some time, many years, they all ended the same." I tapped my head with my finger. "The flashes… the visions won in the end and the seer did not." I nodded. "So many I read about that became void, no longer meant for society…" I sniffed, not liking that tears still fell, "that's what the books said."

I stood up, not able to sit still for a second more. "How can I be a mate for Victor?" I touched my arm, "and take his mark if I'm to be like that." I nodded and looked at her through watery eyes. "To live that many years just…" I paused to find the word, "assures I will end up that way and leave him with a mate that speaks and moves no more."

She jumped up and hugged me tight. I felt more tears fall. I didn't understand all of it, but I hadn't ever felt this kind of pain before. I felt like I lost something I didn't even have.

My face was wet when she released me, hers was too, as her blue eyes searched mine. "You have to tell him." She tried to smile, but it didn't work that way. "Explain it like you just did to me." She nodded. "Maybe there's a way." She stepped back and hugged her arms around her. "They've lived for freakin' ever, Crissy, there *has* to be a way." Her voice shook as she spoke.

I inhaled sharply and wiped my hand over my face, trying to remove the tears, then nodded. She was right. They had been around since any world knew, they would know something. "I will tell him." I took another deep breath, feeling better not still. "When other things are resolved and he has the time…"

"No." She spun back to me and grabbed my hands. "Now. Nothing is more important to him, or to me, than you."

I looked down at her hands and remembered when I looked at my gloves. "I will need more gloves." I told her. I saw the confusion in her eyes. "I read to get the mark the flesh of palms must join." I felt my cheeks heat. "And other things." I pulled my one hand free and held it open in front of her face. "If my palm flesh is covered it can't happen."

She looked at my hand, a strange look in her eyes. "I should have looked for the instruction manual." She snorted and then nodded, giving me that look she did when she made a promise I knew she would keep. "I will get you a pair of gloves in every color of the rainbow if you need them."

I smiled, she always knew what to say to put me at ease. "I would like more colors."

Releasing my other hand, she nodded. "Call Victor, talk to him."

I looked around. "Yes. But not here." I thought of the big room they called mine and shook my head. "I need to take him to my quiet safe spot, where we are from."

"You have a safe spot there?"

I nodded. "Yes." I bit my lip. "He's not going to like it though.

Daxx laughed. "He'd climb Mount Everest for you."

I wasn't sure where that was, but if she said it then it must be so. "I will get him to take me back, so we can go there to talk."

She hugged me quickly. "I need to go cry on my mates' shoulder."

I gave her a startled look. "Are you okay?"

Her mouth formed a soft smile and she nodded. "I will be."

After she left I went back to my bedroom and paced. I had

my pack on the bed, ready and waiting. Looking at my phone, I wondered why my stomach felt so nervous to talk to Victor, but I did it anyway.

"Cristy."

"Hi." I looked around the room.

"Is everything alright?" He sounded concerned.

I nodded. "I'm…" I remembered not to say okay. "fine. Are you very busy?"

There was a pause and a door. "No. I'm done in the cells for the night. I was just going to…" he cleared his throat.

I knew he didn't want to say something. "Feed?" I asked quietly.

"Yes. It was a draining night. Then I was going to come and see you."

I smiled. "I would like that. I want to talk."

He sighed. "I was worried everything tonight would be too much for you…"

"No." I shook my head. "It's not that. Well, okay, I don't think I could do *that* every night, but I'm okay. With that." I added.

"If you are certain."

I heard another door close and almost asked where he was going and then I heard the whooshing sound the doors made in the cells. Maybe he was just leaving there now. "I am certain." I took a deep breath. "I will wait at… my room for you."

"I won't be long." He answered and then hung up.

I probably had walked around the room a hundred times in the period it took for him to knock on the door and come in. "Hi." I said and looked at the space around him. The man of justice was gone and Victor, the sweet one was back.

He smiled and noted I was wearing a jacket. His eyes went to my pack. "What did you wish to talk about?" With long strides he came over and leaned down to kiss me on the forehead.

I smiled and then bit my lip. "I'd like to talk somewhere else."

Searching my face for a moment he nodded once. "We

could go up in the tower."

I shook my head and played with the material of his shirt. "I'd like to go to the place I go for quiet… where I live."

The muscle in his jaw jumped a few times, the way it did when he thought something through. "We can do that."

I looked up to see if he looked tired. "Are you very tired after fighting? Too tired to climb?"

Smirking, he shook his head. "I can climb." He tilted my chin up with a finger. "What am I climbing on?"

I wasn't sure what difference that made. "Fire escape." He nodded and released me to look at my arm.

"Where is your transporter?"

I looked at my wrist. "In the bathroom."

He turned and walked that way. "I want you to always wear it when you… cross over to there. So we don't have to go searching, if you find yourself in trouble again."

I thought that was very sweet of him. I held out my arm when he walked out with it in his hand.

He secured it to my wrist and then reached down and lifted the edge of my jacket to be sure I had the belt and little box on. With a nod, he leaned down and picked up my pack and held it out to me. "Where am I taking us?"

I thought for a moment and then told him of a place that would be the closest he would know. "The street by Daxx's."

We reached the roof with the little stoop that I lived under. Out of everywhere I went, here always felt most right, so in my mind I lived here. Ten stories in the air, closer to the sky than the streets below.

"Only I would be fated a mate that is an adrenalin junkie." Victor mumbled as he stepped onto the top of the building.

I looked up at him. "I'm not a junkie." I frowned.

He smirked. "I didn't mean a drug addict, heart, I meant someone that likes danger." He looked back down the stairs and ladders we had just climbed.

My eyes went wide. "I don't like danger. I hide from it."

Chuckling, he touched the side of my face and then moved to walk around the roof and look under the small stoop. "You may think you hide from it." He glanced back to me. "But the fact remains, you run straight for it, without regard for your own safety." He went and looked over the city for a moment. "I can see why you like it here." He sighed. "It makes my tower gift to you seem…" he waved a hand down over the view, "lacking."

I went over and touched his arm so he would look down at me. "I love my tower." I told him.

Smiling, he put his arm around me and pulled me against his side. "That pleases me more than you know."

I wasn't sure what he meant by that, but we were both happy, so that was good. "I showed Daxx my tower tonight." I thought for a moment. "While you guys were doing your interrogation thing." I still didn't know what that was.

He snorted. "Daxx's words?"

I nodded, he was so smart. "She called me Rapunzel too."

Victor looked at me a big smile on his face and then he looked at my hair. "Her way of speaking at times is…" he made a motion with his hand. "unrefined."

I laughed. "Only to you."

Nodding slowly, he hugged me tighter. "Yes, I'm aware." He smiled and then kissed my forehead again. "I seem to be stuck in one era of language and have never quite moved beyond it. Or so I'm told."

I put my cheek against his chest and listened to his heartbeat. "I may not always understand what you say, but I like it."

"That is all that matters to me. Now." Grasping my shoulders, he leaned back and his eyes searched my face for a long time. "What is so difficult to say that you needed to bring me to the place you are the most comfortable in?"

I bit my lip, not even knowing that was why I did it. He was so smart. I took a deep breath and stepped away, I had to move to keep my thoughts clear and focused. "It was so easy to explain to Daxx," I walked a few feet the other way then stopped. "Or she just understands me, maybe." I looked to see he hadn't moved, and knew he wasn't going to follow me as I paced around the roof. "I read many things in those books… from the library." I looked down to see the streets were quiet and then to the sky. The sun would be up soon. "I was quite excited when I read some of it." I turned on the heel of my boot fast and nodded. "I know I am a seer now. That's what the one book told me."

Walking the other way a few feet, I watched him. He made no motion to interrupt my thoughts. I liked that about him, he knew the smallest thing would set my mind in another direction. "I am looking for the words." I told him.

"I know, heart." He whispered in reply.

I don't know why he called me that sometimes, but I liked it. Some of the others called me nice names too. I'd never had a nickname before, well not nice ones. With a quick nod, I moved again. "I read things, sad things." I said quietly, and they were. "Seers minds working, working, see so much." I stopped and looked down at the surface under my boots. "It's very difficult, as you understand, to sort it and focus through it…" I took a deep breath, not understanding why this was so hard when it had been easy with Daxx. My heart felt like it was aching. I looked over at him, standing there just watching me, not judging, just watching. "Seers…" I cleared my throat because it felt tighter, "they can't do it endlessly." I nodded. "And your kind would know as they live many lives longer than others." He took one step then stopped and continued to look at me. Was he sensing how the emotions were filling me? "I read of their fate. Many of them, not just one or two." I told him so he would know, I looked so I would know. "A mind…" I tapped my head with the tips of my fingers. "like mine." I shook my head, "it's not made to see forever without pause." Letting out a too loud shaky breath, I moved quickly in the other direction and then stopped just as suddenly. "After…" I frowned, trying to say it and not feel it, "years and years their minds break. The visions win." I finished quietly. I heard his boots on the rough surface, but couldn't turn to look at him. When he would have touched me, I paced away. "I can not…" my eyes blurred with tears, "I can not take your mark and then leave you with a mate that does not speak or move." I shook my head, angry with the tears and emotions winning when I needed him to know. "That is a burden no one should have to see." I took a shaky breath, afraid to turn and see the hurt on his face that I would have caused.

Gentle hands grasped my shoulders and turned me to face him. I looked up through the tears to see pain in his eyes and more tears rolled down my cheeks. "I'm sorry."

With his thumb, he brushed a tear off my skin. "Are you certain?" He took a deep, ragged breath. "Of what you read? That a way hasn't been found?"

I blinked, more tears falling. "I read all there was on it." I touched the side of my head. "I always remember what I see. In and out of my head."

He nodded. "I know, heart." He pulled me tightly against his chest and held me. I cried more, I couldn't stop it. "You are breaking me," he said softly into my hair. "I will find a way. If I have to have the kings order every inhabitant to search, our realm and all others. I will find a way." His hand stroked down my back in a gentle touch. "Our members of science will be ordered to cease all other studies to find a way to help you."

I wanted to believe it would happen, but even for one that always told the truth, sometimes things just couldn't be. I wanted to tell him he couldn't order his entire world to do this for me, but I knew he found some comfort in this, so I left it. I looked up to see his red eyes looking back at me. "You understand why I can't..." I swallowed the lump that appeared in my throat, "why it isn't right to take your mark."

A tear rolled down his handsome cheek and I thought my heart might shatter. "I do not." He said with so much emotion I don't know how he spoke. "But it must be your choice to accept freely. A decision I can not sway, despite my heart paining inside my chest." He kissed my forehead and I could feel even his lips shaking.

We continued to stand there, our arms around each other as the sun brightened the sky. I felt so much and yet so little at the same time. A void grew inside me and I didn't understand it. I listened to his heart beating for a moment more and then moved a step back. He looked so tired now, and I remembered it was well past his night time now. "You should go rest, Victor." I told him quietly. "There is much still to do." I nodded and backed up another step. "I will continue looking for your brother." I looked down at my hands and saw my gloves, but knew now was not the time to mention why I wore them. "And find his children, and theirs from there." I took a deep breath and then let it out to find I might live through this pain. "We have to find Marcus, I will search my flashes for signs of him." Yes, there was much to do. I looked up at him to see him studying me, the pain still in his eyes.

He finally nodded slowly and held out his hand. "We'll go rest." I looked at the large hand for a moment and then he lowered it. "You are not coming back with me?"

I tried to smile, I don't know if I did or not. "I will be back in a while." I looked around at the early morning light. "I need some quiet right now."

He put his hands in his pockets and looked down at the surface we stood on. "For more than four hundred years I have simply had to tell someone to do something and it was done." He raised his eyes, filled with emotion, to look at me. "I find myself in unchartered territory presently." I watched the nerve in his jaw twitch. "Please, return to me soon..." he came over and tucked the hair behind my ear, "and unscathed." I frowned. "Safely." He told me.

I nodded. "I will." Stretching up onto my toes I kissed his mouth softly. "Go rest, a tired justice would be bad for his people."

He smiled, but it didn't reach his eyes. "The justice without his seer of truth will be far more dangerous for the people." Leaning down, he kissed my lips softly and held my chin staring into my eyes for several breaths.

When he released my chin, he was gone from my sight. I wrapped my arms around my waist in a self-hug and looked out over the city. Going to pick up my pack, I went and sat under the small roof I had slept under many times. I was trying to find something to think, something to see. The one time I needed the flashes to appear and distract me, they would not. A tear rolled down my cheek as I stared, but didn't see a thing in front of my eyes.

Chapter Sixteen

It had been three weeks since I talked to Victor on the roof. When I'd gotten back to the room all the books were gone except the book with leaves on it. I still had not read it. He said we would together, yet if we were never together, how could we? He told me the next day it changed nothing, what I had told him, but it had. I saw him less. He would call or text, but there were no more moments alone.

I worked on tracking Emil. Which was annoying, as Daxx had put it, because neither of us were allowed on the other side alone, and we needed the internet from that side to track Emil. Daxx and I spent many evenings in cafes with Wi-Fi and guards in the last few weeks.

Rafael still went to the club to watch for Emil, but hadn't seen him. A few days ago, visits to my side were canceled completely. Raf had heard that everyone was looking for a petite woman with bright red hair.

They were still checking for Alona's mark on the wall, but there had been no x so far. I hoped the man with the yellow eyes didn't get her, but had no flashes to give me a hint either way.

Since my talk with Victor, I had coaches I spent hours with each day… night. One was a seer and one was a telepath. They were trying to help me find a way to control the flashes. The seer was truly shocked at the amount I saw. I wondered a few times if she saw at all, but didn't want to be rude and ask. The telepath was trying to help me learn to focus. So far, that wasn't going well either.

I spent every free second I had in two places, my tower and the practice room. Daxx sat with me in the tower sometimes, we didn't talk, just sat there.

I discovered the benefits of the practice room were many. I had so much emotion and energy to burn from being restricted that I enjoyed being physical. Everyone took turns working with me, all depending on who had time. I could tell Daxx had shared with all of them what I'd told Victor, and they were being very nice and understanding to me.

I didn't go to family practice after breakfast, I told everyone that was my mind practice time, when I sat in my tower, trying to perfect the latest techniques. We'd had so many failures, that resulted in headaches, feeling ill or me being to frustrated to continue. Soothing music worked for a day or two, but I had to have ear phones in all the time, and would get startled too often, undoing all the good the music did.

Victor would come and watch while I was with my coaches, to encourage me and tell them to keep looking, there had to be a way.

I was siting in my tower now. Not practicing my focus, not working on finding Emil, and not being happy.

My phone beeped, I saw a message from Daxx.

Want company? I'm tired of testosterone.

I sent back, *yes please.*

She must have been messaging from the ladder to the tower, because when I opened the little hatch, she was there.

Sitting down, she looked at me for a moment. "How are you doing?"

I thought of the right words to explain to her but all I said was, "I'm not."

"I know." She nodded and looked around, even though we were both sitting and there was nothing but block walls to see. "I'm going crazy under this house arrest. I haven't been allowed to hunt in Alterealm for a few week now."

"So, what do we do?" I asked her because I had no ideas, but Daxx always did. "I haven't had any flashes that would tell me where to look for those watching me." I shrugged. "I think it's because I haven't gone back there." I played with the glove on my hand. Today they were pink. Then I realized I didn't need the pink gloves if I didn't see Victor. "We don't know where Marcus is either." I blurted out so I wouldn't think of Victor. "I can't find Emil. I know Quinton tries to get me the lists I need, but I don't know which I need, I only know when I see them. If I'm not there I can't see them."

Daxx nodded, she looked tired. "I may have some good news." She told me.

"All the guys… except Victor and Troy agree we should try to stir things up."

I leaned forward. "What things?"

She shrugged and then smiled. "Like go be seen on our side, and see if we can flush out whoever is looking for us."

I bit my lip, thinking about this idea.

"I know it would mean putting you front and center, and possibly in a fight again, but it won't work if you and your hair aren't there."

I looked at her and nodded. "I understand." I wasn't sure I wanted to see another battle again, but for the last several days I hadn't seen anything with my own eyes. "I think I can do it." I sighed loudly, "it is better than doing nothing, and maybe we can go to the other side again."

"Exactly." She huffed out a breath. "Getting Victor and Troy to agree isn't going to be easy."

I nodded, head knowing that it was true.

"Have to you talked to Victor?"

I held up the phone sitting on my cushion. "He calls or messages me. I see him when we eat or when I am with my coaches."

"Really?" She leaned forward onto her knees. "Men are so stupid."

"He was very upset when I told him I couldn't wear his mark." I nodded.

"I know, but he could still spend time with you." She snorted. "Between his bouts of rampaging at least."

"Rampaging?" I didn't understand.

Daxx nodded. "He's in full battle gear more than he isn't lately. Mister Justice twenty-four hours a day." She rolled her eyes.

"Oh." I didn't know what else to say.

"He's just being a man. It's what they do when there is a problem, turn into Neanderthals." She got up and smiled at me. "If we can get all of us in a room, Victor included, do you think you can sit through it?"

"What do you mean? I have been getting better at not wandering while talking." I grinned. "Although every muscle in my body hurting from practicing so much may be the reason."

She laughed. "I understand that. I have an idea, to help convince Victor, but you need to sit in one place and looked bored."

"I am bored."

She gave me a thumb up. "Perfect. Come on let's go see if Raf and Quinton figured out how to get him to stand still long enough."

I stood up and grabbed my pack. "Have Mitz ask them."

"What?" She opened the hatch.

"Have Mitz ask Victor and Troy to be somewhere and then everyone else will be there too." I picked up my pack.

"Oh. You are so smart." She pulled out her phone and typed.

Mitz must have called them all, because when Daxx and I walked into the dining room a short while later all eight brothers stood there. Well, Chase was sitting and looked like someone had dragged him out of bed, but he was still there.

Victor was, as Daxx had told me, in full battle gear, dark and very much the man of justice right now.

"Oh, good, you're all here." Mitz said as she came in the room. She set a large pot of coffee on the table beside the cups already there. Stopping, she clasped her hands and looked around at the men. "Give me a moment, will you. I have some things in the oven to check." She gave Daxx an odd look and then walked out again.

Daxx looked at the chair beside me, then back to me, and

once more to the chair. I remembered she wanted me to sit while we were here. I sat down quickly.

"Do you want a tea, Crissy?" She asked.

I nodded. "Yes, thank you."

"I'll ask Mitz to get that." She said and started toward the kitchen.

"Can you ask her if she has any of those scones left?" Rafael asked.

Daxx nodded.

"I wouldn't say no to that pie from last night, if there's any left." Chase said with a yawn. "Since I'm up now."

"Why are you up?" Troy asked as he stood there with his arms crossed.

Chase lifted his hands in the air and then dropped them onto the table. "I'm guessing I got the same call as the rest of you."

"Does anyone know what this is pertaining to, exactly?" Victor asked, crossing his arms over his chest.

Daxx looked at him for a moment before turning to walk into the kitchen.

"Do you wear the same clothes all the time now?" Chase asked him.

Victor looked down at what he was wearing and then back to his brother. "If you must know, I have several similar outfits."

"All black and brooding no doubt," Chase snorted. "Haven't see you dress like that this often since the last uprising a few hundred years ago."

"I'm certain my choice of wardrobe isn't the reason we were called here." He glanced to the kitchen making it clear he wanted to be somewhere else.

Daxx came out with a cup in her hand, she held it to Victor. "Take this to Crissy while I grab the other things."

He looked at the cup and then took it with a quick nod, walking toward me.

I was going to get up and meet him to take it, and then remembered Daxx wanted me to sit while we were here. Victor set it in front of me. I smiled and looked up at him. "Thank you."

He inclined his head as his eyes searched my face.

I almost breathed a loud sigh of relief to see he still looked at me with that soft look. It was hard to tell when he was always looking at his plate, or to others, when I'd seen him lately.

"How are you?" He asked quietly.

"I'm okay." I told him. "Or as okay as I can be."

His brows drew together. "Things aren't going well with the coaching?"

I shook my head. "No. We're going to try something different tomorrow." I shrugged. "Maybe that will be the one that works."

He crossed his arms over his big chest. "I have the scholars searching still, they are encouraged that they will find something."

I watched his face as he talked. I missed seeing his face, and his mouth. I missed his eyes, too. Green or red, I didn't care. Oh, and his fangs, I missed his fangs well. I realized he was just standing there watching me. I had forgotten to answer again. "I hope they do." He continued to stand there and look down at me, and I would have been happy to do that all day.

"Ok, lets get the negotiations started." Daxx said loudly.

I watched her slide a plate with pie on it across the table to Chase, and then look to her mate.

Troy raised an eyebrow at her and glanced around at his brothers. "If they're all in on it, I have a feeling this is going to be more of an argument then negotiation."

"In on what?" Victor demanded.

"Ah," Troy nodded and crossed his arms and looked at Daxx. "If Victor and I are the only two not aware, then I know it involves you ladies."

Frowning, Victor looked down at me, and then back to Daxx. "Absolutely not." He nodded his head once. "Now, if you'll excuse me, I have somewhere to be."

He turned to leave and I started to get up and Daxx shook her head at me. So, I didn't.

"Victor. Hear us out." Michael called after him.

He stopped in the doorway and heaved a deep sigh before

turning around and walking back in. With a brief look at me, he walked to the other end of the table and sat down. I wondered how he moved so smoothly with all those weapons on his body, but figured he'd had years to practice sitting down.

He motioned to the table. "You may as well all sit, at least make an attempt to keep this civilized."

"Says the barbarian in battle gear." Chase mumbled with a mouthful of pie.

Chairs scraped back and everyone sat down.

"Oh," Mitz came in. "Good then." She nodded.

Victor turned to look at her for a moment. "We'll discuss your part in this trickery later." His tone wasn't as hard as it had been with his brothers.

Mitz smiled and touched the side of his face for no more than a second. "You can discuss it to your heart's content, love, and I may listen." She chuckled and walked back into the kitchen.

I knew it before, but had never seen it with my own eyes to really know, but now I did. Mitz had always been here for them, and cared for them through the years. I must remember to ask her how old she is.

When he looked back from watching her leave he waved his hand again. "Get on with it."

"We... well, the girls... ladies..." Rafael shook his head. "Daxx and Crissy..." he paused and frowned.

"Eloquently put, Raf, that's good." Leone glared at him. "Stop talking."

Rafael leaned back in his chair and crossed his arms. "You explain it then." He told him.

Leone looked to Victor and then Troy, and then shook his head. "I'm just here for backup."

I loved to watch the way they were with each other. Mitz had explained it was banter, or ribbing each other, and it was just how families were, even though they loved each other, they talked like they didn't.

"Good job, brothers." Chase said and took another bite.

Quinton grinned, then shook his head, he looked straight at Troy. "Its not right to confine the girls here. Daxx has a job to do, and she can't do it if she's wandering the halls here."

Daxx nodded and leaned forward on the table. "I almost have the carpet patterns memorized."

I wondered why she'd memorize the carpets and then realized she was being sarcastic, another thing Mitz had explained to me.

"That can't be helped," Troy told him. "Her safety is more important than hunting down offenders."

"I agree," Quinton nodded. "But... if we... or they..." He looked to Michael for a moment.

"You guys are terrible at this." Daxx snorted. "Please don't ever try to win an argument for me." She turned and looked at Troy. "It's bullshit keeping me under house arrest." She pointed to me and then glared at Victor, "And Criss is like a wilting flower, not being able to roam," She waved her hand around. "Look at her, she's been still this whole time." She slapped her hand on the table, "You may not realize it, but constant moving is her thing."

Victor's eyes moved to study me, I couldn't tell what he was thinking this far away, but the muscle in his jaw was twitching. "I am well aware that she needs space to move, but it cannot be helped at this time." He glanced briefly at Troy and then to Daxx. "We have no way of knowing who is looking for either of you ladies, and your..."

"Safety is of the utmost importance, yeah, yeah we know." Daxx finished for him.

Arius, who sat there without moving, finally sat forward. "What if we could find out who was looking for them?"

Troy's eyebrows furrowed together. "How?"

Victor held his brother's stare. "What do you have in mind, Arius?"

"Setting a trap." Leone blurted out.

"I'm listening," Victor said in a low voice.

Rafael nodded. "We need to draw them out, we'd have to find a place that would work..."

Victor held up his hand and Rafael stopped talking. It was amazing how that worked every time. If I did it, no one would even notice. I looked at my hand and opened it, maybe it was because his were so big.

"If you are taking this where I think you are, forget it. I won't allow…"

"Allow?" Daxx stood up.

"Oh shit, now you've done it." Chase pushed his plate away and shook his head at his eldest brother. "One word in the entire English dictionary that sets her off and you, with all your vast knowledge of languages have to choose *that* one."

"Are you finished?" Daxx stood there with her hands on her hips giving Chase an odd look.

He waved his hand motioning to the table. "The floor is yours, proceed."

Taking a deep breath, Daxx turned and looked back to Victor. "It's not up to you." She glanced to her mate. "Or you. I know you want to keep us girls all safe in a bubble, protected and polished, but you can't."

She lost me right after safe. I took a sip of my tea and tried to figure out what bubble she was talking about.

Daxx looked down at me, and gave a nod. "We want to…"

"Are you talking about using yourselves as bait?" Troy asked not letting her finish.

"Great job, Sherlock." Chase said with a sigh. "Nothing wrong with your detective skills at all."

Troy scowled at his brother and then looked at his mate. "Not happening."

Daxx glared at him. "Seriously, with the eight of you and the guards all watching over us, you're worried?" She shrugged. "*I'm* not worried. I'm tired of feeling like I'm a prisoner here and looking forward to kicking the asses responsible." She sat back down looking very upset.

I looked to see everyone was watching Victor as they usually did for the last say and decision. He did not look pleased to be the eldest today. He rubbed a hand over his face and moved it to reveal his eyes on me. "You've agreed to this? To be out in public, being watched to *draw* them out?"

I let go of my cup and pulled my hands into my lap, gripping them together. I looked to Daxx, not sure if I was supposed to be sitting, but I really wanted to get up and move.

It would help, it always did.

"Cristy." Victor said in a softer way.

I jolted and looked back to him. "I am trying, Victor, I really am." I drew my knees up to my chest, hoping that was okay, I didn't get up and wander, so it should be. "With the coaching, and more coaching, one way, then another," I opened my hands and stared at them, "until my head aches and the flashes are then scrambled…" I squeezed my hands shut and remembered to look at him. To answer. "I need to climb, to get high and settle them down," I nodded. "I need to move to sort through them. I love my tower and the ropes too, but they're so closed in, I can't climb as far when there's a lid in the way." I inhaled a big breath. "If feeling the eyes all over me is the only way I can have that space, that silence again…" I nodded. "Then yes, I have agreed."

I stopped and looked to see everyone looking at me. Most of the eyes looked sad, and I paused to think what I had done to cause that. I nodded and glanced around. "I'm okay." I told them, so they would feel better.

Victor cleared his throat. "You should have told me."

I quickly looked back to him. "I… you are so busy." I hugged my knees.

"Not *that* busy, that you couldn't have come to me." He told me and now he too looked upset.

"Yes, and you're so approachable lately, brother, it's silly she didn't try." Chase said with heavy sarcasm.

Victor stood slowly and I watched all his brothers tense.

"Get the maps and we'll find a suitable location to set this *trap*." He gave an abrupt nod and then walked quickly down the table in my direction. He stopped beside me and held out his hand. "Could I have a word with you, please?"

I frowned, not sure what word he meant, but put my hand in his and stood up. Everyone else got up and started talking again. Daxx went to the kitchen and Michael and Leone walked quickly out the other door.

Victor led me out into the hall and then stopped and just stood there holding my hand. His green eyes had so many emotions going through them I wasn't sure what he was thinking.

"I am sorry that I haven't taken the time to properly check on your well-being." His thumb rubbed over the hand he still held. "I have been having a difficult time lately… uncertain how to proceed…"

I nodded. "It's okay. Daxx explained to me that you are just being a man." I smiled. "And when there is a problem you turn into Neanderthals." I frowned. "I'm not sure what an archaic man, I've read about those… has to do with it, but she seemed to think it was normal."

His lips twitched and he smirked. "While I'm sure Daxx's explanation is colorful, if not derogatory in many ways, I still deeply regret my behavior."

I smiled up at him, I loved when he talked all stuffy. I wasn't even sure why he was apologizing, but I liked to listen to him.

"Victor." Arius called from in the dining room.

"Just a moment." He answered.

I knew that meant our word time was over. He started to straighten, I reached up quickly to touch his cheek so he wouldn't leave me yet. I stretched up on my toes and kissed his mouth, then stayed there for a few seconds to look into his eyes.

He leaned down further and kissed me back softly. "We will figure this out, my heart, I promise, it will be so." Kissing my forehead quickly he turned and went back into the dining room.

I stood there for a moment and just looked down at the carpet. It was an interesting design, I thought, maybe that's why Daxx was memorizing them.

"Well, at least I think he gets the picture now." Daxx said.

I turned to see her leaning against the doorframe. I wasn't sure which picture she meant. "He deeply regrets his behavior." I told her.

She snorted. "They always do. Come on let's go have our say in this planning."

"I don't know anything about planning a trap." I told her, following her back in.

"No, but you know how to hide and where the best places

are for you to see in the city." She grinned at me.
    I smiled. "Oh. Yes, those I do know very well."

Chapter Seventeen

Daxx stopped to kneel down, adjusting her shoelace, she said. There wasn't anything wrong with her laces that I could see. She wore her tall flat boots and the laces in them were fake.

While she fixed her fake laces, I turned around to see where the others were. We were on the street and it wasn't quite dark, which is how they planned it, so my red hair was clear to see. I wondered more than once, since making plans the day before, if I might want to try a new hair color soon.

I didn't know where Chase, Arius, and Leone were, somewhere up high so they could watch for any watching us, I was told. Tim and Bronx were hidden as well, their size and appearance would draw too much attention. I had to agree, they looked like pirates from that movie, and we didn't have many pirates on the streets.

In front of Daxx and I was Rafael, Michael, and Quinton keeping watch. That left Victor and Troy to stay with us, but at a distance, or so they were ordered by Daxx. The witches did another fascinating thing, and I was told no one could see them as they were, to everyone else would see normal people dressed in street clothes. I looked again to Victor's large form and wondered how they had hidden the weapons hanging off his body from other's eyes. I also wondered what he'd look like in street clothes. I don't think Victor would dress as the people in this area would, to be honest. I may have to read a book on how the witches did the casting sometime to find out what all it was they could do. It was quite amazing.

"Getting anything?" She asked me as she stood up again.

There was motion from down the street, a gang was gathering. I looked to see if we should run, but Daxx started walking towards it, so despite being scared, I followed.

"Crap," she said glancing back to Troy, "the boys might be cloaked to look the same, but large male strangers hanging out in their turf… this might get ugly."

For once I understood her strange way of explaining things. Turf wars, I had seen and avoided my entire life. I walked faster, hoping it didn't end with blood. It most often did. I knew the gangs around these streets, and some of them weren't as bad as they wanted others to believe they were.

When we reached the crowd, I saw Rafael and his two brothers, they all had that look on their faces. The look that told me if the group hovering near them got any closer, there would be blood on the streets, and it wouldn't be theirs. I looked to Daxx and held up my hand, the way Victor always did and then pushed my way through the crowd. I knew many of the faces here, and they watched *me* with looks I knew all too well. Jumping in front of the one I knew was the leader, I looked at Quinton and smiled briefly and then stretched up on my toes in front of the gang leader's face.

"Don't look, don't look." I said to him and then turned to look back to Raf for a second. "You will see and once you do see you can't unsee it." I nodded my head I continued to stand there looking at the now frowning man.

A few of the people with him backed up a few steps. He looked at Rafael, Michael and Quinton for a minute more then tapped his head in a salute to me. "Got it. They're with you. Peace be with you, Crizzy."

It was what they called me. I was pretty sure it was crazy and Crissy combined, but it was better than many other things I'd been called. I smiled at him in an exaggerated way. "Be free." I told him and then turned and walked over to Quinton. My heart was racing, my stomach filled with knots, but I had managed to stop any violence from taking place.

Rafael winked at me. "Love your ways, little sister." He told me before the three moved back into the shadows.

When I turned, Daxx was standing there grinning at me and Troy just looked confused. She jerked her head toward Victor who looked, unimpressed, I think would be the best word. I exhaled loudly and tilted my head to look up at him. "Sometimes crazy is *all* that works." I turned to make certain the gang was moving on. "They're not as bad as they'd like people to believe, they just act scary and hard." I glanced back to Victor and nodded. "The way you do." With that I turned and started walking again, Daxx caught up to me.

She leaned closer to me. "We need to ditch these two or no one is going to even think about coming after us."

I looked over my shoulder to the large men in our shadow. "I thought the same." I told her quietly. "They look very intimidating."

She snorted. "Ya think?"

I nodded.

"Ok," She looked around. "Where can we go?"

I paused to look around. Watching the two following us pause and just stand there, I sighed and turned back around. "The club." I told her. "It's where Rafael heard people were looking for me."

Daxx blew out a breath. "Yeah, and they're not going to like it."

I nodded. It was true, but it didn't change where we needed to go. "Do we tell them?"

"Oh, we're going to have to try. They're almost on our heels." She said looking behind her.

We stopped just down the street from the club and stood there. I watched Raf, with a big smile on his face, come out of the shadows and go inside. He knew where I needed to be. Michael followed behind him and Quinton stopped to lean on a building near the corner.

I turned around and looked at Victor, he was watching us. "He's not going to like this."

"Just bat your eyes at him and look innocent." Daxx told me.

I frowned. "I don't know how to bat my eyes."

She grinned. "Do that thing where you bite your lip then, that'll work." She nodded and walked over to speak to Troy.

I wasn't sure what she meant, but I thought I'd try it to see if it made him less mad about what had to be done. Going over, I stopped in front of him, he looked down, his eyes searching my face looking concerned.

"Is this too much for you?" He asked.

I thought about it. "I'm okay with it." I told him and then took a short breath. "We need to go in the club," I stopped when his expression hardened again. "Rafael and Michael are inside and you know it's where they are watching for me." I bit my lip and looked up at him, watching to see if it did what Daxx said it should. His hard look softened and he glanced to my mouth before looking back at my eyes. I felt his chest rise under my hand as he took a deep breath. "There is a side door, and one in the back alley with dark halls you can hide in to watch over me." I told him.

He glanced to Troy, who had the same expression on his face. Looking back down at me, he lifted my arm to check that I had my transporter on, when he saw I did, he squeezed my hand. "You stay close to Raf or Michael."

I nodded. "I will."

We watched them walk down the alley beside the club.

"Damn, you're a natural." Daxx said and started walking toward the club.

I didn't know what she meant, but it sounded like a good thing, so I thought it was good I was a natural. Later, I would ask at what.

The club wasn't as crowded as it would be later, but it was still full enough I didn't want to be here. The music was loud and that smell lingered.

"Damn, Jorge isn't working yet, I'd hoped he would be."

I looked at Daxx. "Jorge?"

She nodded. "The bartender."

I looked to the corner I always went to when here and then realized I couldn't, because I had to be seen. Turning slowly, I thought to check for Alona and Emil. Daxx grabbed my arm and pulled me toward one of the tables in the middle of the room. She had no problems with being seen, I thought, as I debated on sitting under the table instead of standing at it.

Rafael was leaning on the bar, a drink in his hand. I looked around and saw Michael was at a table in a darker corner, just watching without an expression on his face. He was very similar to Victor in some ways, but completely different at the same time. His heart was still heavy though, from what I'd seen when his face was scarred. I knew he would be happy some day, but that was for him to discover and not me to tell.

Daxx elbowed me, "I'll be right back. We stand out too much without drinks."

With my eyes wide, I watched her walk away, leaving me in the middle of the floor alone. I knew I had to do this, if I wanted to sit on my roof again, I had to. I held my head up and took a deep breath, refusing to let myself hunch and try to be small.

I looked to the darkened hall that led to the back door I usually came in, and could see a shadow there so familiar, I felt better. Victor watched me. A hand rested on my shoulder and I froze. I watched Troy come out of the shadows and block Victor's path.

"Hey doll, I love the hair." A stranger said to me.

I turned and stepped away so his hand wasn't touching me. I wanted to run, it's what I did, but I forced my feet to stay still. I tried to smile at him, but most likely failed. He was taller than I, which was no surprise. His dark hair was messy and his face was unshaven.

"Here you go." Daxx appeared beside me and set the drink on the table. "Hey." She said to the stranger and I knew the smile on her face was fake. It was the one she gave people before she kicked their butt, I believe would be her description.

I swallowed and turned back to look at the space around the man, while she talked to him. My heart was pounding so loud, I couldn't even hear what she said. His aura was dark and uncertain, so I looked closer. He wasn't evil, like the evil I'd seen, but he wasn't kind either. There was something else and it gave me a bad feeling. I had to tell Daxx, but didn't know how to without saying it in front of him.

"Listen," the man said leaning far too close across the table, "I know a group that throws awesome parties, you two should come along."

I looked to Daxx, watching how she checked him out.

She shook her head. "No, we've got to be somewhere shortly, but thanks." She glanced at me and her expression changed.

I cleared my throat. "I'll be right back." I told her with a nod.

His arm moved out to block my way. "No, no, red, you *really* need to come with me." He glanced over my shoulder and a shiver went over my skin, as his hold on my waist tightened.

"Let go of my friend." Daxx said, in that tone that meant he didn't have a choice.

I glanced to where Raf was and he stood immediately. When the man turned, making me follow, I saw two large men walking between the tables toward us. I had never seen them before, but the space around them was very easy to see, and it wasn't good at all. I turned and Michael was almost to us.

"You should let go of my sister." Rafael was now beside me.

Daxx reached her hand out across the table and I took it quickly but the man still didn't let go.

"I have to take her, sorry, I don't have a choice." The man told Rafael.

Raf glanced over my head and gave the man an odd look. "Okay, I tried to save your life…"

"Release her." I heard Victor growl and the arm let me go.

Daxx was around the table and pulling me clear. Raf stood beside us.

I turned to see Victor holding the man by his head, it was pulled to an awkward angle. The man held up his hand, his eyes were huge.

"Sorry, I was just following orders." He told me.

I turned when I heard a crash to see Michael and Troy grabbing the other two men. I was shaking and just wanted to leave. I looked to Victor who was staring down at the man he held. "I'd like to go back now." I said hoping he'd hear me above the music.

He looked up at me, having heard, and straightened his arm with the man moving along with him. "Raf, take him out back. I can't send them to the cells in plain sight here."

Rafael grabbed the man's arm and held it behind his back and started shoving him to the back door.

Daxx released my hand and I went to Victor and hugged him. He took his little transporter box off his belt and held it to Daxx. "Send all three of them. I want to know where the friends and this *party* is. Have Troy find out."

"On it." She said then walked out the way Rafael had gone.

"We'll go in a moment, heart, I have to talk to Quinton." He whispered against my ear.

I nodded and walked with him to the door we'd come in. The whole time he spoke to Quinton, he held me to his side. We walked away as Quinton called the others to go back.

Once we were in an empty alley, Victor hugged me tight. "Hold on." He told me, so I did.

When I felt the churning in my stomach, I opened my eyes to see we were on a roof. My favorite one of all. I looked around, checking, but knew up here was always safe.

He leaned down and lifted my chin. "Are you alright?"

I nodded. "I was just scared."

His eyes searched my face. "It was stupid to go in there."

"It worked." I reminded him. "They saw me right away."

He put his hands on his hips. "They've probably been parked there these last few weeks waiting." He cursed softly and I was surprised, I'd never heard him swear. "I should have known better." He said quietly and then he looked back to me. "My judgement is clouded where you're concerned."

I raised my eyebrows, a little surprised. "I'm sorry?" I offered.

He looked at me a moment longer and then shook his head. "It is not your doing." With a soft look, he traced over my face. "It's the damn fates' fault." Shaking his head, he reached out and cupped my face in his big hands. "Nothing that happened is your fault or doing." His eyes looked at me with such care. "I have been unreachable quite frequently as of late, that is my way of… processing." He nodded, knowing I would understand that. "Know that if I thought I could resist, I would be with you without pause. Do you understand?" I nodded as best as I could with his hands holding my face. He gave me a little smile and kissed my lips lightly and then released my face and stepped back. "I am always available for you if you need me, heart, you can call me anytime."

I nodded. "Thank you."

He smirked in an odd way. "You don't need to thank me." He backed away a few more steps and then motioned to the area around us. "Stay here, find some peace for as long as you need. I have to get back." Glancing around, he sighed. "Please stay up here, out of sight, we don't know if we ended it tonight. Don't take any chances until we are certain." He motioned to my wrist. "Use your transporter when you want to return."

I looked at my wrist and nodded. "I will."

"Do you have your phone?" I nodded again. "Turn it on, I will let you know what we find out."

"Thank you, for bringing me here."

He stepped to quickly kissed my mouth, hard, and then was gone.

I looked around my favorite space and then walked over to the edge to look down at the lights. I wasn't sure what Victor needed to resist, but I felt like I needed to do more reading about Alterealm, mates and their ways... and butterflies, I decided. To see if Alterealm had any. Maybe that would help, Victor was a confusing man, to say the least.

I'm not sure how long I sat on the roof, but it was quiet. I sorted the flashes and checked for any I really needed to see. It had been weeks since I felt this peaceful, and I was glad for it. I was just sitting there looking at my gloves that I had taken off. They got quite warm after a while, when my phone buzzed beside me.

It was from Victor. *We have a location. We're going in a few moments. Are you well and safe?*

I smiled at my phone. *I am coming back soon. Did you want me to come? I can leave now. I am very well and safe. My mind is quiet.*

I am pleased. You do not need to come with us. I do not want to expose you to that again.

I felt relief, but worry at the same time. I didn't like they were all going again, but I hadn't liked it when I was there either. *I will come back now and wait for you.*

I will dispatch them quickly and hurry back with that in mind.

I smiled again. *Okay. Do it safely.*

As safe as battle can be Smiley face. *We are leaving in a moment. See you when I return.*

Okay. I stared at the screen, waiting to see if he sent anymore, but knew he wasn't going to. I had seen how he was before battle, and he needed to focus and become that cold man of justice. It was sweet, when I thought about it, that he had taken that time to message me. Standing up, I looked around again, hoping I would be able to come back here sooner next time. Opening the device, I pushed the button.

I sat on the floor in that room for an hour. They hadn't returned yet. Even Mitz had come to check on me twice now. We talked for a few minutes and then she went back to the kitchen, saying they'd want something to eat once they were back.

I stared at the middle of the empty room, Mitz said this was the landing room, all preprogrammed transporters brought travelers here, so when they left as a group, they left from here. I just wanted them to come back soon. The thought of one of them being hurt, or worse, just kept going through my mind.

I had just decided to go find a book so I wouldn't worry too much when Daxx appeared on her back in the middle of the floor. I don't know what she was covered in, but it looked a lot like mud. "Daxx, are you okay?" I got up quickly.

"Huh," she said loudly, "apparently, you land the way you were when you pushed the button." She held up her arm to show me the transporter on her wrist.

"I didn't know you used one of those." I said looking down at her. The mud on her face was drying and she was now covered in a light brown crust. Her blonde hair was not blonde right now either.

"I don't normally, but Troy slapped one on my wrist before

we left, because we were going in blind."

I frowned down at her.

"Going in without any intel on what we were getting into. I used it because…" she rolled to her side and I could see blood on her back, "focus was a little off," she said. "I didn't want to land somewhere else."

I dropped to the floor. "Oh no."

"How bad is it? How much mud is in the cut?"

I tried to see, but with the mud all it, I couldn't see where the blood was coming from.

"Mud. We had to fight in *mud*. Talk about slowing our moves down. Help me get up. I want to wash off before my man insists on licking it, dirt and all. Yuck." She shuddered.

I pulled her to her feet, which was hard to do with my hold on her slipping in the slimy film all over her. Her hair now looked like dreads, like the crews on the street.

She hissed out a breath. "Oh ya, he got a good chunk of me. Dammit."

"Where is everyone else?" I looked behind us to check the room as we walked out slowly.

"Don't worry, we were winning. It's easy for giants to maneuver in the mud." She winced with each step.

Mitz came around the corner and stopped, her eyes wide.

"I'll pay for the carpet to be cleaned." Daxx told her.

"She's hurt, Mitz."

"Oh," Mitz hurried over. "Let's get you to your room to get cleaned up." She paused to look long enough to check where the blood was coming from. "I can't tell, dear, how bad it is."

Daxx nodded. "I know. Just get me to some water before Troy gets back."

Mitz chuckled. "He would too, you know, lick it dirt and all."

Daxx hissed out another breath and tried to walk faster. "I know, we have to hurry."

"Where ever were you fighting? A mud pit?"

"Pretty close. Some old, abandoned site outside the city. I think it used to be a sand and gravel quarry, now it's only sludge and mud." She moaned and tried to lift her leg higher. "It was okay at first, but we ended up backing them into it. It was almost to my waist in some places. My legs are going to be killing me tomorrow."

Mitz nodded, "and the mud wrestling jokes are going to be endless."

"Lovely." Daxx mumbled.

I left Daxx complaining about mud while Mitz helped her shower. She sent me to check if the men had returned. I didn't need to go all the way back to the landing room to find out. There were trails of mud leading down every hallway. I don't know whose job it was to clean them, but they deserved a pay raise.

I followed the trail to Victor's room. I had never been in it, but knew where it was. I didn't want to bother him, he was probably tired and muddy. I just wanted to see with my own eyes that he was okay.

I knocked on the door.

"Come in."

I opened the door and went in slowly, he was standing in the middle of his room taking off weapons and layers.

"Crissy, is everything alright?"

I thought that was an odd question considering where he'd been. I nodded. "I was waiting for you in the landing room then Daxx came back hurt."

"How is she?" He paused in undoing buckles.

"Mitz and I had to put her in the shower to see how bad it was. Mitz says it's not too bad and Daxx has had worse." I trusted her judgement.

"Yes, she has, unfortunately." He reached down and undid the strap on his leg and the knife and case slid to the floor.

"I think who ever cleans the carpets will need a raise after tonight." I told him.

He grinned and nodded his head slowly. "I will suggest Troy bring in some extra people to help with that." Another weapon slid to the floor. "I have never fought in anything like that before. Not in all the years I have been justice."

"Do you need help?" I asked watching him try to get his

long jacket off.

"I think it's drying and cementing to my skin."

I went over and tugged at the back so he could slip his arms out.

"Thank you." He looked down to his boots. "We made have to cut me out of my boots, they're lead weights now."

I looked at the boots and had no idea how he was going to manage it.

Shaking his head, he started walking slowly to the bathroom. "I'll just soak them off, perhaps." He paused in the doorway. "I won't be long."

"Did you want something to drink or… anything?"

He smiled. "Some juice, or anything that will wash the taste out of my mouth would be appreciated. Everyone will meet at the dining room shortly."

"Okay, I'll go get that and wait there. Good luck getting the mud off." I turned and went out of the room. I had wanted to ask what they found tonight, but I could see the mud drying as he stood there and decided he might be more interested in talking about it later. He had looked quite funny with the mud in his hair, and all over him, but I hoped whatever they found it meant Daxx and I could go do what we needed to.

Chapter Eighteen

The gathering in the dining room was quick after the mud was washed off everyone. Victor only stayed long enough to wash the taste from his mouth, then went to the cells. Most of the men followed him. I had to wonder if I stood in one of the cells, would I get to see him more. Daxx sat with me for a short time, and then she said she was going to drag her man away from minds because she felt neglected. I completely understood, although I did feel a touch of jealousy that she had an option.

All of them were happy they'd won, but not entirely, because Marcus with the purple eyes hadn't been there. Now, they planned to find the rest of his followers, and all their camps. I kept hoping the flashes would show me how, but so far nothing came to me. Maybe my flashes were broken. I'd never gone this long without seeing something worth writing down.

The next morning, which was really night, I was flat on my back on the mat in the practice room with one foot held in the air, when Daxx came in.

"Is that a new move?" She asked me.

Dropping my foot to the mat, I stayed on the floor. "No. I was wondering if I wore my boots, maybe the weight of them would help my feet hit the floor… first."

She stood over me looking down at me now. "It takes practice. You would have laughed to see me learning how to use the sais at first. Good thing Chase gave me wooden ones to start with or I'd have no arms or legs now."

I sighed and sat up. "I would just like my feet to land first, just once."

"You'll get it. Once you do then you can practice in your street clothes." She looked at the shoes I wore. "It would be even harder with heavier boots on."

I stared at my shoes and sighed again. "Okay, I'll keep trying."

"How long have you been here? I stopped at your room, but your closet was empty." She smirked.

I remembered I hadn't put my blanket and pillows back on the bed. "I didn't sleep much."

"Visions bad?" She squatted down beside me.

I shook my head. "No, no more than normal. I am just…" I lifted a hand and then dropped it not sure how to say it.

"Come to breakfast."

I looked at my hands and then back to her again. "I don't want to sit there and watch him not look at me today."

Daxx got up and held out her hand. "You just have to keep getting in his face, trust me."

Taking her hand, I got up. "I trust you." I shrugged carefully. "And I hurt too much to fall anymore right now."

All through breakfast, the word mud came up. Mitz had been right. I didn't get most of their jokes, but the ones I did were perfectly timed, so at least there was that. My back was so sore I had to avoid leaning back in my chair. I didn't want to tell Daxx, but I must have landed the wrong way when I fell. Was there a right way to fall? I wondered if anyone knew, so they could show me. Maybe that would be my thing, falling well.

Victor wasn't in his battle gear for once, the first time I'd seen him without it for a few weeks, so I enjoyed looking and seeing his form and not weapons of all sizes.

I realized Leone was speaking to everyone and looked up to not be rude.

"All I'm saying is we've taken out what, four, five of their cells now? How many more can they have?" He looked to

Michael. "There's not *that* many missing from our side."

"Maybe they're not missing because they are here enough to be seen." I offered as a possible answer.

Everyone looked down at me and I realized their eyes didn't bother me as much now. I still was a little uncomfortable with it, but I didn't want to hide under the table now.

Chase pointed his fork at me. "Cutie's right. The bastards are here often enough that we don't even know they're missing."

"How many are documented residents from last night?" Victor asked looking to Michael.

Rubbing his hand over his cheek with the scar, as he did often and probably didn't realize, Michael dropped his hand away. "There were only a few we didn't have some kind of record on."

"So where is Marcus getting those that we don't have records for?" Quinton asked.

"Our side." I nodded. "Like Alona, people that don't know there is a *this* side." I took a bite of my toast.

Troy set his fork down and sat back. "How many have been born to the other side?" He glanced to Victor. "Until these illegal devices were made, weren't visits to the other side monitored?" he looked at Chase. "I thought they were monitored."

Chase nodded. "As far as I know they were."

Daxx chuckled. "You guys are too funny, really you are." She looked down to me. "They wouldn't survive on the streets."

I nodded, knowing it were true.

"Listen up." She said sitting forward and resting her hands on the table. "Anything, and I mean anything, in *any* world, can be bought for the right price."

"It's true." I told them. I leaned back, forgetting, and winced and sat forward quickly again.

"Great, so what your saying is our entire security team can be bought." Arius said.

Daxx snorted, "Come on, don't tell me none of you have ever snuck to the other side on the down low."

All of the men became very interested in their plates at the same time.

"There you go." Daxx said and then looked down to me and nodded.

Victor pushed his plate away and sat back. "There could be an infinite number of those like us born on the other side for Marcus to recruit, and we have no way of tracking them down."

"Older ones would be easier than any born recently." I offered. He looked at me, so I nodded. "Like tracking Emil, through name changes." I paused and thought how to explain it. "I found him because with the names he used, there was never any record of death, he…" I sat forward again when I bumped my back. "The people he pretended to be, they just vanished."

He gave me an odd look, his brows drawn together and I knew he was thinking it over when he got up and started walking toward me. "What have you done to yourself? You keep wincing when you sit back."

My eyes went wide, I hadn't seen him watching me. I looked to Daxx for help on what to say.

"She's probably tender." Daxx told him. "I've been teaching her some evasive moves."

He stood beside me now and leaned to look at my back. "Did she cut herself?"

I stiffened, not sure why he would ask that.

Daxx got up. "Maybe a scrape like rug burn from the mat?"

"It's just a little itchy and sore." I told them.

Daxx was looking at my back now too, and all eyes were watching.

"Did you scrape it Crissy? Your shirt is glued to your back in one spot." Daxx asked leaning down.

"I may have, I'm not sure, but that explains why it's itchy." I wanted everyone to start eating again.

"Hmm," Daxx carefully pulled the collar of my shirt out and looked down my back. "Criss come with me into the kitchen please."

Anytime Daxx used Criss instead of Crissy was never good. I set down my cup and got up slowly and took her hand. I glanced to Victor and didn't like the hard look on his face. How bad could my back be from falling?

We walked in the kitchen and Mitz smiled, "What's

happening?" Her expression changed to concern after she looked at Victor.

"Is there a scrape and it's bleeding?" I frowned wishing I could see my back. "It was a little sore yesterday, but sometimes I bump things and don't notice."

Daxx patted the stool by the counter with her hand. "Have a seat and turn around."

Mitz came over with a table cloth and held it in front of me. "To cover up, love."

I took and held it to my chest. Still not sure why they were so upset if all I had was a scrape on my back. They would not be happy to know about some of the other times I hurt myself, I thought, but decided I maybe shouldn't tell them that now.

Daxx looked around the counter top. "Do you have some scissors…"

I felt my tank top being pulled away from my skin and then ripped in half.

"Or that works too," Daxx said.

Then there was silence.

A gentle touch on my skin near my scar, and I tried to look over my shoulder to see what they were looking at.

"Did I scrape it?"

"Have you kept your amulet on at all times?" Victor asked in an odd tone.

"My bracelet from Clairee's friend? Yes, even when I have a shower or bath." I clutched the cloth with one hand and held up my arm so he could see it.

He took my arm gently and turned the bracelet around. "The silver weave is broken."

"Oh. I don't know how that happened." I rushed to tell him.

"Incompetence, but not on your part." He said in low voice.

"Is everything okay in here?" Rafael asked as he walked in.

Victor turned to him. "Find Clairee and her coven mate. Immediately. The weave on Cristy's amulet is broken."

"What?" He came over and then noticed me holding the cloth to my chest, he looked behind me. "Oh shit. What the hell is that?"

Victor glared at him and I heard someone get smacked, most likely Daxx hitting Raf.

I grabbed Victor's arm. "What's on my back?" My heart started racing. "Is it going to burn again?"

Rafael turned for the door. "I'll go get them, Romulus and the doctor too."

Then I knew it was really bad.

"We'll figure it out." Victor told me and moved closer so I could lean against him.

Quinton came in scowling, "Where is Raf running to?" He looked at my back. "How the hell are they doing it? We banished that asshole mage to a cage for the rest of his life."

"Managing what?" Chase asked, leaning against the door. "I was coming to say good night, but it seems I might miss out on some excitement." He frowned and looked from one person to the other and then pushed away from the door to stand behind me. "Fuck. Put her in cold water. Isn't that what Romeo said last time? To slow it down?"

"Will ice work?" Mitz asked moving to the freezer. "Shouldn't we take her to her room? I don't think being on display in the kitchen is wise." She glanced to the door the staff could come through at any moment. She came back over and handed the ice to Daxx.

"Bring it with us." Victor said and swung me up into his arms.

We walked through the dining room very quickly, but slow enough for me to see everyone stand, and not looking happy. I seemed to be the cause of people not looking happy a lot, I thought as we went down the hall.

"Hey." Victor said softly getting my attention. I looked up at him. "We will figure this out." He gave me a little smile, but I knew it wasn't real, and he was only doing it to make me feel better. I wrapped my arms around his neck and leaned my face against his shoulder. He smelled really good, but I didn't think this was the time to tell him that.

I lay on the bed, my feet where my head should go, on my

tummy hugging a pillow. Daxx was beside me putting cold cloths on my back every few minutes. No one was sure what was on my back, not even Clairee. I made Victor let me see when we got to the room. My scar had turned an awful dark color and it was oozing. I still didn't feel it, and I was starting to think not feeling something like that happening was worse than feeling it.

Everyone was here, again. If this kept happening I was going need more chairs in my room. Victor made them all stand on the other side of the room so I didn't feel crowded, but honestly, I was getting used to all of the brothers now. What he didn't know was they all practiced with me when he was out rampaging.

The doctor looked on from a distance, avoiding Victor. It was not his field of expertise he said and left quickly. Romulus looked curious, but even after researching, hadn't been able to find a spell to counter it that I'd live through. So, thankfully, Daxx told him we'd pass trying that one. Clairee and her friend were not pleased to see someone was able to unbind their weave. She said someone was using strong magic to find me, before running out of the room saying they had a new idea and would return shortly.

All I understood completely was no one knew how to stop it, and that Marcus now knew I hadn't died. Victor had barked for a few minutes, while the other men growled puzzling out how that could be.

I remembered my pack. I looked over my shoulder at Daxx. "I forgot my pack."

"I went and grabbed it, little sister." Rafael got up and went over beside the door and held it up.

"Thank you." I told him when he brought it over.

He sat beside me and set it on the floor right in front of me. "I have to ask," he said leaning closer. "What is so important in that pack?"

Several of the others stopped and looked at him.

"What?" He said lifting his hands. "Don't tell me none of you haven't wondered."

I reached over and pulled it closer. "I carry all of my good memories in it." I bit my lip. "I'm not sure what they're called."

"Mementoes." He said with a smile.

"Yes. Those. I keep my notebook of important things I had to see and pencils and other stuff too, but the mementoes are why I like it with me. When I feel really down, I like to look at them and remember the good memories to help me feel better." I glanced around at the others, a few talked quietly or were texting on their phones. "Would you like to see?" I asked him and looked over my shoulder at Daxx as well. She smiled to answer.

"Yeah." Raf said and slid to sit on the floor by the pack.

"Okay." I opened the pack and dug around in it for the bag inside and pulled it out. Reaching in, I pulled out a small bracelet, it was thin and worn. "A sad man gave this to me. He said I made him feel better, so I kept it because I like making people feel better." I nodded and set it on the floor by my pack. I took out a shiny stone next and held it in my palm. "I found a puppy at the park once, when it was still a park and sort of clean." I smiled remembering. "He followed me and we played half the day. I had so much fun." I gave him a serious look. "I never had a dog or cat, but playing with him was so much fun. He was lost and his people came and found him." Putting the stone on the floor, I pulled out the next thing. It was a penny, I showed him. "I found this the day I realized I wasn't crazy." I nodded and gave him a wide-eyed look. "For years I thought they were right and I really was, then I was sitting on a step and something I'd seen… inside my head, happened right in front of me, and I knew then I wasn't." I put it on the floor.

The next thing I pulled out, I looked at Daxx again. "This hat Daxx gave me the first time I saw her. Right off her head. I had seen her… not with my eyes," I explained to Rafael, "before, but didn't know she was going to be so nice." I put the hat on the floor. "I also have a hat if my head gets cold."

Rafael nodded and gave me a nice smile.

Reaching in, I pulled out the bow that had been on my pack. "This was on my pack when it was left at my door. I kept it because I'd never had something this new before." I looked over at Victor, "and because it was from Victor." I set it down.

I took out the next thing and gave Raf a grin, holding them so he could see. "These are the smiley faces you leave on my cookies. You know you never make it the same way two times in a row." I opened a few and set them on the floor. "See the eyes are all different. I keep them because they're smiley faces, from you, and because they always come with cookies."

He touched them with his hand for a moment and took a deep breath, but then didn't say anything.

Pulling out the last thing, I set the bag on the floor and held the fake flower in my hand. It was a faded blue now, but had been closer to purple when I had gotten it. "When I left where I was and the bus brought me to the city I'm in now, I stood there thinking this is so big and so busy." I turned it in my fingers. "I was going to get on the bus and go back," I shook my head. "Even though I didn't like it there. Then a lady came by and handed me this and smiled, then just walked away." I set it on the floor with the other things. "I knew then, I was meant to be in that city, and I still am."

I looked at the items on the floor and then to Rafael. "I know those are probably silly to you." I motioned to the closet and then the room. "You have always had this and a family." I shrugged as best as I could laying the way I was. "I didn't, so I kept little pieces of happy I found along the way." I looked at him and then to Daxx and sighed. "I'm going to need a bigger bag, because since I found all of you I keep finding happiness every day." I nodded and then glanced to the others to see everyone was looking at me. No one looked happy right now. I looked to Victor, with a sad look in his eyes, and wasn't sure why what I'd told them made him that way.

Rafael sighed, his voice shaky. "If anyone deserves happiness, it's you, little sister." He kissed the top of my head and then walked out of the room.

Daxx cleared her throat. "I need more cool cloths." She got up.

"I'll get them." Leone rushed to the bathroom and Quinton followed.

Chase got up and wandered over to squat down right in front of me. He had a sad look in his eyes, even though he grinned. "I'm beginning to wonder what we ever did without you here."

I smiled. "Probably ate more. There is a lot of eating here."

He chuckled and stood up. "I need a *really* strong drink, after that. Can I bring anyone back one?"

"I'll go with you." Michael said then stopped. "Do you want anything Crissy?" He asked me, his voice sounding strange.

"No, thank you, Michael." I sighed. "I'm just waiting to see what's going to happen." I reached down and started putting all of my mementos back in the bag. Victor came over and sat on the floor, watching me put them away. When I put the bag back in my pack, he reached out and held my hand, resting his head on the bed by mine. I felt better with him close and sighed a long sigh. "I hope they find a way to get that out of my back."

He kissed my hand and then my shoulder. "They'll figure something out. Clairee's coven has been around for hundreds of years."

I glanced to see that Arius and Troy looked very unhappy still. "I think I made everyone sad." I said in a whisper.

"I believe you made everyone think." Victor answered just as softly.

"Is that bad?" I turned my head so I could watch his eyes.

He shrugged. "I suppose it can be, when it's things you haven't realized."

I smiled. He was watching mine. "I like thinking and finding out new things."

Kissing my hand again, he nodded. "I know, heart."

Clairee and her friend came back in the door and looked around. "Should we wait a moment?"

Troy straightened up. "No. What have you found?"

She looked to Victor, a nervous look on her face.

Victor kissed my lips softly and got up. "I'll be right back."

"Oh, good you're back." Daxx held up the dish that held cool cloths. "Do I keep doing this?"

Clairee nodded. "For a few minutes more."

I tried to hear what was being said, but she spoke so softly I couldn't. Troy looked over, with his eyes wide, then Arius did as well. Victor turned and looked angry and then my heart started pounding again. "What?" I asked, hoping it wasn't rude, but it was my back, and I would not know what was going on a second more. If it had been Daxx lying here, I know she would have already threatened to kill someone, so if I seemed a bit impatient, I thought that was okay.

Victor rubbed his hand over his face and shook his head to something they said. He had that look on his face as he walked back over, the look that told me I wasn't going to like what he said. Squatting down in front of me he took both my hands in his.

"They've come up with a way to get rid of whatever was done to your back. To get rid of any remaining magic there." He released one hand and brushed the hair back from my face. "With your resistance to magic, however it has to be a more permanent, intrusive method."

I frowned. "What do they have to do?"

"They have to put a rune on your back, over it." He glanced to Daxx briefly. "It has to be in your skin so it's permanent."

I know my eyes were as wide as they could go now. "How?" I bit my lip knowing before he answered I wasn't going to like it.

"Either a witch's tattoo... made with a small pen like instrument or..." he exhaled slowly, "it has to be burned on."

Daxx gasped from beside me.

I closed my eyes, not wanting to look at her, or anyone, for a moment. Opening my eyes, I shook my head. "I just..." I let go of his hand and sat up awkwardly, pulling the blanket with me. "I need to get up for a minute." I nodded. Kneeling, I crawled off the bed and bunched up the blanket so I could walk. I had barely coped with the magic when it had burned before. I paced over to the wall and then turned and went the other way. How was I going to cope when I was *really* being burned?

My heart was beating so fast in my chest, I almost couldn't breathe. A tattoo... with needles marking my skin... was that better than being burned? I didn't know. I'd tried to avoid both the whole of my life.

Turning, I looked at the floor and took a deep breath.

Shaking my head, I walked to the bathroom, avoiding all eye contact. I closed the door softly and went to the tub and climbed in and just sat there.

I heard the soft knock on the door and knew it was probably Daxx. The door opened and she stuck her head in.

"Can I come in?"

I nodded, but stayed where I was, hugging my knees and the bunched-up blanket to my chest.

She came over and climbed in the tub with me and sat down. Only here, I thought, in the tubs they have could we both sit in it with so much room to spare.

"What do I do?" I asked her finally. "I'm not brave enough to choose either way."

She touched my knee and leaned closer, with pain in her eyes. "I don't think anyone is brave enough for that." Huffing out a breath she leaned back. "I couldn't do it. Not awake."

I shook my head. "I can't take drugs to put me to sleep." I touched my head. "Then there's no control and they would wake me… and I wouldn't *be* asleep." I shook my head fast. "I know. They tried to drug me before."

"Could someone help you control them? Like Victor did after you took his blood?"

I bit my lip and then closed my eyes. "I don't know if he could control that much." I looked at her. "How long will it take?" I took a shaky breath. "I just can't feel it when it happens. I know I can't."

"No one expects you to." She touched my knee again. "Do you want me to go get Victor and ask if he thinks he can do it long enough?"

I nodded.

"I'll be right back." She got out and went back into the room.

I could hear them talking out in the room and was glad Daxx was explaining, because I was having trouble thinking clearly enough to speak right now.

The door opened and Victor came in, closing it behind him. He walked over and I was surprised he did what Daxx had, and got in the tub with me. Sitting down, he pulled me into his lap and held me in his arms. If we weren't here for the reasons we were, I might find it a little funny.

"Daxx explained."

I nodded.

"For the time it will take to put the rune in your skin, I believe I can control the visions." He said softly against my hair.

"What if they're too much for you? I will wake up because of them." I looked up into his green eyes and there was such pain there. Pain for me, I realized. No one had ever felt pain for me.

Victor shook his head softly. "I will manage, don't worry that I can't."

"At what cost to you?"

He kissed my forehead and smiled. "It's only for an hour, heart, I will be fine." He ran his hand up and down my arm softly. "If you're concerned, we can have Arius on hand. He believes he could assist for a few minutes if needed."

"How? I don't really understand what he can do." I watched his eyes move over my face.

"He can control minds in a way that they have to follow what he decides."

I raised my eyebrows and looked at him. "That is a strong power, it's good that he has a pure heart."

His lips quirked. "Don't ever tell him he has a pure heart, it will crush his ego."

I smiled. "I know. He likes to think he is a scary man, but I see what's true."

He chuckled softly. "Best keep that quiet until the time you need to put him in his place."

I nodded. "So, he could take control of my mind if I wake up too soon?"

His eyes went serious again. "He believes so. Then, he could tell you not to feel the pain."

I bit my lip and thought about how that made me feel. "I don't know if he could control mine, and I hope I don't wake up to find out."

"You'll take my blood and let the doctor put you to sleep?" His eyes held mine, waiting for me to answer.

"Yes." I nodded. "But when it's done and I wake up, you have to let the flashes come back. I didn't like how tired you were when you did it before." I stretched up and kissed his mouth softly.

"I will go tell them to get the doctor." He stood up, lifting me with him and stepped out of the tub. "I'll be right back." He set me on my feet and kissed my forehead, then went out of the room.

I went to the mirror and turned so I could see my back. It was an ugly sight. The evil ooze ran down my back, making me feel very unclean. Taking a deep breath, I gave myself a little nod. Whatever had to be done to get rid of this was what I would do.

Victor came back in and glanced in the mirror as he closed the door. "An hour from now it won't ever do that again." He told me. Bending down, he pulled the knife strapped to his ankle out. "Do you want the witches tattoo?"

I nodded. The idea of having it burned in just felt like I would regret it every day after. I pulled the blanket and tucked it around me.

"I'll tell them." He pulled his shirt over his head and I bit my lip, knowing the reason wasn't for me to stare at him, but couldn't help it. His chest was wide and muscles were everywhere.

He tipped up my chin and smirked at me. "Now is not the time to look at me that way."

I felt my cheeks heat. "I can't help it."

He pulled me closer and held the blade against his chest. "Let's get this over with."

"Okay." I huffed out a breath, and squeezed my eyes shut as he started to cut into his skin.

With a chuckle, he pulled me closer. "Come here."

I opened my eyes to see the blood, and didn't hesitate, knowing he healed too quickly. I licked my tongue over the blood running down, then placed my lips against his chest. Sucking gently, I swallowed the blood and thought that this somehow felt right. He pulled my hips, so our bodies were close and I didn't hurry to finish. I needed to find a way to get him this close when the situation wasn't so serious was the last thought I had before I realized he'd healed. Resting my cheek on his chest, we stayed like that for a few moments more.

Leaning back, he touched my cheek with his hand softly, like I was made of something fragile. "Ready?"

"No, but I don't think I have a choice."

He leaned down and kissed me softly, twice, and then straightened up. "Let's go get settled and wait for the doctor." Turning, with his arm around my shoulder we both walked to the door.

The room was quiet and I didn't look to see how many were still here. Someone had made it darker and I was happy not to see. Victor lifted me onto the bed and then stretched out beside me, pulling me so I was over his chest. I leaned my face against him and listened to his heartbeat and each breath he took.

Victor traced his hand up and down my arm. "Just close your eyes and settle. I'm going to start blocking the visions."

Taking a deep breath, I let it out slowly and closed my eyes. It was very quiet in the room.

"After, when you start to wake, you'll take more blood, so it will heal faster. The tattoo will heal, closing in the magic, then it will be over."

His voice was so soft and soothing it was very easy to relax, well, as much as someone could with evil ooze on their back as they waited to get a tattoo.

"The doctor is here now, keep your eyes closed and just relax."

I had to fight to stay calm, just knowing the doctor was near. Victor's hand moved up and down my arm a few more times before gripped it with a firm hold, there was a pinch and slight pain and I knew I'd just gotten the needle, and there was no time to change my mind.

"It's going to be fine, my heart."

Was the last thing I heard and then darkness took me.

Chapter Nineteen

I don't remember going to sleep, or getting the rune tattoo put in my skin. My head was fuzzy and I woke to a drink of water, and then I remember the taste of blood and being held close by a warm body.

When I opened my eyes the next time, I was alone in the bed. Looking around I saw Daxx and Mitz sitting on the couch watching me. I lay there for a moment more to take a look around in my head, the flashes were there and there was no wall that I could find.

"Victor had to go feed and replenish a bit." Daxx came over and sat on the bed. "How are you feeling?"

"My head is a bit fuzzy." I told her. "Did it work?"

She smiled. "Yes, and it's all healed now. Victor gave you blood twice, to make sure."

I frowned. "I only remember once."

Daxx chuckled, "I think you were mostly still under the first time. He insisted on it so you'd feel no pain."

"Oh." Holding the blankets, I sat up slowly and then looked down to see I had a shirt on again. "The ooze and magic is gone?"

"It is. There is no spell, cast, or any of that other crap they can try to get through that rune mark. Ever."

I smiled. "I'm happy about that."

She nodded.

Mitz came over and smiled in her caring way. "You'll need

something to eat and drink, love, I'll be back with it."

I sat back carefully and noted it didn't hurt at all. I smiled. "I think Victor's blood made all my sore muscles better too."

Laughing Daxx sat further on the bed. "Their blood is awesome, isn't it?"

"What time is it?" I bit my lip. "Is it night realm time or day realm time?"

"I still hate that time thing. It's day realm time, soon to be night realm. I was waiting for you to wake before I went to grab a nap." She yawned.

"Thank you. I'm glad I didn't wake up alone." I looked at the pillow beside me to see the indentation from Victor's head.

"Mitz and Chase basically dragged him out of here. He really needed to go feed and rest. Giving you blood three times and holding your flashes the whole time drained him."

"He's okay?"

She leaned back and looked at me. "As okay as a big dominant man can be, that had to watch his mate go through what you did."

I looked at her for a moment thinking about what she said. "He's not okay."

She grinned.

"Knock, knock." Chase called from the door. He walked in and smiled. "Thought I'd see how you were doing."

"You spend much more time on this side, Chase and you're going to have to become a nightwalker." Daxx told him.

"Blasphemy." He shook his head. "I couldn't live over here with all the drama." He chuckled. Standing beside the bed, he looked at me for a moment. "I finally persuaded Victor to rest for a few hours, and told him I would call if he was required. Is he required?"

I sighed, "I'd like to see him, but he should rest."

"How are you feeling?" His grey eyes moved over me slowly.

"I'm okay." I touched my hand over my shoulder. "It doesn't hurt." I looked at Daxx and then under the blankets to see I whoever had put my shirt on had put shorts on as well. "I'd like to see it though." Pushing the blankets back I moved over and got up. "It's on *my* body, but I'm probably the last one to see it."

Daxx followed me in and flicked on the light. "Turn around and I'll lift up your shirt for you."

I took a deep breath and turned so I could see as much of my back in the big mirror. I bit my lip as she lifted the shirt and then stared at what I saw. "I've seen this before." I said quietly. "Inside my head." My scar was healed over as it had been, before the ooze started coming out of it. A black symbol was in the middle of it now. It was a half of a circle with no bottom, another circle filled inside, and a triangle was in that, then a mark through it from one side to the other. "I know I have," I told her and pulled my shirt down and went quickly back to the room.

Rushing over, I found my pack beside the bed and opened it, searching for my notebook. Dropping the bag, I sat on the bed and flipped through the pages as fast as I could. "That symbol, it's been in my head for…" I raised a hand to the air, "a long time." I looked to Daxx, "just after I saw you… in my head, it came to me." Flipping more pages, I stopped and tapped the page with my hand. "Here. See, it is the same." I held the book out to Daxx.

She came over and took it, looking at my drawing and then a glance to Chase as she nodded. "It's the same."

"I didn't know it was for me." I said and took a shaky breath. "Nothing ever came with it to show that it was." I watched Chase study the book with his brows drawn together. "I don't usually see… me."

He handed the book back and sat on the bed. "Is there anything else in there that might fit now?"

I hadn't thought to go through them and search for pieces that fit, not after all this time. "I don't know. I would have to look at each one and remember if it's happened before or after I put that one there."

He glanced to the thick notebook and shook his head. "That's a lot to sort through, cutie."

I nodded. "But what if other answers we haven't been able to find are right there waiting to be found?"

"Is that possible?" Daxx asked.

"Is what possible?" Victor asked walking in.

Chase turned to him slowly. "That was a short rest."

Victor came over, his eyes on only me as he did. "I thought I would rest better here, so I wasn't laying there wondering."

I smiled at him. "I'm okay now."

He sat on the bed and I had to think it was a good thing that the bed, like everything here, was a big as it was.

"Now, is what possible?" He asked again.

"Oh." I held out the book and pointed to the sketch I had made years before. "I saw the rune on my back, soon after I saw Daxx. I just didn't know it was meant for me."

He took the book and looked at it for a moment. "Is there more in here about it?"

I frowned. "I don't know. Chase wonders if there might be more that I've written down that would fit together now." I bit my lip and then nodded quickly. "Maybe I have had answers all along for the things we can't find."

Victor had a strange look on his face. "It wouldn't even surprise me if it were true." He touched my cheek softly and then looked at Chase. "I thought you were going to call me when she woke up?"

Chase smirked, "No, I believe I agreed to call if you were required, not when she woke up."

Victor gave him an unhappy look and then turned back to me. "Is it feeling alright now?"

I nodded. "It doesn't hurt at all."

He smiled and leaned over to kiss my forehead again. "Perhaps a day without falling on the mats would be advisable, just to be sure."

I glanced to see Daxx roll her eyes from where she sat behind him. I smirked. "Perhaps it is."

"Alright, love, I have a light meal and some juice." Mitz stopped in the door and looked at the others sitting on the bed with me. "Should I have brought more?"

For the rest of that day, after it was night again that is, Victor stayed with me. We had very little time alone though, as everyone had to come and check on me once or twice to make sure I was still okay. I was, and glad to be.

It was still nice to spend that much time with Victor. We played cards, which I found out I wasn't good at. We walked the halls and he showed me behind some doors I still hadn't seen. He even told my coaches we wouldn't be practicing today.

I wanted to go through my book of seeing, but he said it could wait one more day. He hugged me or held me, and kissed me many times, but always stopped and then backed away.

Daxx gave me a thumbs up when he wasn't looking on her way out the door before dinner. I wasn't sure what it was for, but made a note in my head to ask her later.

When it was time to sleep, Victor lingered long after saying he was going, and I should rest, and I thought he was finally, *finally* going to stay with me.

Sadly, I was wrong.

The next day, I didn't see him at all the whole day. He was gone again, doing whatever it was he did.

That was three days ago, and I'd seen him a whole of an hour in that time. I stood in my room after the coaches left and stared at the dish of small balls the telepath had left. She used them to show me focus, I don't know why. I couldn't juggle them with my mind. Or my hands, I discovered, having tried then crawling around to find them all.

Turning, I spotted one I had missed and went over and picked it up. I wasn't going to try juggling again, but I did bounce it off the wall, and then the floor and found myself standing there doing that over and over again. The rhythm was soothing, and I realized I was sorting through flashes faster than ever before as I did it. I caught it and stared at the little red rubber ball. Was it something that simple? I paused for a moment and checked in my head again, just to make sure I hadn't just wanted it to be that easy. There were just as many flashes as always.

Turning back to the wall, I tossed the ball and caught it, then bounced it on the floor, caught it and started again. Yes, it was easier to focus on the flashes without really trying, as my hands went through the cycle of moves. Catching it after ten times of wall to floor to wall again, I stood there. I would keep the ball with me today and keep trying it at different times to see if it worked all the time, or just this once.

Tucking it in my pocket, I wondered what I should do now. Daxx and Rafael were getting me more lists from our side of the longest living people, so we could test that idea of mine… that finding others born on that side would be easier that way.

I couldn't look for Emil right now either, because I needed Quinton for that, so I could go over and use the internet. Victor hadn't liked the idea, but Quinton said he wouldn't leave me alone for a second, and we'd come right back after.

I decided maybe I could find someone to help me practice today. Nodding to myself, I grabbed my pack and went out the door.

I moved along the halls quietly, although it wasn't hard to do here. The carpet, endless miles of it, covered the floor. Only in the tunnels had it been left uncovered, which I thought was probably because they were tunnels and not halls.

If Michael wasn't busy, I was hoping he could help me with the defensive moves we'd tried. I had practiced them yesterday for an hour or so, but they were the kind of moves that needed someone practice with. Alone, I just felt like I was dancing without the music.

Passing Victor's office, I saw the door open and paused just long enough to glance in, only to see it was empty. He must be rampaging again. I nodded. I still wasn't sure exactly what that was, but Daxx assured me again it was his way of working things out. Maybe I needed to learn how to rampage, I had many things to work out.

Michael's office door was open a few inches, so I tapped it with my hand, making it seem as if I had knocked, and kept going. Others were in his office, making it seem small. I hoped I didn't interrupt what they were doing. Leone and Michael stood talking quietly behind his desk. I looked around at the others, feeling all eyes on me. I was getting better at being watched, but I don't think I was ever going to like it. I knew two of the men to be guards, but we'd never spoken. I thought of introducing myself now, but if I were disturbing an important meeting, I should just speak to Michael and then leave.

Quinton was leaning in the corner, and I hadn't even seen him with all the big bodies in such a small space. I was getting used to men that towered over me, even if I thought it just wasn't right to have so many so tall meaning the rest of us had to constantly look up. Stepping quietly around the guard, whose name I didn't know, I bumped into a third I hadn't even seen. It was silly really, to miss a body this size. I looked up to tell him I was sorry. I didn't like being touched without warning, so doing it to another person was just rude.

The breath got stuck in my throat as I looked around him to see. It was a habit, I did to any I saw, most times I didn't even know I was doing it, until I did. The space around him was dark and the color that only showed with lies, so many lies. His brows drew together as he looked down at me, but a look of something bad was in his eyes as they moved over me.

"Sorry." I said in more of a squeak. I turned and gave Michael a wide-eyed look, and wanted to tell him what I saw, but my heart was pounding and my mind rushing too fast to speak. I spun on my heel and went back out his door and then stopped and stood there trying to decide what to do.

Turning back the way I came, I started to run to get far away.

"Cristy."

Victor's voice boomed out behind me and I stopped to turn and see him coming from his office door. I froze, wanting to get away, but needing to see him more.

With a frown on his face, he walked quickly toward me, his green eyes moving all over me.

"What is it?"

I held up my finger over my mouth, not wanting the man to hear. Then I pointed to the Michael's door that someone had closed and covered my mouth so I would blurt it out.

He reached me quickly and leaned down close. "What has frightened you?"

I shook my head and grabbed his arm, turning to run to the practice room. Once through the doors I spun around and looked up at him. "The man. With Michael." I nodded. "He's not who he seems to be." I shook my head. "He shouldn't be here."

"A traitor? In the inner chambers?"

I nodded. "Yes." I put my hand over my fast beating heart. "The space around him so full of lies it's black all the way through."

He touched my cheek softly, his green eyes searching my face and then nodded. Pulling out his phone, he tapped the screen and put it to his ear. "Michael. How many guards are there with you?"

He nodded his head. "Bring all of them to the practice room. Now. Cristy saw a traitor in one of them." He looked impatient. "Yes, ours."

Putting the phone in his pocket, I noticed he was in battle gear again, and found it odd I hadn't noticed before. He reached down and lifted my shirt to see if my belt and cable box was on me.

"Climb." He told me.

I didn't stop to ask him why, I turned and ran for the ropes. I paused at the middle one and shook my head and went up the one Victor had climbed that day to help me. When I reached the top, I went up on the beam and hung a leg over each side, resting my feet on the knot at the top. When I looked down I saw the door open, and in came the guards and everyone else that had been in Michael's office.

"Whoa, boss," one of them said. "You guys have all the toys in your gym."

Quinton smiled and Michael gave a shrug, but both were tense.

Leone glanced around and saw where I was, but made no motion to let the others know.

"Justice, are you here to teach us some new moves?" One of the guards I knew said to Victor.

"Something like that." Victor said and a shiver went down my spine from his tone.

Everyone walked further into the large room, except Michael who stood by the door. I could tell by the way he stood, he was tense and ready to stop anyone who might try to leave.

Victor walked along and I couldn't understand why he was just pacing around, until I realized he was turning their backs to hide where I was, but so he would still see me. I tried to exhale and settle my nerves, the guards all wore their weapons, and the only other person with any I could see, was Victor.

When the three men turned to watch him, he pulled both of his swords from the straps on his back and the sound the blades made against their case was loud in the silent room.

"We've been told," he said in a low dangerous tone, "they've managed to get someone inside the inner royal halls." He walked along and stopped in front of the first man, holding his swords out as if he were warming up to swing. His eyes glanced to me and I realized he wanted me to tell him if that was the man. I shook my head quickly. Pacing a few more feet, he paused again. "We are going to have to examine each staff member and guard that works in this part of our realm." Turning, to face the next man his eyes flicked up to me. I shook my head quickly once more. I could see his eyes harden and the justice side appear as he stepped over to the last guard.

With a motion, so fast, his blades were raised and crossed in a way so the man of lies neck was between the blades. I held my breath unsure what he would do. "Ethan, Anthony, take this traitor to the cells."

Leone moved fast and took the man's sword as the other two guards pulled theirs and held them on the man.

I watched Victor's jaw clench, the space around him now cold. He glanced to me then stepped back and cased his blades and watched the men lead him away. When the door closed, he walked toward me quickly. He held his hand up to me. "Come down."

I did as I'd practiced and balanced over the beam, so I could grasp the rope with my legs. In a move, less awkward then the first thirty or so times I'd done it, I got down to the rope and quickly started for the floor.

When I was closer to the bottom, large hands grasped my waist and Victor lifted me down to set my feet on the floor. "Are you alright?"

I looked up to his concerned eyes and nodded. "I am

now."

"I can't believe it was him," Michael said walking toward us. "He's been with us at least ten years."

Victor made a noise that didn't sound good. "We're going to have to check all guards and staff, from both sides, that have access to the inner chambers."

Leone stood there, leaning on the sword from the man. "How?"

"That's close to two hundred people, Victor." Quinton added.

He nodded. "I am aware of the numbers." His green eyes looked to me briefly. "If Cristy hadn't discovered him," he waved a hand around abruptly, "anything could have happened." He motioned to Leone with his head. "Call Troy. I want to know what is inside that traitor's head. Has he been sharing the layout of the chambers, the schedules? We need to know now."

Leone nodded and pulled his phone out then walked away.

Heaving a loud sigh, Victor looked down to me. "How close do you have to be to see the… aura, around a person?"

I looked from him to the other men watching me, waiting for an answer. "It isn't always the same." I clasped my hands and looked down at my red gloves. "If it's pure or good, I can see it from a far distance." I frowned and then looked up. "What do you want me to do?"

"She can't meet two hundred people, Victor, she'll have a panic attack." Quinton said.

Victor glared at him. "I'm aware of what she can and can not do, Quinton. I wouldn't ask her to walk up to so many strangers." He jerked his hand to the door the guards had gone through. "We have to do something though, because clearly we are working alongside them and didn't even notice."

I didn't like seeing him this upset, so I stepped closer and put my hand on his arm. "I can try to meet that many people." I told him.

His green eyes caressed over my face, and he exhaled quietly. "We'll find a way, so it doesn't upset you."

I nodded.

"What if we have department meetings?" Michael suggested. "Crissy can be present but not stuck in the middle or anything."

Quinton nodded. "Yeah, for those she can see far away we'll dismiss until we're down to any that are spies."

"It could work." He nodded abruptly and motioned to the door. "Go get those set up. I want as many as we can manage done today. That guard had free run of our halls and knows where each one of us sleep."

Michael and Quinton nodded and then quickly walked toward the door. Leone came back over and nodded.

"I heard. I'll go wake up Chase. He's going to be thrilled with this." He turned and left too.

Taking a deep breath, Victor finally looked back to me. "I don't like asking you to do this." He said quietly, "but it's the only way to ensure we all stay safe."

I bit my lip and thought about it. "I want everyone to be safe." I took a deep breath and let it out slowly. "Will you be there when I do this?"

"All of my brothers and Daxx will be present." He paused. "We need to do the guards first, I want to know who among those we can trust." Going over, he picked up my pack where I'd left it when I went to go get Michael.

"Victor?" He held my pack out to me.

"What is it?" Concern filled his face.

I clutched my pack to my chest and held his eyes with mine. "I miss you." I nodded hoping he'd understand and then pointed from him back to me. "Like this, not on the phone."

I watched his proud shoulders drop. "I am sorry for that."

I shook my head. "It's my fault, I upset you."

He moved so fast and took my chin in a firm hold. "It is not your fault, any of this." His touch softened as he searched my face. "I'm am running from myself, I admit, but you are not to blame."

I frowned, not understanding how he could run from himself.

He smiled briefly and released my chin. "I didn't mean it literally, heart, what I'm saying is I'm avoiding being alone with you because I do not trust myself, and do not wish to do anything that would compromise your freedom of choice." He leaned over and kissed my mouth quickly and then straightened up.

I still didn't know what he meant, but knew he was telling the truth and it was nice he didn't want to do that, I thought. Putting my pack on, I glanced to him again. "How am I going to check so many people?"

Touching my shoulder lightly he started walking toward the door. "I'm still puzzling that out. Let's go meet with the others and see if anyone has a feasible method."

After a family meeting in the dining room, that included me, Troy came back from the cells and reported that the information he'd seen in the bad guards' head lead him to believe there was a whole network of people inside passing information along. So, the meetings were all planned for today.

With all the brothers, Daxx, Tim, and Bronx dressed for battle, the meetings began. I don't know how they did it so quickly, but supposed when your King ordered something it was done. I'd never known a king before, and now I knew two.

We did the guards from both sides first and found one more from the day side. Troy and Raf had to hold onto Chase so he couldn't get to the man until they got him out of the room. Victor was beside me the whole time, Arius was on my other side and the rest were spread around the room.

As we walked to the next one, I glanced behind me to see what, to me, looked like the army in black following me. I glanced up at Victor. "Who are we seeing next?"

"Housekeeping for the Night realm."

I nodded. "At least they won't be armed." I looked at the weapons on him that I could see. "How do you walk with all that on?"

Arius chuckled beside me. "Practice, many, many years of practice."

"I keep forgetting how old you are." Which I thought was okay, it was the first time I had to remember their ages were in the hundreds, not decades.

"We're not old yet." He grinned and glanced to Victor. "Well, some of us, at least."

I smiled and looked at Victor, "some things get better with age." I nodded.

He grinned and looked at Arius, but didn't say anything.

I stayed silent for the rest of the walk, the flashes were many tonight and I needed to sort them, as much as I could. A few, I thought had come to me more then once, but I'd need some quiet time to figure those out, and the safety of everyone here was more important. A stick and book, a grey street sign and a purple door, but underneath. None of them fit.

Victor pulled me aside as the others went in the room. "The visions bad?" I must have looked surprised that he knew. He smiled. "I observe you often and have realized you get this look when you're more inside your head than out."

I could honestly say no one had ever noticed that before. I didn't even know I did that. "There's many, I'll sort through them when I have some quiet." I motioned to the room we stood outside. "This is more important right now."

His green eyes studied me thoroughly for a moment. "If you need some time in between let me know."

I nodded. "I will." Taking a deep breath, I looked at the door. "Maybe there will only be those two guards." I said trying to feel hopeful.

"We can hope, but I doubt that's all."

I felt the same, but didn't want to say it out loud.

Chapter Twenty

Four hours later we had done both sides of all staff that had access inside the royal chambers. There had been five more that were loyal to Marcus. People that we'd seen every day, they had smiled, and cleaned or cooked for us when none of us knew.

The flashes were coming more often now, with my mind tired from seeing so many people and the spaces around them.

We sat in the dinning room, but for once no one was eating. That was a rare thing here, I thought. I sat with them at the same end of the table beside Daxx with Rafael across from me.

I saw a grey street sign again, but signs weren't grey. There was green or blue, sometimes white, but never grey. The purple door again, not as a door should be though. I looked down at my hands and tried to stay focused on what the others were saying.

"Seven people, we've seen every day for years." Chase mused quietly.

"I still can't believe two of the guards we trained with for years were among them." Leone said rubbing his hand over his head.

"A stick and book, but not a novel that you see in the store. The stick isn't a stick either but carved..." I looked up to see everyone looking at me. "Sorry, I thought I said that in my head."

Rafael smirked at me. "It was a great tension breaker, little sister." Everyone else smiled and I felt my cheeks heat.

Victor leaned back and looked to each person for a moment. "We're going to have to change rotations and routines for a while." He nodded to Michael. "We don't know how much Marcus knows."

I stared at the wood of the table in front of me. Marks in the wood that were carved… like runes of some sort. *Marcus*, of course. The flashes, it made sense now. I kept seeing a cane. "Would Marcus have to use a cane now?" I tilted my head, "a long one like a…" I searched for the word, "like a staff, only not as tall?" I shook my head and reached for my pack so I could draw what I'd been seeing. "I keep seeing something and it didn't make sense until I pictured Marcus, then remembered what happened to him the last time you met." I looked at Daxx, she had told me with great detail how he'd lost his foot in their battle.

Finding a pencil, I opened the book and put my head down to focus and draw what I'd been seeing. "I don't know why I'm seeing it, I haven't been able to fit the pieces together, but it's been in my head many times today."

"Would it be because we found his spies?" Quinton asked me, leaning down the table.

I paused and looked up. "I don't think so. How could he know we did? We caught them before they knew we knew, so I don't think they had time to tell him." I looked back down and continued.

The room was silent as they all watched me, and I paused when I noticed, then was surprised to realize it didn't bother me. That was something I had to think through the next time I was in my tower. "Too many pieces. More pieces to see…" I mumbled. Shaking my head, I set the pencil down. "I can't see it all now."

"Just relax and maybe it will come." Victor suggested.

Getting up, I got the ball out of my pocket and looked around. I turned in a circle slowly. There were portraits all over the walls in here, so I couldn't bounce the ball off their faces. "Give me a minute." Without explaining, I went to the kitchen and found a bare wall. I started bouncing the ball in the cycle I had in my room. "A stick and book, grey street sign and a purple door… they all fit but how?" I murmured to myself.

I nodded and threw the ball some more. "A staff like a cane with runes carved in it… a spell of some sort I'm sure." I bounced through twice more while sorting and then stopped and looked at the ball.

Bouncing it again. "The book isn't a book, but a journal that's very old… not printed but written because it was seen." I reversed the direction of the throws. "Written like a prophecy in a leather-bound journal. Need to find out what prophecy he's trying to break."

More bouncing, a little faster. "Grey street signs, but the street signs aren't grey." Bounced slower again, too chaotic with the fast rhythm. "A sign that isn't grey, but white only seems grey under a street light." I rocked my head to the motion of the ball. "A sign that isn't grey but a sign is something used for directions, so you find your street. Grey street. That was so obvious I didn't see it."

I caught the ball and nodded once, then threw it again. "Okay." Wall to floor to wall again. "Purple door. Purple is no longer my favorite color for reasons that are carved into my back. Purple, mage… a magical place? A door to go through?" I reversed the rhythm of throwing. "Or is it as simple as a purple door on grey street at night?" I bounced it harder, trying to see. "Underneath the door doesn't make sense… unless it's a tunnel and the door is above."

I caught the ball and held it in my hand. "Oh, I *know* where Marcus will be, and what he's doing. I have to go tell them."

I spun around and then jumped and screeched when I saw all of them standing there, silently watching me. "I…"

"I think we just witnessed genius at work." Quinton said.

"We caught it all, little sister." Rafael smiled at me.

Troy shook his head and glanced at Arius, whose mouth was open. "Amazing."

Daxx held up her hand. "You started with a stick and a book, a grey street sign and a purple door and now you know where Marcus will be?"

I nodded and felt my cheeks go hot. "And he's trying to change a prophecy, so we need to find out which one."

Daxx's mouth opened then she shut it. "Oh, my god, when we were fighting him," She looked at Troy, "he said something about that." She waved a hand around. "I thought he was just spouting off crap, because we were kicking their asses. Go team royal and all that."

"What did he say?" Victor asked.

She held her hand on her head. "Just a sec." She glanced at me. "I don't have Crissy's brain so I'm going to need a minute."

I laughed. "You don't want my brain, trust me."

Victor came over and opened my hand and looked down at the ball. "Is this a new method your coach is trying? I saw the bowl of them in your room and wondered."

"Oh." I shook my head. "No, she brought those to float around with her mind, to show me focus." I grinned. "I was trying to juggle earlier and they went all over." I held up the red ball. "Then I found this one and was just bouncing it and realized it made it easier to sort through my head. The ones that don't matter just sort of... disappear." I stopped talking because he was just standing there smiling down at me.

"You may have found it on your own." He said, kissing my forehead and then hugged me.

"Found what?" I hugged him back.

"A way to cope with the visions so they don't overwhelm you." He kissed the top of my head and then leaned back and looked at me.

I frowned. "I've only done it today. How will I know if it is the way?"

He thought for a moment. "I suppose, we'll just have to see if you blackout, or if you have problems sorting and keeping up." He kissed me again. "But it feels like you've done what the scholars and overpriced coaches could not."

I looked at the ball my hand. "That's pretty good for a little bouncy ball."

Victor chuckled and nodded his head.

"I've got it!" Daxx yelled and then frowned. "Sorry. I almost had a meltdown trying to remember." She pointed a finger at me. "I have no idea how you keep it all in your head." She huffed out a breath. "Marcus said, I too have a prophecy to avoid bringing to reality." Nodding she smiled. "Whew."

"Okay, so, we need to have the scholars go through them and find that one." Troy said and then looked from Daxx to me. "And we need to know where there's a Grey Street, ladies."

Daxx looked at me. "Grey Street. It rings a bell, but I'm going to need a map."

I nodded. "I don't look at street signs."

Leone snorted. "Little hard to see from the tops of buildings, huh?"

I laughed quietly. "Yes, they are." I bit my lip. "Above won't help this time though, I think it's a tunnel, maybe that's why he's so hard to find."

"Can you draw out the runes on his cane or staff?" Michael asked.

"I think so." I bit my lip and then looked at the ball in my hand. "If not I know a good place to bounce this now."

Mitz got off the stool. "Just let me know when, and I'll try not to need in the freezer." She pointed to where I'd been bouncing it. On the freezer door.

"I'm sure we can find her many places to bounce Mitz, can't have the food preparations interrupted," Chase said and patted his stomach. "Okay, I'm going to go back to my side and I suggest you all have a nap sometime soon." He turned and waved his hand. "Let me know when we're going to Grey Street, I'm very curious to see what's behind or underneath the purple door."

"I'm going back to the cells to look in some heads and see if I can't find out more. How they got word to Marcus… something." Troy said rubbing the back of his neck. "I think that tomorrow, after breakfast, we need to sit down and figure out a game plan. We are being pulled in so many directions now it's unsettling." He looked at me. "Crissy is the only one capable of processing so many things at the same time."

I shrugged. "I have a whole bowl full of little bouncy balls if you'd like one."

They all laughed at that.

Daxx and I rushed down the hall.

"We're only five hours late," she shrugged, "Clairee is waiting in your room."

I glanced behind us again. "How did you know the men wouldn't go to bed?"

She rolled her eyes in that way she did when we talked about men. "New bad guys to interrogate, battle to be planned… I just knew."

"I don't think I'll ever understand them." I sighed.

Laughing, she pulled me the last few feet to my room. "I didn't say I understood them, I don't think anyone can."

Clairee was sitting on the couch waiting for us. "I didn't know what color, so I brought a few."

I looked at her brown hair, a color she didn't like, and then to Daxx's blonde hair and nodded. "I don't think I want something people will notice or remember." I touched my bright red hair. "This color has brought too many problems with it."

"If we go too light, the red may be hard to cover, you could end up with streaks of pink." Clairee said, taking my hand and leading me to the bathroom.

"Streaks are ok." I bit my lip, feeling nervous but excited at the same time.

"What is your real color?" Daxx asked hoping up on the counter.

I shrugged and then smiled. "I haven't had my real color in so long I don't remember."

We all looked in the mirror and studied my hair.

"Anything but bright, I can work with that." Clairee said with a grin.

"What if Victor doesn't like it?" I asked.

Daxx snorted, "the way he looks at you, we could shave your head bald and it wouldn't make a difference."

"I don't think we'll try that." I said with my hands on my head.

"He sees what's inside, not the color of your hair." Clairee assured me.

I let out a long breath and pulled off my pack and jacket. "Okay. Let's do it. Then I want a nap."

Daxx nodded. "The last few days are killing me. I don't know what time of day, or night, it is any more." She gave me a thumb up. "Thanks to you though, we may be able to catch Marcus."

Clairee paused and looked from me to Daxx. "That would be a blessed thing. Restore some normalcy around here."

I giggled. "I don't think anything here is normal."

A while later we all stood and looked at my hair in the mirror. It was a dirty blonde, with some brown streaks and lighter at the ends. Clairee was right, there was pink here and there. I loved it.

"You are just cute no matter how you cut it, Crissy." Daxx told me with a grin.

I didn't know about that. "I can be more invisible now."

"The way you hide, I don't think that's possible, but if anyone is looking for that girl with the bright red hair now… she's gone." Daxx nodded.

"You look lovely." Clairee told me.

I smiled and touched my hair. "Thank you."

"I need to sleep." Daxx said, giving me a quick hug and walking out.

Clairee nodded. "I think it's going to be more of a nap." She glanced at the watch she wore on a chain around her neck.

After she left I still stood there looking at the new me. I think I liked her.

Chapter Twenty-One

I was nervous when I went to breakfast the next morning, not sure if anyone would think my new look was strange. Well, it wasn't a new look I guess, I still dressed the same. I had my notebook in my hand when I walked in, so I'd remember the drawings of the runes I had seen.

"Whoa, little sister. You took cute to a whole new level." Rafael smiled at me in his way.

I smiled back and sat down next to Quinton. I still hadn't found the chair that felt the most like me.

Chase came in and gave my hair a touch as he went by. "Looking good, cutie." And went to his chair.

Everyone was smiling and looking at me, so I hoped that meant it looked okay. I heard Victor's voice in the kitchen and wondered what he'd think.

He walked in and stumbled over something for a step and then stopped and just stared at me.

"Lift foot, then step." Chase told him.

Leone laughed. "There's a little drool on your chin, old man."

Victor turned slowly and glared at them and then went and sat down quickly. When he did, he looked back at me again and smiled, but didn't say a word.

"If we can make this a meeting-while-we-eat, I'd appreciate it." Chase said. "After being dragged from my bed, *again*, yesterday, I'm feeling a little sluggish now."

Troy nodded. "I'm all for that and if we can try to have a day without some sort of emergency, I have plans to have a nap with my mate at some point."

Michael snorted but didn't say a word.

"Mhmm, I'm sure napping is the plan." Chase said with a big grin.

"Don't make me stab all of you." Daxx told them pointing her fork at them.

I took a bite of my toast and noticed Victor still looking at me, more then his plate. "I sketched out the runes I saw on the cane." I told them before taking a bite of my toast.

"We'll have to see if Romulus recognizes them." Victor said, still watching me.

"I found Grey Street." Daxx said while sipping her coffee.

Arius yawned. "We'll locate the purple door tonight and set up a watch, but still need to figure out the tunnels under it." He motioned to Rafael.

Raf nodded and rubbed the back of his neck and then looked to me. "Anything to add to that? A date stamp would be good."

"I know most of the tunnels under the city." I stopped and looked at him. "They don't come with dates." I told him. "That would be too easy."

"Right. Where's the fun with easy, Raf?" Quinton said and rolled his eyes at his brother and then turned to smile at me. "After watching you process last night, I've realized you're a genius, and if you weren't distracted by visions all the time, you'd just make us feel stupid."

I thought about that and frowned. "You are all smarter than I am about many other things." I nodded. Other things. "Oh, while I was looking at the ceiling last night, I had a thought…"

"Only one?" Rafael asked.

"Must have been tired." Daxx teased.

I rolled my eyes the way she always did to me, and then sobered when I remembered. "I saw Daxx's tattoo and then I met her. I saw the rune that is now on my back. So maybe there are other signs in here I have seen, but didn't know I did, but will now." I nodded and looked at Leone. "Maybe I've seen the flavor that will be who you need."

Leone started choking and quickly set his cup down.

"Swallow, then breathe." Chase told him with a smirk on his face.

"You think you've seen our mates?" Arius asked.

"Make mine with long legs and tall boots." Chase winked at me.

"I don't make them." I grinned. "They're already made, I just see them." I sighed. "Or a sign relating to them."

Chase nodded his head quickly. "Well, think legs when you see mine please." He looked around and then sighed loudly. "This war and spy stuff is really cutting into my dating life."

"I will try." I told him and sipped my tea, hoping someone would talk about something else now.

Victor looked at me again and I wished I had sat closer so I could figure out his thoughts.

"I have gone through the lists of people that have lived long on the other side then just, more or less, vanished." Michael leaned down to look at me. "Its looking like Crissy's theory is right after all."

"That's good, right?" I asked and he nodded. "Well, not if they're working with Marcus… although then we'll know how many there are… but we could find the lost people that should be here and not over there." Lost people. "Oh, I am down to the last decade and should know who Emil is now… very soon."

"And you had time to do all of that when?" Quinton asked me, tilting his head and brows drawn together.

"I don't sleep much." I said quietly.

Chase snorted. "Who does anymore?"

Victor sat back for a moment and stared at his plate. "If the God's favor it, pray Emil is on our side."

"Shit, wouldn't that suck." Rafael said softly. "To find our brother on the wrong side of this war."

The idea was very sad, even for me. "I will not go through my notebook today, just keep looking for him." I nodded to Rafael. "I saw him in that scene shown to me, there were no bad omens… so I don't feel he is against you, just unknowing." I offer a grin.

"What of the elders and scholars?" Troy asked Victor. "Do they have any insight on how a mated male even managed to have a child with another?"

Victor shook his head slowly. "Nothing definite." He said with a serious tone. "It seems they've heard speculation that a second mate is an extreme rarity that can occur." He frowned. "I've told them to look at facts, and not speculation."

"Maybe it's in the prophecies." I offered.

"Mmm," Victor said, his green eyes coming back to me. "I've suggested they look there as well."

"Okay, is it just me or is cutie… the little one that hides and rarely speaks, doing all the talking today?" Chase asked while waving his fork around.

"Mhmm, she is." Rafael agreed.

"I think someone is getting used to you guys… which I really don't know if it's a good or a bad thing. You have so many bad habits." Daxx smiled at me.

I knew they were teasing, and it was the first time I could remember knowing it was done in a loving way. I set my cup down and looked at each one for a second, then shrugged. "Maybe I just didn't want to hear more mud jokes today."

Victor started laughed and raised his cup to me.

"Burned." Raf said with a grin. "So, glad you're on our team, little…" He turned his head and glared at Victor, *"sister."* He finished quietly.

Victor raised an eyebrow at him, but didn't say a word. I wasn't sure, but thought they might be doing that thing where they talk in their heads to each other, which was quite fascinating.

"Okay, what else do we need to cover people? I'm fading fast." Chase leaned down in his chair.

"Ah, still no Alona or Emil at the club." Rafael said quickly.

Michael nodded his head. "Right, we're down to missing ten illegal devices, but if they've figured out a way to make them over there…"

"Or recruiting from that side." Leone added.

"We're not out of the woods yet." Michael finished.

I wondered what the woods had to do with the illegal devices.

"We're no further ahead." Victor said looking at me.

I smiled, just at him, when I realized he paid such close attention, he knew when I got lost in their talk. "Thank you."

He picked up his phone and looked at it.

"We may need Crissy to show us the tunnels." Raf said and everyone was silent and looked at me.

"Let me know when. Okay, I'll see you all later. I need a nap now or I'll be sleeping under the table and the last time that happened Mitz found me and threatened to beat me with a rolling pin." Chase said, getting up with a big yawn.

"Could be because you were drunk, half naked and had been missing for three days." Troy said with a smirk.

Chase snorted. "I was only fifty, give a guy a break. It took me three tries to land somewhere I would be less compromised as well." With a wave, he walked out of the room.

Victor stood up. "I have to get to the cells." He looked at Arius. "The guy you *spoke* with yesterday would like to have a chat.

Arius got up. "I think I'll tag along for that."

"I'll be there shortly." Michael said, and started eating what was left on his plate quickly.

"I'm going to take my lists up to my tower and look for Emil's name." I nodded and got up and picked up my notebook.

"Talk to you later, Rapunzel." Daxx said as I went toward the door. "How come she has her own tower and the huntress doesn't even have an office?" She asked her mate.

"Maybe the huntress doesn't need one because she's always in mine." He told he in a light tone.

Smiling to see them so happy, I went out and headed to my room for the lists.

I was so excited, I clutched the papers and ran to tell Michael. I finally knew who his lost brother was, right now. Today. I paused and realized I'd left my pack in the tower.

Shaking my head, I kept going. I went around the corner near his office and then stopped and didn't move. Leone and Michael rushed out of his office and then the door slammed, but they stood there. I backed up, so I was hidden by the corner.

"He is *so* out of control." Leone said while staring at the closed door.

Michael nodded. "He has a right to be upset... I get that," he motioned to the door, "but this..."

"You have to go tell him." Leone gave him a small push toward the door. "Smack him in the head, maybe it will help." He nodded.

Michael side-stepped and then looked down at his hand and put it behind his back. "Why me?"

Leone turned and looked at the door then back to him. "It's *your* office."

Michael rubbed the back of his neck. "I can get a new office." He waved a hand around. "We have halls of rooms here." He shook his head quickly. "I'm only three hundred and sixty, far too young to die so soon." He nodded.

"Let's go see Chase, he's not afraid of him." Leone suggested. "He should be awake by now." He shrugged, "or we'll just drag him out of bed. I'm willing to chance it."

Michael nodded slowly. "Chase isn't afraid of anything he should be. I still say mother dropped him on his head when he was a baby."

A loud crash and a scream that sounded like a wounded animal came from behind the door. Both men turned and ran down the hall.

Biting my lip, I went over to the door. I knew Victor was inside and needed me. I wonder what had happened. Turning the handle, I went in quietly.

"I said I wanted to be alone." He growled.

I looked around to see papers on the floor and what had been a shelf in the corner was in pieces on the floor. "I don't think you do." I said softly.

He spun around and looked at me. His eyes were red, and so full of pain. "I can't be near you right now, Cristy... you should go. I'll come find you later."

I looked around at the mess on the floor, and set the papers on the desk that looked like they were cleared with the brush of a hand. "I don't want to go." I stood there and looked at him.

He clutched his head in both hands for a second and looked down at me. Then he spun around and put his hands on the wall. "You have to. I'm not able to be this near you when…"

"When you're in so much pain?" I looked at the air around him. "I can see it you know. You're disordered inside, and that's something you don't do very well." Stepping closer, I watched his back rise and fall with each deep breath he took "A man that is so used to order, pieces falling at his command, doesn't do well when chaos won't listen."

"With his seer of truth… at… his… side… the justice will prevail throughout the years of time that remain." He took a shaky breath. "That is part of my prophecy." He spun around and held his hands out. "Only you're not at my side." He slapped his hands against the leather on his body. "I know it's not your fault." He clenched his jaw, then heaved another deep breath. "I can't find those that wanted you, those responsible for hurting you…" He growled, a sound of sorrow in his throat. "I can't even let you have your freedom that you so desperately need to be who you are. Since that moment I laid eyes upon you, passed out in the filth of an alley, there has been no peace or rest inside me. Each day only gets worse."

The pain in his voice made my heart ache.

"I can't hold you without shaking. I can't see you without pain in my heart, because I know now—after centuries of denying, that you do exist and are meant for me." He took a ragged breath and shook his head. "Inside of me, the need grows more. A force I cannot control… pushing me to claim you as my own and cherish you as a long-awaited mate should be." He put his hands on his hips and looked to the floor. "I do not trust myself. I cannot be too near you right now, so please…"

"I'm not leaving." I said, stepping closer. Something Daxx said came back to me, when she told me to get in his face more.

Maybe I wasn't close enough. "I didn't say I couldn't be yours, only that I can't wear your mark right now."

His eyes, still red, watched me as I moved closer. "I cannot touch you and promise not to mark you, the need is too strong."

I was less than a foot from him now, looking up at him. "You won't." I said softly and held up my hands to show him the gloves on them. "You can't… if the flesh of our palms can't connect."

Slowly his eyes searched my face and looked to my hands. He shook his head. "It still isn't right to ask…"

Reaching up, I put my fingertips over his mouth. "It is for me to choose." I moved until I was close enough to feel the heat of his body. "I want to be with you. I want you to feed from me." I nodded. "I can't bear your mark right now, but I never said I wasn't yours… or you weren't mine. I've never felt safe, or like I belong, more than I do then when I'm near you."

He frowned and looked down at me. "What are you saying?" His voice was so quiet I almost didn't hear.

"Victor. Shut up and kiss me."

His eyes flicked to my mouth and he barely shook his head. "If I do I won't be able to stop…"

"Then don't." I told him never knowing a feeling to be more right.

With a move so fast, I didn't see it coming, I was in his arms, my feet off the floor. He grasped the back of my head and crushed my mouth with his. This was not a careful kiss, but one of great need as his tongue stabbed into my mouth and took my breath away. I could feel his sharp fangs, and heat moved through me, making me ache and want.

When he boosted me up higher on his body, I wrapped my legs around him as best as I could with all of the weapons he wore. Turning, he leaned me back against the wall, leaving no space between us. His mouth lifted from mine and we both panted for air before his fangs traveled down over my jaw to my neck and he hovered there.

"Not here." He said with a growl in his voice.

Wrapping his arm under me, he turned and kicked something out of his way to reach the door. He opened the door and started down the hallway, I kept my legs locked around his waist, not wanting to let go long enough to walk beside him, in case he changed his mind. "You have so many weapons on. I can't get close." I gasped as his teeth scraped along my throat. He growled in answer.

Reaching down between us, I undid the buckles and straps that held the long blades on his back. It slipped free and they hit the floor. He kept walking with sure strides. Leaning to one side, I pulled the curved knife from his hip and dropped it. When it clattered against its case as it hit the floor, I nodded and leaned the other way to pull the two blades he had there free. The transporter box was next. It hit the floor harder then the rest, and I peeked over his shoulder to make sure it hadn't broken. His tongue ran along my jaw and I decided I didn't care if it did. I just wanted to hurry so when we reached wherever he was going, there wouldn't be time for him to think.

I found three more blades of different kinds on him, that I could reach. As the last one hit the floor, Chase came around the corner and stopped to watch us walking by him.

"Not now, brother." Victor growled.

With an eyebrow raised and smile on his face Chase looked at me and his brother's back. "I see that, brother." He looked at the trail of weapons. "I'll just pick these up then, so no one falls and gets stabbed, or dies." He laughed.

I didn't get to see if he did or not, as Victor grasped the back of my head and pulled my head to his, our mouths clashed like his blades did in battle. I heard a door shut loudly, but kept returning his hungry kisses, I felt like I was starving for him by now.

Victor stopped walking and lifted me from him, I realized I was standing on his bed. His red eyes held mine as we both breathed hard.

"Be sure." He gripped my waist and stood there waiting.

Reaching, I pushed the jacket over his shoulders, down his arms. He shook them free and I found two more blades on his arms. As I unbuckled the one, he did the other. The weapons landed on his jacket.

"You wear too many things." I said as I started on the

buckles on his vest.

He brushed my hands aside and took over. "Easy access is not what it's intended for."

I stood and watched as he peeled off the layers, and a few more blades, until he stood naked before me. Feeling my cheeks and body flush, I let my eyes wander over him. Muscles over muscles in the most perfect way, I thought as I licked my tongue over my lips.

With a soft growl, he gave me a gentle shove and I fell back onto the bed. He pulled my boots off and tossed them on the floor and then made fast work of my belt and pants. I pulled my shirt over my head, he had my bra undone before I could pull my arms free.

"You are perfect." He whispered as he knelt over me, his eyes moving over me slowly.

I was feeling nervous now, which was silly, this was Victor, but I didn't know what I was supposed to do. He leaned down and kissed my hip and then across my waist, tiny light kisses that filled me need. By the time his warm breath was over my breast, I was shaking and breathing so heavily I wasn't sure if I was really getting air.

His hot mouth closed over one nipple and he sucked gently, I gasped and gripped his hair with both hands, not wanting him to move away. I could feel his fangs against my skin and it heightened every need.

When he lifted his head, he watched my face closely as his hand moved down between my legs and he stroked the wetness between my legs. I raised my hips, needing more.

"I need to know now," he kissed me in a gentle way before looking at me again. "Is this the first time?"

I nodded my head, biting my lips from what his fingers were doing to me.

"I'll try to go slow." He didn't wait for a response. His mouth was over mine, kissing me with such and urgency I didn't know if I would survive the way it made me feel. His hand kept moving and I moaned, needing more.

When he pulled my legs open and our bodies touched, I tried to move closer. He moved his hand and held my hip so I couldn't move. I was panting and whining by the time I felt him against the wetness between my legs, and then his mouth moved over my throat and I moaned again.

He pushed inside me so carefully, I didn't know how, if he was feeling half as much as I was. Grasping my hair lightly, he pulled my head to the side to expose more of my throat, and when his fangs punctured my skin he thrust deep inside me.

My head was now spinning and I thought I was on fire from all the sensations at the same time. I heard myself make noises as I moved my hands over every part of him I could touch. Each time I gasped, he moved faster and then my body exploded with so many feelings and sensations, I cried out his name against his shoulder and felt him tense and still.

Panting, I lay there, my hands still moving over every part of skin with in reach. Never had I felt something like that.

"Give me… a second and I'll move… so you can breathe." He panted, heavy against my ear.

I shook my head and swallowed, taking tiny breaths trying to get air. "This is good." I told him.

For several minutes we lay there, our breathing the only sound filling the quiet space around us.

"Did I hurt you?" He raised himself up and kissed my forehead, then slowly moved off of me.

I gasped at the new sensations that movement created, and shook my head. As he rolled to his side, he pulled me with him so all of our bodies were still touching. I liked that. We were both hot, but I wasn't going to move away from him just to feel cooler.

He kissed my mouth softly, and then smiled at me. "I will never tire of you crying out my name that way."

I felt my face flush and bit my lip. Name… "Emmett." I said.

His muscles stiffened and he raised an eyebrow at me.

I smirked when I realized the timing was very bad. "I just remembered. Your brother Emil's name now is Emmett."

He closed his eyes for a second and then looked at me again. "My heart, we need to discuss your timing when sharing what pops into your head."

Victor smiled at me again, and I felt relief. "That's why I came to look for Michael and found you destroying his office."

"Mmm," he kissed me once more. "While I'm thrilled to know who my brother is right now, I have other things I need to deal with first."

I frowned. "Oh."

He flipped me on my back and licked my neck gently then started to move down my body. "I want to be sure you're not injured."

I didn't know what he intended until his breath touched my thigh and then thought Emil had been lost for three hundred years, he would be okay for one more day.

When we walked in the dining room for dinner, my head was still dizzy from the hours spent with Victor. We didn't move from his bed, except to spend some time in the tub. I had to stop by my room for dry gloves, then we walked the halls, stopping often to kiss before realizing we were starving.

He led me to the end of the table where he sat, and pulled out the chair beside him, so I sat down. I hoped Leone wouldn't mind that I was in his chair.

Chase came through the door from the kitchen a big grin on his face. "Your weapons are in your office." He said and then sat down and winked at me. "Tamed the beast, I see."

I felt my face flush and didn't know what to reply, so I just smiled and then looked away.

Leone came in and paused when he saw where I sat. I could tell he wasn't sure if he could sit beside me without worrying he couldn't resist me.

Daxx came in, and without a word, came and sat beside me and Leone looked relieved. He left an empty chair for her mate, and then sat down. She winked at me and then reached for a roll. "Did anyone do anything they were supposed to be doing, today?"

Troy came in, a big smile on his face, with eyes only for Daxx.

"I was dragged out of bed, *again*." Chase said looking at Victor. "To come take on big brother and settle his ass down."

He shrugged, "little cutie beat me to it."

Victor looked from him to me, then grinned. "I'm sure she had more success than you ever could."

"Well," Michael came in carrying a platter from the kitchen, "now that all of the banter is finally out of the way, we need to figure out a plan for the tunnels." He glanced to Arius as he came striding in the other door. "We got lost in them today."

Rafael was next through the door. "Is that where you went to?"

Arius nodded and then frowned. "It's a maze down there."

"They can be confusing." I told them so they'd feel better. "I was down there for a week one time, because I turned the wrong way."

Quinton came in and yawned. "Is this day over yet?" He stopped and looked from Victor to me and then grinned again. "Thank the gods." He went and sat down.

"You look tired, brother. Not enough sleep lately?" Chase said with a fake snarl on his face. "I know that feeling myself."

"Oh, brother." I glanced to Victor, having forgotten again. "I know who your brother is now. Emmett." I nodded. All stopped, and then looked at me.

"Do you have an address for him?" Troy asked, a serious look on his face.

I sighed, "I do, but I'm not sure it's real, but now that I know who he is, it will be easier to find him." I looked at Michael. "I left the papers on your desk." Then I remembered how his office looked when we left it. "I will get them when Victor goes to clean up his…"

"Rampage." Leone finished for me. He glared at Victor and then turned to get some food.

Victor cleared his throat. "I will make certain the office is returned to its proper state, after we eat." Turning, he smiled down at me and then reached under the table and rested his hand on my thigh.

Just a touch from him gave me feelings I'd thought would be tired and unresponsive after the day we'd had. I smiled at him, and bit my lip for a moment. "I'll help you." I told him softly.

He glanced at my mouth, with the look, a look that I now knew what it meant, filled his eyes as he looked at me.

I'd never felt this kind of happy in my life, and knew I would do whatever it took to have it always.

Chapter Twenty-Two

Two days later, when I walked into the practice room, everyone was standing there looking at me. I looked behind me, in case there was something I hadn't noticed. I stopped and gave a little wave. "Hi?"

Rafael laughed and started walking toward me. "Ready for your test?"

I swallowed. "Test?" Everyone started to move around on the big mats, so they were spread out all over and not standing close together. Feeling like I should do something, I dropped my pack and bent down to adjust the strap that held my knife. It didn't need adjusting, I just needed time to catch up. I stood up. "I'm not very good at tests." I told him. "The teachers said I didn't study, or focus." I shrugged. "They were wrong, I remembered everything, but their questions were never simple, each one had multiple answers that were all correct."

Quinton started laughing. "I want a brain like yours."

I frowned. "No, you don't."

Daxx came over and took my hand. "He didn't mean with all the visions, Crissy, just that brilliant part of it."

"Oh." I looked over and smiled at Quinton to let him know I was sorry. "What…" I looked around at everyone again. "What is the test on?" I bit my lip and hoped I knew the answers.

"We were having a discussion before you got here and someone…" she stopped and looked right at Victor, "who we'll call grumpy bear, said you are not ready to show us the tunnels on the other side."

I leaned closer to her and whispered, "he kind of sounds like a bear with all the growling he's been doing."

She laughed and I looked to see several of the men trying not to smile.

"So, you need to prove that your escape and evade skills are pure awesomeness now." She pushed me so I was standing on the edge of the mat, the others spread out in front of me in a line. Taking my pack, she walked over and set it by the wall of weapons.

I adjusted my belt and little box to avoid looking at everyone. "I have been practicing, a lot." I looked over at Victor and then waved my hand around, "while you're out... rampaging at the world." I glanced to Daxx, and shrugged having used her words.

His mouth quirked, but he didn't smile. "I don't think..."

Chase snorted, "That's obvious."

Victor gave him a hard stare and then sighed. "Fine." He gave each brother a cold stare. "No one touches her."

Rafael lifted his hands and then dropped them. "Defeats the purpose of a test if we all stand here and just stare at her."

Victor growled, "I don't..."

Moving quickly, I went over and rubbed my hands on his chest. Smiling at him. "Please go stand by the target board. I want to show you that I have been learning as much as I can." I stretched up on my toes and kissed his mouth softly. "Please."

His green eyes searched mine for a minute and then he nodded. "If it's too much say so."

"I will." I nodded and watched him back up then turn and stand out of the way by the target. I held up my hand. "One second please." I ran over to my bag to get something Leone had made for me. We had practiced with it for hours. He had one, and some day I wanted to be as good with it as he was. "I didn't know there was a test," I glanced back at them. "I wasn't prepared." I pulled it out and attached it to the back of my belt so it would be out of the way.

I looked to see Leone smirking when I walked back over.

"Okay." I gave Daxx a nervous look. "What are we doing?"

Daxx looked around at the way the guys were spread out. "If they catch you for longer than three seconds, you fail. We can't chase you, but the area two feet all around us we can move in." She glanced to Victor. "If you reach Victor, you win."

"Oh." I nodded. "Good motivation." I looked down to figure out how much space that gave each of them. They had big bodies, long arms. This was going to be hard.

She laughed. "I thought so." She backed up so she was one more body standing in my way to reaching him. "You got this."

I looked at the other end of the large room where Victor stood, and he nodded his head as encouragement. "I got this." I whispered. "Um, any means that I know to get there, right?"

Daxx smirked, "Absolutely. Whatever you can use out there to get back in one piece is allowed."

I nodded and gave my arms a shake, to get ready. Quinton and Rafael were the first two, then Daxx. After that it got harder.

"Stop over-thinking and just do it." Quinton told me as he widened his stance, his arms out ready to grab me.

I nodded and started running at him. Just as he would reach for me I stopped as fast as I could and covered my mouth, looking as scared as I could manage, which wasn't hard, because I had spent my life looking afraid.

"Aw, hun, it's…."

I ducked under his arm then rolled to get away further. I saw the grin on Rafael's face as he'd watched how I'd gotten by his brother. Just when he thought to reach for me I stopped and put my hand to my head like I would if I were in pain.

"Shit. Crissy?"

With a smirk, I dropped and went between his legs and moved fast. Daxx was next and she knew my tricks and her look said she wouldn't fall for them. When I had a few feet before I reached her, I glanced to my left, then paused and looked again.

"Oh, no." I said.

"What?" She turned to look and I bolted by her. Troy was next and I had no special cheats I could use on him, other than his size. Climb them like a tree Daxx had told me many times and then I remembered the ball in my pocket. Pulling it out, I threw it at him. It hit him in the chest giving me enough time to slide by him close to the floor.

"Damn." I heard him say.

Chase and Michael were next, standing closer together.

"Bring it, cutie," Chase said with a grin.

I ran faster, needing more speed. I thought, *like a tree*. As he reached for me, he bent his knees, I used it to step on and launch myself up. Putting my hands on his shoulders, I flipped over him, then used the momentum of coming down to land both feet on Michael's chest. He fell, I kept going.

"Yes!" I heard Daxx yell and felt pretty excited about it myself.

Arius was next and I'd practiced a lot with him, so he knew so many of my moves, I had to think fast. I glanced up remembering where the lowest beams were. As I got closer, I reached behind me and pulled the pulley off my belt. Grasping the handle on it I flung it up with the fast motion, just as Leone and I had practiced, and the weight flew up and spun around the beam and then started to retract, and I leapt over top of Arius as it did.

Jumping to the ground, I approached Leone and he looked entirely too happy. I didn't know what to try next. He was the last one, but I kept running. "Touch me and I'll bite you." I called to him. He straightened, shock on his face, so I rolled by him and came up in a crouch just past him. Grabbing my knife, I flung it up toward the target and heard it *thunk* as it hit the middle.

Jumping up, I ran toward a wide-eyed Victor. I squealed and jumped up into his arms, wrapping my legs around his waist. Then I dropped my head to his shoulder and tried to remind my body how to breathe. I heard everyone clapping behind me and turned to look back at them.

"You so cheated." Leone said walking over, but he was smiling.

"Daxx said *whatever* I could use." I told him as I tried to catch my breath.

"I have no words." Victor said sounding as breathless as I

felt.

Leaning back, I looked at him. "I have worked *very* hard. I was tired of always being afraid."

"So I see." He kissed my mouth quickly. "I am amazed." He glanced to the others and lowered me so I was standing in front of him.

Daxx did a fist pump and then grabbed me and hugged me. "That flip was *so* frickin' good..."

Troy stood there, the small red ball between his thumb and finger. "I was taken out by a rubber ball." He smirked at me and held it out to me. "My ego is crushed."

"Yours? I don't even know how she took the first three of us out." Rafael said.

"With your minds." I told him and nodded.

Quinton shook his head. "You have definitely mastered the art of distraction."

I shrugged. "My mind has been distracted my entire life."

"You will bite me?" Leone stood there with his hands on his hips. "What was that?"

I shrugged. "I don't know, but neither did you, so it worked."

Arius pointed to my pulley that now lay on the floor behind us. "When did you pick up that trick?"

I bit my lip and looked at Leone. "Leone and I decided *up* was my thing." I nodded. "I still have to practice keeping the pulley with me after I come down though."

Arius shook his head. "I'm glad you're on our team." He smiled.

I took a deep breath and looked around at them. "I may not be able to swing big scary weapons, but I would protect each of you as you would me. No matter what." I threw the ball up and caught it and then again. Processing, processing.

"So, grumpy bear," Daxx looked at Victor, "can we go for a hike in the tunnels and maybe catch a bad, bad mage?"

I nodded. "I want to go." I looked at Victor as he thought it over.

"Do the transporters work in the tunnels? Sometimes, deep underground they don't." He glanced to Michael.

He frowned. "We didn't think of testing them. We can transport." He looked around as his siblings. "With all of us there, she'll be safe, Victor."

The nerve in Victor's jaw twitched as he thought about it. "I want Romulus and the witches to make certain that the cell they say is Marcus proof, IS, without question." He glanced to Daxx. "My transporter to the cells will be programmed to only transport there, leaving you all to do any and all of the other dispatching."

Daxx nodded. "I can handle it. I'll just have to fight less, pop more."

I bit my lip and looked to the others, all busily thinking of other possible scenarios. I hadn't told them why I was late. "I may know more." I told them quietly. "I woke up to the flashes, so many today."

"Are you alright?" Victor asked, his eyes quickly assessing me.

I nodded. "I needed some time to process and sort them through."

"Any why didn't you mention this instead of their test?" He asked looking unhappy.

I moved over close and rested my hand on his chest. "I can do more than one thing at a time."

Rafael snorted, "or in your case, thirty, unlike the rest of us sloth-brained beings."

Victor placed his hand over mine, against his heartbeat and looked at me in that loving way his eyes always held, only now I knew what it was. "What did you see?"

"A battle below…" I held up my hand when he started to speak. "That I was present for. A room with a spell…" I glanced to Daxx. "That the greasy mage will be needed to break."

"Romulus." She said looking unhappy with the idea.

I nodded. "A witch with a staff that glows light, comes from and the army in black…" I looked around at them, "that's how I see all of you. Stopping them all." I let out a shaky breath. "There was blood, but I am thinking there always is when all of you are in what I see."

Michael smirked. "As long as it's not ours, I'm good with that."

"The witch, was she ours or his?" Troy asked.

"His." I said quietly.

"So, we need to bring a witch and a mage with us." Arius asked while looking very serious.

I nodded. "I believe that's why it warned me of both being needed, so we don't fail."

Victor paced away and stopped looking at the wall. I could see everyone watching him with nervous expressions.

Daxx motioned with her head for me to go to him, so I did.

I touched my hand on his back when I reached him and he put his arm around me but didn't turn back to the others.

"I do not like taking you into something so volatile, heart." He reached and tipped my chin up, so I was looking in his eyes. "I do not know if any would be safe were something to happen to you."

"I'll be okay." I told him and I knew it was true. "I'm not afraid now, I know more…" I bit my lip for a moment. "And I've seen things to tell me it's true."

His green eyes searched my face, with so much worry.

"I've seen fields of butterflies since I came here, such a peaceful thing to see." I told him. "I saw you happy, inside my head, and I know I must be okay or you wouldn't be." I explained. "I've even seen a baby."

His brows drew together and he looked at me carefully.

"I don't know who's it was, but those are all good signs."

"A baby? Like one baby or two?" Chase asked.

I turned to see everyone look at Daxx.

She shook her head. "Hell no. Twins, in two hundred and forty-nice years. That's it's for me."

Troy hugged her tightly and everyone grinned. I didn't know what that meant, but I made a note in my head to ask later. Turning, I looked back up at the man holding me close. "I need to be there Victor, I don't know why, but I do."

"We have to trust what she saw, Victor, despite all of us wanting to keep her in a *bubble*." Daxx said in a more serious tone.

I still didn't know what this bubble was, but she said it like it was a place I wouldn't enjoy.

Victor's big chest rose as he breathed deeply. "Get Romulus and the strongest witch in the coven. We'll pay a visit to Marcus once everyone is ready." He grasped my chin in a gentle hold. "You will take no chances that are not necessary." I nodded as best as I could and he kissed my mouth hard, before releasing me to walk over to the target and pull out my knife. "Rafael, find a larger blade that she is comfortable handling, to strap to her thigh. It has to be short enough to lay flat as she moves, I don't want her hindered, but I want her to have a backup in case she needs it." He came over and knelt before me and put my knife back in the case strapped to my leg and then looked up at me. "You'll carry it for my peace of mind, and if any get too close to you, I'll know you have something to protect yourself."

I nodded and touched his hair with my hand, then hugged his head as he leaned into me.

"Come on, little sister, lets find you the right blade." Rafael said as he walked by to the wall of weapons. "We'll practice a bit so you know how to handle it and get it out fast."

Taking a deep breath, I released Victor and followed him. I didn't know if I could use it on another person, but to be honest, knowing I wasn't completely defenseless did settle my nerves. The pieces in my head didn't tell me if we'd be successful in the tunnels, or if we'd get Marcus into a cell. What I had seen gave me all we would need, so I had hope.

Chapter Twenty-Three

I stood in the landing room, watching the others coming in and getting ready. Mitz was even here. I noticed she spoke to each brother, to her they were sons. She smiled and said something to Daxx, who laughed and then nodded her head.

When she came over and stopped in front of me, I was surprised. I wasn't a warrior going off to battle, if anything I was the least of all in this fight.

She hugged me quick and then touched my cheek. "You bring them all home to me." She said and then walked away.

I looked to Rafael, standing closest to me.

He shrugged. "I know you don't see it yet, little sister, but you are part of the family now, and a very important one."

I started to answer him and then Victor walked in. He glanced to each person in the room as he walked toward me, I knew he was assessing that all were well prepared. He stopped in front of me and looked to the blade strapped flat to my left thigh and gave Rafael a quick look.

"She holds her descender and the pulley both in her left hand so we practiced reaching across with her right. It's a smooth motion, and one she can do quickly if needed." Rafael said then nodded to me and moved over to stand near Quinton.

I looked up to Victor and tried for a smile, but wasn't sure if I made it work. "I'll be okay." I told him.

Reaching in his pocket, he pulled out a preprogrammed transporter. He took my wrist and undid the one I already wore. "I had them make the signal on this one stronger, so it can reach the edge where the realms touch, so it may work in the tunnels." He put it on my wrist. "If it doesn't at first, do all that you can to get closer to the surface, then try again."

I looked at it and nodded. "Okay." Then back to his concerned eyes. "I don't plan on leaving your side, though I probably won't need it."

Looking around, he frowned. "Bronx will be here shortly. You be sure to stay close to him."

"I will." I touched his arm. "Everyone comes home." I told him.

The commotion paused when Romulus and the quiet witch that had helped me came in. She looked perfectly calm, the mage did not.

"Its nice, to see someone more nervous then me." I said quietly to Victor.

He offered me a small grin and then grasped my chin lightly and kissed my mouth hard. "If things go bad, hide."

I nodded. Of course I would, no one was better at hiding than me.

Bronx and Tim came through the door with Chase, who looked so happy to be going to battle again. Coming over, he winked at me and opened his arms wide. "Where to this time, cutie? I can't wait to see."

Daxx came over to listen as well.

I bit my lip and thought for a moment, finding the best place to go in. "Under the fish factory is the best place, we'll have to run for a bit, but it's better then going to Grey Street and being seen."

"Perfect," she said with a grin. "Only one trip then, because all of us have been there." She looked around to Troy and sent him a smile. "Bring my blocker for me." Then was gone.

Troy cursed under his breath for a second and then put his hand on Tim's shoulder. "Don't dally, she'll find trouble without us." He told them and then the two were gone.

"Ready?" Victor asked with a brow raised.

I nodded and touched him, waiting for my churning stomach to know we'd arrived.

I ran quickly through the tunnels, not needing to pause to think which way to go. I had meant it when I said I knew them, and I did. We went down several levels, on broken stairs and across a small waterway that hadn't been used for at least a hundred years. The others behind me didn't make a sound. I stopped once or twice to make sure we stayed close together. Michael was last, watching behind us the whole way. Romulus looked tired from the short run, and I bit the side of my cheek so I wouldn't grin knowing the going down part was easy, the going up side wasn't going to be.

When we paused by a tunnel that was the first of many levels to go up, I held up my hand. Glancing behind me, I saw everyone looking and watching. Reaching into my pocket I pulled out a small pack of candies. I paused near a darkened corner until I heard movement in the shadow. Shaking my head, I glanced to Victor so he wouldn't react to protect me. An older man, of an uncertain age came out… it was hard to tell age when you wore extra clothes and had dirt on your face.

"I have missed you." He said with his rasping voice. "You've been gone for a long time."

I held out the packet and gave him a smile. He took it and looked so pleased. "I wasn't here." I told him and grinned.

He looked to the others, with one brow raised. "I saw nothing but the empty tunnels here today." He stepped back into the shadows.

I motioned for everyone to go up the ramp, we had several levels to run to reach the place beneath the purple door.

"Love your ways," Rafael winked as he passed me.

When we reached the end of a tunnel that split both ways, I stopped and pointed to the left. "Beneath the purple door is that way, not too far." I said in a whisper. "There are two tunnels that split from a big open area, and one narrow one that's a dead-end between them."

I looked around to make sure the mage was hearing me. "The dead-end is where the magic creates a door." He nodded with a serious expression on his face. I turned to the witch with the pure air around her. "The path to left of the dead end is where I saw the witch with the staff of light."

"Do you know what is down either tunnel?" Quinton asked crouching low and watching around the corner.

I shook my head. "Followers, I don't know how many. Coming and going as they use those tunnels beneath the purple door to get in and out of the city, unseen."

"Lots of bad guys, got it." Daxx said and patted her transporter box. "I hope my batteries are fully charged."

Michael smirked. "It runs on your energy, huntress."

"Really? Okay then, good to go." She smiled at me. "If Crissy had one we could send them to the moon with her energy levels." Pulling one of the blades from her back, she pointed it toward the tunnel we were to take. "Shall we?"

I heard several more being pulled, but didn't pull mine.

Romulus and the witch, whose name I still didn't know, moved to the front with Michael and Leone, then nodded and started walking slowly. I glanced to see Victor, with both long blades pulled, he nodded for me to follow, so I moved after them.

As we reached the open chamber, I looked around to see a ledge above the door. I watched the others move to cover the two paths while the mage started waving his hands toward the dead-end space. I climbed the uneven stones and got on the ledge, to stay out of the way. Once settled, I saw Victor glance right at me, he'd known my every move without having to watch me.

All I knew was if I was down there with them, he would be distracted worrying about me, so I took me out of the battle and planned to stay on the ledge until told to do otherwise.

I watched Romulus moving his hands so very slowly, it was graceful, the way he moved. I hadn't read about what mages could do, but it was on my list to learn more. The sound of blades clashing made me jump, and I turned to see many bodies rushing into the space from the tunnel on the right.

Biting my lip, I stayed still so no attention would be drawn to me.

"Romulus, you think you're a match for me?" A voice

echoed through the tunnels.

I turned to see Marcus, his black hair with the white streak standing in the dead-end tunnel, his dark purple eyes glowing in the dim light. He leaned his elbow on the cane with the wide handle, so both hands could be free. When he started to move them, I saw Victor position himself closer, and held my breath.

"Even if you take down this barrier and imprison me, you're too late. They will complete their task without me." He said with a sneer.

Romulus didn't speak, only focused on his movements and I had to wonder if it was working, but it wasn't something an eye could see.

I didn't know what that task was, but clearly, we needed to find out. I saw Daxx and Tim fighting side by side, he would distract them and she would use the transporter, with a 'pop' they were gone.

Rafael and Leone were with the witch and I couldn't see them. Troy and Chase looked like a reflection in a mirror, as they fought three at once, pushing them back toward the tunnel they'd come from. Quinton and Arius fought back-to-back, keeping the men from getting to the tunnel we'd come from and escaping. I looked below me to see Bronx blocking the way and thought even if they got by, the pirate would slow, or halt, their departure.

A light from the left tunnel flashed and I knew the witch with the staff was there, battling with the one on our team.

Several more followers came out of the other tunnel, forcing our people to step back. I didn't like the numbers we were up against now. Daxx was no longer fighting, but dashing among them, while the brothers distracted. She used the box, cutting down the numbers quickly. I sighed in relief to know she was able to do that, and wondered briefly if Victor could have a transporter to the cells made for me. That was something I knew I could do.

I watched Daxx slide to pop one more then heard a sound below me and turned to see Bronx facing the tunnel we'd come from. He backed up a step, his sword drawn and then a noise like a whip came from the tunnel and his sword hit the floor. He grabbed his arm, blood was flowing through his fingers.

I looked to see if one of the others had noticed, but they were all busy. He staggered back and a tall man walked past. The only weapon he had, that I could see, was a long whip coiled carefully in his hand. Climbing down quickly, I rushed to Bronx. I didn't know how bad his arm was, but knew I didn't have time to check. I pulled the knife from his hip and cut the strap from the sword case and quickly wrapped it around his arm. He nodded and straightened up, holding the injured wrist to his chest and then picked up his sword in the other.

I turned to see where the man went, he was going straight for Romulus. The mage didn't notice as he continued weaving his spell. He was sweating and shaking and if the expression on Marcus' face meant anything, I'd say our mage was winning.

I saw Tim stagger back a few times, trying to hold three others from reaching him. "Go help Tim." I Told Bronx and moved back against the wall. He gave me a look, but went. Even with only one good arm he was more help then I could have been.

Everyone was busy fighting for their lives, and the man with the whip only had one person between he and Romulus. Victor. I bit my lip so I wouldn't shout a warning. I heard Daxx swear and Troy roar, but couldn't look away.

Marcus laughed and did something briefly and I watched Victor fall to the floor. The man with the whip raised his arm. Grabbing the knife from my case, I rushed toward him. I slid beneath Chase's raised blade, jumped over a heap that may have been a body, and flicked my knife toward the man with the whip. He cursed loudly and fell to one knee. As I went by him I saw I'd landed my knife in the back of his thigh.

Flipping around, I stopped where Victor struggled against the magical hold. Crouching low, with a wide stance, I pulled my new blade from its case, and held it toward the man holding my knife with his leg. He would have to go through me to harm Victor.

He sneered at me and pulled the blade free, holding it toward me as he struggled to get up. If he lashed out with his whip, I had no defense, not that I could catch the knife if he tossed at me either. If he got to his feet, I couldn't do a thing. Before I knew what I intended, I reached with my other hand and pulled the pulley off my belt and flung it toward him, when it wrapped around the leg that was holding him up, I pulled as hard as I could and he went down, flat on his back.

Glancing quickly to Victor, I saw he was moving to get up and wondered if Romulus had managed to break whatever Marcus had done. The look on Victor's face was lethal as he got to his feet, his eyes moved over me looking for injury. Pulling me to my feet, he gave me a gentle shove in the direction of Chase, who moved to stand in front of me with his blades both drawn.

I watched Victor step over to the man with the whip, he reached down and pulled him to his feet by his hair, as he drew the thin curved blade from his hip. "The judgement is death for threatening my mate." He spun with the man so I couldn't see, then growled with a sound that sent a chill through me and the man dropped to the floor, blood spilling out around him.

Chase backed me up closer to the entrance again and stood there, assessing anyone near. "Climb." He said over his shoulder and I looked to see a large man rushing toward us with a huge axe with blades on two sides. I needed no more instruction, I turned and went up the wall as fast as I could.

When I was back on the ledge, I turned to see there were few left from the other side. Bronx wasn't looking good, but he was still on his feet. Marcus howled like he was in pain and I turned to see him struggling to stop whatever Romulus did.

Victor screamed, a warrior's cry, and bolted through the space where Marcus stood, and he was gone with a 'pop'. Not pausing for a second, Victor spun back, giving our mage a gentle nudge into the space that had been protected. "It all goes back so you can figure out what he was doing."

Nodding Romulus moved out of my sight. Victor stepped out and picked up his blades, rushing to help Chase with the giant swinging the axe.

I looked to see the others all closer now, and only three more left from the other side. My heart was beating so fast, I was sure it was going to jump right out of my chest. Had we actually done what we came here to do? I heard someone shout from the hall with the witch and then sighed in relief when Rafael came out with a woman I'd never seen, tight in his grasp. He walked right over to Victor and gave a slight nod then raised his sword to help Chase, as Victor used the box to dispatch the bad witch to the cell that held Marcus.

When the last follower vanished, I climbed slowly down. I rushed toward Bronx and turned to look for help. Quinton stood there, his hands on his knees trying to catch his breath. "Quinton, Bronx was cut by that whip."

Straightening, he came over and looked at the still bleeding arm. "I'll take him back." He touched his shoulder, and they were both gone.

I turned slowly and saw four bodies on the ground, and was surprised I didn't feel sad for them. Victor came over, his green eyes assessing every inch of me. Holding out something I realized was my knife, I took it and ducked down to put it back in its case. He reached down and grasped the back of my neck in his big hand to pull me back up faster. Giving me a hard kiss on the mouth, he whispered against it. "I'll be angry with you later because you put yourself in harm's way, but for now I'll thank you for saving me." He wiped my face and I knew I had blood on me, as they all did.

I hugged him tight. "He was cheating by using that whip." I told him.

Victor chuckled and then straightened up to look around at the others.

"Seriously, Mitz has got to stop feeding us heavy foods." Arius said as he squatted and rested back against one of the walls. "I feel like I just ran a marathon."

"Whew." Daxx huffed out a breath. "That was better than the mud, but we could have used a bit more space to maneuver."

"Anyone catch little ninja's moves?" Michael asked and then crouched down and held out his sword as I had done over Victor.

"I did for a second, almost got decapitated for it." Troy said.

Chase chuckled. "That move to knock him on his back was…" He shook his head, "it brought a tear to my eye."

I looked at the man that Victor had killed for threatening me. I knew he had to be cold when he was in battle, and that in his life had killed. I wasn't sure at this moment how I felt about it. I may have saved him, but if that man had gotten up… Victor had saved me too.

As if sensing what I was thinking, he turned and hugged me into his body and then my stomach flipped and I knew we were back in the landing room. He leaned down and kissed my forehead. "I saw you save your guard too, so don't think we won't be discussing this sudden heroic streak."

I thought he was seriously upset until I saw his lips move, like he was hiding a smile. "If you weren't so busy looking around you, may not have gotten knocked off your feet." I said.

I heard laughing and turned to see Troy and Daxx standing there. "She put you in your place, brother." Troy said with a big smile. He sobered and gave me a quick nod. "It takes magic to knock our justice off his feet, but I thank you, little sister, for keeping him safe."

I nodded, but didn't know what to say, so I said nothing back.

"Let's get this blood washed off, then I have to go have a conversation with Marcus." Victor said.

"I'll meet you at the cells." Troy told him as they were walking out.

Taking my hand, Victor starting walking out of the room. "Any insight into what he meant when he said they would complete the task without him?"

I shook my head. "I haven't seen anything to let me know." I bit my lip and looked down at the blood on my clothes. "I can go to the library and see if the not-real-librarian knows of any prophecy that could give us an idea."

"The scholars have been looking." He said, opening a door for me that lead to our rooms.

I thought for a moment. "Sometimes they over-think things that are right there, plain to see."

He chuckled. "It would entertain me greatly if you were

able to solve this when they haven't been able to."

"Not fond of scholars?"

He stopped outside my door. "I am fond of learning, just not rambling as they tend to do."

I nodded. "If the teachers I had taught as much as they talked, I might know more."

Kissing my brow softly he grinned. "If you knew any more, heart, I'd never keep up." He looked at the door behind my back. "If I come in to help wash off the blood…"

"I'll never get to the library, or you to the cells." I felt my cheeks heat.

"Exactly." He kissed my mouth once, and then again. "But we could be a few moments late." Leaning closer, he nipped at my neck and backed me up against the door.

"Go *in* the room." Michael said as he stalked by us. "Make it fast. I want you there when we separate the witch and Marcus."

I felt the door behind me open and he pushed me gently inside. "You can't be late." I told him even though I had not wished for him to leave.

"I won't be. We'll shower together… to save time." His green eyes started to turn and he grinned at me with a mouthful of fangs.

My cheeks heated as I stared at his mouth. "Okay."

Chapter Twenty-Four

For two weeks, there were no battles. I could honestly say I wasn't upset with that. Victor and his brothers were not happy, though. They'd learned nothing useful from Marcus, or the others that had survived that fight. Each time they thought they had a location, it would be empty when they got there.

I wasn't getting any important flashes to help, only static, as Rafael called my constant unhelpful ones. I also hadn't found Emil yet and had decided he could hide even better than me. To feel like I was doing something important, I'd been focusing on tracking his children instead.

Victor and I managed to find more time together and for that I was happy, although I saw him fighting his instincts and staring at the gloves on my hand, when he thought I wasn't watching.

I came down from my tower after an hour of sorting, a little disappointed there were again none that I'd need. As I headed to breakfast, Daxx caught up with me.

"Anything we need to know?" She asked.

I shook my head. "Nothing again today."

"I can't say I'm minding the break," she grinned, "I actually get some time with Troy, but I'd still like to know what Marcus' minions are up to out there."

"I never thought I'd be wishing for pieces to fill my head, but I find I am. Not knowing is very stressful."

"I hear that." She walked for a moment looking at me.

"How are things with Victor?"

I felt my cheeks flush. "They are good. He wants me to share his room."

"I can see that."

"Is it a good thing?" I had never had a real room to share before, so I didn't know if that changed anything.

"If you want it to be."

I held out my hands and looked at my gloves. "He stares are these when I'm not looking."

Daxx sighed and put her arm around my shoulders like she did when she had something serious to say. "The need to mark your mate is very strong in the men. They can't help it."

I nodded. "From what you told me, when that happened to you, I understand that now."

"You are very lucky he loves you as he does and is waiting… even if it's not as patiently as he thinks."

I smiled, knowing it was true.

She released my shoulder and tucked her hands in her back pockets. "Do you have control over your visions now?"

"I think I do, as best as I ever will." I confessed.

"Then take a chance, trust fate. She seems to know what's best for us even if we don't."

I sighed. "I read the prophecy for Victor and I have no doubt it's me."

She chuckled. "I never did get past the part about the kings."

"It can be quite puzzling, I suppose."

"What does it say about Victor?" She smirked. "I know you remember it."

I smiled. "The justice of righteousness will find, when he's not looking, a woman that sees all good and all evil from within. She shall hold a place in his heart as no other could. With his seer of truth at his side, the justice will prevail throughout the years of time that remain."

Daxx stopped and looked at me. "That one is so simple. Why couldn't the huntress part be that simple? I had to choose between twin kings." She snorted. "Of course, the seer of truth… that's you."

I nodded. "I know it is."

Her phone rang, she kept walking as she checked it. "Yes! I have a bail-jumper on the other side. I need to kick some ass."

We walked in the dining room and all the men were already there. The air around them was all much the same. Frustration and worry. They all stood as Daxx and I sat down. I still didn't understand it, but Mitz said it was manners, and it had taken her and their mother many years to program them that way. If Mitz said it was so, then it must be true.

"Anything interesting today, little sister?" Rafael asked as he poured his coffee.

I shook my head. "Nothing again today."

"Maybe it is fate's way of telling us to practice harder, we were a little sloppy last time." Michael said as he grabbed some toast off the plate.

"There was nothing sloppy about me." Chase said with a smirk.

"Yes, you should all practice. However, Cristy and I won't be there today. I have some place I'd like to show her." Victor said smiling at me.

"You do?" The last time he had somewhere to show me, it was my tower.

"I do." He nodded. "If you have time to spare."

I thought for a moment, I had nothing but time as I had no job, I didn't need to hide. I nodded. "Of course, I have time for that."

"I'm intrigued." Daxx said and then looked at Troy.

He raised his hands. "I'm sorry I don't provide towers and have special places to go… I'm running half a kingdom."

Daxx frowned and then laughed. "I was going to say I have a bail-jumper to track down."

"Oh." Troy nodded. "Take Leone with you."

She raised an eyebrow. "I don't need help to track a jumper on my side."

"I know you don't need help, but until we know what the worm in our cells has going on out there, you don't cross over alone." He picked up his coffee and took a drink.

"Fine." She said and glanced to me and rolled her eyes.

I smirked. This was their routine. I glanced to see Victor not eating as much as he usually did. "Are you okay?"

He smiled. "Yes, we're transporting quite a fair distance and a heavy meal doesn't sit well, even for someone that's done it more times than I could count."

"Now I'm really intrigued." Daxx nudged my arm. "Take pictures I need to know where your grumpy bear is taking you."

She called him my bear or grumpy bear more than she did Victor now, I thought is was cute, but couldn't tell him that.

I nodded, hoping I remembered how to do that with my phone. "I will."

Victor had been serious about how much your stomach churned when going far away. He made me sit down and put my head on my knees until it settled, when we got there.

"It's taken me a few weeks to find this place, and several accidental landings in wrong places." He said softly as I sat there hoping my stomach would settle down. "I had to find somewhere I knew Marcus' reach could not stretch to."

Lifting my head slowly I looked around to see we were sitting on a hill, in a field. When I looked to the bottom of the field I saw butterflies. Hundreds, maybe even thousands of orange butterflies, all filling the air. I stood up slowly and took a few steps, then remembered and took out my phone and handed it to him. "Take pictures for Daxx and for me?"

I moved down the hill slowly toward them, they were fluttering everywhere. It was like what I'd seen in my head, though I had no idea Victor was the key. As I got closer, I put my arms out and walked right through them, they were everywhere around me. Some landed on my arms and face, but I didn't care. This was the most amazing thing I had ever seen. In, or out, of my head.

I turned slowly, my arms out and looked back to see Victor following me with the phone raised, and hoped his pictures were perfect so I could look at them always. When he got closer, I smiled and had to pause when a butterfly landed on my nose. Reaching slowly, I brushed it away and the others that were on me took flight back into the air.

Moving cautiously so I wouldn't step on any in my path, I went back to him and jumped up to grab his face. I kissed his mouth hard. "I don't know what to say… this is…" I couldn't find the words.

"The look on your face says all I wanted to hear." He told me.

I turned and looked back at them and then pointed to the hill. "I'd like to watch them for a while, without disturbing their dance." I took his hand and he paused and reached up to my hair, then held out his hand and a butterfly sat on it.

"You had a hitchhiker." He grinned and raised his hand so it would fly away.

We walked back up holding hands and sat on the top of the hill. Inside I'd never felt more right than I did now. The signs never lied. I got on my knees and looked at his green eyes. "It has to be here." I told him quietly and took off my jacket.

His brows drew closer. "What does?"

Sitting back down I pulled off my boots and then turned to look at him. "You need to mark me while we're here."

His eyes searched my face and he seemed unsure what to say, which was quite odd for Victor.

"You're sure?" He finally asked me.

I nodded and pulled off one glove and then the other, then got to my knees again and took off my shirt.

He looked around us for a moment and then back to me with a grin. "If any tourist happens along, butterflies won't be the only thing they get a picture of."

I felt my face go red and then shrugged. "I don't care. It has to be here and now."

Without a word, he took off his boots and then his shirt. "If I'd known I would have brought a blanket…"

I took off my pants and then knelt there in front of him and helped him undo his pants.

When we were both naked, he lay back and pulled me on top of him. He grasped my face between his palms. "I've waited forever for you." He kissed me with such passion I thought I might cry.

It only ever took a few fevered kisses from him, and I

needed more. He knew my body and just what I wanted every time. In a few short moments, he grasped my hips and helped me to kneel over him.

"We'll do the blood bonding in the privacy of our bedroom," He told me as he guided me to lower my body to take him inside me. "I don't need some tourist thinking we're doing some satanic rite on this hill."

I nodded, and then gasped as he filled me. "I need your mark on me." I whispered breathlessly.

With a growl his eyes were red and he pulled me down for a kiss. Grasping my hair, he stopped as our breaths were touching. "Fuck it," he said, "I'm binding you to me in every possible way. I've waited five hundred years to have you." He kissed me hard robbing me of air.

When he released my head, he had a knife in his hand and cut into his chest. In one fluid motion, he had me on my back, his hand grasped over my head. "Take my blood now." He whispered and thrust into me.

I put my lips over the wound and took in the taste that felt like home into my mouth. He held my hand tighter and rocked our bodies harder then his fangs sunk into my neck and the whole world exploded. My arm was burning, and my head felt dizzy as I rose higher, reaching to climax. I could feel him inside me in more than one way and felt filled and a completion that I had never felt before. When the wound sealed, I lifted my head away and bit into his neck as the first spasm hit me.

He growled in my ear. "Mine for all eternity."

I don't know how long we lay there breathing and floating, but I knew I finally had a home and love I'd never had before. We could stay here forever and it didn't matter. I lifted my left arm and saw an intricate design all over it, even onto my palm.

"I'm trying to find the energy to move." He said with a chuckle. "No one ever warned me how paralyzing it was."

"I could run to the moon right now." I smiled and looked at my arm some more.

Propping himself up on his elbows he looked down at me and smiled. "Of course, you could. You never tire."

I looked at his arm to see a pattern the same as mine. "I

wonder how it knows what marks will work for each couple."

Slowly moving off me, he groaned. "I don't think you'll find a book about that. Only the fates know that."

"Mmm," I sighed, "that's too bad. It's quite fascinating."

He handed me my clothes. "Let's get dressed before we get caught."

I'd forgotten I was naked laying in a field. With a giggle, I sat up and looked around. The butterflies were still filling the air. I got dressed quickly.

He pulled me back into his arms now that we weren't naked.

"Thank you for bringing me here." I stretched up and kissed him.

He held his arm out and turned it a few times. "I honestly believed I'd never see this on my body." Leaning up on one elbow he looked down at me. "I spent decades hoping and then waiting many more." He kissed the end of my nose. "Then I grew bitter and decided I didn't need to wait for a prophecy to come true. A hundred years later, not one of my brothers had settled down, and I knew the prophecy was true." His green eyes looked lovingly over my face for a moment. "I still don't think I believed there was one for me until I watched this little woman flit all over Daxx's apartment with flaming red hair."

I grinned. "I bet that was a shock."

He chuckled. "That's putting it mildly." He kissed me quickly. "I had this incredible urge to protect you, and wasn't even sure if I liked you… then I realized you had endured more than I in my long life, and continued to believe there was still good everywhere." He traced his finger lightly over the tattoo up my arm. "I thought for certain the darkness would swallow me." Pausing, a strange look crossed his face. "I have fed off the evil in my cells for three hundred years, believing it was how I'd become cold enough to do what I had to."

"It's a very lonely job you have. Your brothers help, but in the end, it's just you to know the right from the wrong."

He watched me for a moment. "It wasn't until I understood all that goes on in your head… every second of every day, then I knew I somehow had to have you. That you were the good to balance out all the bad I have seen."

I rolled my eyes at him. "I told you that you could have me and you ran and hid from me after that."

Rubbing his hand over the back of his neck, he shrugged. "I didn't want to hurt you, or force you to decide."

"And you thought you had given into the darkness? That doesn't sound like it to me." I touched his cheek softly.

His phone beeped. He reached around and picked it up off the ground. "You would think there was a limit to how far the signal goes." He sighed after he checked it. "I have to get back. There's information on a possible location in Alterealm with more of Marcus' followers."

"Are they hiding there while you look on the other side?" I sat up and looked around for my phone.

"It's possible, I suppose." He shook his head. "I feel like we're chasing our tails the last few weeks."

I smirked. "I'd like to see that." I nodded. "You with a tail and chasing it."

He stood up and scooped me up into his arms. "One last look at your butterflies, heart."

I turned and looked down the hill. "I will always remember."

Chapter Twenty-Five

The next day, I tracked Daxx down. She was in the kitchen with Mitz, who smiled in her way, and looked at me arm. Softly saying something about it was about time her boys settled down. I don't know if she knew the boys the same way I did, but I don't think finding their mates was going to settle them down at all. In fact, all of them were out chasing down locations that may have more of Marcus' followers.

"Tea?" Mitz asked me as I sat down.

I shook my head. "No. I'm fine, thank you."

"What's wrong?" Daxx asked, "You have that focus face thing going on."

"My what?"

She grinned. "You get this look when something is bugging you."

"Oh." I nodded. "Something is. I woke up feeling like I need to go over to the other side today, but I don't know why."

"A bad feeling?"

I thought for a moment. "No, just… you know that feeling like you know you were supposed to do something, but don't know what?"

She nodded. "Story of my life." She laughed.

"I was going to ask Victor to take me to my roof over there, but he's busy… they're all busy today."

"I don't know about a roof, but I can take you." She glanced at Mitz. "I know they won't be happy we're alone, but we survived years without their interference, so a quick trip won't hurt." She glanced at my wrist to see I wore my transporter.

I nodded. "Okay. Maybe to the fish factory, I can check the wall for Alona's mark."

We sat at the factory by the river for an hour. There was an x on the wall, but no Alona. It still felt like this was where I needed to be.

Daxx's phone rang and she winced as she answered it. "Hey. Any luck?" She held her finger over her lips to me. "Oh. Good."

I glanced down at the water and looked in my head, trying to see if there was something I needed to know. There had to be a reason I had to be here today.

"Uh, yeah. I'll meet you there is two minutes." She tucked the phone in her pocket. "I have to go, he's heading to the dining room right now to meet me."

I looked behind to the building again. "Can I stay a few more minutes? I really think this is where I'm supposed to be."

Biting her lip, she stood up and looked around. "Five minutes, then get back before anyone notices."

I nodded, "Okay." Then she was gone. I looked around again and then got up. I thought maybe I'd check the other side of the factory and the reason I was here would come to me.

I wandered over, being careful to not be seen, then stood in the shadows watching all around. There were a few people walking along by the empty parking lot, but none of it seemed like anything I needed to know. I had just decided I should go back as I promised Daxx, when someone stood up near the river at the other end of the building. I hadn't seen them until they got up because there were hidden by an old ramp. They had long dark hair. Moving quickly, I went toward them.

It was Alona. I rushed toward her. I pulled out my phone and dialed Victor.

"Cristy, heart, I'll be back in about ten minutes." He told me.

"Oh good." I kept walking toward her, she turned and saw me and stood there with her hands on her hips. "I had a question."

"What is it?" He sounded like he was walking fast by the way he was breathing, or maybe he was riding on a horse, I wasn't sure.

"If I push the button to pop back and I'm touching someone, will they come with me?"

"Yes… hold on, you're on the other side?"

I nodded. "Okay, thank you." I hung up. Before I got two steps it rang again. It was Victor. Silly man, if he'd just wait ten minutes, we could talk face to face. I tucked the phone in my pocket.

Alona really didn't look happy with me. She looked over her shoulder, like she was going to leave. I moved faster and then the expression on her face changed.

"Crissy?"

I remembered my hair wasn't red and nodded.

"I have waited here *many* times and no one showed up." Alona told me looking very upset.

I huffed out a breath. "Things got a little crazy. Mages and witches and runes… it's been quite a time."

She shook her head and blinked a few times. "That man from the club, the bald jerk, he keeps turning up everywhere I go. It took me several cabs and detours to get here alone."

I frowned. "That's not good. You need to talk to my friends about it."

She flung her arms open. "Which is why I keep coming here. You said mark the wall. I did and no one has shown up."

I looked around. "You were so well hidden, I don't know that they would see you, even if they did come to check."

She huffed out a breath. "Then call them. I'm here now."

"I think I should take you to them where I know it's safe and no one is watching or following you."

She looked around for a second and then sighed. "Where are they, will it take long to get there?"

I shook my head and opened the case on my transporter. "Not long at all." I stepped over and put my arm through hers and then pushed the button.

We arrived in the landing room and I frowned, would my stomach ever get used to this? I let go of Alona, who looked at me with her eyes huge. I was just happy I found her. Now, if I could find Emil, I would be very happy.

I closed the case on my transporter and wondered if Victor could get one for me that popped me to my roof top and back. If they managed one way, how hard could a two-way be?

Arius came running into the room, then slid to a stop. He held a transporter like mine in his hand. He walked slowly toward her, a cautious expression on his face. "How do you feel?" He asked Alona. "Any pains?" He looked worried.

I remembered Quinton doing that and had forgotten. I bit my lip, maybe I should ask what happens if you have those pains they ask about. They didn't sound like a good thing.

Alona looked from me to him, looking very upset. She reached up slowly behind her back and stood there breathing heavy. "I feel… confused…" She put her hand over her stomach, "and I want to throw up." Stepping back a few feet, she glared at Arius. "Where am I? Who are you?" She turned to look at me. "Crissy, what the hell is going on?"

Prologue

Clutching her daughter to her chest, she opened the door wide enough to peek out into the hall. Eva was shaking with fear. How could she have forgotten to keep her arm covered? The exhaustion must be wearing on her to overlook such a thing. Checking three times to be certain none of the other boarders were awake and the hallway was empty, she slipped out the door and bolted to her room.

Closing the door quickly, she turned and set the infant in the middle of the bed. They had an hour to get to the train platform, she wasn't taking a chance on being late. It had been nerve-wracking few days, waiting to get papers signed that would clear them for travel.

She had been terrified through the entire process that they would ask her to remove her jacket. When the doctor had finally decided she and her child hadn't been exposed, and were displaying no symptoms of the virus, she had almost fainted with relief.

Her heart skipped a few beats, thinking what would have happened if they'd been denied. There were camps filled with those afflicted. And each time the medical trucks passed, they carried others to the quarantined areas. It was horrifying, what the country was going through. To survive the years of war and then have millions fall ill with some deadly influenza. She only glimpsed the headlines of the newspapers as she passed them in her travels, but it was everywhere, it seemed.

Moving to the mirror, she studied her reflection. Her cheeks were hollowed and dark circles were under her eyes. The months of stress and worry were catching up to her. She sighed, her white cotton shirtwaist wasn't stained, but the wrinkles were adding up. How many days had she been wearing it now? If there had been more time, she would have given it a rinse, but she couldn't risk missing one of the few trains still running out of the city. "Lord knows my brassiere and bloomers are in desperate need of a rinse as well," she whispered to the scared woman looking back at her. Smoothing a hand down her skirt, she smiled, thankful it was a little longer then current fashion dictated, as her stockings were beyond any condition that a mere washing could remedy.

Her heart ached as she looked at the tattoo covering the length of her left arm. She touched it gingerly and closed her eyes, willing the tears not to fall. He had to be all right. She didn't know what was taking so long, but she knew that he would come back to her. When he did manage to cross back over, the caretaker of their building would give him the message, then he would come and get Alona and her. *Please, Levi, come soon.*

The baby's soft whimper made her open her eyes. She turned and smiled. "Not to worry, love, your daddy will find us at your aunt's." Going over, she sat on the edge of the bed and looked down at her child, her whole world. "We have to go, I don't have a choice. The sickness is spreading, and if we stay here any longer," She let out a ragged breath, "we won't be able to get out." Alona was a beautiful baby, she looked so much like her father. Picking up her bonnet, she placed it on the child's head, over her thick black hair. "You're my strength, little one, never forget that." The baby watched her with pale eyes. She was certain they were going to be the same pale green his were, well when his weren't red that was.

Leaning down, she kissed the soft cheek. "I would be lost in a sea of despair if I didn't have you my precious Alona." It was the truth. The only thing that had prevented her from dissolving in the constant pain of being without him, was their child. While she'd been growing inside her, Eva knew she had to overcome the feelings of grief and continue on until he returned for them.

Tucking the blanket around the baby, she reached over and picked up her worn satchel. Getting her coin purse out, she dumped the contents in her hand and counted. The train fare was going to cost nearly seven dollars, which was the most expensive thing she'd done in as long as she could remember. After that they'd have to get by on what was left, which would be a week's grocery money, maybe two, if nothing unexpected came up. Putting the money back in the purse, she snapped it shut and tucked it safely into her bag.

"You'll like it in the country, doll, once you learn to walk, there's so much to explore." She gathered up the few items not in the suitcase and folded them. Glancing around to be sure nothing was missed, she picked up her jacket and gloves. It was quite warm today, but she had no choice, her arm and hand had to be covered. Telling those curious enough to ask that her husband had died in the war was one thing, and that usually brought a halt to any further questions. Explaining why she had a tattoo that covered the length of her arm, well, that was unexplainable. The scandal it would cause would not end well, something like that was unheard of and completely unacceptable. Levi had said in his world the tattoos were a wondrous and cherished thing. She couldn't wait to see his world.

She missed him with all she had. For months she'd worried that something had happened. Was the outbreak where he was too? Had something happened to him? He told her he would know if she was harmed through the connection of their tattoo, so she had to hold onto the belief that the connection went both ways. She knew he lived, but couldn't understand what was taking him so long. He had to go back to arrange for her to come with him, then they could be together always.

Until he did return, she had to make certain their child was safe and happy. They hadn't discussed children, but he was such a loving man, Eva was sure the surprise of being a father would be something he would welcome.

Tucking her hair up under the embroidered velvet toque, she studied the woman looking back at her. "Just a few more days and you'll be safe, and won't have to worry about someone finding out." She nodded to herself and then turned to pick up her daughter. Cradling her in one arm, she smiled down at the beautiful face as she made sure her mouth was lightly covered by the blanket. They'd managed to avoid infection this far, she wasn't taking chances. Hooking the satchel on the same arm, she opened the door and picked up her case. Taking a deep break, she exhaled and stepped out into the hall.

She had to hold onto the hope that her sister was well. If the sickness had reached the country, there were no other options to take… they'd be lost.

Chapter One

I had spent close to one hundred years staying away from anything that would draw the attention of others. Which, due to the fact I didn't age, was not an easy task. Six months ago I'd moved, an unfortunate necessity, done so people didn't notice that I didn't age. Since then, staying in the shadows didn't seem to be working.

It started when a crazy woman with fantastically bright red hair, and a chaotic array of emotions grabbed me in the club and dragged me out. Since that moment, everyone seemed to be noticing me.

I thought she was completely bonkers, who wouldn't be with so many emotions oozing from her every pore, until I discovered what she said was true. Someone did appear to be after me.

I spent three weeks going to an abandoned fish factory, after painting an x on the wall. Insane, I know, but I did just as she'd told me to do, if I needed help. I went there because the chaotic one had told me her friends could help me, and that they were like me.

That, as far as I knew, was impossible. Yet she knew my eyes changed to red, and when they did my mouth filled with fangs. If I hadn't felt the truth seeping from her, I would have walked in the other direction. After many years of believing I was the spawn of Satan, I was too curious to not find out. I needed to know if it was true. Were there others like me?

When she finally showed up at the factory today, minus the red hair, I thought I'd go meet her friends and see for myself. Of course, I thought the meeting would take place in some out of the way café or concealed location. I did not foresee being zapped, or whatever had just happened, to some room in the blink of an eye.

Now I stood in an empty, drably beige room, unable to figure out what was going on and feeling nauseous in the worst way. I looked at Crissy, she was closing the lid to the watch thing on her arm that she'd pushed to bring us here. I debated on grabbing it from her and pushing the button, so I could get back home to pack up and move, again.

A tall man with gorgeous, long black hair that rivaled my own, came running into the room. He slid to a stop and crouched down with his arms out giving me a cautious look, like I might bolt for the door. And go where? I thought.

"How do you feel? He looked me up and down, his grey eyes filled with worry. "Any pains?

He had one of those watches like Crissy's in his hand. Did I want to try to grab it? He was a large man, so maybe not in my current state. I stared at him for a few seconds and then reached for the blade on my back. Closing my hand around the handle, I scowled at him. "I feel… confused…" My stomach lurched again, so I put my other hand over it hoping I didn't throw up on this stranger. "And I want to throw up." I backed away from him and watched him carefully. "Where am I? Who are you?" I looked to person responsible for this. "Crissy, what the hell is going on?"

Crissy blew out a breath and nodded. "I know. Transporting sucks. My stomach still hates it."

"Transporting?" I glanced at the man again, then shook my head. "Like *beam me up*, transporting?" She gave me a blank look, so I looked to the man to see him smirking.

"No." He sobered. "Not like that at all."

"It's okay, this is the best place to meet, no one can follow you here." Crissy tried to reassure me.

I was debating on giving her friend a few more moments to convince me. That I couldn't pick up any emotions from his was… unusual, to say the least. I could see emotions going through his eyes as he studied me but couldn't *feel* any of them.

"Cristy." A large, redheaded man came running into the room. With the way he was dressed, he looked like he was going to battle. And I don't mean military dress, I mean Samurai meets Blade, black leather, head to toe, large sharp weapons sort of dress. He immediately went to Crissy and hugged her into his large body and kissed the top of her head. *That* I hadn't anticipated. The gentle expression in his eyes bought him a minute's free pass before I lost it on him, or everyone else.

"I will get to the *why* and *how* you got to the other side… later. My heart stopped when you hung up." He touched her cheek in a loving way.

Crissy bit her lip and looked up at him. "Sorry. I just knew I had to go back today, but I didn't know why. Until I did." She smiled at him while pointing at me.

He straightened away from her and gone was the softer look.

Replaced with an ice cold assessment, but once again, I could only see his emotions and not feel them.

He looked me up and down for a moment. "Clearly, she is meant to be here, or she'd need a device." He raised an eyebrow at me. "How are you feeling?"

I glared at him, "Like I've entered the twilight zone."

The one with the black hair snorted but didn't comment.

"Victor, she was waiting for me. She keeps seeing that guy that chased her—" Crissy sighed, "from when I got my scar."

He hugged her against his side but was still rigid standing there. "Has he approached you?"

I shook my head, "I don't hang around to give him the opportunity to strike up a conversation."

He inclined his head, saying nothing else.

"Crissy, are you all right?" The woman that had come to get Crissy when she passed out in the alley came running in.

She stopped when she saw her and placed a hand over her heart. "When Victor went screaming by to get here, I thought you'd been…" she paused when she saw me. "Oh. Awesome! You were finally there."

"So, it seems." How many people had Crissy told about me?

The blonde cleared her throat and looked at the others, "So, maybe we could… oh I dunno, go to the dining room, or somewhere other than the landing room?" She rolled her eyes at me and mouthed 'men'.

I couldn't pick up a single emotion from her either, which intrigued me even further. I'd never been near this many people and not sensed emotion. "I would like to know more about this man following me." I looked at Crissy. "Why is he following me?"

She pouted, "I don't know. It hasn't shown me that, but I do know he's not good."

I looked at her, unable to figure out what she meant. "If you don't know, who does?"

"I know who can find out." The black-haired one said. He grinned at the one still holding Crissy close. "We can get Troy to ask his buddies we picked up after Criss was hurt."

My head snapped back to Crissy. "They hurt you?"

She blew out a breath. "Some magic," she waved a hand around, "whatever it's called, was stuck in my back." Frowning, she glanced up at her man before looking back to me. "It hurt so much. It's gone now, the rune has locked it out forever." She nodded.

If I hadn't felt the truth oozing out of her and all over me, I would have demanded they please take me home. I didn't know what she was talking about, but I was living proof that other types were possible in this life. I held up my hand. "I will just… take your word for all that."

The blonde exhaled loudly and then stepped over and put out her hand. "I'm Daxx. I never did thank you properly for keeping an eye on Crissy when she blacked out in the alley."

I looked at her hand and then shook it briefly. I still picked up nothing from her, a very rare occurrence. "Things tend to be eventful when Crissy is around."

She snorted, "You have no idea." Turning, she motioned to the man that had come running in first. "This is Arius," then to Crissy's man, "and his brother Victor."

Both men inclined their heads briefly but made no move to come closer.

"Let's go to the dining room, grab a coffee or something and figure out why those guys are after you." She suggested.

Before I could decide, another tall man came in. He had short black hair and pale blue eyes. My only thought was that I was usually the tallest person in the room. Seemingly, the males here were all of the large variety.

He stopped in the door and looked me up and down. "Is this who we've been watching for all these weeks, Crissy?"

Crissy nodded enthusiastically. "I brought her back, she said they're following her."

Raising an eyebrow, he glanced at the device Arius held then back to me. "Obviously, she's meant to be here."

At some point, I would have to clarify why they kept saying that. I turned back to Daxx. "You said something about coffee?" I still didn't know where I was, but I wasn't leaving until I knew what the hell was going on, and if they could tell me *what* I was while I was here, that would answer a question that had plagued me for seventy-eight years.

About the Author

J. Risk is a pseudonym used by Jacqueline Paige

I wanted to write a story that would fit into new adult levels as well as adult. Something that was serious with fun elements-- paranormal / fantasy that everyone could read and enjoy.

I've decided to use J. Risk as the pen name for this to separate this series from my other writing which is definitely adult reading material.

Jacqueline Paige lives in Ontario in a small town that's part of the popular Georgian Triangle area.

She began her writing career in 2006 and since her first published works in 2009 she hasn't stopped. Jacqueline describes her writing as *all things paranormal*, which she has proven is her niche with stories of witches, ghosts, psychics and shifters now on the shelves.

When Jacqueline isn't lost in her writing, she spends time with her five children, most of whom are finally able to look after her instead of the other way around. Together they do random road trips, that usually end up with them lost, shopping trips where they push every button in the toy aisle, hiking when there's enough time to escape and bizarre things like creating new daring recipes in the kitchen. She's a grandmother to six (so far) and looks forward to corrupting many more in the years to come.

Jacqueline loves to hear from her readers, you can find her at

http://jacquelinepaige.com